Water
damage
2/8/18 pd for
pg 433-end. GR

05/11

W9-CEV-678

ABIGAIL

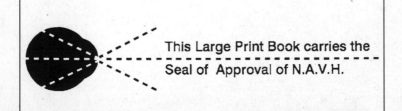

This Large Print Book carries the
Seal of Approval of N.A.V.H.

THE WIVES OF KING DAVID, BOOK 2

ABIGAIL

JILL EILEEN SMITH

THORNDIKE PRESS
A part of Gale, Cengage Learning

GALE
CENGAGE Learning·

Detroit • New York • San Francisco • New Haven, Conn • Waterville, Maine • London

050711

GALE
CENGAGE Learning·

© 2010 Jill Eileen Smith.
Unless otherwise indicated, Scripture is taken from the HOLY BIBLE, NEW INTERNATIONAL VERSION ®. NIV®. Copyright © 1973, 1978, 1984 by International Bible Society. Used by permission of Zondervan. All rights reserved.
Scripture marked NKJV is taken from the New King James Version. Copyright © 1982 by Thomas Nelson, Inc. Used by permission. All rights reserved.

Thorndike Press, a part of Gale, Cengage Learning.

ALL RIGHTS RESERVED
This is a work of historical reconstruction; the appearance of certain historical figures is therefore inevitable. All other characters, however, are products of the author's imagination, and any resemblance to actual persons, living or dead, is coincidental.

Thorndike Press® Large Print Christian Historical Fiction.
The text of this Large Print edition is unabridged.
Other aspects of the book may vary from the original edition.
Set in 16 pt. Plantin.

LIBRARY OF CONGRESS CATALOGING-IN-PUBLICATION DATA

Smith, Jill Eileen, 1958–
  Abigail / by Jill Eileen Smith.
    p. cm. — (Thorndike Press large print Christian historical fiction) (The wives of King David ; bk. 2)
    ISBN-13: 978-1-4104-2953-7
    ISBN-10: 1-4104-2953-9
    1. Abigail (Biblical figure)—Fiction. 2. Bible. O.T.—History of Biblical events—Fiction. 3. Women in the Bible—Fiction. 4. Large type books. I. Title.
  PS3619.M58838A62 2010b
  813'.6—dc22   2010026912

Published in 2010 by arrangement with Revell Books, a division of Baker Publishing Group.

Printed in Mexico
1 2 3 4 5 6 7 14 13 12 11 10

To my beloved, Randy — a man after God's own heart and a wonderful example of what it truly means to be called husband and father.

And to Jeff, Chris, and Ryan — follow hard after Jesus to do His will, and live the dreams He has given to you. Your mother's heart trusts you all to His care.

■ ■ ■ ■

Part I

■ ■ ■ ■

Now Samuel died, and all Israel assembled and mourned for him; and they buried him at his home in Ramah. Then David moved down into the Desert of Maon. A certain man in Maon, who had property there at Carmel, was very wealthy. He had a thousand goats and three thousand sheep, which he was shearing in Carmel. His name was Nabal and his wife's name was Abigail. She was an intelligent and beautiful woman, but her husband, a Calebite, was surly and mean in his dealings.

1 Samuel 25:1–3

1

Maon, 1017 BC

"Rumor has it David is in the area not far from here. If you but say the word, Father, we could leave Simon for good and join him. I hear he has women and children in his company now. Mother and Talya and Abigail would not be out of place."

Abigail nearly sloshed water over the sides of the bowl as she stood in the courtyard straining it through a cloth for tomorrow's washing. Her brother's oft-repeated plea shouldn't surprise her. She'd heard it many times in the past two years since the king's son-in-law had run off and surrounded himself with disgruntled men. So why did the thought cause her heart to beat faster and her limbs to tremble now?

"Ah, Daniel. Always you bring my failures before me." Her father's exaggerated sigh carried to her from the roof, where her parents, Daniel, and his wife Talya sat talk-

9

ing in the early light of the moon. She could imagine the slight shrug of his weary shoulders, the look of defeat in his eyes. Why did her brother insist on pushing his point? If he wanted to run after David so much, then go! But leave her father, leave all of them, in peace.

"You have not failed, Judah. You are a good husband, a loving father."

"Yes, yes, you need not appease me, dear wife. Every day I watch my Abigail grow lovelier, and do you not think I regret what that man will do to her spirit once she lives under his roof? Ach! You mustn't tempt me, Daniel. To run away . . . It is far too appealing."

Silence followed the comment. Abigail sucked in a breath, disbelieving. Was Abba actually tempted to do as Daniel suggested? He'd never indicated such a thing in the two years since her childhood betrothal to pay off her father's debt — a betrothal made before she had reached her full maturity, before her womanhood had come upon her. She fingered the sash at her waist, her heart thumping an erratic rhythm. The change had been late in coming, but six full moons had passed since then. Six months of knowing her betrothed could come at any moment.

"But Father, if you know things will only get worse when Abigail marries that fool, why let her? Surely there is a way to stop this, to undo the damage before it is too late." Daniel's voice dropped in volume, and Abigail strained to hear. She crept closer to the stairs leading to the roof and placed one foot on the bottom step.

"There is nothing to be done. Don't you think your father would have gotten out of the agreement if he could?" The voice of her mother, Naamah, was stern as always, giving Abigail a measure of hope. Her father would not give her to Simon's son Nabal if he truly feared for her future. He would have gone to the elders, found some other way to pay Simon off — *something*. "But I'll admit, David would be a far better master than Simon of Carmel."

Her mother's admission, so unprecedented, sent a chill down Abigail's spine. She gripped the wall for support, her limbs suddenly unable to continue the trek to the roof. Why were they talking like this? Nabal could come at any moment, even this night. How could they even speak of running away? What would become of her?

"Perhaps I could take the case to the elders . . ." Her father's voice pierced her in its stark uncertainty. Never had he sug-

11

gested such a thing. "They may agree to a termination rather than a divorce . . . Abigail would carry the stigma, though, and I cannot provide for her forever."

"I will provide for her." She barely heard Daniel's declaration above the pounding in her head. Divorce? No man would want her again. She would remain alone and barren, her life wasted.

And what of Nabal? Sudden doubt assailed her. Brash, deceitful son of Simon. The picture of kindness at their betrothal — but if her brother spoke the truth, the man carried an impulsive, explosive temper. Hadn't she sensed it in the look he gave her when he took her aside into the privacy of the grape grove at the community wine treading? She pulled in a steadying breath, remembering the flush of shame — and pleasure — she had felt in the moment of his possessive kiss. What began as a tender, heady feeling of love's awakening had turned aggressive and harsh. She pressed two fingers to her trembling lips.

She couldn't deny it. Nabal was an attractive man. Of medium height, his muscles were not strong like Abba's or thick cords like Daniel's, and his hair was darker than her chestnut tresses, black as a goat's skin, his eyes the color of an onyx stone. Sandwiched between his mustache and beard, his smile brooded something dark, mysterious. She'd heard the way the virgins giggled at his princely manner and flirtatious looks. If she had not known he belonged to her, she might have wondered if he had set his eye on one of them. And the knowing, the realization that he was bound to her, had made her proud. Someday he would come for her and carry her off on a jewel-bedecked camel to share in the wealth of his estate, to share the intimacies of his love. Intimacies he had already hinted at . . . if she had not pushed him away that day.

She grasped at the fringe of her shawl, cinching it tight, shivering more from the flash of anger she recalled in his eyes than the night's damp, cool breeze. She'd almost ducked and run from him, but his grip on her arms had held her secure. He wouldn't have slapped her for refusing him, would he? He would wait for the proper time, until she was truly a woman as she was now. He knew all he need do was come for her. He wouldn't force her among the grapevines.

She shook her head, determined to clear it of the disturbing thoughts. Father may entertain traitorous ideas of annulling her marriage, but how did she dare? She had already allowed too much . . . and Nabal would collect on her father's promise one way or another. Of that she was sure.

Lord, help me.

"If we run after David, how will that improve a thing? His enemies are around every corner. We would never know peace again." Her mother's words stilled the restless pounding of her heart. Yes, this was what they needed — wisdom — to talk sense into her brother, whose own logic was tainted with living under the oppression of Simon's employ. And her father whose weariness grew greater with every passing day, his regret palpable.

"Your mother is right, Daniel. I'm too old to live my life on the run, not to mention what it would do to your mother. We would only slow David down."

"You are far from old, Father. The freedom alone would renew your strength."

"Would you have your child born in a cave, my son?" Her mother's severe tone returned. "Talya is better off here, until she is safely delivered."

Abigail released her grip on the wall and stepped back onto the stones of the courtyard. The discussion would turn to other things now. Too many infants lined the crevices in the burial caves near their home — brothers and sisters she and Daniel

14

should have shared. Daniel wouldn't chance his future or Talya's health after such a declaration. Their mother knew how to get her way.

Abigail's sandals trod softly across the court and into the small house, and she eased the door shut behind her. Two years she had waited since her betrothal, and now at fifteen summers since her birth, she was ripe with longing for a home of her own. At three and twenty, surely Nabal longed to marry, to procure sons.

When, Lord? When would her bridegroom come for her?

She brushed a strand of hair out of her eyes and pushed aside Daniel's comments of Nabal's churlish behavior. When they married, things would be different. She would help Nabal see the error of his ways, gently point out how people lost respect for men who were rude or unkind, help him change.

Things would be better. They had to be.

With a heavy sigh, she glanced about the dark room, then settled onto her mat, listening to the muffled voices of her family on the roof. Uncertainty niggled at the back of her thoughts. Everything had seemed so possible until now. Until she had heard her father's doubts and her mother's agreement.

Until the possibility of annulment seemed a reality. Until running away to join a band of outlaws sounded more appealing than marrying her husband.

2

Abigail removed the evening bread from the clay oven in the courtyard and stood. One hand shading her eyes, she gazed toward the town of Maon, where her father, Judah, trudged the narrow path, a lone lamb draped across his slumped shoulders. Defeat shadowed his dear face, and when he glanced up and noticed her, he looked away as though he could not bear the shame she knew he bore.

"Any word, Abba?" That night on the roof, despite her silent protests, Daniel had finally convinced her father to seek the dissolution of her marriage to Nabal. Apparently, Nabal had been caught in a drunken brawl and nearly beat a man to death, which had prompted Daniel's renewed concerns and convinced Abba to act. He had spoken to the elders a week ago. Surely they must have come to a decision. But her hope, which was thin and brittle at best, cracked and splintered at the distinct shake of her father's head and the look of intense remorse in his eyes.

"Simon is too powerful, Abigail." He reached for her then and placed a gentle, rough-worn hand against her cheek. "One of the elders must have brought my request before him . . ." He looked away toward the distant hills, shaking his head again. "Ach . . . we knew it was impossible from the start." He attempted a shrug, but the lamb's body prevented his shoulders from lifting. On closer inspection, she noticed the lamb's splinted and bandaged leg.

She reached to pat the animal's head, looking from the bandage to her father's face. "How was she hurt?" Instinct told her the answer, but she waited to hear it from him, knowing he needed to talk about something normal, something besides the foreboding truth that hung between them. "Did a wolf or a bear get her, or did she run away too many times?" Sometimes Abba was forced to kill a rebellious lamb, one who would not learn obedience, but often he would first break the leg of the runaway, then carry the ewe close to his heart until it healed, to teach her obedience.

"She is the youngest yet the most stubborn of Nabal's flock. A lion almost got her, but Daniel was quick to stop him. That boy would do well with his own flock, if Adonai ever sees fit to give him one. He is the best hireling Simon and Nabal have."

Abigail looked into the large, frightened eyes of the lamb, almost hearing the pitiful cry she must have given, the betrayal and hurt she must have felt when Abba purposely broke her leg. She cringed at the thought, imagining what it must be like to be so rebellious, to suffer such consequences.

"Nabal will come day after tomorrow." Her father's words jolted her, sending her stomach into a spiraling dip.

"So soon, Abba? Then there is no hope of a termination, or of going after David as Daniel suggested?" She bent to kneel beside the lamb content in her father's lap, and gently dug her fingers into the soft wool. She might have preferred a broken leg herself if it would have meant keeping her close to her father a while longer, despite her earlier thoughts that she would prefer a home of her own. She didn't want to leave now. Not after her parents had expressed such doubts, after there had been such hope that she might marry someone other than Nabal.

Her father patted Abigail's head, shifting

the cloth that covered her dark reddish-brown tresses, keeping her beauty safe for her husband. "I have failed you, my Abigail. My little lamb." He cleared his throat as though to say more would cost him, and when she lifted damp eyes to his, she saw the grief he bore.

She buried her face in the animal's wool, suddenly wanting to be anywhere but here. She had less than two days to prepare to become Nabal's wife. Two days to mourn the freedom she knew in this house, to grieve as Abba did now, knowing neither of them could undo what had been done.

Nabal would come for her, and she would become his wife. And there was nothing they could do to stop it.

The shofar blew in the distance, announcing Nabal's coming.

A hush settled over the courtyard as the neighing of horses and the sound of rowdy, loud male voices carried through the open windows.

"Behold, the bridegroom comes!" The voices of her ten virgin maids took up the traditional chant. "The virgins hold their lamps to light the way. Expectantly the bride awaits, till she hears the trump of her beloved." Abigail's heart throbbed beneath the multicolored robe that flowed in folds to her ankles and spilled over the wedding bench. She fingered the ruby pendant, Nabal's betrothal gift that rested between her breasts, trying to see through the hazy curtain of her veil.

His insistent knock made her feel faint. The room tilted.

"Who knocks on my door?" Her father's strong voice quoted the prescribed words, but his tone held no anticipation or joy.

"Your daughter's beloved, my father." Nabal's words slurred ever so slightly. Had he been drinking already? "I have come to take my bride to be with me in my father's house."

Silence met her ear, and for a weighty moment Abigail sat, hands clasped, nerves taut like strings stretched across a lyre. At last, her father cleared his throat and opened the door. "Welcome, my son." It was the polite thing to say, but Abigail knew Nabal would never hold a place in her father's heart the way Talya did.

Nabal's voice came to her above the pounding of her anxious heart as he made small talk with her parents and the handful of well-wishers filling the house. They would feast on sweet cakes and drink the wine her parents had been hoarding until at last he would come to the dais and take her hand.

"Abigail, he's coming this way." Her cousin Leah's whisper made her throat go dry. He'd just arrived. He was supposed to greet her family in the Lord's name and kiss her father's cheeks and offer gifts to her mother and linger with her brother and . . .

She smelled his heady scent before she heard his heavy footfalls across the court-yard. His gilded leather sandals stopped before the dais. She looked up, catching a filmy glimpse of his multicolored robe and turbaned headdress secured with gold-studded rubies. He wore golden wristbands and a wide golden chain about his neck. He smelled of rare spikenard, and he smiled as he parted the flimsy veil and knelt in front of her.

"Everything is ready. Will you come?" His tone came out as more of a demand than a question. And of course, she had no choice.

"I will come." The words, barely audible even to her, caught in her throat. She cleared it and swallowed but did not repeat herself. His fingers now holding hers in a possessive grip told her he had heard.

The veil fell back across her face as he pulled her to her feet. The sudden action made her dizzy again. She had eaten little since early morning, and now her appetite fled completely. She grasped Nabal's hand for support, afraid she might faint. He didn't seem to notice as he pulled her past the decorated court through the house to his waiting horse. She stared up at the beast, her thoughts whirling.

"Are you ready to go for a ride, Wife?" He chuckled. "Wife." He tested the word as though tasting it, then looked at her with a sweeping glance that made her cheeks burn. "Let's go."

"But what of the others? Mama has prepared food, and the neighbors have waited so long, and we're supposed to take time to talk and eat and laugh, and the maidens are supposed to carry torches and lead the people to your father's house, singing love songs along the way —"

"They'll come. Your father knows the way. He will lead them." He climbed onto the horse's back and bent to reach for her hand as one of his men came up and helped boost her into Nabal's arms.

He leaned forward, his face next to hers. "I'm supposed to steal you away, little girl. You're not afraid of me, are you?"

She shook her head, simultaneously thanking God for the veil that hid her gaze and begging forgiveness for the lie. Fear of Nabal mingled with fear of the horse until she worried she would be sick. "I've never ridden a horse, my lord." She was supposed to ride a jewel-bedecked camel — and she was not a little girl!

His eager hands went around her waist. "Just don't look down."

She could feel his hot breath on her neck, the scent of wine from his lips mingling with the spikenard. He had been drinking, which was sure to make him even more unpredictable.

Oh, Adonai, please be with me.

He slapped the reins, and the stallion jerked forward. Abigail stifled the urge to cry out. Nabal's laugh merged with the roaring in her ears. She had to stay focused, stay alert. It would do no good to appear as weak as she felt. His arm tightened around her waist. He took off down the trail ahead of his men, leaving her father's household and the wedding party in his wake.

3

The horse slowed to a trot as they neared the gate and stopped outside the torch-lit courtyard. Servants swarmed about carrying trays of food and drink, burning cones of incense to keep mosquitoes at bay. A male servant helped Abigail dismount. Nabal jumped to the ground behind her. "Take her to the tent, Zahara." His command was directed at a pretty, foreign, dark-haired female servant who gave Nabal a look that seemed much too familiar.

Abigail glanced from Nabal to Zahara, then down at her dust-covered robe and disheveled veil that the wind had whipped and plastered to her face. She could still taste the grit from the sand they'd traversed. Nabal had taken to the outskirts of town to race over rough terrain as if bandits were at his heels. No doubt he had heard of her father's request to back out of the betrothal. Surely this was why he had whisked her away from her father's house in such a rush as well. Did he mean now to take her to the bridal tent without the final blessing of the priest and the witness of the townspeople?

She felt the pressure of his hand at the small of her back, urging her to follow the servant. "May I make myself more presentable for you first, my lord?" She had to stall him, to allow her father time to catch up. Surely Daniel would have hopped a donkey and would be fast on their heels.

Nabal's hand moved from her back to her shoulders. He turned her toward him, then slowly lifted her veil. The moon cast his already narrow face into hard, angular lines, accentuating his frown. He wasted no time lowering his head until his lips claimed hers. "You are plenty presentable already, my dear." His fingers dug into her shoulders, and he pulled her close, his mouth pressed against her ear. "Never question me, Wife."

He released her then and pushed her from him. She stumbled, reeling from the obvious threat, still tasting his wine-coated breath. Zahara caught her arm and gently tugged her away from Nabal toward the sprawling house.

Zahara moved past the outer courtyard down a long corridor of rooms. She glanced behind her, then leaned closer to Abigail.

"Whatever you do, do nothing to anger him."

Abigail's empty stomach turned to stone, but she nodded as though she understood. Daniel had been right all along to call Nabal a fool.

"If you do what he asks, everything will be all right," Zahara whispered in her ear. The servant paused at the end of the hall, then opened a door that revealed an inner court the likes of which Abigail had never seen. Flowering plants and trees ringed the smooth stone walkway. Whitewashed stone benches were spaced at various intervals. Musicians tuned their instruments in one corner of a large circular area, and a white tent bedecked with colorful ribbons stood alone and foreboding in another. Abigail shook loose of Zahara's arm, unable to move another step. She could not enter the bridal tent without the priest's blessing. Before Yahweh it wouldn't be right.

"Come." Zahara urged her forward, but Abigail's feet refused to budge. "Please, you don't want to anger Master Nabal." Zahara's tone rose ever so slightly, at last penetrating her consciousness. The woman's fingers closed over Abigail's as a sense of numbness moved through her. She allowed the servant to lead her into the marriage tent. Three more maids suddenly appeared to fuss over her. They sprinkled the carpeted ground with almond blossoms and lighted five clay lamps set about the spacious, gleaming tent. A fresh sheet spread over a raised bed took up the center of the room, and a flask of wine stood near its head.

As if in a surreal dream, Abigail felt the maids remove her veil and wedding robe, stripping her down to her white linen tunic. Cinnamon-scented oil was poured over her skin and rubbed into her neck and shoulders and down her arms. Someone pulled the combs from her elaborately styled hair, which Talya had taken great pains to put together, then wound the long tresses up again, fixing them with one large shell comb.

"Master Nabal likes things done a certain way." Dissatisfied with the first attempts, Zahara wound Abigail's mass of hair a different way. "Too many combs will frustrate him." The combs were meant to remind him of Yahweh — seven, the number of perfection.

Abigail sank onto the bench Zahara indicated and closed her eyes, her mind unwilling to register the movements around her. The other maids scurried about the room, checking and double-checking each thing, then bowed to her one at a time and slipped from the tent until only Zahara remained.

"You must give him the respect he desires." Zahara knelt at Abigail's side and bent close to her ear. Their gazes met, the implication in the woman's words hitting Abigail with the force of a warrior's blow.

"You've been with him."

Zahara raised a brow but said nothing, neither confirming nor denying Abigail's suspicions. Would she share her husband with this foreign servant?

She drew a sharp and painful breath, and she placed both hands on her knees to keep herself erect. "Why is he doing this? Why does he not wait for the priest's blessing?"

Zahara shrugged as if she didn't know the answer, but her expression told Abigail she knew far more than she let on.

"Please, do not keep things from me." She glanced beyond Zahara to the tent's opening, imagining that she had seen movement, but the place stood empty. Blessedly, they were still alone. She released a long breath. "Tell me what you know." As mistress of Nabal's house, shouldn't she be able to command a servant? But her voice shook with uncertainty, and she knew she would never sound as self-assured as Nabal did the moment he'd crossed her father's threshold.

Zahara cast a quick look behind her, her dark eyes giving Abigail the slightest glimpse of fear. "There is little to tell. The master heard a rumor . . ." She glanced toward the tent's door again, then crossed her arms. "He said he would not be defrauded — and that your father would pay for his attempt to renege on a promise. The master takes no chances."

"Someone told Simon of my father's request." She already knew Nabal's father had a strong hold on one or more of the elders, and his influence had sealed her fate. Abba had said so from the beginning.

"He is coming. I must go." Zahara's urgent whisper shoved Abigail's thoughts back to her surroundings.

Voices drifted to her from outside the tent, one unmistakably Nabal's.

"Do not fear." Zahara stood, patted Abigail's shoulder, and moved toward the door, offering Abigail a parting look that spoke of one who had not always been a servant. A servant who might be hard to control.

But Abigail had other things to worry about right now. She told herself to breathe in and out as her eyes fixed on the tent's opening, her heart hammering to the beat of the distant drum. How had it come to this? For months after her betrothal, she had longed for this day, had spoken of it with her cousins and imagined what it meant to lie with a man. The old women had plenty of advice, and most of it made no sense then. *Duty* was a word they'd often repeated in her ear. But what of love? Nabal had spoken so sweetly of it at the betrothal and later that evening in the olive grove behind his home, when he'd coaxed her to kiss him.

Laughter, low and harsh, followed a remark she couldn't quite hear, and footsteps sounded on the stones of the courtyard. Her parents loved each other. Surely Nabal would show her the same courtesy. Zahara had said to respect him, but already she had lost what little respect she'd had.

Zahara. Was the woman as familiar with Nabal as she let on? What else did Abigail not know about the man? If the elders had recognized early on, if her father had known . . .

A man-sized shadow blocked the moon's eerie glow at the entrance to Abigail's woven prison. Soft and haunting music grew louder as the tent's flap fell behind Nabal, enclosing them both in lamp-lit darkness. Sweat broke out across her forehead, and her limbs suddenly felt weighted as he sauntered closer.

Oh, Adonai, what do I do?

His dark eyes moved slowly over her, his smile broadening with every step. "You truly are the fairest maiden in Maon, perhaps in all Israel." He spoke with the look and confidence of ownership. "Not even the women in the king's household compare to you, dear . . . wife."

He knelt at her side while she still sat on the bench, his gaze searching hers, filling her with a deep sense of dread. What Zahara hadn't said spoke volumes to her now. Nabal would treat her kindly if she never questioned him and never gave him a reason to think she wasn't utterly devoted to him. His fragile ego would make him violent if she ever tried to challenge him . . . or change him.

Despair washed over her in waves as Nabal pulled the shell comb from her hair and dug his fingers into her thick tresses. His breath came hot on her neck as he drew her close. "You are denied the priest's blessing because your father tried to cross me." His whispered words added to the pain he was inflicting as his hands gripped her arms, and he forced her toward the bed. He released his grip for a moment and bent to rip the white sheet from the mat, the sheet that would go to her father to protect her purity. "And your father is denied any recourse against me." His sneer made her blood grow cold.

"I'm sorry, my lord." She choked back a sob, hoping her response would appease him. But he seemed oblivious to her words.

When he had finished with her, he tied his princely robe around his waist once again and strutted from the tent. Abigail pulled a pillow to her chest and curled on her side. She would not cry.

Neither would she respect or forgive him.

4

Daniel picked his way along the dry wadi of rocks and sparse grass, glancing every now and then to make sure his flock followed. He used the staff as a walking stick, his wary eyes scanning the steep hills on either side. In the rainy season, water would rush through this gorge in a life-giving stream, a satisfying place to water the hundred sheep in his care. But during the summer months, he had little worry of being washed away in a sudden cloudburst. He was more concerned about marauding thieves than changes in the weather.

Word had it that David's men were in these parts. Some said the malcontents who had joined the king's son-in-law in hiding were no better than the Amalekite or Moabite raiders who camped out in these hills and struck unsuspecting shepherds.

Daniel felt the leather pouch and sling at his side. Little good they would do him against a band of men, but he'd put up a fight if they tried anything. Right now a fight, or at least its aftermath, might cool the hot blood pumping through his veins.

Wind whistled down to him from the cliffs above, tensing his already overwrought muscles. Was that truly the wind, or a mimicked whistle call of bandits? He stopped to listen, glancing behind again to make sure the sheep still followed. Nothing.

He stood for the space of a few more breaths, waiting, then continued walking. The uneven ground made slow going, but the path to water and away from Nabal's estate was worth the trek.

How could his father have allowed Abigail to marry that fool? He clenched one hand around the staff and jabbed it hard into the ground. If the townsmen hadn't stopped him, he would have cut Nabal's throat after what he did to Abigail. She deserved better. She deserved a normal, traditional wedding ceremony. She didn't deserve a man who strutted about disdaining her family, her femaleness, her innocence. She deserved a man who would protect and treasure her, not mistreat and use her.

He cursed under his breath, though he knew no one could hear. His father felt some misplaced loyalty to Simon and his worthless son, but Daniel did not. If David and his men were hiding in these hills — he prayed to God they were — then he would find them and take Talya and join them. Whether his father agreed with him or not.

David poked the fire with a long olive branch, stirring the embers. Dusk settled like mist across the expansive wilderness, caught between day and night, then falling swiftly to darkness. Patches of conversation drifted to him from fires at the mouths of other caves where his men and their families lived in hiding from their mad and jealous monarch. How long until Saul finally caught up with him? How long could he live on the run and ask those loyal to him to continue the fugitive lifestyle?

He turned the stick over, then dropped it beside him. In the distance a mother scolded a whiny child, while another hushed giggles that could easily turn to shouts and laughter. In the wilderness he shouldn't worry about noise giving his whereabouts away, but spies were everywhere, and the less the sound traveled, the better.

A sigh escaped him. He lowered himself to a large stone and rested his elbows on his knees, watching the sparks fly upward.

"May I get you anything, my lord?" His

wife Ahinoam squatted in the dirt beside him, her beautiful face showing the strain of worry. "A cup of water perhaps? There is still some in the jug."

He shook his head, offering her what he knew was a less than convincing smile. "I'm fine. Thank you, though."

She nodded and stood. "If you don't need me then, I'll be in the cave . . ." Her voice trailed off, and she turned at the commotion of loud male voices coming toward them.

David stood, his hand on the dagger at his waist. "Go quickly." He touched her shoulder in a reassuring gesture, but his hand glanced off her as she lifted her robe and rushed to do his bidding. "Who goes there?" He drew the weapon and stepped away from the fire's light, where he was better hidden by the shadows.

"Joab, my lord. And Abishai. We've got company."

"Friendly?"

"We don't know yet."

David sheathed his dagger and stepped back into the circle of the fire pit as his two nephews stepped forward, pulling a lone man with them.

"Who are you?" David studied the young man clothed in shepherd's garb, minus the

37

usual pouch, staff, rod, and sling a shepherd would carry. He shifted his gaze to his nephews and noted the man's tools tucked into Joab's belt. The man's hands were bound behind him, and Joab's thick hand was wrapped around his forearm.

"My name is Daniel ben Judah, my lord. I've been searching for you to join your band." Daniel held David's resolute gaze. His muscles worked along his shoulders, and he strained against the men holding him, but he made no attempt to free himself. "I have heard that you allow men who are in debt or discontented to join forces with you, and that women and children are also here. I would like to bring my family and help you in your cause to take the kingdom."

"I do not plan to take the kingdom." David's gaze moved from Daniel to his nephews. Joab stood a head shorter and Abishai a head taller. Both men had muscles of bronze, but by the looks of young Daniel, he could have given them quite a fight if he'd wanted to.

"My mistake, my lord, but whether you plan it or not, certainly King Saul assumes this is your intent. Why else would he want to kill you?"

Why else indeed? "The king is troubled."

David stroked his beard, liking what he saw in Daniel's eyes. The youth was forthright, probably a bit hotheaded by the way he clenched his jaw, but no more so than half the rest of the men under his command. "How many are in your family?"

"My wife Talya, who is with child, and my parents, if I can convince them to come. I would bring my sister . . ." He broke eye contact with David, and a pained expression crossed his face.

"Did something happen to your sister?" Perhaps she was ill and couldn't travel. It was none of his business, but something in the man's look roused his curiosity.

Daniel looked at him again, his gaze steely and angry. "She married a fool." Daniel followed the explosion of anger with a curse and spat into the fire.

"To hear the women talk, most men are fools." David tried to lighten the mood, but Daniel's look told him his comment had not hit the mark.

"Not like this, my lord." When he said nothing further, David stepped closer, assessing Daniel.

"Why would your father choose such a man? Is your sister displeasing to the eye that no one else would have her?"

"My sister is quite fair, but my father had

little choice."

"There is always a choice." The words came out more bitter than David intended, but he knew all too well the price he had paid for his own poor choices. "If you have differences with your father, work it out before you come." He had more domestic squabbles going on around him than he needed. "How do I know you're not simply here to spy on us? If I let you go in peace, you could tell Saul where we are, and frankly, I'm weary of running. I want to stay here for a while. How do I know I can trust you?"

Daniel held David's steady gaze, then bowed his head in an offer of respect. "You don't. But I am telling you the truth. Send one of your men back with me if you don't believe me."

David glanced at his nephews. "Cut him loose." He picked up the olive branch and stirred the ash at the edge of the fire. "Go in peace and bring your family."

"Thank you, my lord." Daniel shook his arms free of the ropes the moment they were loosed and accepted his possessions from Joab. "It may take some time to convince them all to come, but I will come. You can count on it."

David studied the ground, making circles

in the dirt. "I can't promise you will find us again. I cannot promise we will sleep here another night. I'm like a partridge in the mountains, quick to flee and hopefully hard to spot." He lifted his gaze along with the stick and pointed the glowing edge of the branch heavenward. "Only God knows how long this will continue, Daniel." He looked at the man. "Are you prepared for such a life? Would you offer such instability to your family?"

Daniel's defiant posture softened, and his gaze held the slightest hint of doubt. "Anything is better than working for a man who is both foolish and cruel."

"So your sister married a fool and you work for a fool. One and the same?"

Daniel nodded. "Yes, my lord. My father was forced into service years ago to a wicked man. Rather than decreasing his debts, Simon of Carmel found ways to defraud my father again and again until finally Simon manipulated my father into giving my sister to his son as his wife. So my sister is trapped in marriage to a fool, and my father and I work for one. I cannot save my sister, but if we leave, perhaps I can save my son the same fate."

David lowered himself back onto the stone and clasped his hands in front of him. He motioned for Daniel to sit beside him. "If you leave this man's employ, will you be putting your sister at greater risk?" It was a question he'd asked himself a hundred times since leaving Michal in her father's care. He had surely left her at risk by fleeing. If he had taken her with him, she wouldn't be resting in another man's arms.

"My sister, while I care deeply for her, is no longer in my power to help. I pray God she is well, but my concern lies now with my wife and unborn child and my parents. These are in my power to save if you will allow us to come, my lord. Please understand, if I could help Abigail I would."

The man was right, of course. A married woman belonged to her husband and his family. Daniel's sister was bound as surely as a slave was bound to his master.

David studied the fire, reminding himself that the night he escaped Saul's house had offered him little choice as well. If Michal had run with him, Saul's guards would have caught them both. He could be dead by now or, worse, imprisoned somewhere or sold into slavery like Joseph of old. Running was the only alternative, and Michal would not have survived this lifestyle.

He looked the young man over again. His muscles were no longer taut and strained except for a telltale clenching of his jaw. Sweat dampened his tunic and glistened beneath his tan turban, probably from both nerves and the heat. "We will remain in this wilderness of Ziph for as long as we can find food and safety. If you wish to join us, I suggest you do so quickly. If we flee, there is no telling if we will return, and trying to find us — I'm afraid I cannot leave you word."

"I understand." Daniel rested both hands on his knees and pushed to his feet. "If it pleases my lord, I must return to my sheep. I will gather my family and come." He bowed, and at David's nod he left the campfire and slipped into the night.

5

Nabal lifted a goatskin flask to his lips and squeezed the last drops into his mouth, cursing the pittance that was left, then wiped his mouth with the back of his sleeve. "Tomorrow, you say?"

The swarthy messenger nodded, his greedy eyes visible in the torch-lit night. They moved from Nabal's face to the pouch at his belt. "The men of Ziph have pinpointed David's location, and some have already headed to Gibeah to bring word to the king."

"But the others will be here?" He reached into his pouch, pulled out two silver coins, and placed them in the man's grasping hand. "I expect the information I seek for the price you're robbing me." Rumor had it that David's men were in the hills where Nabal's shepherds roamed. Some said they protected his sheep and were a contending force against marauders. The malcontents would expect compensation of some sort, as if they deserved such a thing.

"You'll get your information. And when the king fastens the son of Jesse's arrogant hide to Gibeah's gates, you can be as close as you like to watch." The man sneered, raising Nabal's respect for him. They were alike in their hatred of the king's son-in-law and the rogue men who followed him.

"See to it." Nabal lifted the flask again to his lips. Finding it empty, he spat into the dirt, turned his back on the messenger, and walked toward the kitchen. He needed more wine.

"Your father would be proud," the man called after him, his tone laced with sarcasm.

Nabal whirled about too fast and lost his balance, but he managed to right himself, ready to swing his fist into the man's arrogant face. But the man had already mounted his horse and kicked its sides, laughing outright and galloping down the road toward the gates of Nabal's estate.

Insects buzzed with the onslaught of darkness as Nabal stared after the man, heat coursing through him. His father would not have been proud. He had died with a curse against his only son still warm on his lips. His father had named him *fool* — and had done everything possible to make Nabal's life miserable. He was glad the man was dead. He did not deserve Nabal's respect. He was a self-righteous hypocrite much like the king's son-in-law and all of the men who followed him.

Heart pounding and throat parched, Nabal squeezed the flask and slammed it to the ground. Straightening, he stomped toward the kitchen. Heat from the ovens drifted to him, and he heard Abigail talking to a servant. He swore under his breath. He should have known she would be overseeing tomorrow's meal preparation. Another self-righteous hypocrite, that one. Always running her mouth off. If not for her beauty . . . He let the thought drop. She would give him a son one day. Women did have their uses. Though after six months of marriage, he wondered what was taking her so long. He flung his shoulders back and put on his most commanding air as he walked under the arch into the spacious kitchens.

"Woman, bring me more wine." The servants jumped at his barked order, but Abigail merely turned, walked to a stone trough in the far corner, and retrieved the skin. She took her time coming close to him, as though she were the master and he the servant.

When she reached him, he snatched the

flask from her arms, yanked the leather strings that bound it tight, and poured the contents into his mouth, spilling some onto his beard. He gulped more than he probably should have — he'd already finished one flask earlier in the day — but he was tired of incompetent messengers and arrogant women.

Abigail backed away from him, retrieved a linen cloth, and handed it to him. He wiped his mouth on his sleeve instead, then gripped her arm, digging his nails into her flesh.

She winced, but her gaze did not waver. Definitely self-righteous — and disrespectful.

"My lord, please, you're hurting me."

He stared at her, his vision slightly blurring, seeing the woman whose father had tried to defraud him, whose brother disdained him, who too often tried to change him.

She twisted her arm, trying to break free. He released his grip, and she rubbed the place where the imprint of his nails still remained. He looked at the goatskin flask in his hand.

"Don't you think you should save some for later, my lord?"

Did the woman know how to be quiet?

Must her every word be a reason to condemn his actions? Her disdain was inexcusable.

"Don't think your beauty will always save you from my wrath, Abigail." A headache began at his temples, and he rubbed them, willing it to subside.

"Did I offend you, my lord? Forgive me, it's just . . . you look ill, my lord, and I thought —"

"Silence!" She jumped at his command. Good. It was time she learned some obedience, and it was time he taught it to her. He shoved the flask into her hands. "Tie it." Her hands shook as she hurried to obey him. When she finished, he took it from her, set it on a table, and grabbed her arm.

Abigail winced at the bruise he was giving her. Nabal's firm grip tightened, his foul breath close to her face. His menacing look made her heart race like a thousand galloping horses, her stomach tripping in dread. He dragged her out of the kitchen toward the gardens at the back of the house, a place she had been often but never with him. A secluded place where she'd once sought refuge.

He turned his face to the side and spat into the bushes lining the cobbled walkway, then shoved her ahead of him toward the seclusion of the trees. She stumbled toward a handful of torches that lined the edges of the garden and cast eerie shadows over the stones. They were the only lights dispelling the blackness that not even the stars chose to witness this night.

"I've had enough of your prattle, woman!" His sandals scuffed the stones behind her as though he had tripped, and Abigail regained her balance and stepped to the side, afraid he might land on her in his drunken stupor. If only she had stayed out of sight. If she had hidden in her rooms instead of checking on the food supply for his feast, he wouldn't have happened upon her there, wouldn't have spoken to her, wouldn't have elicited the response she had given that had gotten her into trouble. Oh, when would she learn to curb her tongue?

A litany of foul words spewed from Nabal's mouth as he righted himself and came toward her again. Another bend in the spacious garden and they would be at the old olive tree along the wall that bordered Nabal's property. This private garden had been her sanctuary — something she had often needed in her six months of marriage — when he had turned her away from his bed to punish her for some unknown slight, or when she needed to lick her wounds after she found him with one of the servant girls. This had been her safe place, a place he had never bothered to follow. Had someone betrayed her and told him her secret?

She slowed her pace, but he was quick to grab her wrist and pull her to the end of the walk, where the olive tree spread its branches in a gnarled, shaded greeting. He whipped her around to face him, a sliver of moonlight setting his dark, narrow face into a grotesque mask. Her heart beat faster, if that were possible, as she met the hatred in his eyes. He reached above him to rip a thin branch from the tree, giving it a quick yank to try to pry it loose from the larger branch it clung to. His struggle brought forth a string of curses, as though the old tree would battle her husband for her honor.

But even the tree betrayed her after a moment when Nabal finally staggered backward with a jolt as the branch gave way. A wicked gleam filled his gaze as he held it above her head. He had slapped her now and then and had found other ways to humiliate her or mistreat her, but until now he had never beaten her.

"Please, my lord, what will people say if they knew you struck your wife? Surely the laws of Adonai forbid such a thing, and if my father got wind of it, or the priests —"

A cackling laugh escaped his lips. "There are no priests, my dear wife — you forget King Saul killed them all, and who would dare tell your father? You?" He laughed again, but this time it was throatier and more vulgar.

"Yes, my lord, but if the servants become aware that you would lay a hand on your wife, they may turn against you, and then who would help you to shear your many sheep? And you cannot forget that Adonai is watching, and you would not wish to break His law and —"

His palm connected with her cheek so fast she didn't see it coming. "Adonai would not expect a man to put up with a woman's insolence." His snarl sent another puff of foul breath toward her.

Tears sprang to her eyes, and she raised her arms to protect her face, tasting blood on her lip. Why, oh why, had she opened her mouth again? There was no talking to him when he was like this, but how else was she to convince him to let her go if she did not speak? Try as she might, she had never learned to be meek and silent, though her mother had often warned her that her tongue, however wise her words might be, would get her into trouble one day.

He turned the olive branch over in his hand, looking from it to her, as though savoring the terror she knew must be evident in her eyes, despite her desperate attempt to keep him from seeing her fear. "It's time you learned to respect your husband, my dear wife." He spoke with a sneer and a tone that held no respect for her at all.

"Please don't hurt me." She covered her face with both hands as he towered over her. She was at his mercy, with no escape from him.

Nabal's thoughts churned through his head like a torrential wind come down from the hills into the valleys, rushing forward and pushing him to act. The woman his father had dumped on him was beautiful, he'd give her that, but her devotion to Adonai and her clever way with words had annoyed him from the moment she'd opened her mouth at their wedding feast. She could barely speak a sentence without some reference to Adonai, praising Him for His creation or reminding Nabal of one of His laws. Her father had been a fool to allow a woman to learn the law of Moses, and his father had proved his utter disdain for his own son by binding him to such a God-loving woman. He deserved better. He deserved a woman who would worship his every word.

He laughed aloud, though the sound was bitter, and stared down at Abigail now, who crouched before him like a frightened animal. She deserved everything he planned to give her for that brazen tongue. He had half a mind to cut it out of her and be done with her pious nonsense, but he couldn't quite bring himself to permanently mar her beauty.

Which was why he stood hovering over her, turning the whip in his hands. She was right about one thing. No one should know about this, least of all her father, though he doubted the man would ever hear of it. He was too big a coward to do anything anyway. The thought bolstered his confidence — and his anger at this woman who had caused him so much grief.

She covered her face now, hiding what little the moon would reveal of her beauty. Beauty that did not move him as it once did. He slapped the whip against his palm, enjoying the way she winced each time she heard the smack. He would put the blows in places that wouldn't permanently harm her, lest she be unable to give him the son he needed when he so desired. Her clothes would hide any bruises or cuts, but he would definitely have his way with her to-night.

She would not get away with her insolence. He would see to it.

The first blow jolted Abigail, stinging her forearm. Instinctively, she covered the spot with her hand, but he was quick to deliver a succession of follow-up blows, whirling her around and placing each one in a different spot. Fire coursed through every limb, and she cried out, begging him to stop until her voice grew hoarse.

"Silence!" He bellowed the word after each of her pitiful cries until her common sense finally kicked in, and she clamped her mouth shut no matter how severe the pain. When she crumpled to the dirt, covering her head with both hands in a gesture of self-protection, he growled some unintelligible sounds like a wounded animal.

Oh, Adonai, help me. What have I done to deserve this man?

She'd asked the question a thousand times since her wedding night. Despite her father's attempt to dissolve her marriage, she knew he expected her to live well, never needing anything, never knowing she would want for peace and safety every day of her life.

"Get up!" Nabal's demand cut through

her thoughts. He yanked a clump of her hair and pulled.

"Ow!" Her unintended cry was rewarded with a slew of curses.

"I told you, stupid woman, to be silent!" He tossed the whip into the bushes and pulled her toward him. She tasted his wine-soaked breath as his mouth came down hard on hers. Before she could respond, he ripped her torn clothes from her and forced her to the ground again.

Moments later he stood, looked down on her with a satisfied smirk on his face that he had finally humbled her, and walked away, leaving her naked in the dirt.

She fumbled blindly about for her robe after he was gone. She thrust a trembling arm through each sleeve, cinched the robe closed, then fell once again to the dirt and wept in silence.

6

David pushed his weary limbs from the hard-packed earth and stood, glancing down at his sleeping wife Ahinoam. Light flickered from a clay lamp embedded in a crevice of the cave's rock walls and cast shifting shadows over her huddled form. Even in sleep her brows wrinkled and her hands curled into tight balls at her sides. He was a fool to have jumped into marriage with a woman of whom he knew nothing. If he'd waited, sought wise counsel . . . He sighed, shaking his head. One did not consult the ephod and invoke Yahweh's pleasure on matters of the heart.

Still, finding out more about her would have told him she was weak and as frightened as a skittish gazelle. Her worries zapped what little strength he had left. If not for his overwhelming desire to satisfy his own needs, to replace what he had lost in Michal, he would have been better off without a woman to drag him down.

He moved from her side and pulled his robe over his tunic, frustrated with his train of thought. She stretched as he wrapped his leather girdle about his waist. In some respects, women did have a calming effect on the men, kept them stable. A few even seemed to have a measure of common sense, like Joab's wife Marta. Though he wouldn't trade Ahinoam's fear for Marta's common sense. Marta came with a sharp tongue and a beaked nose, neither of which he found appealing. Better to suffer through Ahinoam's weakness. At least she was pleasing to look at.

With deft fingers, David quickly tied the sling to his belt and slipped the sword into its sheath at his side. Ahinoam stirred, then sat bolt upright.

"Is it morning already, my lord?" She snatched the robe from beneath her and pulled it about her, looking up at him with wide, anxious eyes.

"It's still night. Go back to sleep." He couldn't tell that for sure in the recesses of the cave, but no one else stirred about them, telling him dawn was far off.

"But where are you going?" Her whispered words held a thread of panic, raising his ire. "Has the king come back?"

"I'm not going anywhere. Go back to sleep." He kept his voice low, but he couldn't keep the irritation from his tone. She was far too clingy and needy, but to tell her he wanted to sleep by the fire rather than hold her in his arms would bring him more grief than he cared to handle. "I'll be back soon." It was a promise he didn't want to fulfill, but when she nodded and lay back down, looking hurt and lonely, he knew he would return before the sun came up.

He picked his way past sleeping comrades by the muted light of a few more clay lamps set in various niches along the cave walls, past family groups huddled together for safety and warmth. If he had any sense of decency, he would be doing the same — keeping Ahinoam safe, or at least giving her a sense of safety, however false. But his own restlessness would only add to her fear. And his.

The mouth of the cave grew closer, where a fire still burned and sentries stood watch. Temperatures in the desert at night made the fire a welcome sight. He approached, cinching his cloak tighter at the neck and glancing at the guards. One snored while the other stood with his back to the fire, gaze facing the plateau where the town of Ziph stood in the distance.

David scuffed his toe along the ground as he approached the guard to alert him of his presence. "Quiet tonight, Benaiah?"

"Yes, my lord. Nothing moves that I can see." Benaiah stood a head taller than David, his burly frame filling out his tunic and straining the seams. Benaiah had been with him four years now, ever since the day he had run from his service to King Saul to report the loss of Michal to David. David had always liked the young guard, and since that day when Benaiah's disgust for Saul had matched David's own, he'd become a trusted ally.

Benaiah dipped his head toward David in a gesture of respect, then flicked his gaze across the expanse of desert once again. Spies could move along the plains at night with little fear of being seen, despite David's diligence at placing sentries in pairs at eight locations going north, south, east, and west. "Trouble sleeping, my lord?"

"No more than usual." David ran a hand through his hair, unable to stifle a yawn. Stars seemed closer here in the hill of Hakilah with no houses or trees to block the view. "Sometimes it's easier to sleep under the stars than in a cave." He nodded toward the fire. "Wake me if there's trouble."

Benaiah acknowledged David's comment

without a word, then walked to the edge of the cliff to peer down the mountainside. David stretched out before the fire and rested his head on a smooth rock. Tongues of flame licked the animal dung and dry sticks they'd managed to scrounge up, sending sparks into the sky. David's gaze followed the sparks to where his heart turned heavenward.

O Adonai, how long? Will You forget me forever?

Samuel's anointing seemed a lifetime ago, and every good thing that had followed, a fading dream. Already he had waited eight summers since the day the prophet had come to his father's house seeking to anoint the next king of Israel. Where was Adonai's promise now?

How much longer, Lord?

The scent of cinnamon used to remind him of that day. If he closed his eyes to think on it, he could almost feel the oil running down his hair into his beard. Now the scent merely reminded him of Ahinoam, who'd once mixed the spice into her perfume — back when she lived with her uncle in happier circumstances. Ahinoam, whose fear had become his own.

I'll die one day at Saul's hand.

The thought came to him unbidden,

tightening the muscles in his stomach, draining his blood. Impossible. Yahweh would not have sent Samuel to anoint him only to abandon him now. Surely not.

But the unsettled feeling remained.

He turned on his side to face the fire and closed his eyes. Fitful dreams mocked him until the gray edge of dawn poked through the black horizon. He rubbed the sting of sleep from his tired eyes and forced himself to rise. Blinking hard to adjust to the darkness beyond the fire, he searched for a glimpse of Benaiah's stoic form. When he did not see him at first glance, he walked to the edge of the rock cliff and peered down the trail to where the guard made his rounds. He caught sight of him several paces away, a hand over his eyes as if trying to see farther into the distance.

David trained his eyes in the same direction, instinctively searching the plains for any sign of movement in the predawn stillness. He walked closer to where Benaiah stood but stopped short of him when the moon's retreating light illuminated the place at the foot of the hill. A moment later, Benaiah turned and met David's gaze across the space between them. Someone was coming.

David nodded at Benaiah, who quickly

scooted farther down the hill to assess what they'd seen. David crouched low, following at Benaiah's heels. At another clifflike overhang, David got down on his stomach and moved to the edge, peering into the valley below. There, hundreds of black goat-hair tents spread out like a thousand mammoth anthills. *Saul.*

"He's called out the entire standing army," Benaiah whispered, his breath close to David's ear.

The standing army consisted of three thousand of Israel's mightiest men — minus David, his six hundred followers, and Jonathan. His friend would never join in Saul's madness to seek David's life. But there were obviously plenty of those who would, men whom he'd once commanded, who had followed his leadership with excitement, even joy.

Whose fickle hearts now marched after Saul to hunt him down.

"Let's go." David scooted away from the edge. When they were out of the range of vision to those below, he stood and hurried back up the hill, Benaiah's footfalls right behind him.

When they reached the fire pit, barely winded, David rushed past it into the mouth of the cave. "Awaken my nephews and the three mighty men at once, then get the rest of the camp moving." He glanced at his faithful guard, unable to hold back a heavy sigh. "Someone told Saul where we are. There is no other way to explain how he got so close undetected."

"The Ziphites have been less than friendly." Benaiah scratched his beard, then moved to do David's bidding.

"Indeed. Or our young visitor was not as honest as he appeared." David moved to the back of the cave to meet with his leaders, wondering if he'd misread the shepherd Daniel who'd looked so honest and determined to claim allegiance. Had he been duped by a master deceiver, or did the man truly hold kindness toward David in his heart?

7

"Take the women and children to En Gedi."
David paced at the back of the cave, stopping every few seconds to face his advisors.
"It's me Saul wants, so I'll stay behind to
draw him out. One or two men can evade
an army better than hundreds of women
with babes on their hips."

"There isn't time, David." His nephew
Joab sat rubbing a grinding stone across the
blade of his sword, sharpening it. Three
other advisors did the same. The noise
grated David's already heightened nerves.
"Saul's army is too close. They will see the
women or hear the children and intercept
them before we can get down the mountain.
Saul would like nothing better than to
kidnap them all and hold them for ransom.
He knows you wouldn't allow an enemy to
take what belongs to you, so he'd use it to
his advantage."

"Or he'd kill them all as he did the

priests," Benaiah put in.

David glanced at Abiathar, the lone member of Ahimelech's household who had escaped the killing of the priests of Nob, murdered at Saul's command. He looked at Abishai, Joab's brother. "Put the women and children in the back of the largest caves, along with the animals and the supplies. Spread men out in strategic places to guard them, but leave some men in the caves with the women to keep them quiet."

His gaze shifted to Asahel, Joab's youngest brother — the one with feet as fast as a gazelle — and to Eleazar, one of his mighty men. "Each of you take two hundred men and circle in opposite directions behind Saul's army. See if you can divert them away from the women."

He ran a hand through his hair and cast a pointed look from Joab to Benaiah. "You two, and the rest of you" — he took in his small band of mighty men with one glance — "will come with me. We're going to climb up the back of the mountain and see if Saul will follow. Saul's commander, Abner, is sure-footed, but he's out of practice. They haven't fought a real war since the king decided I was sweeter prey than the Philistines. Let's give them something to chase."

Joab set down the grinding stone and

slipped the sword into the belt at his waist. "Lead on, O mighty king."

He took two steps forward, but David caught his shoulder with one hand, making him stop midstride. "Only God is mighty, and I am not king. We are at Saul's mercy here. If we escape, it will only be by God's grace." He held his nephew's hardened gaze. A self-made man, Joab didn't put much stock in Adonai's ability to deliver. Sometimes of late, David had a hard time disagreeing with him.

A commotion coming from the mouth of the cave interrupted Joab's response. One of the sentries approached, out of breath. "They are coming, my lord. Saul's men are even now climbing the hill headed in this direction. We need to flee!"

"Go!" David's command had barely left his mouth before his men dispersed, rushing to do his bidding.

"Which way?" Joab asked when they had reached the cliff and looked down at Saul's men picking their way up the mountain.

David glanced at the outcropping of caves at their back where Abishai stood giving quiet orders to the two hundred men in his charge. Frightened women and children hurried alongside goats and donkeys on the path to join the others already in the largest caves.

"That way." David moved in the opposite direction, leaving the place they'd called home for the past few months behind, wondering if anything would ever be right again.

"Saul is too close, David," Joab said when they paused for breath an hour later.

"I think we're all aware of that fact, Nephew. What do you suggest we do about it?"

David took a sip of water from the pouch at his waist and wiped his mouth with the back of his hand, then took off walking again. The terrain along the mountain made running impossible, but they'd managed to go faster than David had expected. Unfortunately, Saul's men had shortened the gap between them. If they gained any more distance, they'd be within an arrow's shot. He could only hope Asahel and Eleazar would somehow bring up the rear and send some of the three thousand warriors in the opposite direction. Hadn't Gideon of old conquered the enemy with fewer men?

He glanced behind him at his own determined men, quickening his pace to urge them to do the same. "If we stop now, we might as well surrender."

"In another hour we won't have a choice." Joab jogged to catch up with David.

Ire prickled the hairs on the back of David's neck. "So what do you want me to do? Shall I walk down the mountain and let Saul's archers have at me? Or maybe you want me to just lie down at Saul's feet and wait until I feel his sword pierce my neck?" He sprinted forward, not wanting a reply. Anger spurred him on.

Joab caught up with him again. "Of course not, David. Every one of us believes you will be the next king of Israel, but we could get on with that a lot sooner if you'd just let one of your men shoot one of our arrows at the old king and be done with this nonsense. We're running away instead of fighting. If we fight, I promise you I will take him out with one shot." He huffed the words at David's side, falling back when they came to a narrow path circling the mountain.

"I do not doubt your military prowess, Joab, but I've told you before, I will not kill the king."

"You don't have to. I'll do it."

"I am responsible for your actions." He caught Joab's determination and matched it with his own. "The answer is no."

He moved ahead, his side aching from the

climb. When he reached a wider plateau, he paused to look behind him. Saul's men were gaining. How was that possible? But there was no mistaking Abner's plumed helmet or Saul's standard-bearer leading the king behind him.

He looked ahead again. If he took the path to the summit, Saul could wait him out, trapping him here until they ran out of supplies and starved. There would be no way down the mountain without one of Saul's men spotting them. If he took the road leading to the valley floor, the men Saul left at the foot of the mountain would surround him. Saul's men would be rested and able to travel quicker, swooping down on him and his exhausted, hungry men. There was no way out short of the grace of Yahweh.

O Adonai, my enemies surround me. Keep me as the apple of Your eye; hide me in the shadow of Your wings from the wicked who attack me, from my enemies who surround me. They have tracked me down, and now they surround me, with eyes alert, to throw me to the ground, like a lion hungry for prey. Rise up, Adonai, confront them, bring them down. Rescue me from the wicked by Your sword.

Sweat greased his back and his forehead, and he wiped his brow again, warring with indecision. Benaiah joined him, his longer legs carrying him faster than Joab's, his presence comforting.

"If you have a suggestion, I'm listening." David glanced at his guard, impressed with his obvious strength and quiet confidence. This was a man he would keep close, one who could be trusted.

"We should head toward the valley. It may be that the others will have pulled Saul's men away from watching us. But at least there we may find numerous places to hide. Here we are trapped." Benaiah glanced toward the path as the others joined them.

David acknowledged Benaiah's advice with a nod. Joab might disagree, and there was wisdom in the abundance of counselors, but David was not in the mood to hear Joab's opinion yet again. He moved away from the group to the edge of the cliff, the breeze cooling his skin. They would have trouble keeping warm at this elevation. Benaiah was right.

He turned to move toward the path leading downward when a whizzing sound whooshed past his ear.

"Get down!" David flattened his body to the dirt in one instinctive motion, sensing that his men had done the same. He lifted his head and took in the group. "Anybody hurt?"

Benaiah pulled an arrow from a clump of dirt and crawled toward David. "We're fine." He laid the arrow beside David. "Let me volley one back at them. They'll think twice before they shoot again."

David shook his head. "You might hit the king. I can't risk it."

"You would risk our heads instead?" A murmur of agreement followed Joab's angry retort. The thirty now crowded closer on their knees. "At least let us shoot toward them to slow them down so we can escape."

David met Joab's heated scowl with one of his own. He swiveled his gaze to Benaiah. "You can shoot over their heads. Two shots. And make sure you are far from Saul's armor bearer, since Saul will undoubtedly be right behind him."

Benaiah offered David a brief nod and crouched closer to the edge, nocked the arrow into his bow, and let it fly. Shouts came from below, and David moved closer to see the damage as Benaiah readied the second arrow. But the commotion didn't seem aimed in their direction.

"A runner comes," one of the men said. "See there, he's heading toward the king."

The faint sound of Saul's name being

called carried to them. David put up a hand to stop Benaiah from loosing another arrow. Benaiah let the bow go slack as the thirty gathered around David, watching as the runner finally made it to the king's side, out of breath.

"My lord king. Hasten and come! The Philistines are invading the land."

Tense silence broken only by heavy breathing filled the air around him as David held his breath, his head cocked to listen. He half expected Saul to ignore the Philistine threat — however foolish that might be — considering the king's fierce hatred of him. But to his immense relief, Saul turned around and headed back down the mountain, his men surrounding him as they hurried forward. Abner took a last look toward the plateau where David and his men stood watching. Another hour and Saul's men would have intercepted them.

Abner lifted one hand to his helmet and deftly bowed, acknowledging defeat. David ignored the salute, knowing how close they'd come to capture. This would not be the last time he faced this foe.

"Are you ready to rejoin the others, my lord?" Benaiah asked after the last of Saul's troops had faded into the distance and the sun began its descent toward the valley floor. "They'll wonder what happened to us."

David closed his eyes against the angle of the sun's glare and drew in a long, slow breath, letting the tenseness of his muscles ease. "And we will tell them of Adonai's deliverance. From this day forth, this hill shall be called *Sela Hammahlekoth* — rock of parting, for it was here that the Lord Almighty parted us from our enemies."

"Until next time." Joab turned from the group and headed down the mountain.

David watched him go, thinking to argue the point, except for the unfortunate fact that Joab was right.

8

Palm trees and the sound of rushing water greeted Daniel as they approached the Crag of the Ibex, and relief flooded him at the sound of women and children talking and laughing nearby. Shepherds and travelers often stopped at this oasis on the shores of the Salt Sea, but surely these people were with David. He couldn't bear to put Talya through any more aimless searching if he happened to be wrong.

"Wait here." He gripped the reins of Talya's donkey and pulled the animal to a halt among the shaded, overhanging rocks. He motioned for his father to stay with the women, and despite his father's recent protests that he was perfectly capable of keeping up, this time he did not argue.

Daniel released a deep sigh, then gripped his staff and trudged ahead toward the sound of the women and children. He worked his way down a steep incline and rounded a bend out of sight of his family. He lifted a hand to his eyes, squinting against the late afternoon sun, and searched for something familiar, some way to tell whether this was indeed David's camp. After two months of searching, this had to be it. Laughter floated up to him from the pool below, where two young boys ducked in and out of the waterfall. He took another step closer.

Rough hands grabbed him from behind, pinning his shoulders back. He attempted to whirl about, to defend himself with his staff, but the brute holding him disarmed him, and a moment later he felt the point of a knife blade beneath his chin.

"State your business."

The gruff voice was one Daniel didn't recognize, and the oaf was bigger and taller than the two men who had escorted him to David the last time. He forced his muscles to stop straining against his captor, not relishing the thought of feeling the life force flow out of him should the man's weapon slip and cut his throat.

"I'm here to pledge allegiance to David. I've brought my family. They are waiting near the Crag of the Ibex. Please, I've come once before. David will remember. I am Daniel ben Judah. I mean you no harm."

His words came out all in one breath, his heart hammering despite his silent command telling himself to relax.

The man's heavy breath heated the back of Daniel's neck as he leaned in close. "There are many spies these days siding with Saul, giving out David's whereabouts. Why should he trust you, Daniel ben Judah?"

"Because a spy would not bring his wife who is heavy with child to a fugitive camp. Or his parents. He would act alone and expect Saul to reward him. He would not join the camp of his enemy." David thought him a spy? What had happened to change his good opinion in the short months since they'd met? A trickle of fear snaked through him, but he steeled his expression, determined to show this brute guard a confidence he did not feel. "Take me to David. I will answer any question he poses."

"We shall see. If you wish to see another dawn or that wife of yours again, do not try anything foolish." The man nudged Daniel forward down a dusty, makeshift path, past the refreshing pool to the mouth of a large cave hidden from easy view. A fire burned at the entrance, and the man grabbed an unlit torch and touched it to the flames, then pointed toward the back of the cave.

76

"Keep walking."

Daniel obeyed, his fear mounting. What would he do if he couldn't convince David that he was not a spy or in cahoots with Saul? He couldn't return to Nabal. He'd be left with virtually no options.

After a series of twists and turns, the narrow passages opened up to a spacious area, room for forty or fifty people to sleep on the smooth, dry ground. Sleeping mats, baskets, clay urns, and leather pouches were strewn about along the walls while a group of men were huddled in a circle playing a game of Senet. Daniel recognized David sitting off to the side, smoothing a piece of balsam wood with a cloth.

"David, we've got company."

David's hands stilled, and he lifted his head to meet first the man's gaze, then Daniel's. His once amiable expression was now one of wary skepticism. He set the wood aside and stood, wiping his hands on the cloth. "Daniel ben Judah, if I am not mistaken."

Daniel nodded. "Yes, my lord. I told you I would come. It took time to gather my family and sell what I could to gather provisions, but I have brought my family with me, and we have finally found you." He dropped to his knees and bowed his head, his heart throbbing in his chest. "If you will have me, I am my lord's servant."

"How is it that right after you left us the last time, Daniel ben Judah, Saul knew exactly where to find us and nearly caught me? If not for the Philistines and their sudden desire to attack the land, my body would be food for the carrion birds. It is curious, is it not, that you found us and then Saul followed soon after? Now, I've been thinking, either you both talked to the same spy or one of you told the other. Which one do you think makes the most sense to me?"

The gaming stopped, and the room grew still at David's words. Daniel sensed all eyes on him and felt the heat of David's glare. He could barely breathe past the heavy weight of what he should say next. One wrong word could cost him and his family their lives.

"Perhaps my lord would consider a third option." He lifted his gaze to glimpse David's expression. When he saw the slightest flicker of interest, he took courage. "Another way to look at this is that I happened upon you by chance as I led my sheep to pasture. Since I'd heard rumors that you might be in the wilderness, I wanted to find you. But when I did find you, I did not tell King Saul, nor would I. Saul no longer follows the ways of Adonai, and I can no longer support him as king. That is the truth."

Daniel held David's steady look, unable to read into David's thoughts. After an interminable silence, David nodded to the guard still holding Daniel. "Release him." The guard's grip fell away, and he took a step back from Daniel, but he did not leave.

"Where is your family?" David's tone boded neither friendship nor hostility, only curiosity.

"I left them at the Crag of the Ibex. By now they will be wondering where I am."

David glanced at the guard. "Bring them here." He gave Daniel an appraising look. "We shall see if you speak the truth."

9

Abigail approached the audience chamber where Nabal's bellowing laughter clashed with the flutist trying to be heard above the din of male voices. She paused, not sure she carried it within her to face him like this. He'd been drinking on and off from early morn and was nearly inebriated now. The men with him rested heavily on the oriental couches, one by one turning her way as she stepped over the threshold. She caught their lewd glances and averted her eyes, waiting for Nabal to notice her.

His gaze settled on her, and for the space of several heartbeats he said nothing, studying her as if he'd forgotten why he'd called her here. His dark hair hung forward, covering one eye, and he held a silver goblet carelessly in one hand. A smile, like the kind he used to send her way before he brought her to the marriage tent, raised the corners of his mouth. She released a slow, steadying breath.

He leaned back against his gilded chair, crossed his long legs in front of him at the ankles, and held the goblet to his lips, his eyes clearly assessing her. At last he motioned her forward, then spread one hand in an expansive gesture, a man in control of his surroundings.

She moved slowly and bowed at his side, touching her head to the cool tiles.

"Men of Ziph, my wife Abigail." Nabal's words slurred as he spoke, and she felt him move beside her until his hand rested on her shoulder. "You may rise, Wife." Moisture spewed from his mouth, landing on her veil as she lifted her head. He swiped his lips with the sleeve of his robe.

Abigail leaned back on her heels, careful to keep her head lowered. "How may I serve you, my lord?" She longed to be anywhere but here, frustrated that her wavering voice betrayed her frayed nerves.

His fingers lifted her chin. "Look at me, Wife." His smile faded, and his eyes grew dark, brooding. She did as he asked, fear pricking her heart at his sudden change in tone.

Nabal leaned away from her, tented his long fingers beneath his chin, and studied her for a suspended moment, then looked toward his guests. "My friends here tell me that the son of Jesse was in these parts and that your brother was seen in the hills where he was hiding." He swiveled his gaze again to face her. Silence pulsed between them until Nabal closed the distance, his hot, wine-soaked breath touching what little skin was exposed on her cheeks. "Tell me, Wife, why would your brother, my servant, be keeping company with malcontents and enemies of the king?"

His nose nearly touched hers now, and his hand shot forward to grab her wrist. She recoiled, unable to stop the reaction as he pulled her to him until she was pressed against his knees with no escape. Would she be held responsible for every choice of her brother or father? She was paying the debts of her father even now and in every moment in the years to come, as long as she or Nabal lived on the earth. And her children would pay the price for generations to come.

"Speak up, now. Tell my friends what you know. Your father is determined to defraud me, leaving you to pay his debt." He sneered even as his words slurred again, and Abigail wondered how he could think coherently with so much wine clouding his mind.

Perhaps he would forget everything when

the drink wore off. But that did little to help her now or release her from his grasp. She turned her wrist in an attempt to free herself, surprised when he let go without comment. Perhaps he did not wish to make a scene in front of these men — a small consolation for their unwelcome presence.

She lowered her gaze and lifted her hands in supplication to him. "My lord, I am not aware of my brother's comings and goings. I am your servant, my lord, and am not privy to all that goes on outside of your household. My brother does not tell me what is on his mind, but I know he would not do anything to purposely injure anyone or harm the king."

"Keeping company with the son of Jesse is injury enough. I do not take kindly to men running away from their masters to live in the wilderness and feed off the well-being or kindness of others. Such men will find no support from me!" The cadence of his voice rose with every word until the room echoed with his shouts.

"Yes, my lord." But he already knew her father and brother had run off after David. Why did he bring it up again now? To make a show in front of these men?

Abigail clasped her hands tightly, trying desperately to remain calm and praying he would allow her to escape this room and the oppression mounting in her. Nabal's lack of compassion for those less fortunate than him was no secret. Even Simon, for all his faults, had possessed a kinder spirit than his son. Had he not chosen the name Nabal to spur his son to repent of his foolishness? At least if the rumors could be believed — the rumors that said Nabal's birth name was something far more noble, but that his father had changed his name at Nabal's entrance into manhood, because his mother had raised a fool. Rather than Nabal feeling shame and living to prove his father wrong, he had done everything in his power to live up to his moniker.

"You may go." Nabal reached for his chalice. "But see to it that if you do hear from your father or brother, you report to me immediately." He held the cup to his lips. "Understand, Wife?" The command dripped with sarcasm. His look sent a shiver through her.

"Yes, my lord."

He turned away then, back to his men, resuming the laughter and gaiety as though she had never interrupted them. Indeed he was a fool.

She rose slowly to her feet and backed away from him. When she reached the door, she turned to leave, but Nabal's words arrested her.

"My brothers, you do me great honor by keeping me informed of these things. Up until now the son of Jesse has eluded the king's grasp, but rest assured, he will be found again, and the next time we will act quickly."

Abigail stepped beneath the arch and into the hall, her ears attuned to her husband's speech, her heart beating hard.

"And next time you see my wife's father or brother, come and tell me. They think they have slipped from my grasp, but my arm is long, and though we must search throughout Judah, we will find them."

Abigail drew in a quick breath, certain Nabal had spoken loud enough on purpose for her to hear. He may have been drinking, but he still knew what he was doing. And if what he said was true, he was one of David's many enemies who were looking to turn him over to King Saul. Which meant her parents and Daniel were no safer now than they were when they had served in Nabal's sheepfolds.

10

Dawn crept over the rise of the Judean wilderness north of En Gedi. Daniel yawned, ran a hand over his beard, and squinted north and east. Sand covered the expanse in every direction, except for rare spots of green where trees dotted the valley floor, watered by floods and the spring that fed En Gedi on its way to the Salt Sea. His turn as lookout came with a heady sense of relief that David fully trusted him now, though to his chagrin he knew that trust would not have come as soon as it did without his mother's quick convincing. David had a soft spot for a woman's impassioned words.

Despite the slight embarrassment, the thought drew a smile to his lips. He'd done the right thing coming here. His son had been born that first month, and that fact seemed to lift his status in David's eyes. In the year since then, he'd been treated with a certain respect.

He straightened, unable to deny the feeling of pride he still felt at having produced a son. Talya was a good mother, though his own mother seemed to think she needed a lot of instruction. He shook his head. The lookout post was a great reprieve from his mother's clucking tongue.

Rustling sounds drew his attention, but it was only a pack of conies playing chase among the underbrush. He bent to retie a sandal and picked his way farther up the hill to the top of the ridge. If Saul and his standing army came this way, they would undoubtedly come through the valley.

He shaded his eyes as his gaze swept the road that edged the barren hills to the valley floor. He paused, squinted again, then moved closer, his heartbeat suddenly picking up its pace. The size of the group took his breath. Men stretched out across the ravine like a river of hungry locusts, Saul's standard and the banners of the Israelite tribes waving in the wind.

He stepped back on instinct. Had the men spotted him? Had he compromised his family's safety by coming here? How quickly doubt pressed in on him again. He knew Saul had managed to find David in the past, but somehow he hadn't expected it here.

This oasis had given them all such refuge among the caves and trees and in the refreshing pool and falls of En Gedi. He had almost become accustomed to safety.

Cautiously, he moved forward again and peered down at the Israelite army — Saul's choice soldiers once loyal to David. He did a mental head count, marking their location. They would find David's camp too soon. Their respite would be short-lived.

"How fast were they moving?" David crossed his arms over his chest and stroked his chin with one hand, his gaze meeting Daniel's. He ignored the sinking feeling in his gut.

"They got an early start, as they were on the move at dawn. But it's slow going across the sand with that many men. I'd say we have some time."

"But not enough to move the women and children."

"Probably not."

The scent of baked flat bread filled the entrance of the cave where David stood. He clasped his hands behind his back, moved away from his small band of advisors, and walked to the winding road that led around the falls to the Crag of the Ibex. He pulled in a deep breath, then moved farther up the ridge to where the cave was hidden by the falls. He sniffed again and released a sigh. Good. The scent of the water masked that of the bread. But the sight of women drawing water from the stream and the children racing up and down the shore made him pause. They would be visible from a distance. The only way to protect them would be to hide everyone in the caves and hope they wouldn't end up trapped there. David knew the women were a steadying force for his men, but at times like this he questioned his own sanity in allowing them to be part of his band.

He ran a hand through his hair, fighting weariness, a weariness that dogged his every step. At the crunch of sandals on stone, he turned. Benaiah and Joab approached.

"If you see something I'm missing, now would be a good time to tell me."

Benaiah stepped closer, his gaze sweeping the hills. "Saul is likely to come around by the path of the sheep pens rather than take the hillier side to the falls. It's not as narrow and easier for his men to set up camp."

"It only takes a few archers to wind their way down the gorge to find us. But if we risk leaving the opposite way we think they'll take, they'll see us."

"Divide the group and draw them away

from the women like we did the last time." Joab's tone held a hint of impatience, as if David should have figured this out already.

"As usual, Nephew, you are right. We will leave the women and children where they are and put them far back into the cave." Ahinoam wouldn't like the closed-in feeling, but she would have to live with it. "Tell Abiathar and the rest of the men to stay with the women. Joab, you take the thirty to a cave on this side of the hill. Benaiah, get Abishai. Daniel, bring the three mighty men to join me in the cave at the Crag of the Ibex. If He is willing, the Lord can save by many or few. Let's hope He is willing."

David stood just inside the recesses of the cave, looking out at a family of goats picking at the tufts of grass found here and there among the sand-coated rocks. He closed his eyes and leaned against the cave's wall, his stomach rumbling. Hours had passed since the morning meal of goat cheese and flat bread, and he wondered how long he would have to make the dates and almonds in the sack at his side last.

Birds twittered in the trees outside the cave, and as he walked toward the entrance, he ducked out of the way of a row of sleeping bats. Another thing Ahinoam feared, though he failed to understand her worries. If she was an insect, a bat might cause her angst, but this type cared little for men or women.

He glanced at the horizon, where the sun had begun to leave its midway point in the sky. His eye caught movement coming his way. Benaiah. Good. His faithful guard would not come without something to tell.

"Saul has broken camp and as we suspected is headed this way. They're at a fast pace, so I suspect they'll be here within the hour. What would you have us do?"

David glanced beyond Benaiah at the eastern sky, his thoughts turning heavenward. How often had he led his sheep through steep valleys or near rough waters of a recently flooded wadi, only to see Yahweh protect them from the predators that lurked in the mountain passes or calm the restless current? Even in the valley of the shadow, God was with him. Surely He would deliver David again from the man who sought his life. He had to believe that. But the struggle to do so grew tougher with every passing year.

O Adonai, You are my refuge, my portion in the land of the living. Listen to my cry, for I am in desperate need. Rescue me from those who pursue me, for they are too strong for me.

There was no escape apart from Adonai. Alone, he would not get far, and though the stronghold wasn't an impossible distance away, the climb to the mountaintop fortress would take days. His enemies would surround and overtake him first.

He looked at Benaiah, then back at the sky, his heart surging with hope. "They've laid a snare for me, but God is our refuge and strength. We will hide in the cave until they leave."

Benaiah's brows knit, his expression filled with doubt. "If you but say the word, we could go to battle with them. As you said, the Lord can save by many or few, and we're better at secret tactics than they are."

"And risk killing the Lord's anointed. You know my answer to that." David joined the rest of his men in the back of the cave, his hope mingling once again with despair.

Daniel drew a groove in the floor as he paced from the back of the cave to within a long stone's throw of the cave's entrance. The space, illuminated by a few clay lamps, held a handful of David's men, all of them anxious and tense, ready to jump up and claw their way out of this stifling place at a moment's notice. Daniel consoled himself that he would be the first, warding off the closed-in feeling with this frantic activity.

He glanced at David, who sat with his back against the cool limestone, eyes closed. Their leader gave the impression that he hadn't a care and could sleep through an earthquake. His apparent peace was the exact opposite of what Daniel was feeling now. How long did David expect to sit there doing nothing? What if Saul found Talya or his son? His heartbeat kicked up a notch as he envisioned the worst — Talya ravaged by enemy warriors. Surely not. These men hunting David down were fellow Israelites, not some foreign enemy.

He stopped midstride and swung around on his heel, turning back toward the cave's mouth. There had to be something he could do — anything to dispel the tension knotting every muscle, worrying every thought. If he crept closer to the entrance, perhaps he could get an idea of what they were up against. It had been hours since they'd last heard from a lookout. What if Saul had captured them? Why wasn't David allowing him to take a turn? Maybe David's trust wasn't so certain after all.

The thought depressed him even as a new determination to do something, to find out

93

what was going on, pressed in on him. He reached the limit of the lamp's shadowed light and paused, then felt along the wall of the cave. He followed the natural bend and moved toward the late afternoon light coming through the opening. Squinting, he stopped and waited for his eyes to adjust to the darkness, then continued forward slowly, one foot in front of the other, keeping his head tilted, listening.

A heavy groan made him pause. Silence met his ear, then more indecipherable sounds. An animal? He crept closer. His eyes fully adjusted to the darkness now, and the sight before him stopped him cold. There hunched on a sitting stone was the king of Israel, his back to Daniel, his robe splayed out around him, his crown slightly askew as he rocked back and forth, grunting. What providence was this? The man was close enough to touch with no one guarding him.

Giddy laughter bubbled to Daniel's lips, but he clamped a hand over his mouth to stifle the sound that would give him away. Surely God was smiling on David. He had given his enemy into his hand! How easy it would be to thrust a dagger into the king's side or lop that crowned head from his shoulders and take it to David. The thought

94

made his heart thud harder and his knees almost weak.

It *would* be easy . . . but what if David thought otherwise? No, first he would bring the news to the men and convince David that God was the one who had delivered Saul into David's hands. Then he would gladly thrust a blade into the old king's side. And place Saul's crown on David's head.

"David!" A touch on David's arm startled him awake. He looked up, senses on instant high alert, to meet Daniel's excited expression. "The king is here," he whispered, bending low, "at the mouth of the cave, without a guard, trying to relieve himself."

Saul was here? Unguarded? Impossible. David rubbed his eyes and pushed to his feet. The other men crowded close. One look into their eager faces told David they had heard.

"This is the day of which the Lord spoke when He said to you He would deliver your enemy into your hand, that you may do what seems good to you," Benaiah said, one hand touching the hilt of his dagger.

"It's a perfect opportunity, David. Kill the old king and be done with it." Abishai grabbed a clay lamp in one hand and pulled the blade from his belt with the other. "Just give the word, and I'll do it for you."

David examined the group, noting the affirmation in each nod, in each weary but determined expression. These men had been with him nearly from the beginning, and they longed as he did to go home to a normal life, one that didn't keep them on edge or force them to run from place to place. He'd lived the life of a fugitive for nearly seven years. To end it all would be such relief.

"I'll go," he said at last, knowing they looked to him for some type of decision. If anyone raised their hand against Saul, it should be him, not his men. He would be blamed for it, was already accused of seeking Saul's life, so why not?

He removed his dagger and touched the tip, checking for dullness. It would do. Turning, he held up a hand to keep the others from following. He would make his way in the darkness, lest Saul notice the added light. His heart beat slowly in thick, heavy thuds as he eased his way along the cave walls. Rounding a bend, he looked toward the entrance. Sure enough, there sat the king of Israel on a sitting stone, trying to relieve himself.

A thousand emotions rushed in on him as he moved on lithe feet ever closer, until he stood almost near enough to touch the man. *Kill the old king and be done with it.* Abishai would have already thrust the blade into Saul's back. Hadn't he caused them enough misery? If Saul were dead, Jonathan would bring him back to the palace, he'd be reunited with Michal, and he would ascend the throne without further bloodshed. Saul's death would be the end of his persecution. He would be king in Saul's stead.

The thought brought a swift ache to his heart. Things could be so different. Life wasn't supposed to be this way. God's promise of the throne wasn't supposed to include living like a fugitive. *Where are You, Lord?*

A groan followed by muttered curses jolted David's thoughts to the present. The last thing he needed was for Saul to alert his guards. In one swift motion, he cut the edge off Saul's robe and tiptoed backward, farther into the shadows.

Guilt lapped at him like ripples on the Jordan as he made his way back to his men. Saul was the Lord's anointed every bit as much as he was, and David had no right to disrespect him or his position as king. If Saul was bent on seeking David's life, then Saul was the one making a fool of himself. David could not allow himself to stoop to

Saul's level, and cutting off his robe was doing just that. He knew better. He shouldn't have done such a thing, despite what his men might think.

As he approached the light, he turned the piece of robe over in his hand. The woven threads hung loosely, already fraying in the place where his blade had touched. His men rushed forward at the sight of him.

"Did you kill him?" Daniel asked.

"Where is his head?" Abishai scowled.

David held up a hand to quiet their whispers. "The Lord forbid that I should do such a thing to my master, the Lord's anointed, or lift my hand against him, for he is the anointed of Adonai." He held the piece of robe out for them to see. "I could have killed him, but I will not do it."

Silence followed his remark, but the disbelieving and frustrated stares spoke volumes. He released a slow breath, knowing there was little he could do to appease them. They disapproved of him. Maybe they would desert him as well.

Despair cloaked his thoughts, and he turned to go back to the cave's mouth. "Come," he said, motioning for his men to follow. They moved as a group, saying nothing as they crept along the rough walls. He stopped within sight of Saul, but the king still appeared unaware of their presence. Saul stood, dusted off his robe, and walked into the sunlight.

David straightened his back and followed Saul out of the cave. He could feel the presence of his men keeping close, but they stopped short of exiting with him.

"My lord the king," David called once Saul was well out of physical range. Saul turned, and David dropped to his knees and bowed his face to the ground. Then he stood so he could speak loudly enough to be heard by Saul's men, who were now visible on the rocky ridge.

"Why do you listen when men say, 'David is bent on harming you'? This day you have seen with your own eyes how Adonai delivered you into my hands in the cave. Some urged me to kill you, but I spared you. I said, 'I will not lift my hand against my master, because he is Adonai's anointed.'" David's breath came fast, the words spilling from him. He held the cut piece of robe high in both hands so Saul would not mistake the markings. "See, my father, look at this piece of your robe in my hand! I cut off the corner of your robe but did not kill you. Now understand and recognize that I am not guilty of wrongdoing or rebellion. I have not wronged you, but you are hunting me down to take my life."

He held out his hands in supplication. "May Adonai judge between you and me. And may Adonai avenge the wrongs you have done to me, but my hand will not touch you. As the old saying goes, 'From evildoers come evil deeds,' so my hand will not touch you." He met Saul's gaze then, a feeling of deep sadness filling him. This pursuit was so futile, such a waste of time, energy, and resources. And for what? The man was a fool, chasing the wind. "Against whom has the king of Israel come out? Whom are you pursuing? A dead dog? A flea? May Adonai be our judge and decide between us. May He consider my cause and uphold it. May He vindicate me by delivering me from your hand."

Throat parched and words spent, David let his arms fall to his sides, defeat settling like a boulder on his chest. He and his men were surrounded now, at Saul's complete mercy. He'd played the fool himself coming out here like this to speak to the king. Any moment now an arrow could take him down, and the king would have his victory. But at the same time, as close as he stood to his enemy, David felt inexpressible peace.

"Is that your voice, David my son?" Saul's words carried to him, broken by the king's loud sobs. An awkward stillness surrounded the craggy hills. Even the goats seemed to pause at the guttural weeping.

Abner, Saul's cousin and commander, stepped to the king's side and placed an arm around his shoulders in an apparent attempt to hold him up. Saul shrugged him off and straightened, his head bent low in an unusually humble pose.

"You are more righteous than I," Saul said. "You have treated me well, but I have treated you badly. You have just now told me of the good you did to me. Adonai delivered me into your hands, but you did not kill me. When a man finds his enemy, does he let him get away unharmed? May Adonai reward you well for the way you treated me today."

Saul dropped to one knee, hands extended. Was he bowing to his rival, the man he hated most on the earth?

"I know that you will surely be king and that the kingdom of Israel will be established in your hands. Now swear to me by Adonai that you will not cut off my descendants or wipe out my name from my father's family."

David studied Saul's posture, an odd mixture of distaste and pleasure filling him. Behind him, he could hear the whispers of his men. They would tell him not to promise such a thing to the man. But it was Jonathan's face he saw as he watched Saul begging for mercy before him. Jonathan, with whom he had made a lifelong covenant.

"I will swear it," he said, knowing he could never destroy Jonathan's seed, or Michal, should he ever see her again. He was making no promises to the rest of Saul's house, but the king need not know it.

His words seemed to satisfy Saul, who rose and nodded his appreciation in David's direction. Then the king of Israel turned and gave orders to his men to return home.

When they cleared out, David would gather his men and find a better stronghold.

11

Abigail set plates of goat cheese, dates, and cucumbers on the low table, placing them just so, then stood back to examine her handiwork. In the month since she had learned of Nabal's determination to pursue her father and brother, she had done everything in her power to please him, to be visible when he was around rather than ducking into corners and avoiding all contact. Despite her aversion to raising a fool for a son, she wanted, needed, a child. If she could only distract Nabal with a son, then perhaps life would become easier for them all.

She rubbed the ache in her lower back and fought a sense of despair. This morning had shown once again that she did not carry Nabal's child. Another month of enduring his insults, another month of trying to appease. Surely a child would change things. If only God would have mercy and grant this one request.

She turned at the sound of a groan. Nabal stumbled into the dining area and sank onto the couch beside the food-laden table. His hair looked disheveled and his beard unkempt. Bloodshot eyes looked up at her, and a pained expression crossed his face. He looked in her direction, then turned his attention to the food set before him. She hurried to pour him a goblet of fresh goat's milk and some herbs for the headache she knew had come from his night of wine bibbing.

He accepted her offering without comment and rubbed his temples in slow, rhythmic motions, his morning repast only half-eaten. "I'll be gone — I don't know how long — maybe a week or more." He met her gaze, then let his eyes roam over her, his expression telling her he was still hungry, just not for food. "If you weren't so quick to run your mouth off and could be trusted, I would take you with me." His smug smile turned to a sneer. "The last thing I need is a God-loving woman making a fool of me."

Heat filled Abigail's face, and she quickly ducked her chin to avoid eye contact, her hands clasped in front of her. *She* was a fool? Only in regard to thinking he would ever change!

"I need you here," he added, his voice gruff. Of course he did, to make sure the servants obeyed his every whim, and he knew she would make sure of it. He would take it out on her if they didn't.

"Yes, my lord." She glanced up, letting her gaze skirt his as she looked beyond him. "Will you need anything before you go, and what would you have me do while you are away?"

He took a piece of linen and wiped the milk from his mouth, then dropped it on the table and stood. "Zahara will tell you what to do." How he loved to toy with her authority over the servants and to suggest he had relationships with them, which she found questionable at best. Despite Zahara's hints to the contrary, Abigail had yet to catch him with Zahara in his bed. Still, somehow she wondered . . .

He walked around the table and came closer until she could feel his stale breath. His fingers stroked her cheek, then lifted her chin so she would meet his gaze. It was on the tip of her tongue to tell him she was unclean, but before she could open her mouth, his lips silenced her. She felt his arms go around her, and she fought nausea at the taste and odor of his breath. Normally he did not repulse her so, but then he'd never kissed her like this the morning after he'd been drinking.

He pulled back and took her face in his hands, then deepened his kiss. Panic pushed through her that he might demand more than she could give without breaking Adonai's law. But a moment later he released her, his passion apparently abated. "That was so you'll miss me." A cocky smile wreathed his face, and he touched her nose with one finger in a gesture of affection, then walked away, leaving Abigail feeling angry and bereft.

"Do you suppose something has happened to him?" Zahara asked a month later as Abigail twisted yarn through the distaff from the wool of Nabal's many flocks. The new, multicolored robe they were weaving was one he had commissioned through Zahara the night before he'd left them. The intricate design rivaled a garment fit for a king, which fit Nabal perfectly, since he acted like one.

"You said he was checking the sheep and paying a visit to the king in Gibeah. Such a journey can take time." It still irritated Abigail that Zahara had been the one to convey this information, something Nabal should have told her directly.

"His visits are usually shorter." Zahara threaded red yarns through the weaver's loom, her back to Abigail.

As the sun warmed this section of Nabal's spacious roof, silence fell between them, provoking Abigail's long-held curiosity. She cleared her throat. "How did you come to be in this house, Zahara? You are not of our people, so how did Master Nabal come to make you his servant?" The questions had burned in her heart since that first day in Nabal's house when she'd sensed this girl held her husband's interest in a way she could never seem to do.

Zahara focused her attention on the loom as though she didn't want to answer, but at last she straightened and looked up. "I was captured as a spoil of war. Nabal's father bought me." She met Abigail's gaze, then quickly lowered her head back to the loom, but not before Abigail caught the bold gleam in her eye.

"I see." Part of her felt compassion that the girl had obviously lost her family, but she chafed against Nabal's obvious favor toward her. He even went so far as to make Abigail, mistress of the house, feel like she was somehow beholden to the girl. "What happened to your family?"

"I don't know. My home is here now."

Abigail studied Zahara, catching the defiant tilt of her chin before Zahara respectfully lowered her head. "Tell me, Zahara, how is it you have been with my husband all these years, and yet you have not given him a son?"

The girl looked up at that, surprise etching her features. It was a risky question. Abigail didn't know for sure that Nabal had been with Zahara. But a part of her told her he had.

"I could ask you the same question, my lady." Zahara made no attempt to hide her disdain in the lifted brow and scorn twisting her normally pleasant mouth. A strand of her raven hair slipped from beneath the linen head scarf. The jewels Nabal had given her enhanced her dark, exotic beauty. She was dressed in robes nearly as rich as Abigail's, and her manner when Nabal was not around bordered on arrogance.

"We're talking about you. What is your precise relationship with my husband?"

Zahara reached for another colored thread, her movements exact, not missing a beat, while Abigail's thread knotted, forcing her to stop to tug it loose. "There are ways to avoid giving a man a son," Zahara said, sidestepping the answer Abigail desired. Her voice was a mere whisper.

Abigail's hands stilled, the distaff slowing. "What do you mean?" Had the girl done something . . . Impossible! And yet . . .

Zahara continued to weave the thread as though nothing they had said held any importance. She met Abigail's gaze. "My people are schooled in many arts, some of them more practical than others. Women can learn to manipulate men, and there are ways to remove things that are unwanted through certain herbs . . . if the woman would prefer barrenness to the burden of bearing the child of a man who does not deserve an heir."

Abigail's heart skipped a beat as she looked at her maidservant in disbelief. "You would kill an unborn child to keep Nabal from having a son?" For all of Nabal's cruelty, only Yahweh had the power of life and death.

Zahara lifted one shoulder in a shrug, her defiant gaze never leaving Abigail's. "So you have been with him, but you have destroyed his seed?"

"You are putting words in my mouth."

"Then speak plainly and tell me the truth."

Zahara looked beyond Abigail as though seeing something in the distance, then slowly brought her gaze around to Abigail's once again. "Can you honestly say you would want that man to father your child, my lady?"

The thought had never occurred to her otherwise. Nabal was her husband, after all. But the girl was successfully avoiding a direct answer to her questions and, in the process, doing a remarkable job of making Abigail question her own desires and motives. But what choice did she have? She had no other hope.

Abigail lifted the distaff and turned it to spinning again, meeting Zahara's gaze. "Of course I would."

"I know what Nabal did to you, my lady. I know what he has done to others. A man like Nabal does not deserve sons." Silence hung between them, broken only by the sounds of the distaff and loom and birds twittering among rustling oak leaves.

Abigail's stomach pitched, the familiar sense of despair swirling, spiraling downward with the weight of Zahara's words. Was she right? Should a man like Nabal not father sons? But if not for Nabal, she would never become a mother. Could she live the rest of her days without life's greatest gift?

The thought made the despair deepen. She looked at Zahara, noting the slight defiance in the way she held her shoulders back and in the uplifted tilt of her jaw. Was she trying to manipulate Abigail as she had Nabal all these years? Yet her words and tone spoke kindness and concern.

Abigail rubbed her left temple, her thinking muddled. Had Nabal been with Zahara, or was Zahara only trying to make it appear he had, toying with them both?

Adonai, give me wisdom. No telling what Zahara's pagan influence had done to Nabal. Didn't the law warn against taking foreign wives so they did not turn a man's heart from Adonai? Was Zahara a foreign wife or concubine? Was she responsible, at least in part, for Nabal's behavior? Then why would she seem to care how Nabal had treated Abigail?

Even if she tried, could she discover the truth? Nabal wouldn't care at all for the truth, and he certainly would not change his actions or put Zahara out of his house.

The thought brought a dull pain to Abigail's heart. She ached for justice — both for Nabal for his selfish cruelty, and for Zahara if she was guilty of destroying Nabal's unborn seed. But at the same time she wanted them both to repent, to bring them both to the knowledge of Adonai's peace.

Law warred with mercy in her heart.

111

David wrapped his arms around Ahinoam's waist, her back to him. He breathed in the sweet scent of her golden brown hair as his gaze swept the vast wilderness below. Barren red clay stretched in every direction, the narrow paths easily visible from their privileged perch. They were safe here in the stronghold of this mountaintop fortress. Something his timid wife should appreciate.

"A man feels rather small compared to all of this," David said, bending close to Ahinoam's ear. "When I consider this, then look up and see that the sky is bigger still, everything else seems so insignificant. What is man that Adonai is mindful of him?"

Ahinoam rested her head against David's chest. He drew in a contented sigh as he took it all in, threads of a song weaving their way into his mind.

"The desert is big, like it goes on forever," Ahinoam said, her voice carrying the same awe he felt. He squeezed her closer. Perhaps they had something in common after all. He nibbled her ear, pleased to hear her musical laughter, laughter he had heard too little of late. Someday things would be different. Someday he would give her everything she needed to keep the smile from

112

ever leaving her face.

The early morning breeze brushed the strands of her hair against his arm. He turned her to face him and kissed her forehead. "It is good to see you at peace, my love." He smiled down at her, then released his grip and turned for one last look at the valley floor.

She stepped away as if to attend to her chores, then stopped and looked at him, indecision crinkling her brow. "David?"

He looked at her again. "Yes?"

She chewed her lip, glancing beyond him, then lowered her head. "What happens when we run out of water? I don't mean to worry you, my lord, but some of the women were voicing their concern this morning, and they asked me —"

"Maybe you should stop listening to their worries."

Guilt nudged him at his own sharp tone and her startled intake of breath. He shouldn't snap at her so, but even on a good day Ahinoam had the ability to strip him of his confidence, to remind him, however subtly, of his inability to protect her, to protect them all.

He walked away from her toward the edge of the precipice and looked into the distance toward the west and north, then examined the road below once more. Movement caught his eye — a lone person trudging up the side of the mountain, leaning heavily on his staff. Saul would never come alone. Had God sent the prophet Gad again as He'd done the last time they'd stayed in this mountain fortress to tell him to move?

A troubled breath escaped him, and he glanced back at Ahinoam, half expecting her to have gone back to the shelter. Seeing her still standing there awaiting his answer, he walked toward her and touched her shoulder. "Go back to the women and tell them not to worry. We may not be here long enough for water to become a problem."

"What do you mean? Are we moving again so soon?" Her voice rose in pitch, and her alarmed look made him wish he could retract the words. But he couldn't keep the truth from her, so he was better off telling her.

"I don't know, Ahinoam. I don't know from one day to the next where Adonai will lead me. We are safe here for now, but tomorrow He may tell me to leave this place for another. You might as well get used to it."

He bristled at the look of hurt he got in response, then watched her turn and rush back toward the sea of tents. David sighed, then went to find Benaiah and Joab to meet whoever it was coming to call.

12

Her spinning and dyeing finally finished, Abigail sat alone beneath a makeshift tent on top of the roof, pulling colored strands of thread through the weaver's loom. Normally she would share the task with Zahara or one of her other maids, but this morning she'd come up here at dawn to enjoy a bit of solitude.

Nabal's return three weeks earlier had caused activity to swell throughout the household. Sheepshearing time was still five months away, but in the meantime there were olives to press into oil, dates from local farmers to press into cakes, and grapes from area vineyards to be made into wine and dried into raisins. And in the midst of it all, Nabal wanted his garments finished for the celebration after the shearing was over. The whole town would be present to hear him boast over all the things his hands had made.

A shiver worked through her at the thought. Nabal's pride surely could not be pleasing to Adonai. A man's pride was a curse, if her mother was to be believed, and while Abigail knew all men needed to feel important and respected, she wondered where the line came between the need and the desire for more than they deserved.

Adonai, why doesn't he see it?

Of course, she couldn't tell him. Just as she could never bring up the questions she'd raised with Zahara, despite the implications, the desire to know. She wasn't sure why she tormented herself so. He was rarely kind to her and did not know the meaning of love. They barely tolerated each other. The last thing he would want was to be bothered with the petty worries of a woman.

And Zahara's own change in demeanor had puzzled her. She'd been kinder since that day, easier to be with. The tension had somehow lessened despite the unanswered questions hanging between them.

Birdsong came to her on the morning breeze as she knelt on the roof, working the loom. She whistled a tune in response, mimicking the melodic call of finches and swallows, pleased with her ability to sound so like the birds that often perched on the parapet to watch her. She smiled, humming

117

to herself, then paused.

Hoofbeats coming hard and swift drew her attention. Curious, she stopped the loom and pushed up from the floor. She smoothed her skirt and stepped out of the protection of the tent, then walked to the parapet to look in the direction of the sound. She could see a fair distance from the roof. Terraced gardens rose up and around the house, while Nabal's land in the valley below boasted an olive grove, a vineyard, and cornfields. Storehouses and stables surrounded his house, large enough to host a small entourage.

The horseman stopped at a feeding trough long enough to give the animal a quick drink, then trotted up to the courtyard. Abigail gathered her skirts and hurried down the stone steps to the court as Nabal's servant met the messenger.

"Tell my lord Nabal that the prophet Samuel has died. All Israel is gathering at Ramah to bury him in the tomb of his fathers." The messenger's words rang out through the courtyard. Nabal stepped out of the house to meet him. Abigail moved closer, careful to stay out of sight.

"When?" Nabal tied the belt at his waist, and his hair was missing the turban he normally wore. He looked disheveled, as though he had just awakened, though Abigail knew he had been up for hours.

"The prophet died this morning, my lord. The school of prophets sent runners throughout Israel with the news. We had planned to bury him at his home in Ramah by sundown but wanted to allow the people time to come and mourn. So we will bury him before sundown the day after tomorrow."

"Will the king be there?"

"I assume so, my lord."

Abigail's thoughts wandered. Would David bring his men to mourn the prophet as well? If Saul was there, it would be a great risk. But if he came despite the risk, perhaps she could see her family again. If Nabal would let her go with him. If Nabal planned to go at all.

Please, Lord, let it be so.

The messenger turned his horse around and kicked the animal's sides, galloping through the gate. Nabal stood staring after him for a moment as though caught in indecision. Abigail stepped from the shadows and approached him.

"Will you be attending the burial, my lord?" She kept her voice gentle, knowing how it was with him most mornings after he'd been drinking.

He looked at her and rubbed a hand over his face. "I have no use for prophets." He spat in the dust near her feet. "But if the king is going, then I have no choice." His gaze flitted beyond her in the direction of the retreating messenger, then back to her. "Gather your things and be ready to leave before the sundial moves to the next notch. You're coming with me."

Abigail nodded her acquiescence, hid a smile, and hurried to do his bidding.

The cry of mourners met Abigail's ears as they approached the city of Ramah. Crowds lined the streets while merchants hawked their wares even amid those who had come to grieve.

"Rare spikenard from the Far East for the beautiful lady," a man said, thrusting an alabaster jar toward Nabal as his gaze skirted past him to Abigail. "Or perhaps you would like these silver earrings. Your wife would be the envy of every other man's wife in town." The man smiled, showing uneven, yellow teeth as he opened a cloth and spread several pairs of sparkling silver earrings before Nabal.

Heat flamed Abigail's cheeks as she watched Nabal dismount his donkey to bargain with the man. They weren't here to make purchases, but Nabal had a weakness for crafty salesmen. Moments later, he tucked two packages into his animal's saddlebag and remounted, kicking the donkey's sides to move forward. Abigail quietly urged her donkey to do the same, feeling the crush of people on each side. Were the gifts for her as the man obviously intended, or would Nabal give them to Zahara or to some friend or ally to buy their allegiance?

Nabal glanced back at her, then pulled the reins, taking a narrow side street away from the throng. They wound around the dirt roads and up a hill until they reached the outskirts of town, where they gained a foothold to look down on the procession, surrounded by others who had the same idea — to get a better view.

Weeping and wailing pierced the air as the crowd parted for the men carrying the bier with Samuel's body, which was wrapped in spices and white linen. The men marched slowly and sang a funeral dirge until they came to a cave set in the side of the hill. The smoke gray basalt seemed a fitting choice for a tomb — a depressing color, matching Abigail's somber mood.

She let her gaze move from the prophets carrying Samuel's body to the people lining every space in front and behind the cave. If her family were here, finding them would be nearly impossible. Her heart sank at the thought.

Nabal moved his donkey closer to hers, and she felt the heat of his stare. She looked at him, surprised at his troubled expression, not sure how to respond.

"I have no use for funeral dirges." He held her gaze, but his dark eyes revealed nothing. "They sang them for my mother." He turned his head away from her then, as if his admission embarrassed him. "I have no use for them." His rigid back and the firm set to his jaw were telltale signs that he was craving wine and barely holding his anger in check.

"I'm sorry for your loss, my lord." She moved her hand to touch his arm, then thought better of it.

His gaze swiveled back to hers, the hard lines of his mouth softening ever so slightly. He nodded, acknowledging her comment. He opened his mouth as if to say more, then turned away at a commotion coming from the direction of the burial cave.

She followed the sound, squinting against the sun's glare, trying to see. King Saul stood in full regal garb surrounded by a large retinue, hands lifted above the crowd.

"We mourn a great man today — Samuel, prophet of Adonai, judge and ruler, and the man who anointed me king over you." He paused, and the crowd quieted. Prince Jonathan stood to the king's right, his posture humble, his gaze solemn. Jonathan would not turn Samuel's funeral into a focus on himself, but it was obvious Saul was the one in control here.

"Though Samuel and I had our differences in recent days, I am certain he would want us to remember better times, when the kingdom was not filled with strife and discontent." Saul's declaration pricked her heart, filling her with unease. The honeyed words were aimed against men like her brother and father, and the king's own son-in-law. "Let us therefore remember Samuel's life not as a prophet and judge, but as a man who strove to unite us as one people under one king — a king who stands humbly before you now." He bowed his head for a brief moment, then moved an arm toward the bier bearing Samuel's lifeless form. "Let us mourn for Samuel, and remember all he did to honor his people."

No mention of Adonai or of how Samuel had rejected Saul as king, when Abigail was just a girl. But if what she knew of Saul was accurate, she should not be surprised that his "humility" was merely disguised arrogance.

"Once they roll the stone over the cave, we'll pay our respects to the king," Nabal said, coming up beside her again. His troubled expression had been replaced by a self-assured smile as he looked her up and down, then handed her one of the packages he had purchased from the greedy merchant. "Put these on. I want you to make a good impression on the king." He placed the packet in her hand and walked back to his donkey without another word.

Of course Nabal would be concerned with appearances. It was why he had come. But she felt awkward and foolish adorning herself when she was here to grieve. They ought to be tossing ashes on their heads and wearing sackcloth. But Nabal would never stoop so low, even for her.

She pulled aside the folds of soft cloth to reveal two shiny silver earrings. She inserted the rings into the holes in her ears, then tucked the cloth into her saddlebag, scanning the crowd once again. Even if she found her brother, she would never be allowed to speak with him. Nabal would have her father and brother taken captive for deserting him if he knew.

Perhaps later.

The thought brought a bit of comfort, but deep down she knew she was playing the fool. She was here to support Nabal, not worry about her family. If Adonai willed it, she would see them despite the crowd. But why would Adonai care about one woman's desires?

She pushed the thoughts from her mind as she kicked the donkey's sides and followed Nabal. They wound their way back down the hill as the prophets carried Samuel's body into the tomb and then heaved the large round stone to cover the opening and shut him in.

Daniel watched as the stone fell into the groove cut for it, sealing the cave's opening. He glanced to his right at David, who stood beneath the shelter of a terebinth tree, arms crossed, gaze fixed on the crowd. His stoic stance masked the emotion Daniel had witnessed the day the prophet Gad brought the news of Samuel's death. David had torn his clothes, and later that night when they had all made it safely down the mountain and camped in the clefts of the hills, he had composed a song and taught it to the prophet. David stood listening now as the school of prophets sang the song in layered harmony one last time.

A surge of pride rushed through Daniel that David's presence here, though hidden, was felt by every man close enough to hear the song. Someday, when David was king, all Israel would be able to hear the music that made him famous among the men who supported him now.

His gaze skipped beyond David to the crowd. There below them, King Saul's retinue took up the place closest to the burial cave. The king's son Jonathan stood nearly as tall as the king, his manner stately and somber, and somehow appeared more sincere than the king. Daniel looked back at David again, certain David had seen his friend. David turned his head at that moment and met his gaze. He moved his head, motioning Daniel forward.

"What can I do for you, my lord?" Daniel asked, stepping beneath the shelter of the tree camouflaging David.

"Jonathan is here." David unfolded his arms, then crossed them again.

"Do you want me to bring him to you?" The task would not be an easy one, but he would do anything for David.

Silence followed his question as David's gaze swept beyond him to some point in the distance. "I would not ask it of you. It's too risky."

It would be difficult to get close to Jonathan without his bodyguards stopping him. But he was willing to try.

"The guards do not know me, so maybe there is a chance. Benaiah or Joab would be spotted at once, but I was never part of the king's household." He met David's serious gaze. "Let me try."

David studied him for a long moment, and Daniel felt as though the man could read into his soul. At last he nodded, his expression grim.

Daniel slipped from beneath the tree's limbs and made his way down the hills with purposeful strides. A donkey brayed, and a baby's piercing cry made him glance that direction. But the child wasn't his. Talya was safely back with his mother and the other women in a protected area south of town.

Daniel felt for the dagger at his waist along with his other valuables. In a crowd this size, funeral procession or not, there were always people who would snatch a man's worldly goods from him without his notice.

His sandals scraped the dark sand and rock as he reached the base of the hill. Saul's attendants had the king surrounded, and Jonathan was no longer visible. The way parted as he drew nearer, and he noticed a line of men moving forward, each paying their respects to the king. Where were Samuel's sons and the rest of his family? They were the ones who deserved such respect, not a king whom God and Samuel had rejected. But it figured that Saul would use Samuel's death to his own advantage.

A burly man brushed against him, bumping him into the man beside him. "Sorry," the man said as he shoved his way past, toward the head of the crowd.

"Sure you are," Daniel muttered under his breath, careful not to be overheard. He straightened his shoulders and stood on his toes, trying to see over the heads of the taller men in front of him.

Irritated with the whole situation and anxious to find Jonathan and get out of this crowd, Daniel's impatience grew. As he approached the king's armor bearers and flag bearers, Daniel straightened his robe and tunic and raised his head, hoping his bearing exuded confidence and made him look as though he belonged. He slipped in unnoticed among the first batch of men and spotted the prince standing several paces beyond at the king's side. A startled intake of breath made him turn. A partially veiled woman stood beside him, her hand pressed to her mouth.

He turned to her, then stepped closer. "Abigail?"

She nodded, then shook her head and pointed to the man in front of her, holding a finger to her lips to silence him. Nabal stood two paces ahead, dressed like a prince himself, his shoulders flung back, his bearing proud.

Daniel inclined his head to show her he understood, then moved to within touching distance of her. No one would notice with the crowds so thick. If only he could speak to her. But a discreet hand on her arm was the best he could do without Nabal overhearing.

He glanced at her every now and then, longing to speak. *Are you well?* His eyes asked the question he could not voice. She gave the slightest nod, but he didn't miss the longing, the deep need, in her expression. Would he see her again? She'd never even had the chance to meet his son. Somehow he must convince David to camp near Nabal's estate so he could bring Talya and Micah and Mama to meet with her.

Nabal's turn came to stand before Saul, and Daniel slipped away, listening as Nabal proudly introduced his beautiful wife. Daniel caught a glimpse of Jonathan, but the prince had turned his gaze toward the hills.

Unable to risk exposure for Abigail's sake, in defeat Daniel moved back through the crowd to David.

■ ■ ■ ■

PART II

■ ■ ■ ■

One of the servants told Nabal's wife Abigail: "David sent messengers from the desert to give our master his greetings, but he hurled insults at them. . . . Now think it over and see what you can do, because disaster is hanging over our master and his whole household. He is such a wicked man that no one can talk to him."

1 Samuel 25:14, 17

David had just said, "It's been useless — all my watching over this fellow's property in the desert so that nothing of his was missing. He has paid me back evil for good. May God deal with David, be it ever so severely, if by morning I leave alive one male of all who belong to him!"

1 Samuel 25:21–22

13

Abigail strode through the storehouse, clay tablet and thin reed in hand, making sure the numbers matched what the young man in charge of the place had recorded. Nabal would inspect the records soon enough, and she wanted to make sure there were no mistakes. A sigh worked its way through her, and she struggled to fight off a feeling of unease. How naive she had been the day of Samuel's burial six months before, hoping for a glimpse of her family. How idealistic the imaginings of her youth when she had believed that she alone could curb Nabal's churlish behavior. Her brief glimpse of Daniel had only heightened her homesickness, and Nabal was no kinder than he'd ever been.

She closed her eyes for the briefest moment, remembering, heat pouring through her. Three years of marriage had done little to erase the shame of her wedding night, of the way Nabal had treated her since, of the beating and the humiliation . . . If she had learned to curb her tongue sooner, had realized that a man's ego was a fragile thing . . .

She blinked, forcing her attention to the baskets of parched corn before her. The memories were best held close enough to rein in her actions and her words, but far enough not to wound her again. The physical scars were reminder enough.

She jotted a few markings on the tablet and allowed herself to feel a small moment of pleasure. Despite her disappointing marriage, Nabal had become almost manageable since the day he had so wounded her, almost as if he regretted his actions, though his caustic tongue told her otherwise. While his attitudes were often deplorable, her husband was not unattractive, though he came close the mornings after he'd drunk too much — his breath alone could skin a coney. But at other times, especially in the early days when she'd blotted out the things that troubled her most about him, she had actually dreamed of love. Now she dreamed only of peace and did all in her power to make sure it didn't elude her.

She scratched her temple with the end of the reed as she walked toward a row of corn

134

and turned to the one with pressed date cakes, then went on to count the row of raisin cakes and figs. The sheepshearing feast would begin at sundown, when Nabal returned with his shearers after the last of the three thousand sheep had finally been shorn. Rowdy men would fill the house and courtyards, and wine would spill in abundance from silver goblets to bearded lips. Nabal would be drunk each night. His unpredictable wrath was the one variable she struggled to understand, to appease, to vainly hope to control. If only she could find a way to rid these storehouses of the wine . . .

She shook her head, trying to clear it of the troubling thoughts. So many emotions warred within her, threatening her sense of well-being and her fragile peace. If she could just keep things running smoothly, keep everyone fed and safe . . .

She ran through her mental checklist again, glanced at the tablet, and added the markings in her head. Everything was in order here. She had spared no expense, considered no detail too inconsequential. Perfect.

Satisfied with her calculations, she placed the tablet on a low table near the door and stepped into the sunlight. The expansive courtyard spread out before her, where harpists and flutists and a drummer practiced for tonight's entertainment.

Please, Adonai, let everything go well.

She skirted the edge of the courtyard, smiled in quick acknowledgment at the servant who was arranging flowers and cones of incense around the court's perimeter, and moved to the back of the house, where the smoke from twelve roasting and dressed sheep rose to meet her. The scent tantalized her empty stomach, reminding her that she needed to hurry inside to oversee the rest of the supper preparations. Sheepshearers came in growling like she-lions from all the hard work.

She lifted her robe from her ankles as she stepped nearer the open pits spitting fat from the lambs. The slow roasting, smoking, and salt would help preserve the meat for the days to come. Nabal's feasts tended to last at least a week, two if he was in an unusually generous mood.

Three young boys stood watch over the spits. She smiled and nodded to them as she walked among the rows, checking to make sure the lambs didn't burn on one side. When all looked as it should, she walked across the yard toward the kitchens. Zahara met her at the ovens, where several female servants were taking the third batch of bread from the heat and placing it on the stones to cool.

"There you are," Zahara said, wiping her damp brow with the back of her hand. "Jakim is looking for you." She wiped flour-coated hands on a piece of soft linen, her expression worried.

"What does he want? What's wrong?" The young shepherd had arranged the one meeting she'd had with her parents after Daniel had convinced David to move to the wilderness of Maon.

Memories assaulted her at the thought, and she sighed, feeling again the ache that came from missing her father's strong arms about her. She could not tell him of the abuse she suffered in Nabal's house, but she could see by the glint in his eyes that he knew.

They all knew. Or at least suspected. Though none of them spoke of it because nothing could be done to change it.

"Perhaps when you have a child, Nabal will become a decent man," Mama had said, confirming her own silent hopes. But her mother's clinging embrace and the way she avoided looking Abigail straight in the eye dashed those hopes just as quickly. A child would not change Nabal. Short of a miracle, nothing would.

"I don't know what he wants, my lady," Zahara said, snapping Abigail's thoughts back to her maid. Zahara looked toward the front of the house and motioned for Abigail to follow as she stepped toward the hall through the kitchens that led to the main courtyard. "Some visitors came to Nabal by the river where they are shearing. Jakim raced home in a hurry looking for you, but that's all he would say. Come. He is at the well watering his horse."

Male servants rarely spoke to her unless there was trouble. Abigail tucked a loose strand of her thick, ever-straying hair beneath her headdress, smoothing the fabric and wishing the wrinkles of her heart could be so easily pressed into submission. She forced aside her anxious forebodings as she wove her way around the serving girls and followed Zahara. The scents of garlic and cumin mingling with the baking bread, normally appetizing fare, now made her stomach do an uncomfortable flip. Her sandals slapped the rectangular stones of the court as she lifted her robe and tunic and half ran to keep up with Zahara's long strides. They moved past the guards at the gate toward the well at the entrance to Nabal's estate and arrived moments later, out of breath. Jakim stood rubbing down a lathered horse while the horse panted and drank water from the stone trough.

Abigail slowed her pace and released the grip on her skirts. She held Jakim's gaze for the briefest moment before he averted his eyes and fell to one knee before her, arms raised in supplication.

"Please, my lady, you must do something, or every man in Nabal's household will be dead by morning."

Zahara's sharp intake of breath and Jakim's unmasked fear told Abigail that this was no ruse.

"Tell me what happened." She pressed a hand to her throat, feeling the rapid cadence of her pulse. She willed herself to stay calm. Nothing could be so bad that she couldn't, with God's help, figure out a way to fix it. She just needed to listen, to think.

Jakim rose to his feet. "David sent messengers from the desert to give our master his greetings, but he hurled insults at them." He kept his voice low and glanced about as though he expected Nabal to appear at any moment. His actions would have seemed ludicrous if she didn't know for a fact that Nabal had loyal spies everywhere — much like King Saul's supporters who ignored the fact that they served a mad king.

139

"Yet these men were very good to us. They did not mistreat us, and the whole time we were out in the fields near them, nothing was missing." Jakim's voice cut into her thoughts, the weight of his words suddenly registering deep within her. "Night and day they were a wall around us during the whole time we were herding our sheep near them." He shifted from foot to foot, his movements agitated, his gaze darting beyond her as though he feared the rocks themselves would betray him. "Now think it over and see what you can do, because disaster is hanging over our master and his whole household. He is such a wicked man that no one can talk to him."

"What did David request?" The question formed of its own accord as she worked to overcome her shock. She knew the servants did not respect her husband, but it was the first time she had heard one of them speak ill of him in her presence.

"He asked for whatever our master could find on hand to give the ten men he sent. They were looking for food, my lady."

Of course, the need for food for such a large contingent of men and women would be a constant source of concern for David. His unsolicited work for Nabal should have been met with gratitude. Even she knew how easily shepherds could be accosted in the Wilderness of Maon. Barren land made for sharp tempers when food ran short and water ran low.

And then another thought pierced her. Had Daniel been among the men greeting Nabal? Surely not. Surely he would know better. Even after two years away, Nabal would recognize her brother. They'd known each other for as long as she could remember.

She rubbed her arms and looked beyond Jakim to the rock-strewn hills in the distance. Nabal's disdain for David and loyalty to Saul were no secret to those who knew Nabal best. But disdain or not, her husband's actions were grave indeed. Men like David were warriors first and, as with all men, wore the need for respect on their sleeves.

A shiver fluttered in her stomach, and every last remnant of hunger fled. She must act. If Nabal's actions had put their household in danger, then perhaps by God's grace, hers might undo the consequences that were sure to come. Even her father and Daniel would not be able to stop a warrior like David. She knew only too well what it was like to live with an unpredictable, often violent man. And knowing Daniel, he would be only too happy to fuel the king-elect's anger. He would like nothing more than to see Nabal lying in a pool of his own blood.

Oh, Adonai, what should I do?

Zahara's touch on her arm made her jump, drawing her thoughts back into focus.

Abigail looked again at Jakim. "Take two hundred loaves, two bottles of wine, five sheep ready dressed, five measures of parched corn, a hundred clusters of raisins, and two hundred cakes of figs, and put them on donkeys. Go on before me, and I will come afterward." All her calculations on the storehouse lists would be wrong now, and Nabal would surely question her, but she would have to take that risk. She would come up with a solution and an explanation later.

She met Zahara's worried gaze, suddenly wondering who was the bigger fool, she or her husband. What could she possibly say to David to appease him if the food was not enough?

She swiveled to look at Jakim, who was already mounting his exhausted horse. "Hurry," she whispered as he galloped toward the storehouses.

Zahara stepped closer and stared at her as if she had lost her senses. "You would stand in the way of hostile men, my lady? If David doesn't kill you, Nabal will."

Abigail lifted her robe and pushed past Zahara back to the house, her heart pounding harder than her running feet. Zahara was right. There would be no way to explain this to Nabal except to tell him the truth. And once she told him the truth, things would not bode well for her.

Zahara caught up with her as they reached the courtyard. "Are you sure about this, my lady?" Though by her tone, Zahara was not trying to dissuade her. How could she?

"I would rather risk Nabal's wrath than allow our innocent servants to suffer." She offered Zahara a weak smile, stifling the fear that was swiftly and surely stealing her peace. "Come, help me dress in clothes that will catch an angry man's attention. Perhaps God made me beautiful enough to allow me to speak. And if my words fall on ears of hardened stone, then at least I will have died trying."

14

"Gird on your swords, every man of you!" David reached for the blade he had just finished sharpening and tucked it into the scabbard at his side, his hand trembling as he did so. Fierce rage rushed through him. He drew in a deep breath, willing himself to remain steady, to think. He looked up at the ten men he had sent to Nabal, hearing again the rebuff they had witnessed.

"Who is this David? Who is this son of Jesse?"

Nabal would pay for his insults, along with every man who served him.

"Many servants are breaking away from their masters these days. Why should I take my bread and water, and the meat I have slaughtered for my shearers, and give it to men coming from who knows where?"

Anyone who would put up with such a man as master, who would stay loyal to one so worthless, did not deserve to live.

David's indignation mounted, his blood bubbling like hot oil.

"Two hundred of you stay with the women and the goods. The rest of you follow me." He glanced at the eager faces now crowding around him. His gaze caught Daniel, whose father, Judah, had suggested this wilderness hideout and had introduced his men to Nabal's shepherds. Had they known this would happen? Surely they knew Nabal was a fool. Hadn't Daniel said as much?

A stab of mistrust pricked his conscience as he assessed the man. Daniel's gaze held approval, and David's sudden suspicion evaporated. Still, perhaps Daniel and his father were too close to Nabal's household to be objective.

"Daniel ben Judah, come here." The afternoon sun shone down on him, casting shadows among the rocky clefts of the hill.

The crowd parted to let Daniel through. He stood before David, hand on the hilt of his sword as if ready to fight. "Yes, my lord?"

"You know this man's house."

"Yes, my lord."

"Do I have your full support?"

A look of annoyance crossed Daniel's face. "Of course, my lord. I only ask that you spare the women and children. My sister is among them."

"As I intended." Good. He was loyal to his family.

"So what are we waiting for?" Joab's voice came from behind David.

Cries of assent mingled with a handful of chuckles from his men. If they hurried, they could do this thing before nightfall. "Let's go."

He turned and marched along the path that wound down the hill, every step fueling his wrath. "It's been useless — all my watching over this fellow's property in the desert so that nothing of his was missing. He has paid me back evil for good. May God deal with me, be it ever so severely, if by morning I leave alive one male of all who belong to him!"

An intermittent breeze offered little respite from the blazing summer sun, and it lifted Abigail's veil only slightly from her face. Up ahead she could see the outline of the heavy-laden donkeys bearing gifts of food for David and his men. Perhaps it would appease. *Please, Adonai, let it be enough.* She could have given them more, though Nabal would miss what she'd taken as it was. What kind of explanation would she give him for what she had done?

The thought sent a shiver through her

despite the warm day. She drew in a deep, slow breath and gripped the reins tighter. The valley stretched before her as her donkey's sure steps followed the path up the side of the mountain. Behind her Jakim trailed, insisting he come along to protect her while other servants carried the gifts up ahead. But somehow, despite their relative closeness, she felt alone — and in truth, she was. Jakim's life was forfeit if David would not listen to her plea. What were a few men against the hundreds at David's side? Unless, perchance, her brother or father were with David and could speak on her behalf.

Oh, Adonai, give me strength. Let me find mercy in the eyes of Your servant David, and give me the words that will keep him from shedding innocent blood.

What was she supposed to say to him? Her mind tested and discarded a number of possible persuasive words as her hands grew moist beneath the leather reins, her heart thudding harder with each step higher up the mountain. She could do this. She had to do this.

A hawk screeched overhead, a foreboding sound. Moments later male voices accompanied the march of steady feet coming closer. She looked up to where the road bent in a wide curve. Her donkey reached the bend as the marching men drew near with their leader in front, fierce and determined.

David. It had to be.

The sight of the king's son-in-law was nothing like she'd imagined. In the stories she'd heard of him, he was the shepherd and the singer and the man who would kill to marry the woman he loved. The last thought should have warned her of the fierce warrior who strode down the hill, gaze angry and proud. He was more handsome than Nabal, but his expression was as dark as Nabal's had been the night he assaulted her the first year of their marriage.

Adonai, help me!

Her knees grew weak, and she wasn't sure they would hold her, but she reined in her donkey just the same and slipped from its back. David's pace never slowed until he stopped within an arm's length. She sucked in a startled breath. He was so close she could feel the strength of him, smell his sweat. Unable to stand without swaying, she fell to her knees and lowered her face to the dust.

"My lord, let the blame be on me alone. Please, let me speak to you; hear what your servant has to say." She stopped and waited for his response, her pounding heart sounding louder than her breath.

Silence spanned between them like a wide chasm. She felt his touch on her head. "Rise and speak." His voice was quiet and hoarse, as though he didn't trust himself to say more.

She pushed to her knees and leaned back on her heels, her gaze focused on his feet. "My lord, please pay no attention to this man, Nabal. His name means 'fool,' and folly goes with him. But I, your servant, did not see the men my master sent." She pressed sweaty hands along the folds of her robe as the sound of marching came to an abrupt halt behind David. She ignored the muffled sounds of grumbling men.

"My lord," she said, lifting her voice above the din, "since Adonai has kept you from avenging yourself and from shedding innocent blood, may your enemies and all who seek your life be as Nabal."

At his startled intake of breath, she looked up briefly to meet his gaze. Where had such a curse on her husband come from? But the words had been on her tongue before she could stop them. Her hands trembled at the thought. She twisted the sash at her waist, looking once again at his dusty, sandaled feet.

"And now, my lord, may this food your

handmaid has brought," she said, hurrying her words lest he stop her before she could finish, "let it be given to the young men who follow you. Please forgive your servant's offense. Adonai will surely make a lasting dynasty for my lord, because you fight Adonai's battles. May you never be found guilty of wrongdoing. Though your enemies pursue you and seek your life, the Lord your God will protect you, and the lives of your enemies He will hurl away as out of the pocket of a sling. When Adonai fulfills all the good that He has promised you and has appointed you ruler over Israel, my lord will not carry the grief of having avenged yourself or shed blood without cause."

She drew in a deep breath, willing herself to calm down, but she could not stop her body from trembling. Clasping her hands into a tight ball, she looked at him boldly but dropped her voice to a whisper. "When Adonai brings all these good things to pass for you, my lord, then remember your maidservant." She quickly dropped her gaze then and placed both hands on her knees, but not before she caught the hint of a smile on his lips. His anger had been assuaged, her words heard.

Thank You, Adonai. Relief flooded her, and a shiver passed over her.

"Praise be to Adonai, the God of Israel, who has sent you today to meet me." David bent to touch her shoulder, and when she looked up at him again, he offered his hand. "May you be blessed for your good judgment, for keeping me from bloodshed this day, and from avenging myself with my own hands. Otherwise, as surely as the Lord God of Israel lives, who has kept me from harming you, if you had not come quickly to meet me, not one male belonging to Nabal would have been left alive by daybreak."

She placed her hand in his and let him pull her to her feet. She swayed from the sheer relief of his smile, and he quickened his grip on her hand. Heat filled her face at his touch, however innocent, and when she looked into his eyes, she read his frank appreciation that spoke more than he dared say. She quickly dropped her gaze as he released her hand.

"Go home in peace. I have heard your words and granted your request." He stepped back from her and clasped his hands behind his back.

The action made her look up again. His smile had faded, but his eyes never left her face. She nodded in acknowledgment, and the impact of all that had just happened rushed in on her with a force that nearly knocked her to her knees again. David was accepting her gift but sending her home. Home to Nabal her husband. Nabal, the foolish son of Belial.

And come morning she would have to tell him everything.

15

Daniel's heart thumped hard inside his chest as he watched the interchange between David and his sister, and it slowed only a fraction when she concluded her speech and David helped her to stand. Why had she come? If she had let things be, he could have freed her from her impossible marriage to her incorrigible husband. And from the way David was looking at her now, she might even have had a chance to join their band and marry the soon-to-be king. Better to be one of many wives in David's family than to stay married to a fool.

His hands clenched in and out, and he swallowed back the barrage of questions he longed to fling at her. No, she had come out of loyalty, and perhaps she did have a point. It would not bode well for David if he shed blood without cause.

The thought cooled the heat rushing through him, and he maneuvered past a handful of men to David's side. "So we're turning back, my lord?" He knew the answer, but a part of him wanted to hear it confirmed. Perhaps David could be persuaded to kill only Nabal.

"Yes," David said, his gaze still fixed on Abigail. "She is the man's wife?"

"Yes, my lord. Abigail is my sister as well."

The words brought David's head around to meet Daniel's gaze. "Truly?" He looked as though he would say more, then turned away to look in Abigail's direction again.

"She is trapped in a marriage to an evil man. Forgive me for saying so, my lord, but killing Nabal . . . I wanted to free her from it."

A muscle worked in David's jaw, his face grim. Abigail stood beside her donkey as though she was in no hurry to mount. "Unfortunate," he said at last. He took two steps forward, then stopped and turned to Daniel. "See that she makes it safely down the mountain."

Daniel hesitated, weighing whether to speak again, to try to convince David to let him kill Nabal. If Nabal were dead . . . But he could not act on that thought. He would be guilty before God, and Abigail would never forgive him for it, even if it was in her best interest.

154

He moved away from David to Abigail's side. "Abigail, my sister."

She jumped as though startled and faced him. "Daniel!" In the next instant she flung herself into his arms, and he was half afraid she would start to sob, as his wife Talya did now and then. But she pulled back a moment later and held him at arm's length, smiling into his eyes, relief flooding her face. "I had so hoped to see you here. Is Father with you? How are Mother and Talya? It's been so long . . ." Her voice trailed off, and she stole a glance behind him.

"Father stayed with the baggage." He noted the soft blush on her cheeks. Or was it the warmth of the sun? He glanced in the direction of her gaze and saw David still standing where he had left him, watching them.

"You've caught his interest," Daniel whispered. "If you had only let us kill that lout of a husband of yours —"

Her gaze snapped to his, sudden fire in her eyes. "Don't say such things, Daniel! You know only Yahweh has the power of life and death. If Nabal were an enemy such as the Philistines, then you would be justified, but he is just a foolish man. Besides, I have given you what you asked for. Please, do not risk harm on my account. Nabal is powerful and supports King Saul. He would kill you himself or have you killed if you even tried to harm him."

"Not if I killed him first! Do you think we are weak-kneed women?" He couldn't stop the venom in his tone. The last thing he needed was for his sister to berate him in front of David's men.

She blanched, and a stricken look crossed her face. "You know I do not think you are weak, Daniel." She bent her head, her voice low, her shoulders drooping in a sudden gesture of defeat. "I'm sorry."

"Are you going to help your sister mount so she can go home before nightfall, or do I have to do so myself?" David's voice came from behind, startling them both. Daniel turned, but not before he caught the soft gasp from Abigail and glimpsed the definite blush on her cheeks.

"We were just catching up on things, my lord," Daniel said, hurrying to cover the sudden feeling of embarrassment. "She asked about my wife and our parents." He looked from David to Abigail. "She hasn't seen them in over a year."

"Then we will have to arrange a meeting for her." David took the donkey's reins and nodded to Daniel. He seemed anxious to have her go, though his eyes couldn't seem to leave her face.

Daniel settled Abigail on her donkey's back, but it was David who guided the animal. He turned it for the trek down the mountain, then handed her the reins. Five male servants, four on foot and one on another gray donkey, joined her.

"We'll return the animals to you once we have taken the food to our camp," David said, standing beside her as though unable to walk away. "Perhaps we can send your father and Daniel . . . if it's safe." He put a hand on the donkey's mane. "Is it safe?" The look he gave her was one of deep concern, and Daniel knew David had not missed a sentence of their conversation. He knew she was returning to a foolish, evil man.

"Thank you," she said, but Daniel did not miss the glint of worry in her eyes. "The donkeys would be missed."

As would the food she had taken. How closely was she watched? Did Nabal check her every move? The thought sent a chill through him.

"Is it safe, Abigail?" David's use of her given name brought Daniel's thoughts into sharper focus. It wasn't safe at all. Especially for her. He moved closer, wanting to yank her from the donkey and whisk her back to camp with them. Let Nabal just try to take her from them. He would be more than happy to slit the man's throat.

"I will not tell Nabal of our meeting tonight. He will be too drunk to notice." Her words seemed to appease David, but Daniel was not so easily convinced. Should he follow her home, wait in the shadows, and kill Nabal on his bed?

"Then go in peace."

Daniel heard David's words above the thoughts tumbling in his head. As David stepped away from his sister's side, Daniel moved in and grasped her hand. "Be careful, Abigail." He looked at her, but her gaze merely lighted on his, then turned back to the road.

"Pray for me, Daniel." She kicked the donkey's sides and trotted ahead without him.

Abigail returned to the house, hurried to her rooms, and changed back into a fresh, less ornamented robe. She was fairly numb with worry. She would not tell Nabal what she'd done. Not tonight. That much of what she had told David was true. But she would have to tell Nabal the truth tomorrow when the wine went out of him. Otherwise, when he went about his obsessive tasks of counting his wealth, he would find the missing food and blame the servants. She could not have them suffer on her account.

She leaned against the cool limestone wall inside her bedchamber and drew in a long, slow breath. Her life could be over soon. An involuntary shiver shook her from head to toe, and all energy seeped from her like oil through a press. Indeed, she did feel squeezed from every side, torn between loyalty to her family and loyalty to the man she had married. How naive she had been to think she could change him.

The scent of roasted lamb came through the open window, and the curtains fluttered in the cool evening breeze. She smoothed both hands on her gown, stopping at her middle, at the place where a child should lie. Her one regret in all of this was that she had never borne a son. Would Nabal have treated her differently if she had? Could she have earned his affection then? Or was she barren out of fear of him?

Shouts and rowdy laughter mingled with the music coming from the direction of the front courtyard. Nabal and his shepherds would sit around the court on the limestone benches while servants offered them wine and cheese and washed their feet. They would be inebriated before they ever proceeded to the hall where a banquet awaited. Abigail closed her eyes and prayed for strength. Somehow she had to get through this night without a word of what she had done. Could she trust Zahara to keep quiet about it all?

A sliver of doubt troubled her spirit, and she fell to her knees in prayer, hands raised to the only one who could help her now. She rose moments later, her heart strangely at rest, though she knew the peace was only temporary. She stepped into the hall and made her way to the kitchens to finish overseeing the feast. She would stay away from the drunken men and hope that Nabal would not call for her until she could slip back here to sleep in one final night of peace.

16

David picked at a new tune on his lyre as he sat near the fire pit at the mouth of the cave he shared with Ahinoam, his advisors, and their families. His men congregated in groups, some with their wives and children, others playing games together, all satisfied and happy with the gifts that had come from Abigail's hand. David lifted his gaze from the strings, catching a glimpse of Ahinoam where she sat spinning wool and conversing with several women. They were probably filling her ears with complaints for her to bring to his attention again, or giving her more to worry about than she needed. His jaw clenched at the thought and his hands tightened on the frame of the lyre. Would Abigail be so fearful, so easily swayed by the worries of women?

He looked away from his wife and sighed. He bent his head back over his instrument and tried to force a song into his thoughts.

But all he could see was a picture of the woman whose beauty had held him spellbound, whose words had kept him from shedding innocent blood. Why did she have to be another man's wife?

You already have a wife — two, in fact. But kings took many wives. And God had promised him the kingdom . . . someday.

He glanced up to see Judah and Daniel, Abigail's father and brother, approach. His hands stilled on the lyre, and he set it at his feet as they took the empty seats beside him.

"Please don't stop the music on our account, my lord." Judah's mellow voice reminded David of his own father, warming him to the man.

"The song would not come, so it is best to set it aside for now." He smiled at the older man, studying him in a new light. The man's debt must have been great indeed to cause him to give his beautiful, intelligent daughter to a man such as Nabal. Either that or he'd been deluded somehow. "What can I do for you?" No one ever came to him without a reason, without wanting something.

"At the moment, nothing. We were just discussing how we might help my Abigail." Judah sank to the stone seat with the agility of a much younger man, but his eyes bespoke a man who had struggled often and suffered much.

"Help her how? She is under the care of her husband now. She is not your worry." David stretched his legs out in front of him and crossed them at the ankles, folding his arms over his chest. The other men did not need to know that his thoughts had also been on Judah's amazing daughter.

"A man never stops worrying about a child, especially a daughter . . . especially when that man is responsible for her marriage to a fool." The pain of choices past took residence in Judah's gaze. He rubbed one hand over his graying beard and released a sigh that spoke of deep, personal defeat.

"I suppose not." David uncrossed his arms and studied his hands. He looked up and met Judah's gaze. "Do you want to tell me about it?" He would offer once, and though his curiosity wanted to demand answers, he would not pry. A man's business was his own.

Judah clasped his hands in his lap, his gaze focused downward. "I won't burden you with the details, David." He looked up. "Suffice it to say that my father's debt was passed down to me. We were servants of Simon, Nabal's father, my whole life. The debt continued down to Daniel and Abigail until Simon offered me the chance to be released from the debt. He'd seen Abigail's beauty and somehow hoped her righteous spirit would rub off on his son. All I had to do was betroth Abigail to the young man. I knew Nabal was a bit of a rogue, but I did not realize just how mean-spirited he could be. When Daniel finally convinced me to seek to put an end to the marriage, it was too late. Nabal somehow got wind of my desire, announced his intention to come for her, then stole her away. He took her to the marriage tent without witnesses or the priest's blessing, and there was nothing I could do."

David's hands clenched into tight fists at Judah's words, until he reminded himself that he couldn't fix the man's past. He straightened and placed both hands on his knees, unable to keep the fire of indignation from filling him. "If Israel had practiced the Year of Jubilee as God intended, your debt would have been canceled. Your daughter would not have been forced to pay your debt."

"Yes, my lord, but that practice is a mere memory, a tradition of fable. No one considers it important anymore, if they ever did."

"We shall remedy that one day." David

ran a hand down the back of his neck. "But of course, that does not help you now."

"Short of Nabal's death, I fear there is nothing I can do to help my Abigail." Judah's stricken look sent a pang to David's heart.

"If she would have let me kill the fool, we could have brought her here. I'm sure any number of men would find her to be a fine wife." Daniel's impassioned words matched the heat in his gaze. "But she wouldn't let me touch him."

David courted a smile. "She's a bit headstrong, is she?" He watched a look of embarrassment accompany a blush across Daniel's strong features. "Don't worry, my friend, I understand the trial of dealing with opinionated women."

Daniel visibly relaxed and smiled at David in return. "My sister knows her own mind, but she is also loyal and obedient. She is a better wife than Nabal deserves."

"So you've said." David looked beyond him, his gaze resting briefly on Ahinoam, who still sat with the women, spinning wool and listening to their chatter. Why couldn't she be more like this sister Daniel was so quick to defend? "If you're suggesting we send someone to kill her husband, I'm afraid I can't oblige you. I've given the woman my word."

"Would your word change if you knew her life was in danger?" Judah's quiet question stirred David's emotions, troubling him. Who would dare hurt such a beautiful, respectful woman?

"You think the man would hurt his own wife?" He'd heard of such a thing but never seen it. Men didn't talk about their wives unless they had something to complain about, but most of them wouldn't severely hurt a woman. Surely Nabal wasn't that big a fool.

"He's capable of anything. Since his father's death three years ago, he's become the wealthiest, most powerful man in all of Maon and Carmel combined. And he drinks too much. I've seen him beat a man for the smallest slight." Daniel leaned forward on the edge of the stone he sat on, his hands clasped in front of him. "I'm convinced she isn't safe."

David stood, this news stirring his blood. He paced to the fire and then back to his stone seat, then back and forth again. She had never answered his question when he'd asked her that very thing. She had simply assured him that she would not tell Nabal tonight what she had done. Did that mean she would tell him tomorrow? Confounded woman! If her father and brother were right, she had twisted her words to appease him so he would not feel compelled to protect her.

But he did feel compelled, and the need to protect her, to free her from whatever evil Nabal might plan for her, rose within him with a fierceness that took his breath. He stopped at the fire and stretched his hands in a vain attempt to warm the chill working through him. Daniel was right. Something must be done, despite his assurances to Abigail to spare her household.

He turned back to the two men sitting expectantly before him and looked from one to the other. "Take Benaiah with you," he said, his gaze fixed on Daniel, "and watch the house for any sign of trouble. If your sister does as I suspect she might and tells her husband of all that transpired today, and if he responds in anger toward her so as to harm her, then kill him and bring her to me."

"To you, my lord?" Judah looked at him questioningly.

"Yes. If you are forced to kill her husband, she will need protection. I'm willing to give her that." The import of his words hit him full force. Did he truly want to add another wife? But the chances of Benaiah being forced to kill Nabal were slim. "If she is safe, leave her in peace."

The thought left him strangely bereft.

Birds twittered outside Abigail's window the following morning as dawn's pink and yellow hues framed the brightening blue sky. Nabal would not awaken until the sun had moved several notches higher, but Abigail rose just the same, knowing this day would decide her fate. She rolled to the side of her raised sleeping mat and shoved the cushions aside. Sleep had eluded her much of the night, chased away by fitful dreams. But there was nothing she could do about that now.

She stood and walked to the window to gaze at the beauty of the private family courtyard. Signs of Nabal's drunken feast last night had carried throughout the house, even staining the stones of this secluded court. After his shepherds had gone home, Nabal had stumbled into the court and passed out on the ground. The skin of wine he carried splattered its contents, seeping into the limestone. Abigail heard the commotion from her rooms and summoned the servants to carry Nabal to his bed. They began to clean up the mess, but Abigail sent them away. Time enough to scrub the place today before Nabal arose.

She turned from the window and quickly dressed. Zahara, looking haggard, appeared at Abigail's door as she closed the lid on the pot of kohl.

"Did you sleep?" Zahara asked, stepping into the room with a tray of cheese and dates and fresh goat's milk.

"Some. As well as could be expected, I suppose." Abigail took a slice of soft goat cheese and nibbled the end. One thing was true of Nabal — he liked to eat well, and he chose only the best foods for his table. Her parents had never had it so good.

"You won't change your mind? He doesn't have to know, my lady." Zahara's olive skin held uncharacteristically dark circles under her eyes. Did she fear for Abigail's safety or her own?

"You don't need to worry, Zahara. I will not give away your part in helping me." She had decided in that moment on the mountain, when she saw the fierceness in David's eyes, that she would blame no one but herself. No servant needed to suffer on account of her decision. She would bear this trial alone.

"It is you I'm worried about, my lady. He nearly killed you the last time. You know what he is capable of. He'll do it for sure this time." Zahara set the tray on a low table and sank to the floor as though all strength had failed her. "If he kills you, what will become of us?"

So she *was* worried about her future. As Abigail suspected. But then, Abigail couldn't blame her. Zahara had grown more agitated with Nabal in the past few months, and Abigail wondered more than once if she would one day awaken to find that Zahara had run off.

Abigail bent low and touched Zahara's arm, meeting her gaze. "If anything happens to me, do not stay here. Run to David and ask for my brother Daniel. They will protect you." If only she could do the same without telling Nabal a thing. She lifted her head to the window as a sudden, swift longing rushed through her. She shook her head, looking back at Zahara. "Take my maids with you. Do not leave one behind, lest Nabal harm them because of me." If she had to perish, she could not leave these innocent women at Nabal's mercy.

"If Nabal tries to hurt you, my lady, you must not let him. Why should he kill you? We will all run to David at the first sign of Nabal's wrath." New hope sprang to Zahara's eyes as she pushed herself up from the floor. "I will gather provisions and hide them in the stables with the donkeys." She looked to Abigail as if waiting for her approval. "I won't let you stay here, Abigail. You must promise me."

Abigail lifted a brow at Zahara's sudden change in demeanor.

"You do agree?" Zahara lost a bit of her confidence and clasped her hands in a servant's petitioning pose.

Abigail's thoughts rushed in different directions, weighing Zahara's suggestion with her conviction that she should stay and support her husband. But did that mean she should allow him to beat her as he'd done the first year of her marriage? How could she stop him? If he did not lash out at her immediately, he could sneak up on her when she was least suspecting. He could kill her on her bed.

So should she flee the moment the truth of her interaction with David left her lips? She could never outrun Nabal or his men. And if she ran to David, she would still be bound to Nabal. She would never be free of him this side of death. No one would grant her a divorce or want her if she had one.

She looked at Zahara's hope-filled face and shook her head. "Running won't do me any good, Zahara. Nabal would track me down, and it would put everyone in danger."

171

A sigh escaped her as she fingered a plump date, then put it back on the tray. "No, my place is with my husband until death parts us." She watched defeat slowly replace Zahara's hopeful expression. "Let's get to work at cleaning Nabal's mess before he awakens. That will give him one less thing to grumble about." She left the food tray barely touched and went to do just that.

Daniel crouched low, hidden by ancient olive trees near the presses on Nabal's property. Benaiah hunched near him behind another tree as the two of them watched Nabal's house for signs of life. Daylight softened the harsh edges of darkness, and Daniel straightened, rubbing the kink in his back. After a night in the olive grove, he was weary and sore and covered with morning dew.

But as the night gave way to dawn, Daniel's blood quickened, pulsing through him. Today would tell him the fate of his sister. What he wouldn't give to end her husband's life now.

He glanced at Benaiah, who nodded his head in the direction of the house. Daniel followed Benaiah's stealthy lead and crept closer. Servants milled about the outer court, and three women carrying clay jars on their heads walked toward the well just over the ridge. Daniel squinted and assessed the women, confident by their unfamiliar size and gait that Abigail was not among them.

Frustrated, Daniel continued toward the house. He had hoped to snag a moment with Abigail in private to avoid any chance Nabal might overhear. Now they would have to enter the property.

Benaiah swung behind a brick wall enclosing the family's private courtyard. Daniel caught up to him but stopped short at the sight of a man coming their way.

Daniel's hand moved to the hilt of his sword as the servant approached, but a moment later he relaxed. It was Jakim, the man who had protected Abigail on her journey to David.

"Is something wrong?" Jakim motioned both of them to the shelter of a spreading sycamore fig tree. "Is David unhappy with my lady's gift?" His dark eyes filled with unease as he glanced from them to the estate and back again.

"Not at all," Daniel whispered, his own fear causing him to keep checking the house. "I am worried about my sister. Has she told your master what she has done?"

Jakim looked from Daniel to Benaiah, his

eyes widening as insight dawned. "You think she is in danger." It wasn't a question, and Daniel could tell by the man's furrowed brow and worried expression that their concern was not unfounded.

"The possibility didn't occur to you when you told her of the danger you were in? You've been with Nabal long enough — did you think my sister would suffer no consequences for her actions?" The thought irritated him, but at the same time Daniel knew that Jakim had had no choice.

Jakim shook his head, then ran a hand through his shoulder-length brown hair. "I didn't think that far." He glanced behind him again as though he sensed spies approaching. "Master Nabal is not up yet. There is still time to talk to your sister. I will get her for you."

Before Daniel could respond, Jakim turned and jogged back the way he had come.

17

Abigail picked up the last broken goblet from the dining area while Zahara swept the crumbs from the mosaic tile floor. Two other serving girls spread the low table with a clean white linen cloth and set out covered plates of cheese, cucumbers, olives, grapes, and melon. Flat bread fresh from the oven along with coriander relish and honeyed cream were set in bowls near Nabal's seat. Hyssop tea steeped over the fire in the kitchen, waiting to ease the headache Abigail knew Nabal would have after he rose.

She carried the pieces of pottery to a wicker basket for later disposal in a field over the rise. Servants spoke in low voices around her, their wary glances piercing her resolve and filling her little by little with dread. They knew. And they were waiting with bated breath for Nabal to present himself to see what she would do. Why did so much ride on her decision? He must be told or the servants would suffer. But once he was told, they might suffer just the same. There was no safe solution.

Her stomach dipped and swayed in an all too familiar unsettled feeling as she left the kitchen to survey the dining area once more. She turned at the sound of sandals slapping on the stones. Jakim stood closer than a normal servant's distance, his head bent toward her. Startled, she took a step back.

"What is it?" She met his troubled gaze, her heart skipping a beat and her fear spiking.

Jakim put a finger to his lips, making her realize she had spoken too loudly. She glanced hurriedly about, then moved from the dining area to the outer courtyard, motioning for Jakim to follow. "What's happened?" She willed her racing heart to calm.

"Your brother and one of David's men are here. They are just outside the wall, beneath the trees."

She glanced toward the wall where the trees stretched higher, shading some of the court. Why had he come? After so much time apart and so much danger from her husband, why risk coming now?

"They are worried about you, my lady. They want to be sure you are all right."

Daniel must have come to the same conclusion she had — that once she told Nabal, her life would end. But the fact remained, she couldn't let him kill Nabal on the assumption he would hurt her. People could change. And maybe God would soften Nabal's heart. Maybe when she told him the truth, he would react kindly.

She looked from Jakim to the wall barring her from her brother, then back at the house. If she hurried, she could see him and assure him of her safety. She turned to walk toward the gate when Zahara's voice stopped her.

"My lady." The sound of running feet met her ear. She turned back at Zahara's panicked tone. "Nabal is up and in the dining hall and is asking for you."

Abigail's heart skipped, the fear knifelike. A moment passed, and her indecision mounted. Should she run to Daniel and flee or go to her husband as she had planned? She looked from Jakim to Zahara, reading the urgency in their eyes. But urgency to do what? *Oh, Adonai, give me strength.*

The prayer came so naturally, she did not expect the calm that followed. Surprised, yet strangely at peace, she turned slowly, deliberately, toward the house. With one last glance in the direction of her brother and freedom, she moved with purposeful strides to speak to Nabal.

Abigail poured Nabal a cup of tea and walked back to the dining area, pausing at the threshold. She tested the unexpected calm in her spirit, expecting it to take wing and fly away as quickly as it had come. She drew in a slow breath and released it, then summoned her resolve and stepped into the room, setting the tea before Nabal. She took a step away from him just out of his reach.

Nabal looked at her through hooded eyes, accepting the tea from her hand. He sipped in silence, then helped himself to a fat grape, one hand on the fruit, the other on his left temple, rubbing what Abigail sensed was a horrific headache. He should know by now that too much wine left him feeling awful the next day, but that didn't seem to curb his behavior. He spat the seeds onto a glazed plate, then popped another grape into his mouth. "Where were you?"

"In the courtyard, my lord. But I'm here now." He expected her to greet him each morning, something she usually did. Jakim's interruption had changed her routine and would not bode well with Nabal's mood.

"Don't let it happen again."

"Yes, my lord." She moved about the room, removing empty plates and replacing them with full ones. Nabal's appetite was large on mornings like this, so Abigail waited, watching for the look of satisfaction to cross his face.

"I looked for you last night. Why didn't you join the feast?" His deep scowl gave the impression of one nowhere near satisfied.

Help me, Adonai. It's now or never.

"I was tired. I took a journey yesterday while you were with the sheep." She watched as the meaning of her words slowly registered in his dark eyes. "I took food to David and his men. I had heard they were in need and had served you faithfully for months. Since we had plenty, I knew Adonai would want us to share. Besides, I heard evil was plotted against you and your household, so I took the food to them to appease, to keep them from shedding innocent blood." She took a step farther from him, her eyes never leaving his face.

His brooding gaze darkened further. He rubbed both temples, closing his eyes. Silence enveloped the room like a shroud. At last he looked at her again. "You did what?" The quiet of his voice held the menace of a curse.

Calm shattered, she willed herself to swallow the fear his gaze evoked. "I took food to David —"

179

He shoved the bench from beneath him, its clatter making her jump. She backed up another pace toward the door.

"Ungrateful, foolish woman!" His voice dropped in pitch as he stepped toward her, a litany of curses coming at her in a low, fierce growl. The intimidating words along with the murder in his eyes struck terror in her heart. She should run, flee to Daniel. But her feet would not move.

He scooped up a heavy urn from a table near the window and lifted it high over his head. In two strides he would be upon her.

Run, Abigail. Don't be a fool! Her feet finally loosened, and she scooted away from him, then stopped at the threshold at the startled look that crossed Nabal's face.

She glanced behind him, quickly searching the room. Had someone struck him with an arrow or stone from a sling? His eyes lost their murderous glare, their glazed appearance frozen in sudden fear. His arms fell stiffly to his sides, the urn slipping from his hands and crashing to the floor. He pitched forward face-first onto the table, crushing plates of food beneath him.

"Jakim, come quick!" Abigail heard her own voice call to the servant, though she felt like the words had come from someone else. Jakim appeared at her side with Zahara, while four other maids hovered near the door, quietly weeping. "Is he dead?" Abigail asked, barely able to speak above a whisper. She stared at the still form of her husband, his slackened face pressed against the table linen. "Get some men to help you lift him. If he isn't dead, we'll need to call for a physician."

She placed both hands against her cheeks as she watched a sudden influx of men swarm the room, lift Nabal, and lay him on his back onto a cushioned couch. Jakim put his head on Nabal's chest, listening to see if he was breathing, then felt his arms and legs for movement. "He's alive. But his limbs are as weighted as stone."

The announcement filled her with hope and fear. What would she do with a man who could not move?

"Take him to his rooms." Jakim's barked orders barely registered through the haze of Abigail's thoughts. Time slowed as Zahara appeared at her side and escorted her to the family courtyard.

"Come, my lady, sit down. I will get your brother." Jakim's voice came to her from a distance.

Abigail's shaky limbs embraced the chance to sit, to rest on the stone bench and breathe in the earthy scents of almond and oak trees. She shook her head to clear it, hearing shouts of men and whispers of women mixing with the cadence of birdsong. She felt a touch on her shoulder and slowly lifted her head to look into Zahara's eyes.

"There was nothing you could have done, my lady," Zahara said. "Your God struck him down so he wouldn't hurt you."

Abigail held Zahara's gaze, trying desperately to focus. Was that what had happened? Did God strike Nabal for his reaction? Or had she caused his heart to fail because of her outright disobedience?

Guilt nudged her, awakening her spirit and filling her with a sense of despair. She pushed both hands against the smooth stone of the bench in an attempt to rise. Zahara's hand on her shoulder gently forced her to stay put. "Let me get you something to drink, my lady. Don't go anywhere until I get back."

"I'll make sure of it."

She knew that voice. She turned to see Daniel coming toward her. Suddenly fully aware of her surroundings, she jumped up and ran to her brother. When his arms came around her, she fell into his embrace, unable to stop the tears.

"There, there. It's all right, Abigail. Nabal

can't hurt you now." His whispered words soothed her. "God will either take his life or change him. You'll see." He rubbed circles along the middle of her back until her breathing slowed and her tears dried.

"How will I care for him if he cannot move? How will I feed him? What will I do, Daniel?" She accepted a silver goblet of wine from Zahara's hand, then walked ahead of Daniel into the house. "I must see to him."

He hurried to catch up, grasping her elbow. "Let others care for him, Abigail. Why should you trouble yourself?" Daniel drained the cup Zahara had offered him and handed it back to the maid, forcing Abigail to stop her rushed movements. "You have done enough for the man. He doesn't deserve your loyalty."

Abigail looked at her brother askance. "You know that's not true. Before Yahweh, I must honor my vows. He is my husband, Daniel." She picked up her pace again toward Nabal's rooms.

"I know another who would gladly be your husband in his place."

Abigail stopped short. They stood at the fork that opened into a small, private court where the hall led either to her set of rooms or to Nabal's. She glanced at the servants who had accompanied them. "Go on ahead of us. We will follow shortly."

Zahara nodded, a knowing gleam in her eye. She had heard their conversation and seemed pleased with Daniel's words. The thought troubled her, not so much that Zahara approved or that Daniel had suggested such a thing, but that her own heart betrayed her, wanting to know more. How unfaithful could she be? Her husband was not dead and might live for many years. She simply could not entertain such things, despite the rapid pounding of her heart.

"He told Abba and me that he would be willing to protect you, and I don't think he meant that in a general sense. I think he wants to spread his garment over you, Abigail."

She searched her brother's gaze. "Who?" She didn't have to ask, but she needed to hear it just the same.

"Who else? David was pretty taken with you."

"David already has two wives." So why did she long to be the third? *Oh, Adonai, forgive me.*

"Only one now. Michal has been given to another man." Daniel grinned, that annoying, self-confident grin that told her he was right and he knew it.

"Nevertheless, one wife is enough. He doesn't need another." Nabal might never have loved her the way she had hoped, but at least she had been his only wife. Though in truth, she had shared him — if not with the women she suspected he had taken to his bed, then with the wine and the many things that consumed him. She wanted better next time. If there ever was a next time.

"You could do worse, Abigail. David will be king soon, and kings have many wives." His voice still held the edge of confidence, but he looked at her with a hint of uncertainty. "You asked him to remember you when he comes into power. I'm telling you, you have already made a deep impression on him that he isn't likely to forget."

His words sent a strange warmth through her. To know she was wanted, even if the wanting was impossible to fulfill, was an encouraging thought. She wouldn't have to rely on her father's or brother's kindness for protection if she married again — if Nabal didn't recover. The thought cheered her, but in the next instant, the sounds of household servants hurrying to and from Nabal's rooms jarred her back to her surroundings.

"I must go to my husband," she said, meeting Daniel's gaze. "As long as Nabal lives on the earth, he is still my husband, Daniel. We must not speak of this again."

She turned her back to him and moved to Nabal's rooms, leaving Daniel to follow in her wake.

18

Mourning doves sang their melancholy dirge outside of Abigail's window, awakening her with the familiar sense of foreboding she had known since that fateful morn ten days before when Nabal's heart had turned to stone. Days of hovering over his rigid form, his body stretched out on the bed as though it belonged on a bier, his eyes staring above him, unseeing. Were it not for the soft rise and fall of his chest, the physician would have proclaimed him dead.

If only God would have mercy and either set him free from this bondage and let him live or take his life. This state of in between, of waiting and wondering, was taking its toll on her emotions and her disposition.

She ran one hand over her eyes, blinking away the need, the longing, for sleep. Depression sank roots into the soil of her heart, and each day found her less able to fight its growing strength. *Oh, Adonai, how long? Will my life continue in this wait-and-see pattern forever? Have mercy on Your maidservant. I am poor and needy and don't know what to do.*

She squeezed her eyes tight one last time, then rose quickly from the bed. Two of her maids appeared at her door, accompanying Zahara.

"Some of the master's shepherds are here to speak with you, my lady. They don't look happy," Zahara said as she stepped into the room. "Let me help you dress." She walked to the wall where Abigail's robes hung on pegs, paused as if considering something, then chose Abigail's second-best robe. She draped it over one arm and approached.

Abigail met Zahara's gaze, the woman's concerned expression matching the knot in her stomach. Why did she fear? These men had no claim to Nabal's estate or to her. They were hirelings, and they would do as she commanded.

But if she believed that, why did her insides refuse to settle and her blood pump with dread? She didn't want to meet these men. What was she supposed to say to them? She had no answers. Yet she would need to appear in control in front of Nabal's burly shepherds whether she felt that way or not.

She turned to one of the female servants and accepted a chalice of goat's milk from the maid's outstretched hands. She fingered a soft square of cheese on the silver tray but couldn't force herself to eat. Nothing, not even her fear, could pull her from the feeling that her life was spiraling downward, without meaning or purpose.

She placed the cheese back on the tray. "I will eat later." She sat on a low stool and allowed a maid to adorn her hair. Zahara stood in silence, still holding her robe.

"Has there been any change in your master?" She looked at Zahara for a brief moment, caught the shake of her head, then glanced at her reflection in the bronze mirror. The application of kohl did little to hide the despair in her eyes. "I should be wearing mourning robes and sackcloth."

"Would that you could," one maid said as she scooped up the tray of barely touched cheese and dates and headed toward the door. The other maid fitted the final ivory comb into Abigail's hair, then took a step back, holding out the mirror for her to see.

Abigail gave her appearance a cursory glance, then allowed Zahara to help her don her robe and tie the gilded sash at her waist. "There," Zahara said, seemingly satisfied.

"The men will give you their full attention now."

Abigail released a slow breath. "It cannot be any worse than confronting David. I thought he would slit my throat before I had a chance to speak." She offered her maid a weak smile. "I should be used to disgruntled men by now." She turned and walked from her rooms to Nabal's audience chamber, Zahara at her heels.

Three grizzled men stood in the court, one tapping a foot in impatience, another pacing the stone court, and the third sitting on a bench, legs outstretched, as if time held little importance. Abigail's heart skipped a beat, increasing her sense of dread. What could they want?

She stood beside Nabal's kingly chair, unable to sit in the place where he had claimed such self-importance. "Send them in." She nodded to Zahara, who moved to do as requested.

At Zahara's approach, they quickly came to attention and followed her into Abigail's presence. They stood at a respectful distance, straight and proud, obviously unwilling to acknowledge that a woman might hold their fate in her hands.

"How may I serve you?" Abigail asked, meeting each man's gaze without flinching.

"We heard the master has taken ill, and we wondered . . ." The man who had been pacing suddenly looked down at his feet as though he were embarrassed to speak the next words. "We wondered who might be in charge of the master's sheep and goats with the master so . . . indisposed." He glanced up at Abigail, his face flushing crimson. "Some of us were thinking that since the master doesn't have a son, the man who marries his widow would inherit his property, and . . . well, I'm here to offer to do just that — should the master pass on." His grin showed uneven, grayish teeth, and he smelled of a mixture of sweat, sheep, and too much wine.

What would happen to her if Nabal soon died? Her position would be one of a woman of means. If there were no kinsman redeemers to raise up a son to Nabal, she would be free to marry whomever she chose. And as far as she knew, Nabal had no other living relatives. The thought had not occurred to her until this moment. She'd been too absorbed in her own fear and uncertainty. But the idea suddenly held merit, and the thought of remaining alone the rest of her life was an unhappy one at best.

But if Daniel spoke the truth and David

was truly interested in her, she could help his cause. She wouldn't go into the marriage empty-handed or to cover a debt, feeling as though she had no control over her life and was at the mercy of an unmerciful man. Rather, she would add to the wealth David would need to secure the kingdom.

She looked at the man standing before her, his bearing proud and ridiculous, as though he had something to offer her that she would actually want. She'd seen him, all of them, at the various feasts Nabal had held. He was one of those who would do anything to get into the good graces of the wealthy, to further his own station in life, which shouldn't surprise her, though she had never been impressed with the sniveling way some men would acquire such things. Not at her expense.

"As it stands," she said, calmly meeting each man's gaze, "my husband still lives. Now if you will excuse me, I have work to attend to." She waited until the men exchanged embarrassed glances and backed out of the room, then she turned and hurried to check on her husband.

"How is he?" Abigail asked as she entered the room where the morning sun bathed the mosaic floors in welcome light. The town physician had been in attendance each day, his nimble frame bent over Nabal, trying to coax herbs and water past his lips. To no avail.

"His eyes move in quick motion as though he is trying to run from something. But otherwise, he lies as still as stone." The physician looked at her then, his narrow face wreathed in sorrow. "There is no change, mistress."

Abigail stood at Nabal's feet, looking down on him. His eyes moved, met her gaze, and held. A shiver passed through her at the stark fear she saw in this brief window into his soul. She moved closer to kneel at his side opposite the physician. She reached for his hand, shocked at the total lack of warmth in his fingers.

"My lord, I am sorry to have upset you so." The words came out slowly, and emotion filled her throat, choking off her ability to continue. She swallowed hard and wiped the moisture from her eyes with her free hand, then placed it over the other holding Nabal's. "I don't know if you can hear me, my lord" — she moved so that her eyes could connect with his — "but if you can, please know that what I did, I did for the safety of your household. Your insults to David had ignited his wrath. He was on his way to kill you and every man in your house. The food appeased him, my lord, and spared you."

She watched for some sign that he understood, but the fear never left his face. "It is possible, my lord, that you are about to go the way of all the earth. Or perhaps Adonai in His great mercy will heal you and allow you to live. I hope, my lord, that whatever happens, you will seek His forgiveness for the deeds you have done, that He might yet have mercy on your soul." The words pushed forth from her lips unplanned, but as she had that day when she spoke to David, she could not seem to stop them, to hold back the urgent need to be heard before it was too late.

She squeezed his hand but got no response. More tears fell unbidden, dampening her cheeks. She swiped them away, sniffing back the urge to weep.

"You must not trouble yourself with these things, mistress." The physician put a hand to Nabal's forehead, meeting Abigail's gaze. "There was nothing else you could have done. Your words or actions did not do this to Nabal. El Elyon the Most High God Himself struck your master. It is the only explanation."

He moved his hand to Nabal's chest and

leaned over him to listen. Soft raspy sounds came from Nabal's throat, but a moment later they changed to a dry rattle. His chest heaved once, twice, and his stiff body lifted from the bed, then dropped again like a felled tree.

A collective gasp came from behind Abigail. She turned to see Zahara and three of her maids huddled near the door, eyes wide. She looked again at the physician who was making a thorough check of Nabal. At last their gazes met.

"He is dead, my lady." The physician closed Nabal's eyes one at a time, then stepped away to allow her maids to come and prepare the body for burial.

Abigail released her grip on Nabal's cold fingers and sat back on her heels, staring at the man who had wooed her to want him but then controlled and mistreated her. She searched her heart for a sense of grief but found only relief instead. She was free of him at last.

The thought both comforted and terrified her. What would happen to her now? Even as a woman of means with a measure of independence, what good was her life without a husband and children? Who would care for her when she was old? Who would inherit the wealth Nabal had acquired if she never bore a son?

He would be willing to protect you, and I don't think he meant that in a general sense. I think he wants to spread his garment over you, Abigail. Daniel's words came back to her, swirling around her like a feast-day dance. She stood and surveyed the room.

"We will bury Nabal in the cave of his father and mother this afternoon." She glanced at Zahara. "We can be ready by then, can we not?"

Zahara nodded. "Yes, my lady. We can."

"Good. And send a runner to David's camp to my father and brother to tell them Nabal is dead." They should be told, and better that it come from her than to wait for a passing caravan to happen upon them with the news. Never mind that her heart picked up its pace at the thought of what this news would bring. Her brother would insist she join them, and then there was the matter of David . . .

She brushed the thought aside, frustrated with the traitorous bent of her heart. She must focus on what was expedient now for the funeral. Food would need to be prepared and professional mourners called. Nabal would be buried with all the kingly fanfare he felt he deserved. And she would show him respect despite the conflicting emotions

196

that told her not to. But she would not shed another tear for his loss.

And she would not miss him.

David stood at the crest of the hill overlooking the Judean wilderness. The summer heat bore down on him, adding weight to his oppressive thoughts. They should move on to a better place. They'd already been in the area surrounding Maon for months, and if his spies were right, since the encounter with Abigail, the Ziphites had shown enough unrest to convince him Saul would soon be at his back door. He needed another secure location. But there was no place left where they hadn't already been, and with the summer months coming fast upon them, all hope of vegetation and a steady water supply was slim.

Even now the sun's scorching finger had turned the valleys a hazy brown. The few sheep and goats that provided milk for the children would need better grazing land, but to go east toward the Jordan or north toward Jezreel would put him amid towns and land where Saul could readily find him.

He rubbed the back of his neck as he took in the barren landscape, unable to keep his chest from lifting in a troubled sigh. They should have moved on days ago when the spies first brought their report of the men of Ziph, but a second report that Nabal had taken ill had kept him from acting. Wait and see, he'd told himself more than once. But after ten days, the waiting was making him nervous. They definitely needed to move on, but where? Israel had many caves and hidden dwellings, but David was certain he had found them all. And he was weary of them. They needed someplace new, someplace where Saul would not think to look, where they might find at least the illusion of peace.

He turned, irritated that his train of thought had led him no closer to a solution, and trudged the narrow path that went around the hill, back to his hideaway. Benaiah and Daniel met him as he entered the camp.

"Good news, my lord," Benaiah said, matching David's strides as he walked toward the mouth of the cave. "A runner has come from the widow Abigail."

David stopped as Benaiah's words registered. "Widow?" Dared he believe it?

Daniel stepped closer, his wide grin showing a dimple in one cheek and lightening his normally dark eyes. "Nabal is dead, David! The Lord has struck him for his abuse."

David worked at hiding a smile, but it was no use. Laughter burst from him. "Praise be to Adonai, who has upheld my cause against Nabal for treating me with contempt. He has kept His servant from doing wrong and has brought Nabal's wrongdoing down on his own head." He slapped Daniel on the back and motioned for Daniel to follow him into the cave. "Summon your father for me."

"Yes, my lord." Smiling, Daniel hurried to do his bidding.

David's nerves hadn't been strung so tight since the first time Saul had hurled his spear in his direction. He shouldn't be worried. It wasn't like he had never sought a woman's hand in marriage, but this one seemed different somehow. And the fact that he already had a wife had made him pause more than once. He knew the law. Kings weren't supposed to have many wives so that their hearts would stay true to Yahweh. But he wasn't a king yet, and no woman of his would ever lead his heart from the worship of his God.

He shook his head at the impossible thought, then strummed his lyre, his head bent over the strings. There was nothing to worry about. Besides, how many wives were considered "many"? Two should not be an issue.

He plucked another chord and looked up at the sound of men approaching. His mighty men and advisors took their seats around the fire pit, then stood as Abigail's father, Judah, entered the circular area. Would her father approve? Would his daughter accept his offer so soon after her husband's death? Though he'd waited two days to act, he didn't have the luxury of giving her a month to mourn her husband — though it was doubtful she would mourn for a man like Nabal.

His hands stilled on the strings, and he motioned for Judah and Daniel to take the seats of honor beside him. He bent one knee to the ground, then bowed his head, facing Judah. Judah coughed as if embarrassed by David's display of humility, but when David looked up, he saw only joy and pride in the man's eyes.

"Judah, my father, I have heard that your daughter is now free to marry the man of her choosing, as she is no longer a daughter in her father's house but a widow of means. Nevertheless, I seek your blessing, and should your daughter accept, I am willing to place my garment over her, to take her as my wife." He bowed his head again in an act of submission, then looked up and waited.

"My lord, you do me great honor. I would be more than pleased to have my lord, the future king of Israel, as my son-in-law . . . if my Abigail agrees, of course." Judah's mouth held a humorous twist.

David courted a smile of his own. "Of course." He turned to face Daniel, then thought better of it and addressed his nephew Asahel. "Take men with you and go to Abigail, Nabal's widow, and tell her that David ben Jesse would like her to become his wife." His gaze took in the rest of his men. "Any objections?" Every face held approval, but as he glanced beyond the group to the cave's mouth, he glimpsed Ahinoam's stricken look. He should have known this would not be easy for her. He should have told her first in private. And now it was too late.

Commotion brought his attention back to his men. Asahel stood, followed by four of David's mighty men, and left the fire to do his bidding.

At their departure, Daniel approached him. "Why did you not want me to go with them, my lord? Abigail would be more comfortable with me there."

David met Daniel's disappointed gaze, then clapped the man on the back. "You might have persuaded her to say yes."

"Isn't that the point, my lord?"

David smiled. "Of course. But I want Abigail to come because she wants to, not because her brother convinced her." He glanced beyond Daniel, catching sight of Ahinoam hurrying away from the women and into the cave she and David shared. "Please excuse me," he said. He left the campfire and walked into the cave to try to somehow appease and comfort his wife.

19

Ahinoam turned at his approach and ran from him, deeper into the recesses of the cave. David watched her retreat, ruing the day he had taken her to wife, but as her sobs carried to him, he tucked his pride away and strode after her.

Lamplight cast grotesque shadows along the narrow passageway. Ahinoam normally shied away from coming here without him. She hated the caves more than he did. It was one of the very few things they agreed on. He had wanted to give her a fine palace and servants and jewels to adorn her hair, but all they had known since the day Joab had brought her to his camp was a life of uncertainty without a normal roof to protect them. He never should have married her.

The thought had troubled him more often than he could count, and at one time he had actually contemplated allowing her to return to her uncle's house and be free to marry another. But a part of him couldn't bear to give up what belonged to him. It would be like losing Michal all over again.

Ahinoam's crying grew louder as he rounded a bend in the tunnel to where the cave widened into a large room. The place was deserted except for his wife, who now sat in a crumpled heap in a far corner where their provisions lay. The sight of her hair — the color of wet sand — and her luminous, liquid eyes filled him with compassion. She had known the day would come when he would take other wives, but she probably hadn't expected it to come so soon. As long as he was a fugitive, he wasn't yet king, so he was hers alone. And he would have been if not for Abigail. But Abigail's wealth would help feed his men and their wives for years to come, if he could somehow manage to get the animals away from Maon. The trick would be figuring out how to hide thousands of sheep and goats from Saul's eyes.

Ahinoam's soft weeping brought his thoughts back into focus. Somehow he was going to have to convince her that this was a good thing, that despite having to share his time and attention, she would still have all the privileges of second wife of the king of Israel. Surely the promise of future riches and prestige should suffice.

He stepped closer until his shadow fell over her small frame. He bent low, kneeling at her side. She stilled at the touch of his hand on her shoulder. "Ahinoam, please, don't weep." He spoke softly as he'd done so often with an injured lamb, pulling her into his arms and stroking her hair. "I should have told you first. I'm sorry."

He expected his words to appease her, but instead her sobs grew stronger, louder. He held her close, willing his impatience to stay in check. "It will be all right, my love."

She hiccuped on a sob and pulled back, her look telling him his words couldn't be farther from the truth. "How can you say such a thing? You told me I would never lose you, but now you are throwing me away for another without a thought as to how I feel." She flung the words at him, and their barbs hit their intended mark, increasing his sense of guilt.

"I'm not throwing you away. I am just adding to my house, increasing my strength. Abigail's inheritance will make the job of looking for food less of a chore. And one day you will both stand at my side when God fulfills His promises to me." Saying so helped to convince his own doubting heart.

"You mean *if* God fulfills His promises to you. How do we know they are even true,

David? For eight years you have been a fugitive from the king, and there is no sign of that ending. Maybe Samuel was wrong. Maybe you misunderstood him." She spoke quietly, but the words thundered in his heart like a war drum. Hadn't he wondered the same thing over and over again? He'd had such faith in the early days, but this woman had consistently whittled it down until he almost believed her.

Abigail had not agreed. Hadn't she spoken of his coming rule as though she knew it to be true? His heart warmed to the thought, increasing his longing for his men to return with her. Would she come?

But it was Ahinoam he held at arm's length, searching her gaze and seeing the root of bitterness beneath those dark, beguiling lashes. "I didn't misunderstand the prophet, my love, but I will admit I don't understand you. Every time I come to you, you doubt me or fear me or fear what will become of me. I need you to have faith, to believe in me, to believe in Yahweh. Your fear withers my spirit."

She leaned back as though he had slapped her, pulling her arms around herself in a self-protective gesture. "I only fear what will become of us because you keep leading us to places Saul can find us." She looked away, avoiding eye contact, and scooted farther from him into a corner like a startled doe.

He released a weary sigh, frustrated. How was he supposed to get through to her? Nothing he said or did seemed to make any difference. She was beautiful in form but not in spirit. He could share none of his heart with her. The realization confirmed what he'd been pondering for months, and with it came the satisfaction that in Abigail he was making a wise choice.

"I'm sorry you feel that way, Ahinoam. I trust that in the coming days you can have more faith in me than you exhibit now." He stood and looked down on her. "If Abigail accepts my proposal of marriage, she will be joining us. See to it that you make her feel welcome. I will not tolerate animosity between my wives."

The look she gave him told him he wasn't likely to get what he requested.

Abigail wandered from room to room, feeling as though the vast estate would swallow her whole. Nabal's presence, while not something she enjoyed, still gave a certain purpose and life to the house that was now sorely lacking. Even during his illness there had been work to do and reason to do it.

Now, after only three days without him, she walked about wondering what next. *Oh, Adonai, what shall I do?*

She paused at the audience chamber where Nabal had so often sat convening with neighbors or entertaining guests, the place where he'd displayed such self-importance. For what? All had come to naught with his death. His wealth would go to another, not even to his own son.

The thought filled her with an unexpected sadness. She pressed a hand to her middle where a child would never lie, allowing the melancholy to seep into her heart. What would happen to her? Perhaps she should have taken that shepherd's offer of marriage, though the very idea was enough to make her physically ill. Besides, she didn't need a man to survive any longer. Nabal's wealth was security enough.

She moved away from the ornate room, turning her back on the oriental tapestries and carved cedarwood furnishings. The expense of the place could have rivaled the king's palace. Would David find any of it useful?

Servants moved around her, going about their normal tasks as she had commanded them, but with an air of peace the household had never known before. She should find

208

the atmosphere comforting, but thoughts of her family, of David, kept stealing her focus. She had sent word about Nabal's death to Daniel three days ago. Why had she heard nothing from him? Her servants had returned from delivering her message, so she knew David's men had heard the news. Surely Daniel would come to comfort her, to bring Mama and Abba, even if he'd been wrong about David.

Worry niggled the muscles along her shoulders. Was it wrong to want David to do as Daniel had suggested? He had already married two other women, though the king's daughter Michal now belonged to someone else. If Abigail joined their ranks, she knew she would not be the last of David's wives. Her only hope would be to bear a son, someone to love her when David could not. But she'd already proven with Nabal how uncertain such a hope could be.

Frustrated with herself, Abigail walked to the roof and examined the weavers as their hands worked the loom. The garments would bring a goodly sum in the marketplace, as Nabal's wool was some of the finest in Judea. She could use the money to help some of the poor in Carmel and Maon and increase the wages of Nabal's servants.

She moved to her spindle, which had sat

gathering dust in a corner since Nabal had taken ill. She must stop thinking about the future. Each day had enough trouble of its own, so why was she borrowing trouble from tomorrow? She had a household to oversee and plenty to do . . . but a deep longing for her family brought the sting of tears to her eyes. She'd been true to her word and shed no tears for Nabal, but at night when no one was looking, she could not help the tears that came unbidden for herself.

She swiped them away now, clenching her jaw, then sat on a low stool and picked up the spindle. The women gossiped as they worked the loom, and she smiled at their occasional glances her way. When the sun had risen halfway to the sky, Zahara rushed up the steps, out of breath, her hair coming loose from her headdress.

"My lady, some men from David are here to see you."

Abigail's hands stilled even as her heart picked up its pace. David had sent men? Not her father or brother? She searched Zahara's anxious gaze. "How many men? Is my brother among them?" She laid the spindle aside and stood, smoothing her robe as she walked toward her maid.

"There are five of them, and no, your

brother is not among them."

Abigail slowed her pace as she considered and discarded a handful of reasons why they had come. She stopped halfway to the audience chamber to rearrange her veil. "Is it straight? Do I look all right?"

"Of course you look all right. You are beautiful as always, my lady." Zahara smoothed the finely woven head scarf over Abigail's flowing hair, adjusting the ivory combs that held it in place at her temples. "There, that's better." She met Abigail's gaze. "Don't worry. Whatever they want, it will all work out. Didn't your brother say David wanted you? So you will have a home after all."

Abigail saw the glint of something akin to hope stir in Zahara's eyes, and it occurred to her that perhaps Zahara would now want, even seek, a home of her own as well. "I suppose you will want to return to your people?"

Zahara lifted a shoulder in a slight shrug as though the thought had never occurred to her, but her expression was far from indifferent. The thought pained Abigail. She enjoyed Zahara's company, despite the girl's pagan roots and lack of faith in Adonai. "We will talk more of this after we hear what they have to say." She nodded toward the audience chamber, indicating for Zahara to lead the way.

She stopped at the threshold for Zahara to announce her presence, scanning the five bearded men whose company filled only part of the spacious room. Their hair appeared freshly washed, their faces were clean, and their clothes smelled of travel more than sweat and sheep. This was an official greeting to demand such an attendance. She looked into their anxious faces, her gaze stopping with the burly man she had seen with Daniel the last time he had come to see her, the day Nabal's heart had turned to stone.

"Welcome to my home." She glanced at one of her young maids, then took a seat in the chair Nabal had reserved for himself. Her maid hurried away and returned moments later with a bowl and pitcher to wash the men's feet. Abigail glanced at each man, then focused not on the burly man but on the one who appeared to be the leader. "How may I serve you, and why have you come?" She pointed to cedarwood benches that lined the walls, indicating for them to sit. They did as she bid them, and her maid quickly approached the first man and bent to untie his sandals.

"I am Asahel, nephew of David ben Jesse.

212

David sent us to you to ask you to become his wife." The man who spoke was about her brother's age. His medium brown hair fell along his square jaw, his thin frame was muscular and agile, and he bore a resemblance to David except fairer. As he spoke, he held Abigail's gaze, then glanced briefly about the room. Interest flickered in his eyes as his gaze rested on Zahara, then he gave his full attention to Abigail again. "He regrets that he did not allow you more time to mourn your husband, but he is anxious to leave the area. I know this is sudden —"

"No, it is good. There was no need to mourn." She stood, her knees feeling suddenly weak at what she was about to do. Her life would change forever if she did as they requested. Did she truly want to be just another wife of a charming man? But the thought of marrying Nabal's shepherd or living alone the rest of her life answered that question with ease.

She stepped forward, knelt before the leader, and bowed her face to the earth. The man cleared his throat but did not speak. She raised her head and stood again, then took the pitcher, basin, and towel from her maidservant and continued the task the girl had begun. When she finished washing the feet of each man, she handed the towel to her maid and stood, head bowed before them.

"Here is your maidservant, a servant to wash the feet of the servants of my lord." She looked up and caught the wide grin on Asahel's face and the accompanying smiles of the men with him. Even the burly guard she'd seen with Daniel had lost his stoic expression in a soft grin. "Let my maids and me gather our things. Then we will come at once."

"How can we help you, my lady?" Asahel spoke again, drawing her attention. "We will be happy to load the donkeys for you."

Abigail nodded, her heart doing a sudden gallop through her chest and a shudder working through her. "My servant Jakim will help you to ready the animals. My maids and I will gather our things. We will meet by the well."

"We will do as you say." The man turned to his companions. "Let's hurry."

Before the men had finished retying their sandals, Abigail and Zahara fled the room to hasten to David.

■ ■ ■ ■

PART III

■ ■ ■ ■

Abigail quickly got on a donkey and, attended by her five maids, went with David's messengers and became his wife. David had also married Ahinoam of Jezreel, and they both were his wives.

1 Samuel 25:42–43

David thought to himself, "One of these days I will be destroyed by the hand of Saul. The best thing I can do is to escape to the land of the Philistines. Then Saul will give up searching for me anywhere in Israel, and I will slip out of his hand." So David and the six hundred men with him left and went over to Achish son of Maoch king of Gath. David and his men settled in Gath with Achish. Each man had his family with him, and David had his two wives: Ahinoam of Jezreel and Abigail of Carmel, the widow of Nabal.

1 Samuel 27:1–3

20

Abigail's knuckles whitened on the donkey's reins the closer they came to David's encampment. Shadows blanketed the hills as the sun began its quick descent over the western horizon, and Abigail's heart thumped with a strange mix of giddy excitement and dread. She'd caught a glimpse of David's varied emotions the day she'd met him along the path — known the terror of his murderous wrath in his warrior eyes, and the sudden switch to gentle kindness when that wrath had been appeased. Would he ever turn that wrath on her?

A shiver worked through her, despite the many times she'd told herself that David was not Nabal. Somehow she must keep her fear to herself and stop comparing the two men in her mind. *Oh, Adonai, grant me peace.* Her heart fluttered in accompaniment to her prayer as her donkey followed the messengers into the clearing where men and women were separated into groups, the women cooking over open flames and the men sitting about sharpening swords and laughing together.

The donkeys halted near a supply cave filled with leather packs strewn about at one end and animals resting or bent over a large feeding trough on the other. A man appeared near the supplies, and as he drew closer she recognized her brother. Smiling, he walked toward her and helped her dismount.

"Nervous?" he asked, his gaze searching hers. Concern replaced his wide grin. "I know that look. You don't need to worry with David. He is not like Nabal." He rested both hands on her shoulders. "David won't hurt you," he whispered, as if he knew all about Nabal's abuse though she had never told him.

She nodded, her throat suddenly thick with unshed tears. "There is more than one way to hurt a person," she whispered back, leaning close to his ear. "But you needn't worry about me, Daniel. Yahweh will take care of me." She looked at him with tentative assurance, hoping that he would believe her and that saying it would make it so in the deepest places in her heart.

He leaned forward and kissed her cheek.

"You will do well here, Abigail." He smiled again and turned toward the central fire pit. Music from a single lyre floated on the night breezes, nearly drowned out by the din of men's banter and the chatter of the women. "Come," he said, leaving the baggage cave and motioning for her to follow.

She lifted her robe above her sandals and hurried after him. "What of my maids, Daniel?" She glanced back at Zahara and the four other serving girls she had brought with her from Nabal's house. She could have abandoned them to the mercy of the male servants she had left in charge of the place until David could decide what to do with Nabal's estate, or allowed them to return to their fathers' houses and let Zahara return to her people, but she wouldn't risk what might become of them. And she needed the moral support of their presence.

He stopped to look at her. "They will still serve you, I suppose. David will probably let you do as you wish with them. Now come on, Abba is waiting to give you to David, and Mama is anxious to see you." He whirled about before she could respond.

Daniel led her to a large stone where a man holding a lyre stilled his playing at their approach. She tugged her scarf across her neck but left her face open for him to see.

Their gazes met, and his dark eyes held hers. Even in the dim light of dusk and firelight, she could read the sheer delight dancing in their depths. Her knees lost their ability to stand in the intensity of his look, and she sank to the earth and bowed with her face to the dust.

"My lord," she said, feeling that she should say so much more. But where once her mind flowed with words to appease him, now she could think of nothing to say.

His touch on her shoulder made her look up, his tender gaze stealing her fear. He was undeniably handsome, making her pulse jump at his dark, rugged good looks. He held out a hand to her and lifted her to her feet. "Welcome." He searched her face as though wanting to be sure she had come because she truly desired to be here.

"Thank you, my lord." She averted her gaze from his perusal, but his fingers under her chin coaxed her to look at him again.

"You got my message." It wasn't a question, though he waited, clearly expecting an answer.

"Yes, my lord. I accept your offer."

His fingers closed over hers, and his eyes lit with that same fire of longing she'd noticed when their gazes first met. He wanted her, and in that instant she realized she wanted him as well. "You understand my situation?" He spoke softly, bending closer to her ear, as though the question worried him.

She looked into his eyes, unable to pull away, his face so close she could feel his warmth. "You live as a fugitive and have another wife. Yes, my lord, I understand." She drew in a slow breath, willing her racing heart under control. "I still accept." She allowed a slight smile to reassure him and was rewarded with a sigh of relief and an enigmatic grin that stopped her heart.

He stepped back from her and glanced at the men she now noticed sitting in a circle near where he'd been playing his lyre. She recognized her father and had to hold herself in check to keep from running into his arms. His beaming smile told her she had made a wise choice in accepting David's offer. He stood and walked toward them while her mother stood behind him, looking as though she couldn't wait for the men to get on with things.

"Abigail, I have already given David my permission, but Abiathar here is waiting to give you the ceremony you deserve — such as we can offer. You will not be denied the priestly blessing this time." Her father pulled her close and wrapped strong arms about her. Her throat closed with sudden unexpected emotion at the comfort of his embrace. She was safe again, and despite the living conditions, despite the presence of another wife, this marriage would be better.

"I won't let anyone hurt you again, dear one," Abba whispered against her hair.

"Come, come, Judah, give a mother a moment to hold the daughter she hasn't seen in half a lifetime."

Abigail turned at the sound of her mother's voice and fell into her open arms. "Mama!" She choked on the word, fearing she would weep for the joy of being with her family again and spoil the quick work Zahara had made of her makeup for the wedding.

"I'm glad you came." Her mother's tone carried a sense of relief, and when Abigail pulled back and looked into her eyes, she caught a glimpse of something more. Gratitude, perhaps? "Come now, Talya and I have prepared the canopy." She turned and waved Abigail's sister-in-law over. "Bring your maids and follow me."

Abigail hugged Talya and glanced over her shoulder at David, uncertain. He nodded, indicating she do as her mother asked.

"We will come when you are ready." His

dark eyes crinkled at the corners, and his assuring smile bolstered her courage.

"Thank you, my lord." She turned then, confident of his favor, and slipped her arm through Talya's.

"He's nothing like Nabal, Abigail. Daniel thinks the sun rises and sets with David, as though God's favor is linked to the man." Talya leaned close as they approached the cave where a makeshift canopy stood awaiting her. "But his first wife Ahinoam is used to things being a certain way."

Abigail paused to look into Talya's eyes. "What are you saying?"

Talya shrugged. "You don't have anything to worry about. She's a whiny one, and David grows weary of her complaints. He'd been growing tired of her before he met you. But she's been with him for several years now, so she might not be easy to befriend."

Abigail glanced beyond the cave's entrance to the men and women and wondered which one was Ahinoam. Guilt pricked her conscience, but what could she do? It was too late to back out of the marriage now.

"There wasn't time to make something special," her mother said as she came up behind Abigail, "but Talya brought her wedding garments with her when we came."

Abigail turned to see the embroidered, multicolored robe that had draped her sister-in-law at her marriage to Daniel and had been worn since at festivals and other special occasions. "It's beautiful. Thank you." She had left her own wedding garments, the robe and tunic she had worn for Nabal, back at Nabal's house, wanting nothing to do with the memories they evoked. She fingered Talya's robe, then allowed the women to remove her own robe and place the cheery garment over her tunic in place of it.

Talya placed a garland of wild flowers over her veil, then stood back. "Lovely as always." The women surrounded her, giggling and smiling. "Wait until David sees you."

"He will never know such a beautiful bride." Her mother gripped her arms and searched her gaze, her voice low. "You know he will take more wives someday, don't you, child?"

Abigail's heart did a little flip at the implication of what her future held. "I know, Mama." But the knowing didn't stop the uneasy feeling her mother's words brought to mind.

A moment passed, then her mother clucked her tongue and hurried past Abigail toward the cave's entrance. "The man won't want to wait for you forever!"

Her maids laughed, and Abigail felt her face flush even as her heart quickened its pace.

Moments passed, and her stomach fluttered at the sound of the men outside. Her father's voice carried to her but was overshadowed by David's newly familiar tone. They came closer, and a young man stepped forward dressed as a shepherd but draped in the ephod of a priest.

"This is Abiathar, last surviving member of the priests of Nob," David said, one hand held toward the man, the other extended to her. She took it and stood with him under the canopy.

David spread the corner of his robe over her shoulders and wrapped one arm about her waist. Tingling warmth rushed through her at his touch. She hadn't expected the wedding to happen so fast, but then David did not live as normal men.

She listened in silence as her father pledged her to David.

"And do you, Abigail ben Judah, promise obedience to your husband, David ben Jesse?" Abiathar asked.

She met the priest's kind gaze. His pale eyes told her he had seen far too much pain in the world, yet he had somehow survived.

The thought comforted her, infusing her with strength. She could survive too.

"Yes." Abigail looked up into David's shining eyes. "I will strive to please you, my lord." Her words were spoken for his ears alone, and her heart lifted at the delight in his responding smile.

"I promise to protect you, to care for your needs, to cherish you." David tightened his grip at her waist, his gaze never leaving hers.

"Then in the sight of Adonai and these witnesses, I give you Adonai's blessing."

David pulled her to him and kissed her forehead. Cheers erupted around them, and David led her back to the campfire and seated her on the stone next to him. A woman brought a bowl of savory-smelling red lentil stew and a large, round loaf of flat bread and placed them on the small stone before them. David broke the bread, dunked it into the stew, and handed it to her.

"Taste and see that Adonai is good," he said, his smile gentle, his dark eyes searching hers.

She accepted the bread, her arm tingling when her fingers brushed his in the exchange. She lifted the bread to her lips and ate, barely aware of the taste or of the sounds of feasting, laughter, and music floating around them.

"I don't have much to offer you here" — he waved a hand encompassing the area around them — "but what I have is yours." He bit off a large chunk of the flat bread and chewed, silently assessing her.

She glanced around them. "There are more women here than I expected. Does that make it hard for you . . . when the king . . . when he —"

"When Saul tracks me down and threatens my life?"

She nodded, wishing she hadn't brought up such a topic on this day.

He looked beyond her, and a cloud covered his expression for the briefest moment, then lifted. "The women help keep the men calm," he said at last, as though no other explanation was needed. "They are a burden, without question." He turned to her then, caught her hand in his, and smiled. "But a burden worth the trouble." He winked, making her pulse quicken.

She returned his smile, not sure how to take his answer. But of course, the women would slow the men down in the event they had to run. "I hope so, my lord." She did not wish to add to David's troubles, but she was here now and determined to make the best of the arrangements.

Movement caught her eye and she glanced

to her right, following David's gaze. She glimpsed a young woman at the edges of the camp avoiding the festivities, staring at David, her beautiful face wreathed in a frown. Ahinoam. Undoubtedly.

She looked at David, watched his brow furrow and the lines tighten along his mouth. Would he introduce them to each other here? Now? The thought troubled her for the briefest moment, but in the next instant he turned to her, stood, and pulled her to him. "It's time," he whispered. "Come." With one hand on the small of her back, he ushered her ahead of him, away from the fire pit where the dancing and music continued and into the shadowed lamplight of a cave. The slight pressure of his touch sent tingling warmth through her.

After several winding turns, the cave opened into a larger area where several clay lamps dispelled the closed-in feeling. A bed of soft skins lay in one corner, and a small loom and baskets of wool lay propped against a limestone wall in another.

"We normally share the area with some of my advisors, but tonight it belongs just to us." He turned her to face him, his smile boyish and carefree. "I'm glad you came."

"As am I." She shivered as he traced a finger along her cheek, the image of the other woman slowly slipping from her mind.

He bent forward to kiss her. "Are you?" He kissed her again, his lips lingering this time.

"Of course." She smiled, tempted to offer him a teasing quip, but she quickly squelched the thought, not sure she should take the risk. Nabal would have misunderstood and probably slapped her.

He held her at arm's length, his eyes searching, probing. "You look worried." He sounded troubled and the slightest bit annoyed.

"Do I? I don't mean to be, it's just . . ." She looked over his shoulder as he toyed with the edge of her veil. "It's all happened so fast." Was his other wife fearful of him, or did he just find the fears of women irritating?

He took a step back, studying her. "Would you prefer to wait? If I offend you —"

"You don't offend me." Heat filled her cheeks that the conversation had turned so intimate. "I want to . . . I . . . it's just . . . I don't exactly know you." She looked at him then, saw the smile in his eyes.

"Of course not. But we have years to remedy that." He ran gentle hands up and down her arms, then cupped them around her face and kissed her again. "You have nothing to fear from me, Abigail." He pulled back, watching her as he smoothly tugged the veil from her head, then one by one released the seven combs that held her hair back, allowing her thick tresses to tumble to her shoulders. When the last one dropped to the earth at their feet, he tenderly entwined his fingers through the silken strands of her hair. "Let me show you my love," he whispered, his breath soft against her ear.

She nodded, afraid to trust her voice, her heart beating an erratic rhythm. She worked to undo the knot in the belt at her waist, then stilled as his hands covered hers.

"You're trembling."

"Am I?"

"Yes." He placed her hands at her sides and undid the knot, then slipped the robe from her shoulders. He tilted her chin so she would look at him again, his gaze searching.

"Your first husband — were you afraid of him?" His obvious concern warmed her heart. She nodded. "Did he give you reason to be?"

"Yes." She held his gaze, allowing him a glimpse into her soul, trusting him more than she expected she would.

"And yet you defended him."

"I meant to protect the others, and you."

"You mean, you meant to protect the others from me." Silence followed, and she saw mingled fire and regret in his eyes. "You should have let me kill him."

"I couldn't. I —"

"No, you are right. Yahweh had a better plan." He smiled then and turned his head to one side to get a better look at her. "You can trust me, Abigail," he said. "I will never hurt you."

She searched his face and felt her heart yearning for him. "I want to believe you." She lifted her hands and wound them around his neck, drawing herself into his embrace.

"Believe me, beloved." The fire of longing smoldered in his dark eyes as he bent to kiss her again. "I always keep my promises."

21

David half listened to his men as they discussed the latest sighting of Saul and argued over what to do next. He scooped porridge with a piece of flat bread from the common bowl he shared with his men, then tossed it into his mouth. His gaze traveled to Abigail, her busy hands refilling empty plates and replacing fresh skins of water at each man's side. She hummed a soft tune, and when she glanced at him, a smile lit her eyes. He winked at her in return, silently thanking Yahweh for her presence in the camp and in his life. Somehow she had managed to bring peace to the place in the few weeks she'd been here. Even Ahinoam seemed to settle into an unexpected sort of acceptance. Some of the time.

He looked over the area as he sat back and licked the last drops of stew from his mouth, his gaze settling on Abigail's maid Zahara. That one troubled him. Though

Abigail seemed to think the girl was loyal, he had his doubts. Perhaps if they married her off, the wild look he glimpsed now and then would disappear. But the fact that she was a foreigner kept him from suggesting it to Abigail. That, and the uneasy feeling she gave him. Something in the way she watched the distant hills, as though she intended to run off at the first chance. Could she have been one of Saul's spies? Abigail had indicated that Nabal himself had conspired with the Ziphites against him, so why not this foreigner?

She glanced in his direction, and a blush filled her cheeks. She'd caught his perusal. Did she think he was interested in her himself? He looked away, turning his attention back to his advisors to focus on their discussion.

"The scouts' report is clear, David. Saul has made camp beside the road on the hill of Hakilah facing Jeshimon. What would you have us do? He's too close." Joab sipped from his water skin and grimaced. "What I wouldn't give for a good skin of wine."

His comment was met with approval around the circle of his closest advisors. Abigail's store of wine remained on Nabal's estate, and now was not the time to go looking for it. He could use a bit of mind-numbing drink himself right now. But not with Saul on his heels.

"I will go down to Saul and see for myself." He looked at the thirty men who had proven the most valiant and loyal, then stood. He pointed to a newcomer, Ahimelech the Hittite, and four other men, Abishai, Joab, Benaiah, and Asahel. "Come." He checked the sword at his side and left the group with the five men following.

They passed the wives of his advisors sitting in a separate group feeding their children. He would have moved on without a backward glance but couldn't help the desire for another glimpse of Abigail. If the scouts' reports were true and he found Saul this night, he might not return in safety.

The thought stopped him at the edge of the women's circle. He turned, searching for Abigail among them. She noticed his gaze, jumped up, and came to him.

"There is trouble, my lord?" She was already too good at reading his expressions.

He nodded. "Don't look for me tonight."

Disappointment flickered in her eyes for the slightest moment, but her reassuring touch on his arm and warm smile told him she understood. "I will pray unceasingly for Yahweh's protection for you," she whispered, standing on tiptoe to reach his ear.

He bent closer, tugged her to him, and kissed her soundly, not caring who witnessed his affection. "Thank you." He smiled as he released her. "I will return."

"As I would expect, my lord."

He moved away with a flicker of guilt that he should bid farewell to Ahinoam. Irritated with his own sense of responsibility, he glanced back at the group of women and caught her looking at him. He motioned her forward, his guilt increasing at the look of relief on her face.

"Yes, my lord?"

"Don't wait for me tonight. I won't be back until morning." He kissed her then, a soft touch to her lips. He was finding the desire he once had for her waning despite his effort to treat his wives as equals. Soon he might feel the same toward them both, though he sensed that wasn't true. Abigail was new and exciting and was nothing like Ahinoam, and he couldn't imagine himself ever growing tired of her.

Ahinoam stepped back as he released her, and he moved away from the women to join his men, his mind shifting to the task at hand. Saul was out there, and they needed to find him and put an end to this.

But something told him the end was still

a long time coming.

Abigail watched David stride down the path leading to the winding road that wove among the wilderness hills until he was a mere speck in her eyes. Her interest in and deep concern for him still took her by surprise. The feeling had been nonexistent in her marriage to Nabal. Was this love?

Her mother often spoke of her father in affectionate terms and had assured Abigail that such feelings came after the marriage — that beforehand a wife could not be expected to even know her husband, much less care for him. With Nabal there was too much fear for such feelings to exist, too much disrespect and disdain. But David . . .

"Don't expect him to keep you his favorite." The voice coming from behind startled her. She turned to look into Ahinoam's scowling face. "When we first wed, he treated me the way he treats you now. Give him a few months, or perhaps if you're fortunate, a year or two, but soon he'll meet someone new, and then you'll be little more to him than an occasional concubine." The words carried a brittle edge.

A handful of responses, unkind, even damaging, flew to her thoughts, but she squelched each one in turn. The haunting truth of it was that Ahinoam was probably right. When David took the throne as king, other women would vie for his affection, and when war did not conquer their enemies, peace treaties would be linked to marriage contracts. She'd always known it, but the reminder so soon after her marriage left her unsettled, uncertain, and suddenly wondering if she'd made the right decision.

"I'm sure you are right, Ahinoam. David will one day be king, and kings have many wives. We must remember that and support each other. You and I have the unique privilege of knowing David now during the waiting years. We may not be his favorites someday, but we will share memories the others will have missed." The unsettled feeling grew, a heavy weight in her middle, despite her brave words. Sharing David with one other wife would be hard enough, but more than one? How would she bear it?

Her thoughts churning, she forced her mind back to Ahinoam and offered her what she hoped was a kind smile to put her rival's mind at ease. She would need this woman to befriend her in days to come. Somehow she must learn to share David with her and help her to see that she was not Ahinoam's enemy. "I would be your friend, Ahinoam, if you will have me."

Ahinoam's gaze met hers, and Abigail caught a glimpse of her thoughts — a mix of anger and fear. At last Ahinoam shook her head, her scowl deepening. "You are only accepted because your family got in good with David, but don't forget, I'm the first wife here. Don't go trying to usurp my place." She took two steps back and crossed her arms. "If you want my *friendship*" — the word came out tinged in sarcasm — "give me my husband. Your bridal week is up; it is time you share him." She turned and stalked off, leaving Abigail staring after her.

Moonlight created dancing shadows over the hill of Hakilah where Saul and three thousand soldiers spread out on the ground near the road.

"Saul's standard is in the middle of the camp, in the dip in the earth, with Abner's beside it," Abishai said at David's side. Ahimelech the Hittite crouched with them beneath a terebinth tree at the top of the hill overlooking the encampment.

David ducked from the branches and stepped away from the edge to avoid being seen by those below. Abishai and Ahimelech followed, joining Joab, Benaiah, and Asahel, who came from other lookout places along the cliff. "Who will go down with me to

Saul in the camp?" He looked from Abishai to Ahimelech, gauging the reaction in each man's eyes. He would leave the others above, to watch their backs.

"I will go down with you." Abishai spoke first, his hand on the hilt of his sword and his expression eager. Ahimelech took a step back as though relieved that Abishai had volunteered.

"Good, let's go." David backtracked to the winding path, picking his way slowly down the mountain toward the base of the hill. They stopped at the entrance where sentries should have been standing watch. But there was no sign of any guard stirring or safeguarding the king's men.

"What now?" Abishai whispered. David scanned the darkly cloaked bodies of Saul's men stretched before them, lying in small rises and low crevices in the earth. Abishai's voice, though a mere whisper, nearly echoed in the silence. An eerie feeling crept over David.

"Nothing moves," he said as they set one foot in front of the other between the narrow rows of men.

Abishai nodded, his eyes wide. Not even the sound of a cricket interrupted the dark. The only noise was the faint crunch of their sandals in the dirt. An owl swooped above their heads, its distant flapping a muffled ripple in the night's cool air.

David pulled his cloak closer to his neck, a shiver working through him. Yahweh was in this place, walked beside him in this valley of darkness. He could sense Him in the strange silence, the total lack of movement on the part of any soldier in the camp. Every man slept, their breathing soft, as though the army lived yet slept in Sheol, where the dead lay.

They walked on to the middle of the camp where Saul's gold and blue standard stood beside his spear, waving its banner in the night breeze near his head. Abner's red-crested insignia as captain of the guard was emblazoned on his cloak and shield, which lay beside him. But rather than guarding the man he had sworn to protect, Abner showed no signs of life other than soft snoring as he slept next to Saul. The king of Israel lay on his side, arms curled in a self-protective position, and his water jug rested at his feet.

David looked down at the man who had made his life miserable for the past nine years, expecting to feel anger, even hatred. But his heart held only pity.

"David." Abishai touched his shoulder and leaned close. "Today God has delivered your enemy into your hands. Now let me pin him to the ground with one thrust of my spear. I won't have to strike him twice."

David looked into Abishai's eager eyes. He stood poised, one hand closed over the hilt of Saul's spear. How often had David jumped out of the path of that blade when the king had thrown it at him in a fit of rage? In one thrust Abishai could put an end to David's fugitive life, allowing him to pursue the dreams God had promised. The temptation to do just that rushed him like an enemy solider in battle.

Abishai lifted the heavy spear with ease, waiting for David's word.

O Adonai, if only You would let me do this! How long, Lord? Will You forget me forever? The thought had come to him far too often of late. One day this man who lay so helpless now would surely take David's life if he allowed him to live, proving Ahinoam right and giving breath to his own faithless fears.

He lifted his gaze heavenward, his heart yearning for closure, for action, for hope. *How long, Adonai?* But he knew that whether God kept His promise sooner or later, killing Saul was not part of His answer.

"Don't destroy him!" He looked into Abishai's bewildered face, knowing his nephew would never understand. "Who can lay a hand on Adonai's anointed and be guiltless?" He searched for words to explain himself. "As the Lord lives, Adonai Himself shall strike him. Either his time will come and he will die, or he will go into battle and perish. But the Lord forbid that I should lay a hand on Adonai's anointed." He released a breath as Abishai lowered the spear back to the earth and loosened his grip. "Now get the spear and the water jug that are near his head, and let's go."

David picked his way back through the camp and climbed the hill, Abishai at his back, his nephew's silent disapproval weighting the air around them. David pressed on, ignoring the unspoken reprimand, and relief filled him as they joined the others.

As dawn turned the sky from gray to a mingled array of yellow, rose, and blue, David stepped from under the terebinth tree to the edge of the cliff. Joab and Benaiah jumped up to join him, but he waved them back with his hand.

He looked down at the stirring soldiers, memories of once fighting beside them in battle filling his thoughts. He tried to accept the fact that most of them had turned against him and thought him a traitor now. Would he be able to regain their trust and

goodwill when God handed him the kingdom? *If* God handed him the kingdom. Had
he imagined the promise? Had Samuel been
wrong?

Shoving his melancholy thoughts aside,
David drew in a breath for courage, then
cupped his hands around his mouth. "Aren't
you going to answer me, Abner?" His voice
carried below, echoing in the valley floor.
The men looked toward the hills as though
trying to determine the source of the sound.

"Who are you who calls to the king?"
Abner's turban carried the telltale red sash,
making him visible to David even from the
distance. Not exactly a wise move in a true
battle, as it made him a living target. But
the general wasn't likely to care what this
upstart young rival thought, even if he did
once grudgingly appreciate his expertise in
times of war.

"You are a man, aren't you? And who is
like you in Israel? Why didn't you guard
your lord the king? Someone came to
destroy your lord the king. What you have
done is not good. As Adonai lives, you and
your men deserve to die, because you did
not guard your master, Adonai's anointed."
He motioned for Abishai to bring the spear
and water jug. "Lift them high," he whispered, then turned back to Abner. "Where

243

are the king's spear and water jug that were near his head?"

David caught sight of a man moving toward Abner, his gold crown shining in the sun's ever-brightening rays. "Is that your voice, David my son?"

David's stomach did an uncomfortable turn at Saul's tender tone. Too many memories accompanied this man, thoughts of Jonathan and Michal, times of joy and acceptance back when David was young, his future bright.

He swallowed hard, surprised at the sudden emotion he felt, knowing how close he had come to sinning against Yahweh and killing the king. "Yes it is, my lord the king." He drew in a breath, lifting his chin, trying to bolster his wavering pride and confidence. "Why is my lord pursuing his servant? What have I done, and what wrong am I guilty of?" He'd said similar words to Jonathan when Saul had first hunted him down, a lifetime ago.

Would it never end?

"Now let my lord the king listen to his servant's words. If Adonai has incited you against me, then may He accept an offering."

Could Yahweh have done this? Had David somehow offended the Almighty that He should allow him to suffer this way? *Please, Adonai, accept my broken heart on Your altar.*

David stood straighter, making sure his voice could be heard below. "If, however, men have done it, may they be cursed before the Lord! They have now driven me from my share in the Lord's inheritance, and have said, 'Go, serve other gods.' " Was that the answer to get away from Saul's pursuit? Must he run away from this land he loved? "Now do not let my blood fall to the ground far from the presence of Adonai. The king of Israel has come out to look for a flea, as when one hunts a partridge in the mountains." Indeed, he was no more significant, but oh, for the wings of a bird to take him far from this place. He could return to Moab or try again to find refuge among the Philistines.

"I have sinned," Saul said. "Come back, David my son. Because you considered my life precious today, I will not try to harm you again. Surely I have acted like a fool and have erred greatly." Saul's voice broke despite its strength.

David watched Saul's head bow and his shoulders droop as though in grief. He put a hand to his head and looked up once more. Did he honestly think David would return to Gibeah with him? The man deluded himself!

"Here is the king's spear!" David pointed to Abishai, who lifted the weapon again. David met his nephew's gaze and read in his eyes a desire to thrust the blade toward the old king even now. David shook his head and looked back at Saul. "Let one of your young men come over and get it. Adonai rewards every man for his righteousness and faithfulness. Adonai delivered you into my hands today, but I would not lay a hand on Adonai's anointed. As surely as I valued your life today, so may Adonai value my life and deliver me from all trouble."

Saul lifted his hands toward the hill where David stood. "May you be blessed, my son David. You will do great things and surely triumph."

David stepped away from the edge and turned his back on Saul, rejoining his men. Had he been any other man, Saul's blessing might have meant something to him. But David knew how fickle the king could be, how untrustworthy the men who supported him and incited him against David were. Even if Saul spoke the truth, David could not believe him. Saul would never quit his hatred or his pursuit, and David would never kill him. Which meant one of them must move or die. And it wasn't likely to be

Saul.

David walked on in silence until they reached the camp where men and women sat about in circles, breaking the fast from the night before. He moved ahead of Benaiah, who had kept at his side throughout the arduous trek back to the wilderness compound, and stood in the main area at the central fire. He called the thirty together, and they hurried to gather the men and women to listen. Abigail stood near her mother, her face a study in concern. He met her gaze but could not bring a smile to his lips.

When the crowd quieted, he jumped up on a large rock and faced them. "We have come from the camp of Saul, where Adonai delivered him into our hands."

A cheer erupted from the crowd, but David cut it short with a gesture. "But I would not, will not, kill Adonai's anointed." Murmurs turned to stony silence at the announcement, confusion and anger evident among both men and women. Uncertainty settled in his gut until he caught approval in Abigail's eyes, and a sense of peace settled over him. He had done the right thing. "As long as Saul walks the earth, he will never stop hunting me, and since I will never kill him, we will never stop running. Unless . . ." He paused, waiting to make sure he had everyone's attention. "Unless we go where Saul cannot find us. Where Saul would not dare to go. Then we can live in safety and peace until Saul is dead."

"Where will we go?" Joab asked, his usually confident face wreathed in a scowl.

In that moment, David realized that his advisors might not support him, as they had not supported him when he'd first fled from Saul to the king of Gath. But that was before he had a mercenary army at his command. Now they were a force to contend with, a force the king of Gath would be pleased to accept. As these people must also accept if they were ever to acknowledge his leadership as king. They might not like it, but they would obey. He would allow nothing less.

He took his time, letting his gaze scan the crowd and making eye contact with as many men and women as he could. He smiled with a confidence he hoped he would soon feel, determined to make them feel it as well. At last he stopped at Joab, whose scowl had still not left his dark, beady eyes.

"I've given this a lot of thought, and there is only one place to go — a place where they will welcome our military skills as mercenaries to fight their battles . . . or so we will make them think."

Joab's scowl softened the slightest bit, his interest piqued. "You want to take us out of Israel."

David nodded. "Yes. To a place Saul would never go and where we will live in peace." He scanned the crowd once more, his gaze resting on Abigail. "Tonight we will sleep one last time in this place. Then we move west toward the sea — to the land of the Philistines."

22

Abigail carried a large earthenware jug filled with water atop her head from the well to the outskirts of Lachish near the edge of Israelite territory. The six-day journey across the barren wastelands of Judah to this place had been slow going with the women and children and flocks of sheep and goats. David had left some of Nabal's shepherds and servants in Maon to manage Nabal's estate in their absence, but he'd taken some of the herd along to provide for their ever-growing entourage.

Abigail teetered as she lowered the jug to the earth near the campfire, then caught herself before she lost her balance. Ahinoam squatted nearby, flipping flat bread on smooth stones set over a low flame, and lentil stew bubbled in an earthenware pot above another small fire. The spicy scent of cumin made Abigail's stomach protest her self-imposed secret fast. She pressed the back of her hand to her forehead and drew in a slow breath.

Why, Yahweh? Why do You not stop my husband from making a horrible mistake? Why won't he listen to reason?

At least David did listen at first. Six days ago before they left the wilderness of Judah, some of his advisors had tried to talk David into reconsidering this trek into Philistine land. But enough of the people supported him, including Ahinoam, to convince him he was doing the right thing, the only thing to ensure their safety.

Abigail worried her lower lip as she knelt beside Ahinoam to scoop the finished flat bread into a clay bowl, and Ahinoam poured more batter onto the stones. Life would change the moment they set foot on Philistine soil. Would Yahweh go with them? She shuddered at the thought.

"Are you all right, Abigail?" Her mother's voice lacked the sharp edge she'd noted since they left the wilderness. Her parents were not in favor of this move either, but her father would never complain or raise an objection to David, and Daniel thought David could do no wrong. "Here, let me take that." She felt her mother grip her elbow as she took hold of the bowl of flat bread with the other hand. "Sit over there. You look like you're about to fall over."

Abigail held a hand to her middle and moved to do as her mother commanded, her legs struggling to carry her to the makeshift bench.

"I'll take this to the men and be right back. Don't move."

She couldn't move if she tried. *Oh, Adonai, why do You not answer my prayers?* She'd prayed and fasted for six long days, but David's scouts had returned from Gath with the good news that Achish, their king, was quite willing to accept David's mercenary army and was waiting to welcome them at the palace. How would they avoid contamination from idols if they lived in the midst of them? Hadn't Adonai called them out to be a separate people? Did David think himself or his followers immune from such temptation?

"When was the last time you ate?" Abigail looked up into her mother's concerned face. "I've noticed the way you seem to avoid sitting when the women gather to eat. Are you trying to starve yourself, Abigail? Fasting will not change anything."

Abigail would have argued a few days ago, but now, with no answer in sight, she couldn't think of a thing to discount her mother's words. "I had hoped my prayers would keep us from leaving Israel," she said softly, covering her face with both hands. "But Yahweh does not hear my prayers." Her throat grew thick with the emotion she had held in check since David's announcement. She would not give in to it now, but she couldn't seem to stop a few tears from escaping her eyes.

Her mother's strong arms came around her shoulders and pulled her close. "There, there. Everything will turn out all right." She patted Abigail's back. "Do not worry about this so much, Abigail dear. Adonai surely heard you, but sometimes He expects His people to take their own action. Perhaps rather than praying, He wants you to talk some sense into that husband of yours. When David finally listens to you, you'll have your answer."

Abigail pulled away from her mother's embrace to look at her. "David listens to his men, not to me."

"He listened to you before, didn't he — when you stopped him from killing Nabal?"

"Yes, but that was different. Now he is too busy and I am only a wife." She'd done her best to allow Ahinoam time with David since his return from the camp of King Saul, and never told him how Ahinoam had acted toward her. The last thing David needed was a whiny wife.

"You are more than a wife, you are a confidante. David trusts you, Abigail. Surely if you talk to him as you have done in the past, he will hear your words. If you don't speak up, we will end up living among the pagans. For your own peace of mind, eat something and speak to your husband."

She slowly nodded. "The bread does smell good."

Her mother clucked her tongue. "Well, of course it does. Wait there." She moved to the fire where Ahinoam still squatted and snatched a small round loaf, then returned before Abigail could change her mind. "Eat." She thrust the bread into Abigail's hands. "And when you feel your strength return, you must speak to David. I will tell him you need him tonight." She hurried off in the direction of the men's circle.

"Mama, wait!" Abigail called after her, but her mother did not respond. She would push Abigail to do this thing whether she liked it or not. But could she be right? Was God's answer to her prayers to take matters into her own hands and do something to stop this madness herself? Such a thing had seemed so right when she'd rushed off to appease David's wrath, but now she felt uncertain, nervous. How did one appeal to a man who teetered on the edge of discouragement, even despair? David's faith needed an infusion of strength. Strength she didn't have.

She nibbled the bread as she fought her own bout of despair and wondered what she would say to her husband when he came to her.

Stars sprinkled the night sky as Abigail set a three-pronged griddle along the middle partition of the goat-hair tent that separated David's side from hers and Ahinoam's. With the new wealth she had brought to the marriage, they would each have a tent of their own one day, or, better yet, a room or home of their own, but for now, David kept them together in this large enclosure. Who knew what kind of dwellings they would have in Philistine territory?

She closed her eyes, then opened them again, willing her nerves into submission. If only Yahweh would hear her and change her husband's mind. Perhaps if she were a man . . . Did God care about the prayers of a mere woman?

She turned at the swish of sandals on the swept dirt floor behind her and felt David's arms go around her waist, his lips close to her ear. "Your mother said you wanted to

255

see me." He turned her around and kissed her. "You've been quiet on this journey. I was beginning to wonder if something was wrong. Ahinoam finally seems happy, but now all I see is sorrow in your eyes. Are you missing your old home in Maon?" He held her at arm's length, his dark eyes hopeful. "You're not regretting your decision to marry me, are you?"

She shook her head. "Never." She smiled at his boyish grin, wanting desperately to please him. She had no desire to be the one to take the joy from him — a joy he'd had since his announcement to move out of Israel. What if God had spoken to him and told him to do this? Maybe her worry about temptations and false gods was just her own fear of change.

"So what did you want to talk to me about? Your mother made it sound urgent." He let his fingers slide slowly down her arms, then captured both of her hands in his.

She glanced through the tent opening at the pockets of men and women sitting in front of their nearby tents, playing games and chatting by firelight. "Can we go somewhere quiet?" People could overhear, especially Ahinoam, who could walk in on them at any time.

His look grew sober as he studied her again. "There is a place up the hill a ways. Or we can go to my side of the tent." His bed of soft wool was there, but she feared he would be less likely to listen in such an intimate place.

"Up the hill would be nice." She gave him a coy smile. "Then we can come back to your side of the tent."

"Let me get a torch." His eyes lit as they often did when they were alone, as though he could think of no one else but her. But if he walked away . . .

"Is that necessary?" Someone else might grab his attention, and she would never get this chance again. "The moon is nearly full. Isn't that enough?"

He looked doubtful but nodded. He tightened his grip on her hand and led the way up the hill behind their tent. He paused every so often to pick his way with care, then finally stopped in a small rock enclosure. He led her to a large rock to sit, then took the seat beside her. Moonlight bathed his face, and she read concern in his earnest, unwavering gaze.

"What is so important, Abigail? Has someone offended you, upset you? You know you can tell me anything. I will never hurt you." He touched her face with one hand and stroked her cheek with his fingers, his look tender. He was so used to fixing everyone else's problems, sometimes he jumped ahead of them, certain he knew what they wanted.

"No one has offended me or hurt me, my lord. It's just . . ." She glanced down for the briefest moment but couldn't keep from looking into the fathomless depths of his eyes. "Don't you worry about living among the pagans, my lord, about the influence of their false gods on the people? If we are in the Philistines' royal city, we will be surrounded by their gods, and even if the king accepts us, the Philistine people will find us offensive. How will we keep our people from straying away from the true worship of Adonai?"

She fought the urge to chew on her lip as she watched David's expression change. He leaned away from her and placed both hands on his knees, shifting in his seat to look first toward the dust, then toward the stars. Crickets and the whisper of wings moved in the air around them, breaking the silence.

Abigail folded her hands in her lap, longing to undo what she'd said, wanting to restore David's boyish grin and pretend her world was at peace. But she kept silent, waiting for an eternity for David to respond.

At last he looked at her, and relief flooded through her at his tender expression. "I thank God for you, Abigail, for your wisdom and your love and concern not only for me but for all of the people. You will make a wise queen someday, should the Lord give us a kingly heir." He took her hand and caressed it. "I too am concerned about the false gods of the Philistines, but there is no easy solution. What I can promise you is that I will ask Achish for a city of our own, far from the places where most Philistines dwell. Achish will understand our need to practice our faith apart from theirs, and we will still be out of Saul's reach. How does that sound?" He held her gaze, his own so hopeful she couldn't bear to object to anything else, despite the sinking feeling in her heart.

"That sounds good, my lord." She smiled, hoping he would take her at her word and not read in her expression the sorrow still filling her soul.

He let go of her hand and pulled her into his arms, joy lighting his eyes. "You'll see, beloved, this move will be good for all of us, give us the rest we so desperately need. I'm weary of running." He paused to search her gaze. "I need this, Abigail."

"I know, David." She reached up to kiss him, and he bent to meet her lips, his passion drowning out any thought of protest she had left.

23

The palace of the Philistine king sent chills down Abigail's spine. Almost every wall held relief paintings of the gleaming half-man, half-fish idol Dagon. She shuddered as they passed trim, armored soldiers wearing red-feathered leather helmets who flanked the halls and widely pillared open courtyards. How could David trust this man? She felt exposed and vulnerable despite the hospitality and the rich apartment Achish had offered them.

She leaned against a gilded couch, still recuperating from her long fast and the trek through Gath. She'd kept her face veiled at David's request, to hide her beauty from the men of Philistia. Now, in the room she shared with Ahinoam and their maids, she could remove her headdress and veil and let her hair fall to the middle of her back. It felt good physically to unwind after so much running. But her spirit still shriveled in fear of the future.

Her gaze traveled over the rich carpets and mosaic tile floors of the room. Heavy embroidered curtains hung over stone walls and could be drawn across wide windows facing west. They pointed toward the direction of the Philistines' ancestral homes, the islands of the sea. Sculptures and paintings of sea creatures covered walls and sat atop oak tables, with Dagon the central theme of them all.

Their spacious room adjoined David's even larger one. She could hear laughter coming from David's quarters. David's nephews, Joab, Abishai, and Asahel, were his constant companions along with Benaiah, Daniel, and a handful of his mighty men who held counsel with him. A part of her longed to hear their conversation, but she knew David would only tell her not to worry herself over political affairs. Even Daniel barely had time to visit with her these days to tell her what David had planned, leaving her to speculate.

As an Egyptian slave bent to wash her dusty feet, she relaxed and closed her eyes, listening to the chatter of Ahinoam, Talya, and her mother. *Oh, Adonai,* she prayed as she'd done all the days of her fast, *please keep us from being polluted by this place.*

262

Send us far from the pagan influences of Gath. Protect David from the lure of wealth and remind him that You are his keeper and his best defense against all of his enemies.

The king's delicacies that were placed before Abigail in the spacious dining hall that evening, where she and Ahinoam sat at a table across from the wives and concubines of Achish, turned her stomach at first glance. Except for the fruit, dates, figs, and vegetables, the law of Adonai allowed nothing. A roast pig lay browned in the center of the table, while broiled catfish and crabs' legs from the sea filled ceramic platters to overflowing.

Abigail wondered whether David would eat everything Achish offered. She glanced about at the rest of their group seated at long tables all around the room. In his generosity, Achish had invited David's entire entourage to dine with him. David sat at the table nearest the king.

"They keep staring at us." Ahinoam leaned close, the hem of her veil touching Abigail's arm. At David's command, the women had kept their faces covered, allowing only the smallest opening for their eyes and mouth to see and eat — a command she obeyed with gratitude for the protection it afforded from pagan scrutiny.

"If we don't look back, we won't notice. I suggest we eat and keep to ourselves." She picked up a raisin cake and glanced into Ahinoam's fear-filled eyes. The woman had been almost giddy at the prospect of settling down — until they walked the foreign streets of Gath and felt the animosity of the Philistine people as they passed. "It will be all right, Ahinoam. Yahweh is with us."

"Is He?" She waved a hand at the roasted pig in the center of the table. "You know He would not approve of this. There is nothing we can eat!" She glanced toward David's table. "Does our lord eat the king's delicacies? Will he expect us to?" Her words, barely above a whisper, carried a sense of despair.

Abigail looked in David's direction as well, hoping to catch his gaze, but he was caught up in conversation with his men. From a distance it was hard to tell, but the swine looked untouched and the sea creatures still piled high on platters in front of the men. A servant approached David as Abigail watched, and David spoke something in the man's ear. Moments later the platters of unclean food were removed from his table and the tables of all the Israelites in attendance.

"There, see," Abigail whispered, leaning close to Ahinoam. "Adonai is still with us, even in this pagan city." It was a small comfort, but she would take whatever she could get. Somehow, she must endure this country, these people. David had chosen to come here, and Yahweh had not stopped him. This trial couldn't be any worse than living with Nabal's abuse, and yet — she couldn't help praying, silently pleading for Yahweh to intervene and rescue them from this place.

A strand of hair slipped from beneath Abigail's headdress into her eyes as she worked the millstone in a circular motion over grains of wheat, grinding them into soft flour. The kernels were among the many spoils David had retrieved on military raids of foreign towns in the four months they had been in Ziklag. After six months living in the royal city of Gath, David had finally kept his promise to her and brought them to the outlying town of Ziklag, far from the watchful eye of the Philistine king.

She paused, straightened, and looked out over the bustling town, lifting her shoulders to ease the tension. The men had returned the night before from a raid, and David was busy dividing the spoils to send to strategic places in Judah, to friends who had helped him in times past. Squeals of children mingled with the laughter of women as they picked through piles of utensils, clothing, and jewels.

Ahinoam approached with a sieve and settled onto a bench at Abigail's side. "David gave me two new robes and a matching jeweled headdress and earrings last night." She lifted her chin, her expression telling Abigail that she'd been much too pleased to have David call her to his quarters after he'd kissed Abigail goodnight. If he'd come home a week earlier, she would have been his choice, but she'd been forced to tell him she was unclean, leaving him momentarily disappointed. She almost hoped he would sleep alone and wait until she could join him again, but Ahinoam was only too eager to take her place.

"That's nice." Abigail bent over the millstone, letting the grinding noises fill the silence between them. She ignored the clamor of women hurrying back to their chores and shooing children away from the goods.

"What did he give you?" Ahinoam asked, finally breaking the silence. Abigail knew that the woman's interest was only so that she could compare their gifts. While Abigail took a particular liking to the sapphire head-dress David had given her — extracting her promise that she would wear it on his coronation day — she was in no mood for comparisons. It was hard enough sharing a man. She didn't need to compete for every expression of his love.

"About the same as he gave to you," she said at last, deciding that Ahinoam would find out eventually anyway. "Have you seen Zahara?"

"Not since last night before David asked me to his rooms."

Abigail closed her eyes, telling herself to ignore the stinging comments, which were meant only to wound. David called Ahinoam so rarely, Abigail ought to feel pity, not jealousy. So why did the woman's haughty tone trouble her? She would never make David a good wife if she spent her days comparing herself to every other wife he chose to take.

The thought left a hollow feeling in her heart.

"That's strange. Zahara almost always greets me after her visit to the well. But I didn't see her this morning." Abigail forced her mind to focus on her missing maid instead of Ahinoam's bragging. "She must be around here somewhere. Did anyone check her pallet? Perhaps she is ill."

"How would I know? She's your maid."

Abigail stopped the mill and straightened. "Indeed she is."

And the only maid not yet married to one of the eligible men, though David's nephew Asahel had asked for the privilege more than once. He needed a wife to care for his young son after losing the child's mother at birth. For some reason David kept putting him off, as though he didn't want the man to marry Zahara. But the girl had proven to be nothing but loyal. So why did David still distrust her?

Abigail stood and brushed flour from her tunic. "I'm going to check on her."

Ahinoam shrugged. "Suit yourself."

Abigail checked the room where the girl slept and found her sleeping mat and personal items gone. She then stopped at each neighboring courtyard to ask after Zahara, growing more worried with each negative response. Alarm tightened her middle, and sweat covered her upper lip. She wiped it away with the back of her hand, surprised to find herself shaking.

She leaned against the cool limestone wall of the house David had inhabited when the residents of Ziklag had left the town to the Israelites. Where would Zahara have gone, and why? Was she a threat to David? Did David know something about Zahara he hadn't told her?

She drew in a slow breath, willing strength into her weak limbs. She must find David to tell him at once and hope they could find the girl before something terrible happened.

David climbed a low hill and glanced toward the south in the direction of their last raid on the Amalekites. He'd done his best to annihilate the people, to carry out God's judgment on them as Saul was once told and failed to do. But pockets of them still existed, and David worried lest one of them escape and make his way to Gath, to Achish, to tell the Philistine king of David's exploits.

He ran a hand over his beard and sighed. If he had listened to Abigail, they would still be running from Saul with little earthly wealth to sustain them. Coming to Philistine territory had given him the edge he needed to build a better following. More men had joined him here, and the spoils of war had made him stronger.

But a part of him wished he'd had her courage. The lies he had spoken to protect himself from King Achish, leading the man to believe he was killing Israelites instead of

Geshurites and Amalekites, left him feeling somehow bereft and ever more distant from Yahweh.

He glanced heavenward, yearning for that closeness he'd once felt as a shepherd in Judah's hills. Was Abigail right? Though the people did not openly worship foreign gods, had Adonai abandoned them when they entered Philistine lands?

What would You have me do, O Lord?

Even his prayers seemed to reach no farther than his heart. Heaviness filled him. He turned to walk back toward the town and was met by Benaiah, who guarded his every move, and Joab, whose agitated look raised the tension at the back of his neck.

"What is it?" He kept walking as the two men fell into step beside him.

"Achish has sent his messengers, accompanied by palace guards and a small army."

David stopped. Looked at his nephew. "How small?"

"Six hundred men."

David's stomach clenched. So many. "He never sends guards."

"Obviously, this time is different."

Had Achish gotten wind of the truth? Worry gnawed at him again. "What could he want?" The question demanded an answer he would have soon enough. He picked up his pace and hurried toward the gate.

Philistine soldiers wearing the colors and insignia of Achish, king of Gath, stood at attention at David's approach. David's own men surrounded him as he took his seat in the gate and beckoned the king's messenger forward. The man bowed one knee and straightened, meeting David's gaze.

"The king requests that David, son of Jesse, and his men accompany him and the rest of the Philistine army into battle against the Israelites. He requests your presence in Gath immediately."

David steeled his expression, drumming his fingers on the stone seat. His gaze took in the messenger and the band of Philistines spilling out of the gate, waiting to accompany his men. To refuse would be seen as a slight to Achish. His men and their families would never escape if he tried to run. He recognized the formidable Ittai the Gittite, the leader of the king's personal guard, and knew this mission would not end well.

He looked back at the messenger and nodded. "We will come. Just give us time to gather our provisions."

The messenger stepped back and bowed.

"It will be as you say."

When the guards and messengers had left the town gate and joined the soldiers outside the walls, David turned to his advisors. "Summon the men to prepare for war. We return to Gath."

Abigail stood at the threshold to David's rooms, waiting for him to finish stuffing an extra tunic into a sack and double-check the sharpness of his dagger. She walked in when he turned to look at her and handed him a satchel of honey cakes, almonds, and figs.

"Everything is ready, my lord."

He took the satchel, his expression grim. "If only that were true." He reached for her hand and pulled her to him, pressing her head against his chest. "Pray for me, Abigail." His voice caught, and his arms tightened around her.

"Always." She wove her fingers through his hair as he drew her close. His kiss, so ardent, so desperate, surprised her. Did he fear he wouldn't come back? Was Adonai allowing this to punish David for leaving Israel? But she couldn't voice the thought. "It will all work out," she whispered when their lips parted. "Adonai will not abandon His anointed."

His brow lifted at that, and he held her at arm's length. "He will have to abandon one of us, beloved. Saul is my opponent, fighting against the Philistines. If I fight with the Philistines, in truth one of us will die. We are both His anointed."

"But the Lord said you would replace Saul as king, so if one of you dies, it will be Saul, not you." She knew in her heart it was so. It had to be.

"Pray you are right." He kissed her again, then released her. "I must go."

"My lord, there is one thing I must tell you before you leave." She wondered at her own wisdom in light of his irritated look.

"I have to go, Abigail. Is it truly important?" He moved toward the door but paused at the threshold.

She held his gaze, too late to back down now. "I think so." If she didn't tell him, he would wonder why she'd kept it from him.

"Tell me quickly."

She followed him as he walked through the house toward the courtyard where his men waited. "My maid Zahara is missing. It appears she has taken her pallet and few belongings and left Ziklag. I've looked for her everywhere, but she is gone."

He stopped near the ovens where her mother and Talya hurriedly snatched hot loaves from the stones and shoved them into baskets for the donkeys to carry. "When did this happen?" His expression clouded, his brows drawn together in a scowl.

"I discovered it this morning."

He rubbed his chin, then scanned the courtyard. Benaiah, Joab, Abishai, and Asahel stood in the street outside the court beside donkeys, engrossed in some private discussion, while Daniel stood nearby, holding Micah and Talya in his arms. David took two steps toward his nephews, then turned back to her. "There is nothing I can do about it now. She has apparently run off, and that's probably a good thing. I never trusted her." He touched her shoulder. "If she returns, do not accept her back unless she has a plausible explanation for her abandonment. Have one of the young men detain her until I return. Otherwise, let her go. May God grant her whatever she deserves." He bent to kiss her cheek, then turned toward his men without a backward glance.

24

Rank after rank of Philistine soldiers passed by King Achish where he sat on a large rock overlooking the plains of Aphek, their red-feathered helmets moving in the warm afternoon breeze, their proud backs straight, their faces like hardened stone. David stood with his men at the rear of the crowd, his gut twisting, his mind testing and discarding any number of possible ways to escape his fate of having to go to battle against his own people. He found none.

Benaiah moved closer, but even the sight of his burly guard did nothing to assuage the deep-rooted feeling of unease sifting through him. This was surely God's hand of judgment on him for bringing his men out of Israel. He should never have come, never have trusted a foreign power above his God for protection.

O sovereign Adonai, have mercy on me!

The prayer had turned to a plea the moment Achish insisted to his face that he and his men would surely accompany the Philistines into this ill-timed battle. The moment he'd heard his own lips utter compliance, however vague he'd tried to be, guilt and fear had become his constant companions.

They nudged him now as Benaiah came to stand at his side. The only sign of the man's own agitation was the muscle ticking along his right eye. "They number in the tens of thousands," he said, his voice low.

Tension knotted the muscles in David's neck. He folded his arms over his chest and nodded. "Yes. A formidable foe. Saul is ill prepared." The thought should comfort him, for if Saul perished in battle, the way would be clear for him to ascend the throne. Jonathan would see to it. But not if David's own hand carried a sword to war against Israel. The people would never accept him.

"We could help him."

David looked at his guard and lifted a brow. "You're suggesting we go into battle with the Philistines and then turn against them to help Israel?"

Benaiah shrugged and met David's gaze. "Have you thought of a better way to redeem ourselves out of this situation?"

David glanced again at the Philistine ranks, noting the blue and red robes setting apart the princes who governed the outlying Philistine cities. They bowed low before King Achish, then gathered in a group to speak with him. Angry shouts in a tongue he didn't understand drifted across the compound, with Achish's voice drowned out by the Philistine lords. Moments later, the leaders followed Achish into his tent.

David's men huddled into their own tents or gathered at several fires at the edges of the Philistine encampment. A commotion caught his attention as Asahel broke through the Philistine ranks and rushed to his side.

"What did you learn?" David's nephew was quick and unobtrusive, his plain features and agile motion allowing him to move like a fox, virtually unnoticed among the enemy soldiers.

"Achish's army generals do not take kindly to our presence. They are demanding we leave, while Achish is insisting we stay." Asahel straightened the belt at his waist and lifted somber brown eyes to David, reminding him of Jonathan. He couldn't bear to war against the best friend he'd ever known.

"Let us pray Achish loses the argument," Benaiah whispered as Joab and Abishai joined them.

"The men are beginning to grumble," Joab said, stepping up to David. He faced him down, his hawklike gaze boring through David. "If you try to make them go through with this, you may find yourself at the end of one of their swords."

"The Philistines are murmuring as well. They remember the virgins' song, 'Saul has slain his thousands, and David his ten thousands.' " Asahel glanced around as though fearing the enemy might overhear.

"I suspect they liked it about as well as Saul did." David kneaded the back of his neck and looked first toward the Philistine tents, then behind him at his six hundred men. "How many are disloyal?"

"To you or to Israel?" Joab's sarcasm matched his bitter gaze.

"To me." If they would all turn on him in battle, he must do as Benaiah had suggested and turn this thing around to bring down destruction on Philistine heads.

Joab took a step back and glanced in the direction of the men. "Right now only a handful is grumbling, but such talk will quickly spread if you do not reassure them."

Even a handful could ignite flames to the dry brush of fear that David could feel among his men, despite the stoic acts they put on as they passed in front of the Philistine lords. He turned to the four men facing him. "Pass the word among the troops. If

Achish does indeed call us into battle against Saul, we will go. When the battle rages, whose side they fight on will be up to them. As for me, I will not lift my hand against Adonai's anointed." Let Achish think what he wanted in the meantime.

At his word, the men dispersed to do his bidding, while David went into his tent, fell on his face, and prayed.

Abigail awoke with a start, her heart beating with the memory of the wild dream she couldn't shake, the nightmare she had lived with since David went off to follow the Philistines. Something terrible was going to happen, something beyond her ability to control. Would David die as Ahinoam had feared?

From the next room, the sound of Ahinoam retching over a clay pot didn't help to ease her racing heart. The woman had been sick every morning for two weeks now, and Abigail knew Ahinoam's illness had nothing to do with fear. She had to be carrying David's child. Nothing else made sense.

Disheartened by the thought, Abigail forced herself up from her mat and blinked hard, rubbing the sleep from her eyes. Ahinoam stumbled through the arch of the door, sank to her own mat on the floor near

Abigail's, and leaned her head against the limestone wall. They'd taken to sharing a room after David left and Zahara fled, drawing small comfort from each other's presence. How long did it take to win a battle?

She looked at Ahinoam as she donned a fresh tunic and tightened the belt of her robe. She knew the answer. Sometimes David had been gone for a month or more at a time, something she thought she'd gotten used to. Until now.

"Is there something you want to tell me?" Abigail asked. It was time they discussed Ahinoam's condition. As much as Abigail longed to bless David with a son, apparently Ahinoam would have that privilege first. She steeled herself for the answer as she handed Ahinoam a robe. "Well?"

"It's obvious, isn't it? I am with child." Ahinoam's face drained of color, her once haughty expression replaced with worry. "What if David dies and never knows?"

"He's not going to die." Irritation tickled her spine. She was unwilling to admit how close Ahinoam's thoughts came to her own of late. "You must stop thinking like this. David is Adonai's anointed. Nothing will happen to him." It was true. She must believe it.

Ahinoam bit her lower lip while sweat

beaded her forehead. Abigail could see why David had taken her to wife. She was lovely, with hair the color of wheat and eyes the color of husked almonds, soft and round as a doe's. When she wasn't whining or complaining, her laughter could be infectious.

"I'm sorry. I shouldn't worry. I don't want to harm the child."

Yes, the child. David's firstborn. The thought stung, bringing Abigail's own longing for a son to the forefront again.

Shouts from the direction of the city gate interrupted her straying thoughts. Perhaps a messenger, or even David and his men returning. Her father would be on watch now along with a handful of young boys, the few David had left to guard the women. But if David had returned, the guard at the tower would have blown the shofar. Something was amiss.

"I'm going to the gate. Perhaps another quarrel has erupted." If the shouts had to do with the women and their constant quarrels, perhaps she could help. At least the women listened to her most of the time.

"I'll come in a few moments. I don't think I can stand yet."

"Take your time. Eat some figs or drink some goat's milk when your stomach settles. I can handle the women." She nodded and smiled at Ahinoam, hoping the jealous twinge she felt did not come through her tone or expression. David would want her to care for Ahinoam, to keep his child safe.

She shoved the thoughts aside and moved through the house to the courtyard. She stopped, her stomach tightening and then plunging at the sight of men on horseback wearing the red and black robes of foreign Bedouins and riding straight for her. In the distance, the sound of screaming women and crying children reached her ears. She turned and looked down the dirt road to the houses of her neighbors, catching the terror-stricken faces of the women around her and hearing the wild, hysterical screaming as the foreigners tossed the wives of David's men over the backs of their mounts like sacks of grain.

Leather whips cracked against the backs of resistant women. Mothers strained against their captors, clawing at air and desperately reaching for their children. The cries echoed amid the screams as boys and girls were dragged from the houses and thrown into separate wooden carts, whimpering for their mothers.

Abba! Her father was on guard at the gate. Had they killed him in order to enter? The thought sickened her even further, and hot tears filled her throat. She swallowed them down.

Across the street, she glimpsed a handful of young boys sitting on low branches of oak trees and on the roofs of houses, whipping stones from their slings at the intruders. Hope that they might do some good sprang up but then died moments later as burly soldiers swung heavy whips high enough into the trees to force the boys down. Those on rooftops ran from house to house before they were caught and tossed into the carts with the rest of the children, their wrists and feet bound.

Abigail's throat ached and her body shook as she fought an intense urge to weep. The dream — this was her nightmare, not David's. God had been warning her, and now here she stood, helpless to stop them. Wild-eyed Bedouins grabbed her mother, Talya, and Micah and shoved them into an already full cart. Joab's wife Marta, Abishai's wife Deborah, and Ahinoam were each tossed up to a waiting soldier and made to ride in front of groping men on the backs of pawing horses.

Oh, Adonai, protect David's child. God forgive her, she didn't feel so fiercely about the mother, but David would not want to lose a son.

The lead horseman reined in his mount at her side. The man hopped down, then reached a hand up to the woman sitting behind him and swung her to the ground.

Abigail studied the man, then the woman, who was dressed in finer linen garments of brightly woven threads. Jewels adorned her headdress, and her painted eyes and lips gave her an exotic look. Abigail glanced away for the briefest moment, then looked back, a spark of recognition causing her stomach to clench with dread she could not escape.

Zahara.

Clammy fear took hold of her as the burly Bedouin leader who stood beside Zahara walked toward her, turning a whip over in his hand. She fell to her knees and buried her face in the dust. She'd seen that look before. From Nabal.

An arm reached down and jerked her to her feet. "You are the Israelite's wife." His heavy accent made him hard to understand, but Abigail caught enough to discern that the Israelite he spoke of must be David.

"Yes." She swallowed, barely able to choke out the word.

He snarled, leaning toward her until she could smell his stale breath and feel the heat in his gaze. "You will come." He tucked the whip into his belt, and before she could respond, he lifted her over his shoulder. Wisdom told her that to resist would be foolish.

Moments later he stopped and set her on her feet. She stood straight, head bowed. The man on the horse before her was decked out in greater finery than the one who had carried her, telling her that her earlier assumption of leadership was mistaken.

"You will ride with me." His clear diction spoke of education, his stiff gaze of hardship.

She nodded her assent but kept silent, praying, pleading with Yahweh for mercy.

The first man lifted her again — and none too carefully — to the other man, up over the horse's back. The leader's eager hands grabbed her and pulled her close, his breath touching her ear. "Soon you will be mine."

A sick feeling settled inside her. *Please, Adonai, no!*

"Zafirah tells us you are the wife of the infamous David. As I have heard he has many wives, I am sure he will not mind sharing one." His brittle laugh made her skin crawl. "You remember Zafirah, don't you?"

"I'm afraid I do not know this Zafirah, my lord."

"The man who found you first is my captain, Kadar. Zafirah rode with him. Surely you recognize your personal maid."

"Zahara." She understood now. But who were these people and what did they have against David?

"Yes, Zahara." He spat the name as though it tasted like bile. "Troublesome Israelite name. Zafirah suits my sister better, wouldn't you say? And Kadar, her betrothed, thanks you for taking such good care of her." His sarcasm was unmistakable, and she cringed at what Zahara must have told them. But what had she done to cause Zahara to do this, to lead these people straight to Ziklag?

Out of the corner of her eye, she caught a glimpse of the soldiers ransacking their houses, piling possessions in with people in the wagons. Terrified cries still filled the air, and the horse pawed the ground beneath her. Abigail felt the man's fingers probing her through her robe, and panic rose to choke her.

Moments later she saw Zahara approach her brother's mount, heard her angry shouts in a language Abigail did not understand. But the look in Zahara's eyes told Abigail that her former maid was not happy with the man. Her brother seemed not to care, his own response bitter as he tightened one hand around Abigail's waist. He lifted the other hand to his mouth, turning toward the crowd of fellow Bedouins. "When you finish pillaging their valuables . . . burn Ziklag."

Hot tears stung Abigail's eyes.

"Amalek will defeat Israel yet. Today is just the beginning." The words were perfectly clear, meant for her ears alone.

No wonder Zahara had kept her nationality secret. She was of the hated Amalekites whom God had commanded be destroyed. She must have been captured when Saul failed to wipe out her people, and somehow Nabal had purchased her.

The stench of burning wood and bricks filled Abigail's nostrils. She could hear wild, joyous hollering of hundreds of men as Ziklag went up in flames. Moments later the man behind her pulled her against him again and kicked the horse's flanks. The beast took off at a fast gallop at the head of the troupe and marched beneath the city gates, with Ziklag going down in flames behind them.

25

Evening shadows danced in rhythm to the swaying trees above the tents of David's men. Fires dotted the landscape, stretching like stars across the expansive valley floor. David warmed his hands at the small fire pit in front of his tent and listened to the voices of his men. The discontent seemed to have lessened among them, but the clammy closeness of so many of Israel's enemies still felt like thick fog at dawn.

He turned his hands over, examined the calluses in the faint light, and rubbed his thumbs over the rough edges of his fingertips. Warrior's hands. Musician's hands. Shepherd's hands. Were these the hands of a king as well?

A touch on his shoulder made him jump. Annoyed that he'd allowed himself to be so unaware, he looked up into the faces of Asahel and Benaiah.

"You have news."

Asahel's expression was too readable; it was so easy to determine his thoughts and intents. He nodded. "The Philistine lords have left the tent of Achish. The king requests your presence. His guards are headed this way even now."

David looked beyond his nephew toward the Philistine tents, where Achish's guards could be seen coming his way.

"We're looking for David son of Jesse," one said to the sentry at the edge of the Israelite encampment. The sentry turned, and David approached.

"I am David." He crossed his arms over his chest, assessing them.

"King Achish would speak with you. Come." They turned, clearly expecting David to follow.

David nodded to Benaiah and Asahel to accompany him and fell into step behind the Philistine guards. Hair bristled along his arms as he passed beside the enemy soldiers so unprotected.

O Adonai, be my strength.

They trudged up low peaks and then down to a flat plain, at last stopping before the ornate tent of the Philistine king. Two guards decked out in full military garb stood at attention before the door. One nodded to the sentries leading David and stepped aside, allowing the guards and David alone to duck under the flap and enter the wide, elaborate temporary home of King Achish.

David dropped to his knees as the guards took a step back, and touched his forehead to the earth. "May my lord, King Achish, live forever," David said. He rose up on one knee, his eyes still turned to the ground.

Achish held out the royal scepter, and David bent forward to kiss it. Achish offered David a reassuring albeit sad smile.

"David, as surely as the Lord lives, you have been reliable, and I would be pleased to have you serve with me in the army. From the day you came to me until now, I have found no fault in you, but the rulers don't approve of you. Turn back and go in peace. Do nothing to displease the Philistine rulers."

O sovereign Adonai, this is good news.

And yet he could not let the king know how quickly his heart beat with delight, how relieved his soul was to have an escape from this place. He steeled his emotions and pulled his lips into a tight line, averting his gaze for a brief moment, then looked at Achish, unflinching.

"But what have I done? What have you found against your servant from the day I came to you until now? Why can't I go and fight against the enemies of my lord the king?" If Achish had somehow gotten wind of David's true intention to fight for Israel, he had to convince him otherwise, hoping the vagueness of his words did not displease Adonai, who surely had His hand in this.

Achish leaned back among the pillows surrounding him and accepted a silver goblet from an Egyptian slave. "I know that you have been as pleasing in my eyes as an angel of God. Nevertheless, the Philistine commanders have said, 'He must not go up with us into battle.' Now get up early, along with your master's servants who have come with you, and leave in the morning as soon as it is light."

David nodded, too grateful to speak, and masked his expression behind a resigned look. "As you say, my lord."

After a few more parting words, David backed out of the tent and joined his men. Tomorrow they would waste no time returning to Ziklag.

Three days of grueling travel came to an abrupt end. At the Besor Ravine, Abigail's captor lifted her from the horse and set her to walk with the other women down the steep incline and up the other side. Her legs ached and her shoulders drooped in exhaustion as they finally reached the Amalekite encampment.

As far as she could tell, no one from their group was missing or terribly hurt. Amazingly, they had remained untouched. Even her father, whom she'd feared dead, had been visible in the distance, kept apart with the younger men and boys.

She had seen no sign of Zahara again, and the man who'd threatened to take her to his tent had disappeared somewhere in the midst of the other men and women who greeted their return.

Abigail stood at the entrance of a small cave, one of many that dotted these hills, and looked out at the plain spread before her. David would never find them here. They'd come too far in a direction she'd never been before, to a land she didn't know. The thought sank to her middle like a heavy millstone.

Soft weeping made her turn. Ahinoam lay huddled in a corner behind her, knees pulled to her chest, rocking back and forth on the hard-packed earth. Abigail released a slow breath and straightened her shoulders, then walked toward the young woman.

"It will be all right, Ahinoam. David will come and we'll be safe again." She squatted beside her and rested one hand on her shoulder, trying not to notice the protective hand Ahinoam put on the secret place where David's child lay. But her thoughts betrayed her, and jealousy sparked a flame in her heart again. She attempted to douse it to no avail.

"They're going to kill us. I heard one of them say so — after they ravish us." She hiccuped on a sob and pressed a fist to her mouth, her doelike eyes wild with fear. "David will never find us. They'll kill him when he goes to battle against Saul. Don't you see? Our lives are forfeit."

"Don't talk like that!" She hissed the words through gritted teeth, forcing her swift anger in check. Never mind that she'd given thought to the same fears, believing the same truth. Yet she couldn't, wouldn't, give in to despair. Until such time as those fears came to pass, there was always hope.

She looked again into Ahinoam's eyes, reading the complete lack of faith, the desperate desire to give vent to fear. No wonder David grew tired of this woman. Her fear drained Abigail's strength and filled her heart with dread. For the sake of the rest of the women and children, she couldn't let Ahinoam do that.

"Every time you speak of your fear, you upset the other women." Abigail glanced around. Several stood near enough to hear, and by their expressions Abigail knew they weren't far from giving in to their hysteria again.

Ahinoam stopped rocking and met Abigail's gaze. "I'm sorry. But I can't help the way I feel. I just know these things. I've always known."

"And you're always wrong." She drew in a breath and pushed to her feet. "The prophet Samuel anointed David to be king, and Adonai will see to it that His promise is fulfilled. You can either choose to believe that or continue to tear David down with your worries. You're not supporting his faith the way things are now." She sucked in a breath at the shocked look on Ahinoam's face, but she didn't care. "You are carrying David's child and will soon raise a son or daughter to follow after him. Do you want to raise a son worthy to be king after his father or not?"

Ahinoam gave the slightest nod, her eyes wide, as though she'd never considered the possibility before now.

"Then act like the woman David needs you to be, a woman about to be first wife to the king." She gave Ahinoam one last calculated look and whirled about, unable to bear any more of the conversation.

Why would Adonai give David's first child to such a foolish woman? She shook her head and walked away toward the back of the cave, struggling to control her sudden, all-over trembling. She felt the stares of the other women, wondering if her comments would spur them to faith or sentence them to despair.

Despite her fine talk, deep down she wasn't sure what she believed anymore. Adonai had allowed their kidnapping and could as easily allow their deaths. He had anointed David to be king. She had no promise from Him that she would be part of that coming kingdom.

The scent of damp, burned wood and brick caught David off guard. As he ascended the rise heading toward Ziklag, his eyes confirmed what his senses had already told him. Black, rain-soaked soot coated the land where Ziklag had once stood. Now the city gate lay crumpled, covered in ash.

Bile rose up in the back of his throat.

The three-day journey to Ziklag from the Philistine encampment at Aphek had taken its toll on his spirits. Amid the intermittent rain showers, he'd heard the rumors, the discontent, the grumbling among some of the six hundred mercenary men who had once supported him without question. They were divided now, uncertain in his ability to lead.

And now this . . .

He stumbled forward, heard the outcries of the men around him as they surged ahead to the burned-out town. *Abigail! Ahinoam!* Would he find their bodies buried beneath the ash? Would there be anything left to tell him what had become of them?

His leaden feet carried him down the hill alone, now that his men had abandoned him. Remnants of the homes they'd lived in lay in a heap of rubble. Broken pottery littered the streets, and the clay ovens in the courtyards were crushed, unusable.

No sign of the women or children.

A high-pitched wail jolted him out of his stupor as he reached the place where his home once stood. Other cries soon followed, his men giving vent to the pain of their losses. David looked out across the street at the group of men now sitting in the dust, their hair and beards covered in ash, their tunics torn in grief. He swallowed back the bile as emotion rose to choke him. He sank to his knees and scooped ash into his hair, burying his face in the dust and weeping.

Oh, Adonai, what have I done? I have

brought these, Your people, to this foreign land, and now You have taken our families from us. Surely I am sinful from birth and have done evil in Your sight.

The heat of the sun beat on his back, and the taste of dust and ash coated his tongue. His eyes stung and his beard carried the sticky remnant of his tears. The sounds of weeping and wailing rose and fell as the afternoon waned.

Eventually murmurs tinged with anger filtered through his grief, growing closer. He rose from the dirt and moved to the edge of his ruined courtyard, cocking his head to listen.

"We wouldn't be in this mess if we'd never come here."

"David knew the risks and put us in danger to save his own neck."

"He's not fit to lead us or Israel. Let Saul's son be king in Saul's place."

"What of our families? He should pay for their loss!"

"He lost his wives too." David recognized Benaiah's deep, comforting voice.

"He should have lost more."

"I say we should teach him a lesson."

"More than a lesson — he deserves to die along with our families."

The escalating cries for vengeance rose

above the steady, supportive voices of reason. Fear's claws sank into him, digging deeper with each threat, each rising temper paralyzing him.

"Stone him!" The shout reverberated through the street.

"We can't kill him. He is Adonai's anointed." He recognized the voice of his nephew Abishai.

"Abishai is right." Benaiah's booming voice rose above the fray. "God may do worse things to us if we kill His anointed."

The arguments rose and fell, leaving David vulnerable and unable to shake a terror so deep he was powerless to confront it.

O sovereign Adonai, show me what to do.

He glimpsed Abiathar the priest on the fringes of the crowd, looking haggard and far older than his years. Abiathar had witnessed the deaths of his entire family when Saul had ordered the priests slain. This loss of the wife he had found here and the young babe she had just borne had to hit him doubly hard. Would he help David now or be among those who turned against him?

Gripping the crumbled wall of the court for support, David forced his shaky limbs to move, walked across the compound toward the man, and called to him.

"Abiathar, please bring the ephod here to me." His voice caught the attention of his men. They turned to watch the priest, their arguments silenced, the menace in their gazes a wall of stone against him.

Abiathar moved to his donkey and removed the priestly ephod from the saddlebag. He walked up to David.

"Ask the Lord, 'Shall I pursue this raiding party? Will I overtake them?' "

The crowd drew closer, raising David's hackles, but Abiathar seemed not to notice. He took the Urim and Thummin and tossed the stones, repeating David's question. "Pursue them. You will certainly overtake them and succeed in the rescue."

Relief rushed at him, weakening his knees. He gripped Abiathar's arm, searching his gaze. The man spoke truth. His breathing slowed to normal, and he looked at his men. "Did you hear?"

Several nodded, and Joab and Benaiah stepped forward. "Which way do we go?"

David looked out over the land. They had no idea who had taken the women and children or where they would have gone. But an inner sense that he could only believe was Yahweh's Spirit told him to head south toward the Besor Ravine.

"That way," he said at last, peace finally

settling over him. "Let's go rescue our families."

26

David stood at the edge of the Nahal Besor Ravine and looked out over the water, trees, and underbrush, gauging the distance across. While the trees would conceal the movement of his men from any enemies keeping watch from the fields and hills on the other side, the dense foliage and rushing river, risen with the recent rains, would make crossing a definite challenge. If not for the determination coursing through him, he would make camp and rest first. But the urgent need to rescue Abigail and Ahinoam pressed in on him, and he feared what would become of them if he waited.

"Some of the men are too exhausted to go on." Benaiah came up beside him.

"How many?"

"Two hundred."

"Hmm . . ." One-third of his forces. He needed every man to fight. David glanced behind him, then looked back toward the ravine. Lush vegetation bordered the river on both sides. They would have to hold on to tree branches to make it safely across without getting swept away down the river.

"We'll never get the donkeys across those rushing waters." Benaiah cleared his throat. "The men could stay and protect the supplies."

"We hardly need two hundred men to watch one hundred pack animals. And four hundred men may not be enough to conquer and recover all." David ran a hand over his beard. Was Adonai testing his trust?

"Two hundred too exhausted to fight will only hinder us."

David released a weighty sigh, knowing the answer he was about to give would not bode well with the men who would push through any trial, exhausted or not, to save their loved ones. He glanced at his guard and gave him a slight nod. "Tell the two hundred they can stay. Gather the rest and let's go."

Within the hour Benaiah, Joab, and Abishai had enlisted men to help them create a hand-over-hand bridge among the trees. Grumbling and sometimes outright cursing the men left behind, four hundred determined warriors crossed the rushing waters of the Besor wadi. When the last man had made it safely across, David focused his men's anger and attention on the kidnappers.

But as he clawed his way up the hill, a deep-seated fear filled him. Were they going the right direction? Worse, would he find Abigail and Ahinoam unscathed? For though Adonai had indicated that they would succeed in the rescue, He hadn't promised that David would find them as he'd left them. He knew all too well the practices of marauders bent on destroying a town — they killed the men and ravished the women, or they killed everyone, men, women, and children. Such a plan was the only way to ensure their own safety and avoid retaliation. David had instituted a similar plan himself during his months in service to Achish, killing the enemies of Israel and letting Achish think he was destroying enemies of Philistia instead.

He wiped sweat from his brow and shaded his eyes to scan the hills before him. What if the men had already humbled the women — the wives of his men and his own wives as well? A sick feeling settled in his gut. Death was not good enough for such a man.

He fisted his hands and forced his aching legs to continue.

■ ■ ■ ■

Abigail listened to the mixed sounds of the whispering, frightened women around her and the louder drunken reveling of the Amalekites outside the cave. The men and the few Amalekite women among them had begun their celebration long before nightfall. Dusk now blanketed the plain, and the merrymaking showed no signs of slowing. Perhaps this was a blessing, though Abigail knew that depending on his mood, a drunken man could either avoid or abuse the woman who caught his eye.

She stepped farther away from the cave's entrance and tugged her cloak closer to her neck, troubled by memories of Nabal. These Amalekites were more cruel and evil than Nabal had ever been, and by the way the leader had treated her, she knew it was only a matter of time before he plucked her from this group of women and did as he pleased with her.

Adonai, please help us. David, where are you?

Would he come? But how would he ever find them? The women had been ill prepared to leave any type of trail. And though the horses' hooves and footprints had left imprints in the sand, the stiff breeze that had assailed them the last half of the trip and the rains that had come during the night would have wiped away even those marks to show David where they had gone.

Hopelessness filled her. She sank to the dusty ground, pulled her knees to her chest, and rested her head on them, her gaze focused on the cave's entrance. She begged God to keep the Amalekites busy with anything but the women who crouched in fear with her.

A high-pitched female scream jolted her. She glanced around, satisfied that the sound was coming from outside the cave. But had the Amalekites snatched one of the women without her knowledge? She forced herself up from the ground and glanced hurriedly around her, moving to the hidden recesses at the back. Where was Ahinoam?

She came upon Ahinoam curled on her side, sleeping near a wall. Abigail blew out a troubled breath. When her heartbeat had slowed to a manageable rhythm, she walked back toward the entrance, searching the faces of the women as she went and asking if anyone had left the cave.

The screams grew louder the closer she came to the cave's mouth, but the tones were deeper, throatier. She stole quietly to the yawning entrance where the Amalekite guard kept watch, and peered around the one wall that offered a bit of seclusion. Firelight danced in the gathering dusk, but the jovial mood of the camp had changed. Swords clanged in the distance, and the sickening scent of blood drifted to her on the warm breeze.

David! It had to be.

She strained to see, noting the absence of the guard, who must have left to join the battle. She hoped for a glimpse of the men but could not tell friend from foe.

"What's going on?" Her mother's voice behind her made her turn. Joab's wife Marta, Abishai's wife Deborah, and her brother's wife Talya stood with her, followed by a number of the other wives of David's advisors. Her father and the older boys had been separated from them and placed in another cave, probably to keep them from defending the women.

"I don't know." Abigail looked back at the chaos going on in the camp, her stomach clenching at the swishing, thudding sounds of blades cutting flesh and bone. "Someone is attacking the Amalekites."

"David?" her mother asked, her tone anxious.

"We can only hope."

■ ■ ■ ■

The war continued into the night, through the next day, and into the following evening. Abigail slept fitfully in little snatches, taking turns with the women to keep watch over the group and hoping for some sign of David or one of his men. But though they must have taken time to rest from the fight, the men did not come near the cave of the women, leaving them to wonder and worry.

At the end of the evening of the second day, the sounds changed to war whoops and victory shouts. Abigail's stomach did a little flip as male voices grew closer to the cave. She hurried to the entrance and peered into the darkness, and then there he was, standing before her.

"David!" She ran to him, falling into his arms. The stench of his blood-soaked, sweaty tunic nearly gagged her, but she held his face in her hands just the same. "You found us."

He placed both hands on her shoulders and kissed her in response, a bold, passionate kiss. "The men would have killed me if I didn't." He smiled, then kissed her again. "I couldn't let them have you, Abigail. Of course I had to come. You belong to me."

He let his arms fall from her shoulders to her waist.

"Are the boys and men you left to guard us . . . is Abba safe?" Behind them the other women now rushed from the cave in search of their men, while the men moved wearily toward them.

He kissed the top of her head. "Everyone is safe, beloved. Your father and some of the boys helped in the fight." Relief flooded her as David tried and failed to stifle a yawn. "I need to wash before you share my bed." His fingers traced a line along her jaw. "Where's Ahinoam?"

His announcement that she was the one he chose to be with made her heart sing. "She was staying at the back of the cave, my lord."

He looked beyond her, then met her gaze. "She is hiding in fear?"

Abigail shrugged. "Some of the time, yes. I believe she is simply exhausted, as any expectant mother would be."

David straightened, his eyes growing wide. "Ahinoam is with child?" He toyed with a smile, and his eyes lit with delight. "How is she?"

The familiar stab of jealousy stung, replacing her joy of having him to herself this night. "She is fine, my lord." She stuffed her frustration down and took his hand. "Come and see for yourself." She led him toward the back of the cave but stopped when Ahinoam met them halfway.

"David?" She lowered her gaze in a decidedly shy gesture and placed a protective hand on her middle. "Thank God you are safe!"

David released Abigail's hand and stepped toward Ahinoam, pulling her into his arms. Abigail watched the exchange, feeling bereft.

"How are you, beloved?" He kissed Ahinoam with a tenderness that made Abigail's heart ache.

"I am fine now that you are here. I didn't get to tell you before you left. I am carrying your child, my lord." Her words were soft, breathy. Abigail couldn't help but look at her and noted the healthy blush on her cheeks and the joyous smile on David's face.

He placed a hand over the secret place where Ahinoam's child grew. The intimate gesture brought the sting of tears to Abigail's eyes. She turned and willed her mind to focus on other things. Moving a few steps beyond them, she told herself that sharing a man wasn't all that unusual, though no one else in the camp lived with the same struggle. Despite her suspicions of Nabal's unfaithfulness with Zahara, Abigail's heart had never ached as it did now. When David was king . . . would he take more wives? Fear fluttered in her heart.

She leaned against the cave wall, listening to the sounds of men and women reuniting, the squeals of children laughing and singing that their fathers had come home.

David's hands on her waist startled her, but a moment later he wrapped his arms through hers and nuzzled the back of her neck. "Running away from me already?" His lips brushed her ear. "Don't be jealous, Abigail. Now that Ahinoam is with child, I can devote my time to you." His whispered words brought her up short. Was her jealousy so obvious?

She leaned her head against his chest and turned toward him, meeting his gaze. His weary smile melted her heart. "I'm sorry, David. I didn't know my feelings were so visible."

"I see everything about you, beloved." That he used the same endearment with Ahinoam pricked her anger again, but she squelched the emotion. His weary tone and sagging eyelids told her exhaustion was quickly overtaking him. *Beloved* was better than some of the things Nabal had called her.

"You should rest." She faced him then and

took his hand. "Do you want to wash first or sleep?" Love would have to wait until another day.

"Sleep." He tried to stifle another yawn to no avail as he dropped one arm across her shoulders.

She put her arm around his waist and guided him toward the back of the cave where Ahinoam still stood. The two of them helped David out of his cloak and spread it on the ground, the clean side facing up. David curled on his side moments later and slept.

Abigail awoke the next morning before David or Ahinoam. In their relief at being back in the safety of David's company, they had lain on either side of him, taking comfort in his nearness. Now David lay with one arm draped over Ahinoam in a distinctly protective pose. Abigail crept from her spot at his other side and brushed the dust from her robe, looking away from the image of the family they made.

She never should have agreed to marry the man. If she had declined his offer, perhaps her father would have found some other man to keep her, someone who would love her alone. Didn't her parents have such a relationship? Didn't Daniel care for Talya

311

in that way? Why did both the men she had married have a failing that stirred her to despair?

The questions plagued her, causing a frenzied dance in her head, and she hurried from the cave lest she give in to her doubts and openly weep. The pink edges of dawn greeted her, illuminating the surrounding hills and casting blue and yellow hues over the blood-soaked plain. The stench of death nearly overpowered her, and she took a step backward and held a hand to her nose to filter the smell from such a pungent onslaught.

Carrion birds cawed and swooped low, feasting on the bodies of the defeated Amalekites. Was Zahara's body among them? The thought troubled her, bringing with it a host of other thoughts that accused her of her own foolishness. Why hadn't she been as suspicious of the woman as David had been? She should have known that Zahara's loyalties would have stayed with her own people. After all, she was a foreigner who, despite her amiable attitude, denied that Yahweh alone was God. David would have killed her in one of his raids on Amalekite towns — had she been there — in fulfillment of Adonai's curse on the cruel, idolatrous nation.

But what of the argument she had witnessed between Zahara and her brother? Had Zahara simply fled to find her people, never expecting them to use her to lead them back to David and his people? Zahara had often been kind to her. Had everything been a lie? Somehow she suspected that Zahara had tried to stop her brother's actions, and in the end, maybe the reason the man had not hurt her had something to do with Zahara's impassioned words.

A woozy feeling swept over Abigail as she grabbed a clay urn and picked her way along the outskirts of the Amalekite encampment toward the river. They would need water to bake the morning's bread, and perhaps in the process of getting it, she could wash from her skin the blood that David had gotten on her.

Unnatural stillness broken only by the sounds of the carrion birds and meandering river heightened Abigail's already tense nerves. She should have waited for more of the women to awaken rather than come down here alone. What if some of the Amalekites who had gotten away came back to retrieve their belongings, and waited to pounce on unsuspecting men?

A shiver worked through her. She lowered the urn from her head and knelt at the river's bank.

Branches crunched behind her. She jerked upright and pulled away from the edge, her heart skipping a beat. She glanced around, and relief spilled through her. "You scared me."

David moved toward her, still wearing the bloodstained tunic, his face a mixture of pleasure and concern. "You shouldn't be here alone." He stepped closer and squatted at her side, then sat on a rock to untie his sandals. "I noticed you were gone and followed you here. Just because the enemy is dead doesn't mean it's safe, Abigail. You should have waited for the others."

"I'm sorry. Forgive me, my lord. I only meant to get started on the morning meal." His serious expression caused a longing for his approval to sweep over her.

He pulled first one sandal and then another from his dirty feet. "Never mind it now. Just be more careful next time." His smile put her at ease as he proceeded to remove his robe and pull his tunic over his head. Warmth filled her as she watched him slip into the cool water and dunk his head. "Come in and join me." His playful smile sent a flutter to her middle.

"It's too cold."

"It's refreshing." He laughed, the hearty

laughter of a man whose cares are few, whose burden is light. "Come on."

"Someone might see." She couldn't believe he would suggest such a thing.

"There is no one here but us."

"The camp is awakening and the women will be here to draw water soon. They'll see you." She picked up his filthy garments and looked them over. "I should wash these instead."

"Plenty of time for that." He gave her his most charming smile. "We may never get such a chance again."

She glanced behind her toward the camp, then looked back at her husband, who had disappeared from sight. "David?" Panic filled her for the briefest moment until he popped his head from beneath the surface and came up again, laughing and shaking the water from his thick, dark hair. He scooped silt from the bottom of the river and scrubbed it into his skin, all the while looking at her with a gaze that turned her knees weak.

She placed his robe and tunic back on the grass and worked to undo the belt at her waist. She sat on the rock David had vacated and untied her sandals, then slipped the robe from her shoulders. She was about to lift her tunic over her head when the sound of female voices drifted to her.

Should she hurry and join him, not caring what the women might see? Or should she don her clothes again and catch the women before they came too close to give David his privacy? Indecision filled her.

"Come on, Abigail. We're running out of time." His playful tone had turned the slightest bit impatient, and Abigail did not miss the disappointment in his eyes.

"We already have. The women are coming." She lowered her tunic again and put her arms back through the sleeves of her robe. "You'd best get dressed." She slipped into her sandals and quickly tied them. She found his spare tunic in his leather pouch and smoothed out the wrinkles as he shook the water from his hair and beard and stepped out of the river onto the shore. He took the clean tunic from her outstretched hands and placed it over his wet body. He looked so refreshed that Abigail instantly regretted not having joined him. And now it was too late.

As the women approached the water's edge, he pulled his soiled robe over the clean tunic and bent to tie on his sandals.

"I'll wash this for you," Abigail said, clutching his bloodstained tunic to her. She felt as though she needed to do something to redeem the moment.

He looked at her, then glanced at the women behind her and nodded. "Don't come back alone."

At her silent agreement, he turned and moved back through the trees, out of her sight, leaving her drowning in a river of regret.

27

By the time they had gathered the spoils the Amalekites had taken and trudged back along the path they had come, meeting up with the two hundred men at the Besor Ravine, the trek back to Ziklag had taken nearly a week. Now Abigail sat beneath the wide awning of the goat-hair tent she shared with David and Ahinoam, stitching some of the fabric David had given her from the Amalekite plunder. David would need new garments when he took the throne as Israel's king, and somewhere deep inside herself she sensed that time was near.

In the three days since they had returned to Ziklag, the town had filled with men from Judah seeking to help David's cause. They had salvaged the courtyards of the burned-out homes and made camp among the ashes. David's wealth had jumped substantially with the spoils they had taken from the Amalekites, despite the large portions he had shipped off to friends in Judah who supported him.

Abigail fingered the fine fabric and smoothed it across her lap, listening to the midmorning sounds of women shooing children off to play and men shouting to one another across the square or speaking in guarded tones in small groups. She reached for her basket of colored threads and pulled a deep green from the assortment. Threading a slivered bone needle, she worked a leaf design along the edges of the tunic.

Zahara had taught her how to dye the threads to just the right shades back when she lived under Nabal's roof. When Nabal was off inspecting his sheep, Abigail had learned creative stitches to design intricate patterns in cloth — something she rarely took time for in the day-to-day management of Nabal's estate.

Where was Zahara now? A weight of worry pressed in on her at the thought. When finally alone with David, she had asked him for permission to search the dead before they left the Amalekite camp in hopes of finding her, but he had refused. Her jaw tightened as she remembered his adamant response, his stubborn unwillingness to allow her the chance to know what had happened to her maid.

"But my lord, she belongs to me. I'm only asking to find out what has happened to her. If perhaps she is still alive —"

"No one still lives out there, Abigail." His sweeping gesture toward the rotting corpses and his hardened expression told her he would not be easy to convince.

"But you said four hundred men got away on camels. Is it possible she went with them? How will I know if you don't let me check or send someone else to check? I want the chance to bury her, David." She crossed her arms and turned her back on him, her own stubborn defiance surfacing despite the better part of judgment that told her to let it go.

His hands rested heavily on her shoulders, and she flinched as he turned her to face him, but he didn't seem to notice. "She was an Amalekite. She does not deserve a proper burial." He worked his jaw and glowered at her, an expression he'd never directed her way before. He dropped his hold on her and stood looking down at her, arms stiff at his sides, obviously waiting for her compliance. A compliance that she was loath to give, despite her longing for peace.

"I understand that, my lord." She uncrossed her arms and held her hands toward him in a gesture of supplication. "But she was a good servant . . . and . . . and I think her actions spared me a terrible fate."

He quirked a brow at that. "What do you mean?"

"She argued with her brother, the man who planned to take me for himself. I couldn't understand their words, but he did not do as he planned, as he might have done."

David closed his eyes, drew in a slow breath, and released it, but he did not take another step toward her. "I hope what you are saying is true, beloved. But your maid was Zafirah, not Zahara, and an Amalekite spy. I suspected her from the first week she joined us and should have sent her away right then. Despite what she might have said to save you, the fact is, she led those men to Ziklag. She almost cost me your life. For that, she deserves whatever fate befell her." His voice rose on the last words, but when he cleared his throat, his tone grew quieter yet was just as stern. "Put her out of your mind, Abigail. And never speak of her again."

Abigail paused in her stitching and swallowed the rise of emotion evoked by the memory. She'd wanted to ask David how he knew Zahara was a spy or why he'd suspected her, even how he'd come to know her Amalekite name since she hadn't told him. And if he'd known all of this, why had he allowed Zahara to live among them for so long? Or was it just a hunch that happened to be proved right? Chances were, she would never know. As it was, the argument had cost her precious time with him, and she had slept fitfully beside him without the comfort of his touch.

She tilted her head at the sound of children racing down the street and kicking a pottery shard in a keep-away game. Laughter rose from young girls watching the boys play, and a handful of women scolded the boys for coming too close to them as they moved from the river carrying jars of water on their heads.

She started at the sound of David's voice among a group of men heading toward the courtyard not far from where she sat. He hadn't called for her to share his bed since that night, and even from this distance she suspected he would keep his gaze turned away from her at any cost. The inner turmoil this created in her spirit had stolen her appetite for days, but there had been no chance to seek him out to ask his forgiveness.

Though deep in her heart, she still believed she was right — he should be the one seeking her goodwill, not the other way around. But she would humble herself and fall at his feet if she knew it would put an end to their current strife. She was a peacemaker at heart, and her heart told her she needed to act soon.

Shouts caused her to look up again.

"Captain! A runner comes." Asahel, David's nephew, rushed up to the courtyard and stopped near David. "A man enters Ziklag even now. He comes from the battle. There is news of the king."

Asahel stepped aside and allowed David a full view of the foreigner now moving toward them. A Bedouin — robe torn, dust on his head, and out of breath — came to a quick stop just outside the courtyard and fell to his knees before David. He bowed low, his face to the dust.

"Where have you come from?" David asked, crossing his arms over his chest.

"I have escaped from the camp of Israel."

David's hands clenched of their own accord, and he steeled himself for the news, holding his anger in check. "What happened? Tell me."

The man lifted his head and rested on his haunches, hands pressed against his knees.

"The men fled from the battle. Many of them fell and died. And Saul and his son Jonathan are dead."

David's gut tightened and he winced, not wanting to believe. He searched the young man's face for some sign of falsehood. "How do you know that Saul and his son Jonathan are dead?"

The man straightened, fingering a leather pouch at his side. "I happened to be on Mount Gilboa, and there was Saul, leaning on his spear, with the chariots and riders almost upon him. When he turned around and saw me, he called out to me, and I said, 'What can I do?' He asked me, 'Who are you?' 'An Amalekite,' I answered. Then he said to me, 'Stand over me and kill me. I am in the throes of death, but I'm still alive.' So I stood over him and killed him, because I knew that after he had fallen he could not survive."

"And Jonathan?" The question faltered on his tongue, though deep in his spirit, David knew the man had spoken the truth.

"A Philistine arrow pierced him through. That is all I know." The man reached into his pouch, produced a jeweled golden crown and a solid gold armband, and laid them at David's feet. "I took the crown that was on the king's head and the band that was on his arm and have brought them here to my lord."

David glanced at the familiar adornments of Saul, then looked hard at the Bedouin, his mind reeling. The man had admitted to killing Adonai's anointed. "Where are you from?" Had he heard him correctly, that he was an Amalekite? Surely the man was not such a fool as to think David would be pleased to hear such news from an enemy that nearly cost him his life and the lives of his family.

"I am the son of an alien, an Amalekite," the Bedouin said, lifting his chin. His haughty gaze rested on David as though in challenge, as though proud of his heritage. Apparently the man truly was a fool.

"Why were you not afraid to lift your hand to destroy Adonai's anointed?" David took one step back from the man and skewered him with a look. Several of his men quietly surrounded the Bedouin. The man glanced around him, blood draining from his face.

Abishai stood at the back, behind the man, sword drawn. David nodded to him. "Go, strike him down."

In three strides, Abishai moved forward and thrust his sword into the man's back.

"Your blood is on your own head," David said, "for your own mouth has testified against you when you said, 'I have killed Adonai's anointed.' "

The man fell in a heap where he stood, his eyes wide, his face twisted in a grotesque mix of hatred and fear. David gave him one last look, then nodded to Abishai. His men took the body to a nearby ravine and cast it down for the carrion birds.

David sat cross-legged in the dust, his throat raw from weeping, his eyes stinging and swollen. The feeling was all too familiar. Hadn't he and his men dealt with similar emotions just days ago when they thought their wives and children were lost to them? A knot of grief coiled in his belly, and his mind traveled of its own accord to the terrifying moment when his men had come close to stoning him. How much of a difference a few weeks could make! Now they looked at him with expectant eyes beneath their grief, eyes that spoke of the promise of the future kingdom.

A kingdom that now felt suddenly hollow. How could he ascend the throne without Jonathan at his side? He had always expected to have his friend help unite the tribes, to turn the kingdom over to him after Saul was dead. Michal would be restored to him, and he would bring the people back to the true worship of Adonai. Now, without Jonathan's aid, who would accept his rule?

He lifted his head from staring into the ash-coated dirt and looked over the compound in one sweeping gesture. Abigail sat huddled near their tent, a picture of misery. His conscience pricked at the sight of her. He'd been hard on her after the rescue, upset with her desire to seek a maid who had betrayed her. Somehow he needed to make it up to her, to let her grieve in her own way, however misguided she might be.

His gaze shifted away from his wife to the pockets of men and women sitting in small groups, mourning the dead. How many had lost loved ones in the battle? Months would pass before they would know for sure. And how much territory had the Philistines taken from Israel?

David's hands clenched in and out as he considered how close he had come to being forced to fight with them. *Oh, Adonai, how I thank You for sparing us.*

The thought made his heart turn heavenward, and a song of lament formed in his mind. Brushing the ashes and dirt from his tunic, he stood, walked toward his tent to retrieve his lyre, and returned to mourn his friend.

Abigail pulled her cloak about her, cinching it against the evening breeze that blew down from the surrounding hills and sent the flames in the fire pit to dancing. She crossed her legs at the ankles, listening to David strum his lyre. He repeated his haunting lament for Saul and Jonathan over and over until she could match the tune in her head.

"Your glory, O Israel, lies slain on your high places! How the mighty have fallen! Tell it not in Gath, proclaim it not in the streets of Ashkelon, lest the daughters of the Philistines be glad, lest the daughters of the uncircumcised rejoice. How the mighty have fallen in battle! Jonathan lies slain on your heights . . ."

She glanced at her husband sitting across from her. His dark head was bent, his fingers deftly strumming the funeral dirge.

"I grieve for you, Jonathan, my brother. Your love to me was wonderful, surpassing the love of women." He paused, his voice catching as it did each time he uttered the words.

Abigail studied the fire, the words pinning her with guilt. As his wife, she should have loved him without demands, should have somehow offered him a companionship unequaled. Hadn't God said in the beginning that the two shall be one? But David had made their marriage a union of three from the start, since Michal could not really be counted. And yet, only Michal had been his alone, a position Abigail envied. If she had been the first . . . But she mustn't bemoan what she couldn't change.

She shifted her gaze from the fire to David, catching a look of deep sorrow in his eyes. He offered her the slightest smile and held her gaze, and in that moment she understood the meaning behind her husband's lament. David and Jonathan had shared a camaraderie, a brotherhood of friendship and burden-bearing of secrets and trust, much like women shared a common sisterhood, a commiserating of shared worries and woes. She'd had such a thing with her cousin Leah before her first marriage, a lifetime ago.

She inclined her head toward David and offered him her most understanding expression in return, then averted her gaze and toyed with the fringe along the edges of her robe, debating whether to stay and continue to listen to his mournful tunes or move to the tent and find solace in sleep. Undoubtedly, he would grieve alone this night, so he wasn't likely to require her presence.

"How the mighty have fallen, and the weapons of war perished." He strummed one last chord on the lyre and let his fingers fall silent. David's men rose two and three at a time and bid their goodnights, then headed to their tents. Abigail looked up at the touch of a hand on her arm.

"Come with me, Abigail." David held his hand out to her, surprising her.

She felt the warmth of his fingers intertwining with hers as he led her to their tent. He paused at the opening and bid Ahinoam to rest, then tugged Abigail beyond the partition toward his private quarters. Multiple pillows surrounded a plush blanket, offering a soft cushion to cradle them when they slept. The furnishings were a far cry from the goat-hair blankets and cloaks they'd used for coverings when she had first married him, evidence of the many spoils taken in battle.

He placed the lyre in a leather pouch and hung it from a peg, then motioned for her to join him among the pillows.

She knelt at his side and shifted her feet beneath her. "How can I serve you, my lord?"

He pulled her down beside him and traced a finger along her jaw. "Serve me? Surely you must know that's not why you are here." His expression softened as his eyes assessed her. "Something troubles you, though. What is it?"

"This is a difficult day, my lord." She avoided looking at him, though she could feel the warmth of his breath on her cheek and the gentle way his finger loosened the combs from her hair. He sifted the strands between his fingers as they fell to the middle of her back.

"We can comfort each other," he said, turning her chin toward him and leaning closer to taste her lips. "I need you, Abigail." He left a trail of kisses from her lips to her neck, then back again. "Let me love you without words."

She held his gaze. When they were alone like this, it was one of the few times she had to speak to him of anything that troubled her, to ask his favor for things she wanted or to work through a difficulty or misunderstanding she might have with him — as she longed to do with their argument about Zahara. He was asking her to hold her tongue, to let their love speak its own silent language.

Which meant another day or week or month she must wait to bring up the subject, to clear the air between them. Must she harbor her resentment forever? Could she forgive and forget without letting him know how she felt?

He looked at her with an expression that begged her to understand, to act as men acted when they overlooked a matter, as he'd often done when having to deal with two wives and a host of unruly men.

She nodded, her heart suddenly warming to him. She wanted to be the friend Jonathan had been to him, and more. She wanted him to find the love of this woman greater than the brotherly love he'd lost in his friend.

Abigail slipped her arms out of her robe, saw the delight ignite in David's eyes. She lifted her hands to his shoulders, then moved them around his neck in response and kissed him without words.

28

Days turned to weeks, and Ziklag burst at the seams with men from the tribes of Israel seeking to anoint David king in Saul's place. Abigail's time alone with David had been sporadic since the night they'd sought solace in each other's arms, a situation she told herself again and again to accept. If only she could get her heart to allow the inevitable change that was coming — and coming far faster than she ever dreamed possible.

Now, as she sat astride a donkey at the front of the group of women and children on the way to Hebron, she looked toward the hills blanketing their path and the sea of men stretched before her with David riding in military splendor at their head. Fighting men broken in regiments of hundreds made up the thousands of soldiers flanking them on all sides, solid protection against bandits or enemy Philistines come to prevent David's ascension to Israel's throne. Some even feared Saul's tribe of Benjamin would attempt to thwart Judah from proclaiming David king, as word had it that Abner, Saul's cousin, had vowed to do all in his power to put Saul's remaining son Ishbosheth on the throne.

David didn't seem worried. In fact, he was thrilled with the royal garments she had made for him, seeing it as a sign of God's timing. Indeed, it did appear that Adonai was leading her husband, that the fulfillment of His promise to David was near. She smiled at the thought.

"I don't know what there is to smile about." Ahinoam's sharp tongue cut into her musings. "Of course, you don't have to ride carrying an added weight in your middle. If I have to sit on this beast one more day, this baby is going to come before it's due."

Abigail felt the familiar pall of bitterness she experienced every time the woman flaunted her condition. The fact that Ahinoam traveled in misery did little to console Abigail or relieve her of the nagging fear she had carried since the sixth month of her marriage. She was barren. She had to be. In her three years with Nabal, she had never conceived, and now, after nearly two years with David, things were no different.

She glanced at her rival, catching the self-satisfied smirk beneath her gauzy veil. She sensed not for the first time that Ahinoam enjoyed taunting her with her superior status as first wife about to bear David's first heir.

She swallowed the words she longed to fling back at the woman and gazed ahead at the company as they rounded a bend between two green hills. The sun had crested the middle of the sky moments before, illuminating the limestone gates of Hebron.

"It won't be much longer now." She nodded toward the gates. "I'm sure you'll be fine." She glanced behind her at the other women, some of them walking, some riding, some chatting and keeping a quick eye on their children or nursing babes tied to their sides. She hoped to spot her mother or sister-in-law or a friend. But none were close enough to interfere or intervene between David's two wives.

Ahinoam grunted and mumbled something Abigail could not quite understand but happily ignored. She prodded her donkey to move a few paces ahead, hoping Ahinoam didn't notice her desire to get away from her.

"There's talk of David bringing Michal back."

Abigail tugged slightly on the reins to slow her pace again so she could meet Ahinoam's gaze. "What did you say?"

"You know exactly what I said. We aren't even to Hebron yet and it's already started. Soon David will have his palace and his many women, and we'll be relegated to just another ornament at his side." Her bitter words held a fragile edge. "You can't tell me it doesn't worry you, Abigail. We have to present David a united front or he'll allow more women to take our rightful places."

A united front? About what? But it was obvious Ahinoam had given the matter much thought, and even now, despite her occasional haughty air and her worrisome talk, her expression told Abigail that she was scared and lost, needing a friend. Few women spoke well of Ahinoam behind her back, and in an overcrowded women's quarters, things would only get worse.

"You think there is something we can do to stop him from reclaiming his first wife?" She shook her head. "I'm afraid you are mistaken. Once David is king, there will be little to stop him from doing whatever he pleases." She winced at her own bitter tone, not wanting to give Ahinoam any encouragement, but the fact was, men did what they pleased. A king all the more so.

"Then we are doomed." The dejected look Ahinoam gave her squelched the anger her words produced. "He will bring Michal back, she will become his queen, and we will be nothing but concubines to occasionally share his bed." She placed a protective hand over her middle. "The only consolation is that Michal is barren, so whether I'm queen or not, my son will be David's rightful heir."

Abigail fisted her hands around the donkey's reins, gripping them until her knuckles went white. The woman was obsessively self-centered. "We are a long way from declaring David's successor. Let's allow our husband to be crowned king of Israel before we decide which of his sons may one day sit on the throne in his place." She kicked the donkey's sides, harder this time, and moved ahead of Ahinoam. If David fell out of Adonai's favor, as Saul had done when he refused to obey Adonai's commands to kill the Amalekites, David might end up like Saul, without a rightful heir. It was foolish to speculate about such things now.

But a niggling worry irritated her just the same. There was far more truth in Ahinoam's words than Abigail cared to admit.

Though he had never spoken of it with her, Abigail had no doubt that David would one day expect, even demand, Michal's return. Just as she had no doubt that David would take other women to be his wives. To build a family dynasty, a man needed sons — and if her fears were realized, a son was something she could not give him.

David lifted his head to the surrounding hills that nestled the town of Hebron in its own protected cove. The housetop where he stood overlooked much of the city, where caravans of men on horseback and camels continued to pour into the city from outlying Judean towns. The home the people of Hebron had prepared for him was a veritable palace compared to the tents and caves of his all too recent past. And now farmers carried to Hebron wheat and olive oil, pressed dates and figs, raisins and honey cakes, sheep and goats, all for the celebration that would accompany tomorrow's coronation.

He stilled, moving his gaze from the busy workers in the city to the hills once again. Thick, billowy clouds rested atop the highest mount, bright white against the afternoon sun.

Adonai, my help comes from You.

Would he be a good king? He couldn't bear to end up like Saul one day.

Please don't take Your Holy Spirit from me.

He'd done his best to live a righteous life, though his foray into Philistine lands had taught him that he needed to remember to seek Adonai before rushing off to do things he thought best.

Cleanse me, O Lord, and keep me from presumptuous sins.

The sound of footsteps behind him pulled his gaze from the hills back to his current surroundings. Hushai the Archite, the man who had introduced David to his new home and had quickly endeared himself as an advisor, approached.

"My lord, the delegation from Judah seeks an audience with you to prepare for the ceremony tomorrow. Abiathar has some things he wishes to discuss with you as well."

He nodded but found himself drawn once more to gaze over the city that had welcomed him with open arms, allowing the unguarded sense of peace to fill him — a feeling he had not known in a long, long time.

Voices drifted to him from below, from the courtyard of his wives. He took a glance at Ahinoam talking to her maid, the ever-protective hand resting over the place where his child lay. His child. A son, no doubt. The thought brought a smile to his lips. Adonai had blessed him and would continue to bless him.

He took two steps toward the stairs when he caught sight of Abigail sitting quietly in the small garden at the edge of the women's court. Fabric was spread over her lap, and her hands moved with a precise rhythm, in and out. The scene made him pause. She had proven to be a great asset to him in the past two years, always seeking to encourage and uplift, keeping the women calm at times when they could have been a burden, enduring abuse on his account . . . He should have listened to her advice and never gone over to the Philistines. Then she would not have had to endure capture.

A sense of guilt threatened to mar his present peace. He had not been there for her as he'd hoped, hadn't spent the time with her she needed, hadn't comforted her the only way he knew how. She might have been the one to carry his first child if he had. Though if he were honest with himself, he would have given Michal the privilege if Yahweh had allowed it. If their child had lived.

"My lord?" He felt Hushai's touch on his arm.

"I'm coming." He pulled his gaze away from Abigail, vowing to somehow make it up to her.

The new home in Hebron came equipped with a number of spacious courtyards, with wide pillars supporting the roof of a large audience chamber. Men from all the towns in Judah numbered in the tens of thousands, spilling from the chamber to the outer courts to the streets and rooftops of their neighbors. The city bulged with life all the way to the surrounding hillsides outside Hebron's city walls.

Feasting and music and dancing had commenced each night, and this night would be the culmination of their festivities. Abigail held a privileged view in the alcove next to David's audience chamber, where a gilded throne awaited him. She tuned out the whispers of the women about her, focusing her gaze on the front entrance where David's coming would be announced.

"This is so exciting!" Ahinoam spoke in her ear. "Did you think this day would ever come?"

Abigail threw her a sidelong glance. "I never doubted it." God forgive her for the barb, but her rival's attitude was becoming as prickly as an unwanted thorn.

"Well, of course you wouldn't."

Abigail didn't miss the sarcasm but pushed it from her mind a moment later at the sound of the shofar. Flag bearers carrying the standard of Judah marched in rhythmic precision. They paused, waited for the shofar to sound again, and then moved forward three paces. Abiathar the priest entered the hall, wearing the priestly ephod. David emerged following the fanfare, wearing a simple white linen tunic and carrying a shepherd's staff.

A hush fell over the crowd as David reached the step leading to the dais. Abiathar stopped above him and turned to face the people. David knelt before Abiathar and bowed his head.

"Praise be to Adonai, the God of Abraham, Isaac, and Jacob, who has chosen you, David, son of Jesse, to be our king, to rule His people Israel in righteousness and justice. This day I anoint you king over the house of Judah." Abiathar stepped to David's side and lifted the horn of oil.

Abigail's breath caught as she watched the contents of the jar flow out in a thin, amber stream over David's bowed head. David's face shone with a joy she had never seen from him before, and a moment later, as Abiathar prayed, David lifted his hands toward heaven, his lashes glistening with unshed tears.

When the prayer ended, Abiathar accepted the book of the law from a scribe and read, "When you enter the land Adonai your God is giving you, and have taken possession of it and settled in it, and you say, 'Let us set a king over us like all the nations around us,' be sure to appoint over you the king the Lord your God chooses. He must be from among your own brothers. Do not place a foreigner over you, one who is not a brother Israelite."

Abigail listened with interest, watching David's bowed head and hands clasped before him. Surely this time Adonai's choice of David would prove better than the people's choice of Saul.

"The king, moreover, must not acquire great numbers of horses for himself or make the people return to Egypt to get more of them, for Adonai has told you, 'You are not to go back that way again.' He must not take many wives, or his heart will be led astray. He must not accumulate large amounts of silver and gold."

Abigail's heart stirred with the mention of wives. Would David take more than the three he already had, once Michal was returned to him? Would they lead his heart away?

Please, Adonai, may I never lead David away from You.

"When he takes the throne of his kingdom, he is to write for himself on a scroll a copy of this law, taken from that of the priests, who are Levites. It is to be with him, and he is to read it all the days of his life so that he may learn to revere Adonai his God and follow carefully all the words of this law and these decrees and not consider himself better than his brothers and turn from the law to the right or to the left. Then he and his descendants will reign a long time over his kingdom in Israel."

Abiathar handed the book back to the scribe as Benaiah brought the robe Abigail had fashioned for the new king and held it open for David to place his arms through the sleeves. Gold and green fig leaves adorned the purple fabric along the fringes near the sleeves and at the base near the ankles. A golden-fringed sash held the robe in place, and a gilded, jeweled crown was placed on David's head.

"Long live King David!" Abiathar shouted, hands outstretched toward the people.

The shout repeated as one voice from the

cheering crowd, over and over again, until David ascended the step where he had knelt and took the throne.

A lump formed in Abigail's throat as she watched the humble, awed face of her husband. She moved slightly to get a better glimpse of him, her heart soaring when she caught his eye and his ready smile.

She leaned her head against the wall of the alcove and released a slow sigh. The day David had longed for had finally come to pass. He was king of Judah and soon would be king of all Israel. Life had already changed dramatically for her, for them, for their marriage. The question remained, what now?

How did a woman act as a wife to the king?

■ ■ ■ ■

Part IV

■ ■ ■ ■

The war between the house of Saul and the house of David lasted a long time. David grew stronger and stronger, while the house of Saul grew weaker and weaker.

2 Samuel 3:1

Then Joab returned from pursuing Abner and assembled all his men. Besides Asahel, nineteen of David's men were found missing. But David's men had killed three hundred and sixty Benjamites who were with Abner.

2 Samuel 2:30–31

29

The dining hall overflowed with people, the men seated nearest the king and the women at the back closest to the walls. Men's voices rose and fell in boisterous laughter as the food was set before them — platters of meat and fish, dates and figs, leeks and lentils, and wine in abundance. Their conversations drowned out the women's quieter voices, forcing Abigail to focus on her food instead of Ahinoam and Maacah, David's newest wife, and the wives of David's captains seated near her.

The first year of David's rule in Hebron had passed, and war between the house of Saul and the house of David loomed on the horizon, with Abner working to gather support to formally proclaim Ishbosheth king of Israel.

Amnon's childish chatter caught Abigail's attention, and she glanced at Ahinoam's young son, then looked quickly away. She caught sight of Maacah's seductive eyes fixed on David as the woman daintily bit into a fresh date and then slowly licked her lips. The woman had wasted no time squeezing her way into David's affections, and Abigail had no doubt that Maacah would be the next one to bear David a son. Abigail had been married to Nabal for three years and to David for more than three, and she still carried no child in her womb. She had finally resigned herself to the fact that she was undoubtedly barren, like David's first wife Michal.

The thought still pained her despite her resignation, but the sting had lost some of its edge. She picked a fresh date from a platter, her gaze taking in the scene before her. David leaned on a couch of soft cushions surrounded by his closest advisors, his expression thoughtful but distant, as though he was only half listening. His dark eyes looked over the crowd, pausing every now and then to assess a man, then abruptly he turned to show interest to someone seated near him.

Daniel had the privilege of sitting at the king's table this night, and Abigail could only imagine how excited and proud that must make her brother feel. He'd been pining for months, years in fact, to join the band dubbed "David's mighty men," and he'd taken who knew what risks to gain military acclaim and catch David's favor. But other men had always surpassed his prowess, killing more of the enemy or doing some uncommon feat, like Benaiah, David's bodyguard who had killed a lion in a pit on a snowy day.

Somehow Daniel's actions never quite caught David's military eye the way Daniel had hoped, despite his connection to her. Even now, as Daniel sat near the king, she could see David paying little attention to her brother. Had he grown weary of her family as he had appeared to have grown weary of her?

A yearning in her heart made her look away from her husband's handsome face, determined not to give in to the melancholy that threatened her. She should be proud that he had finally achieved his dreams, that Adonai had shined on David with such pleasure. If only the people would favor him a little less, would not consider their daughters as such wonderful gifts to offer their king. She had already endured David's marriage to the foreigner Maacah, and rumor had it that another wedding to the fair Haggith would take place before the month was out.

"Try to at least appear interested in the meal, my daughter. You are a woman of privilege, wife of the king, yet your mouth is curled in such a dour expression. If the king does notice you, he will most certainly not be attracted to such a display." Abigail's mother lowered her body to the end of Abigail's couch and scooted closer to her daughter, placing a comforting hand on her arm. "Be grateful, Abigail dear," she whispered close to Abigail's ear, the scent of honey on her lips.

Abigail straightened and did her best to offer her mother a convincing smile, knowing that David hadn't gotten close enough to notice her moods in weeks. The thought added to the sinking feeling that warred with her appetite. She drew a deep breath and bid the feelings subside, reminding herself yet again that her mother was right. She tasted another date and glanced at her husband, whose attention was occupied.

"I try, Mama." She picked up her silver goblet and gazed at the wine swirling untouched at the bottom. "If only Adonai would grant us a son . . ." She blinked, surprised at the wave of emotion she carried. She swallowed and tried again. "David hasn't called for me in weeks." To admit such a thing made her feel like a failure.

"He is a busy man with far too many demands on his time. I'm sure he still cares for you, dear one." Her mother's tone gentled. She plucked a thick piece of fish from a platter, scooped up leeks and two juicy slices of melon, and plopped them onto Abigail's tray. "You need nourishment. You will waste away to nothing at the rate you are eating."

"I'm not hungry, Mama."

Her mother regarded her, turning her chin to look into her eyes. "Is a son all that worries you, my daughter? Or is there something you are not telling me?"

Her mother had always been a strong woman, having endured the loss of several children between her and Daniel. She would understand Abigail's fears, but the tension she'd always created in Abigail made her reluctant to confide in her. Especially not here. If she were indeed barren, which would be more obvious if David were more attentive, the news would come out soon enough when all of David's other wives began to beget children and she did not. So far, only Ahinoam had birthed a son, and even she had not begat another since Amnon's birth. If Maacah were with child, she would have flaunted it in Abigail's face. Not that she didn't try to keep David to herself every chance she got.

Abigail cast a sidelong glance toward the two women who shared her husband, noting the distance between them and the wall of hostility each put up as an invisible barrier. A deep shudder worked through her, and she leaned closer to her mother. Despite the tension, her mother was someone she could trust.

"It's hard to share him, Mama." She swirled the liquid in her chalice. "I fear we will never . . . I mean, he will never . . ." Heat crept up her neck, warming her cheeks.

Her mother reached for her arm and gently squeezed. "He will, dear. Of course he will. But you must do all in your power to make him want to. Make yourself visible, eat properly, smile coyly at him when he looks your way. There are ways a woman can beguile a man, you know."

"Of course." She knew. Didn't she? She'd seen Maacah use her wiles on David often enough, and he had always seemed powerless to pull away from her, even when his expression told Abigail he might have preferred a quiet evening with her. "I will try harder, Mama." She rested the chalice on the table and patted her mother's hand. "Thank you."

"What else are mothers for? If only your sister-in-law were as willing to listen." Mama lifted her hands in a defeated gesture. "Ach. I try with that one, but she is forever letting that brother of yours do whatever he pleases without a single word of caution. Men don't know their own minds. But you know this, don't you, dear? They need a strong woman to guide them, as you did for David when he nearly went off on a fool's errand to kill your first husband. Where would we be now if you hadn't intervened? David thinks he has troubles with Israel following Saul's son now. Things would be even worse if he'd taken vengeance on Nabal."

Her mother prattled on as she was wont to do, while Abigail's thoughts drifted. She was not willing to get caught up in her mother's complaints about Talya. Her sister-in-law respected her brother, far more than Mama did Abba. She wouldn't fault her for that no matter what her mother said.

"Now your father, he knows when to listen to me. He isn't so foolish that he would go off to war trying to win David's favor, making me worry so. What is wrong with your brother that he keeps seeking some ridiculous military glory? Perhaps if you spoke to David . . ."

Abigail looked across the room again at the mention of David's name, her heart tripping at the sight of him, and in that moment, he glanced her way. Their gazes held, and on instinct she turned her head to the side and lifted a brow, offering him a distinctly suggestive smile. His eyes widened in response, alight with something akin to amusement. He lifted a hand to his beard, toying with a smile. She turned her head and lifted her chin, raising a hand to cover her mouth.

He waved a servant toward him, never taking his eyes from hers despite the tables and men between them. She watched him lean toward the servant and whisper something in his ear. The man bowed and left, and David glanced her way again, gave her a slight nod, then turned back to his advisors. Musicians tuned their instruments and began a lively song, while jugglers and dancers swayed between the tables throughout the hall.

Abigail realized that her mother had stopped talking and was now giving her a look that said she'd seen what had transpired between her and David.

At the end of the first set of songs, the servant David had spoken to approached her table. "My lady Abigail."

She turned to face him. "Yes?"

"The king has requested you come with me."

Abigail rose quickly, but not before her mother caught her arm and half rose to whisper in her ear, "See if you can get the king to keep Daniel from any more military excursions. I promised Talya I would ask you."

The man cleared his throat, and Abigail glanced at her mother, then hurried to excuse herself from the banquet. Did Talya put her mother up to this? If so, why would her mother complain that Talya never tried to talk sense into Daniel?

She shook the thoughts aside, her heart thudding harder in anticipation as she followed the man from the hall down through the family courtyard, to David's private chambers. Female servants met her there and spent the next hour perfuming her body, sweetening her breath, and dressing her in fine white linen.

She felt his presence before she heard him. The chattering girls attending her giggled, then hurried from the room, leaving her alone with him. He stood there, leaning one hand on the threshold beneath the arch leading to his spacious chambers. His dark eyes were lit with pleasure and roamed over her slowly, as though he were savoring the moment.

"It's been too long, Abigail."

"Yes, my lord, it has." She stood still, not sure how to proceed, unused to plying feminine wiles to get what she wanted. She was too used to trying to appease angry men.

But by the look on David's face, he was far from angry. He closed the door behind him and took a step toward her, then another. He removed the gilded leather belt from his waist and slipped the purple robe from his back, flinging it over the couch. He stopped in front of her and pulled her into his arms. His kiss was warm and comforting, like sweet wine for the thirsty.

"I've missed you." He traced a finger down her bare arm. She shivered involuntarily when his hands rested on her middle, and he placed one hand over her womb. "Amnon is a fine boy."

His dark eyes searched hers, and she returned his gaze, wishing she could hide the pain that statement evoked. Why talk of Ahinoam's child now? This was their time, and she didn't want to share it with another.

"Yes, my lord, I'm sure he is."

He pulled the combs from her hair, letting it tumble down her back. "It's time you had a son of your own."

His words and the tender way he looked at her brought a rush of emotions to the surface, feelings she'd locked away for months, unable to say to anyone, even him. She lowered her head, not trusting her voice, and studied her feet.

"Don't cry, beloved." He kissed the tears that had slipped out unbidden and took her hand, intertwining their fingers. "I'm sorry I've neglected you, but I'm here now. Let me make it up to you." He tugged her toward his bed, pulling her down beside him.

Everything she'd planned to say to him the next time she finally had him to herself — the concerns about her barrenness, the pain of sharing him, along with her mother's request for Daniel — fled her mind as she lost herself in his love.

Before the sun rose, David met with Joab, Abishai, and Asahel over a morning repast of sheep cheeses and fruits. The troops were headed to Gibeon, and David wanted to be sure they were prepared to negotiate with Abner, to bring as little bloodshed as possible to their people. The war between Judah and Israel had already lasted a year, and David longed to see it come to a swift end.

He couldn't help but worry about the long-term outcome of such civil strife.

"Perhaps we could pose a champion battle as the Philistines did with Goliath," Abishai suggested, biting off a large hunk of soft cheese. "We just need a giant, head and shoulders taller than the rest."

"Or a young man with a stone and sling." Asahel looked at David and smirked, then laughed at his own humor. David's nephew had been but a child when David had gone up against Goliath.

"Keep in mind that the champion fight was only the start of the battle that day." David leaned back in his chair, stretched his legs out before him, and crossed them at the ankles. "The whole army pursued the Philistines all the way to the entrance of Gath and the gates of Ekron. I know Abner may push you to fight him hard, but I don't want to see our brothers destroyed. Do what you can to minimize the losses." He ran a hand over his beard, thinking not for the first time that life would be so much simpler if Abner would come over to his side and work with him instead of against him. "We need to put an end to the civil war as soon as possible."

"Abner is a fool. He will fight to keep control of Israel until he breathes his last."

Joab stood to pace the room, hands behind his back.

"Abner is ambitious. He knows a good thing when he sees it, and he sees power in supporting Ishbosheth. But he is wise enough to know he can't win forever. In the meantime, I want to keep the bloodshed minimal." David glanced at the window where the sun had now fully crested the eastern horizon. "Your troops will be waiting." He stood, dismissing his nephews. "May God go with you."

Each nodded in respect and headed to the door.

"Report to me as soon as you return." David watched them leave, then returned to his chambers to find Abigail.

The cistern at Gibeon circled down into a black abyss where water collected during the heavy rains and a spring wound its way from the hills leading to the pool. Joab stood facing his two brothers a stone's throw from where Daniel waited with Asahel's troop. Daniel was close enough to hear, though Joab would never actually include him, the king's own brother-in-law, in the conversation.

"We'll divide into three groups and come at them from before and behind, and some will hold back and reinforce whichever group needs the most help." Joab looked at Abishai. "Your men will circle around behind. I'll take the frontal attack." His gaze shifted to Asahel, and Daniel cautiously moved closer. "Asahel, keep your men back and wait for my signal."

"What about the contest the king suggested? Are we simply going to ignore that?" Abishai cast a glance Daniel's way and frowned, then nodded his head in Abner's direction, across the Gibeon pool.

Joab thrust his hands behind his back and tapped a foot impatiently. "Contests don't eliminate the need to fight."

"They can determine the outcome, though," Asahel put in, "as the Philistines can so readily attest — when they will actually admit that they lost a son of Anak to a mere shepherd boy."

Commotion and movement across the pool drew Daniel's attention. Abner's forces moved with rhythmic precision into strict military formation, standing at attention, facing the pool and Joab's waiting men.

Daniel's pulse quickened at the sight, his blood rushing hot through his veins. If they posed a contest, he would fight in it. He would prove to the king that he was worthy to be counted among David's mighty men, that he was not some weak-kneed woman who needed to be kept from harm's way. If he didn't know better, he would almost wonder if Abigail had said something to David to keep him from seeing any real battles.

Daniel leaned his head to the wind, feeling the breeze cool his hot face, the heat not coming from the mild warmth of the sun but from the stirrings of anger in his heart. Abigail would never do such a thing to him. Though Mama might.

He turned at the rustling sound of Abner's men as some squatted and some sat cross-legged among the rough grasses of the plain.

"What are they doing?" Had he missed something while letting his mind wander?

"Same thing we're doing," Asahel said, coming up behind Daniel. He motioned for him to join the rest of the soldiers on the ground.

Daniel knew better than to argue or assert any perceived authority he might have as brother-in-law to the king. Joab, Abishai, and Asahel were the obvious favorite captains in David's army. Everyone else did as they said.

Pockets of conversation filled his ears as he crept from his position toward Joab's men seated closest to the pool. Abner, King Saul's former commander, stood and cupped both hands over his mouth. "Let's have some of the young men stand up and fight hand to hand in front of us."

Would Joab take the challenge? Daniel's pulse quickened, pinpricks dotting his skin. He could do this. He was most skilled with a sling, as any shepherd would be, but he'd had plenty of practice fighting Amalekites and Geshurites under David's command — proof enough that he deserved some recognition. He tamped his anger down and stood.

Such a contest would prove his worth as a man, forever erasing the smear on his family name and making a place for himself without the help of a wife, mother, or sister.

"All right. Let them do it." Joab's response should not have surprised him. This was it then. He hurried forward and stopped a handbreadth from Joab.

"How many men?" Abner's voice carried across the pool.

Joab's hard, beady eyes narrowed. His gaze moved from Abner to the first row of his men, his gaze skimming Daniel's. He crossed his arms over his brawny chest, shifting toward Abner. "Twelve men, one for each tribe."

Despite the fact that this was a civil war and neither side could boast men from all twelve tribes, the number made some kind of twisted sense, perhaps proving one side deserved the support of all twelve tribes over the other.

Daniel stepped closer, drawing Joab's attention. "Let me go." Daniel stiffened at Joab's glower, knowing he would have to fight his commander before he ever fought his opponent. "You know I can do this. Let me fight for David."

Joab's brow lifted, his eyes glinting. He shook his head and waved him off as though he were nothing more than a pesky insect. Daniel paused, stung, his anger rising with the hurried steps of his feet.

"You, you, you, and you." Joab pointed in quick succession to four men, who were quickly joined by eight others Daniel recognized — four each under the command of Joab's brothers. The twelve straightened their military tunics, checked the swords and daggers strapped to their sides, and moved to the edge of the pool.

Flushed and angry, Daniel grabbed hold of Joab's sleeve and garnered a murderous stare for his action. "Listen, Captain, there is no reason for you to treat me like this. I am willing to fight, probably more so than some of the men you just sent. So why do you ignore me as though I am of no conse-

quence? I am the king's brother-in-law!"
He didn't often fling his relationship to Abigail around, and a part of him loathed himself for doing so now, but he was tired of being ignored as though he were nothing. "That reason alone should make you take notice of my ability. I'm as good a soldier as the next man."

Joab bared his teeth, and for a moment Daniel had the impression that if he were a lamb, then Joab was a lion and would rip him in two. "That reason alone is why I ignore you, Daniel ben Judah. How would I face the king again if I was responsible for the death of his wife's brother? Be grateful that the king values your hide so much and stop acting like a lost pup looking for its mother." He whirled about and stalked off before Daniel could respond.

Heat poured into Daniel's face as he glimpsed the smirks of the men around him. There would be no end of taunts toward him now. His humiliation could not be more complete. Why had he been such a fool? Joab was a hard man, and few came against him and walked away with their lives or their reputations intact.

Daniel ground his teeth and slipped away from the onlookers, but stayed close enough to watch the contest that should have been his.

Joab's twelve moved away from the pool to a grassy spot closer to Abner's forces, meeting Abner's twelve face-to-face.

"When I blow the trumpet," Joab shouted, "let the contest begin!"

Daniel's breath suspended, the air prickling, snapping like the prelude to a thunderstorm. The shofar sounded, jolting air into his lungs, He stood, his feet frozen to the dirt. First one, then two, four, six — his gaze darted from one man to another. Arms thrust out, heads yanked forward, swords plunging. Terrifying, haunting screams pulsed in the sun's heat.

Blood spilled onto black earth.

Screams slowly stilled into silence.

Daniel's heart thudded like thick mud, weighting his arms, his legs, sickening him. An eternity passed, or was it only a moment? Shouts awakened his dead ears, and the shofar sounded again.

"Let the war begin!" Joab's battle cry jolted him, freeing his limbs. Daniel surged forward in pursuit of the enemy.

30

David stood at the window of his bedchamber, looking east toward the slowly rising sun. News of the battle had begun to trickle into Hebron, but he was still waiting for a report from his nephews, and the delay had filled him with an uneasy sense of dread.

Abigail stirred in the bed behind him, and servants moved about in the halls, their muted whispers and quiet footfalls breaking the silence of oppression that had settled about him like a cloak. Birdsong greeted him as the pink hues of dawn cast a pale glow over Hebron's mud-brick homes and distant, grass- and sand-covered hills. If he didn't hear something by the time the sun broached midday, he would send scouts out himself to see what had happened to Joab and his brothers.

"David?" Abigail's gentle voice pulled him from his irritating thoughts. He turned to find she had wrapped a thin robe about herself and stood at his elbow. "Is everything all right?"

He drew her to him, encasing her in his arms. There was a sense of rightness about having her here, and not for the first time he wished he had known only her. Keeping her with him these past few days had made it almost possible to blot out the constant need to appease his other wives. If only for a time, he could forget the kingly demands that obligated him to keep peace with tribes and nations through marriage contracts with their daughters.

A sense of uneasiness crept over him, and he wondered again if he was doing the right thing. Hadn't God told kings not to take many wives? And yet he seemed powerless to deny the requests put on him, or his own faithless desires. The kings of surrounding nations had far more wives at their disposal than he would ever allow, and he assured himself that he would never let his wives lead his heart from Yahweh.

He kissed the top of Abigail's head, then rested his chin there. He momentarily appeased his conscience, enjoying the way she fitted against him, as though she was made for this space nearest his heart. "Everything is fine, beloved."

He absently stroked her back, felt her

shiver beneath his touch, and was reminded again of how she had loved him at first with such reservation because of the abuse she had once endured. He vowed to never hurt her that way, to never again allow her to feel the brunt of any man's wrath, to protect her from any further pain life had to offer.

If only he could.

"Something troubles you, David. You tossed and turned in the night, and I wonder if you slept at all." She leaned away from him and looked up, meeting his gaze. "Has something happened with the battle?"

He shook his head, looked at her for a long moment, then glanced beyond her out the window again, which allowed him an expansive view of Hebron and the path leading to the city gates. "Only a few rumors of victory over Abner. But Joab has yet to return."

"A victory should not rob you of sleep. You fear something." She touched his cheek, stroking his beard. "Surely you have nothing to fear. Adonai is with you."

He looked down at her again, the warmth of desire for her filling him. He shifted closer, took her face in his hands, kissed her soft, delicate lips, and sifted his fingers through her rumpled hair. This kiss awakened his need of her yet again, and when she wrapped her arms around his neck in response, he lifted her and carried her back toward his bed, deepening the kiss. He placed her among the soft pillows and slipped his arms from the sleeves of his lounging robe, letting it fall to the tile floor.

An urgent knock at the door jolted them both, bringing David's initial fears of the battle's outcome rushing in on him once more. He pulled away, frowning. "I'm sorry, my love." He released her, snatched the robe from the floor, and donned it as he walked briskly to the door.

Joab and Abishai stood before him, blood-stained, ash-coated, and disheveled, putting David's heightened emotions immediately on edge. "What happened?"

Joab's hard features, always commanding and often bordering on disrespect, looked weary and drawn. His mouth was pulled into a tight line, his cheeks hollow from lack of sleep. But fire snapped in his round, dark eyes, and his hands flexed in and out, his whole body poised like a coiled snake, as though he could barely contain his rage.

"We've walked all night from Bethlehem." Abishai spoke for his brother, glancing beyond David into the room. "But this is hardly the place to discuss these things."

David looked from one nephew to another, reading in Abishai's expression a confirmation of the dread that had awakened him before dawn. "Let me dress." Anticipating his thoughts, his manservant appeared from the hall and quickly retrieved fresh clothes for David to put on. He was vaguely aware of Abigail's soft footfalls and looked up to see her approach.

"Do not trouble yourself to leave on my account, my lord. It is I who should go." She placed a comforting hand on his forearm, her warmth momentarily soothing the beating of his anxious heart. "Call me if I can be of help to you." With that, she turned and walked to a side door, where her own maidservant appeared and ushered her out of David's chambers. A sense of disquiet settled inside him, and it surprised him that he should miss her so quickly, so completely.

Giving himself a little shake to clear his head from the distraction of his beautiful wife, he turned to his servant and allowed the man to help him dress, while Joab and Abishai moved into the room, shutting the door behind them. David deftly tied the belt at his waist and walked across the room to face them. He motioned for them to sit and commanded the servant to bring food and drink to his nephews.

"Now tell me everything," he said, taking

one of the cushioned couches opposite them and tenting his fingers beneath his chin. "Things did not go well, if your appearances are any indication."

Joab cleared his throat, but it was Abishai who leaned forward, his gaze intent on David. "The battle was bloody and not without casualties. Abner lost three hundred sixty men. We lost twenty."

David released the breath he'd been holding. "A victory then." But by the look in Joab's eyes, not one to rejoice in. "What else?" He placed both hands on his knees, bracing himself for whatever news his nephews were slow to tell him.

"Asahel is dead. Abner killed him."

Murder seethed from Joab's dark eyes, and David almost flinched. He wasn't sure which troubled him more — that the lanky, fleet-footed Asahel with the quick wit and easy smile was dead, or that Abner had killed him. Joab's bitter glare made him pause, and he had to remind himself that Joab was on his side. His fierce loyalty was one of the only positive things about the man.

"Tell me what happened." Perhaps the telling of it would ease a bit of the burden and exonerate Abner somehow, who was as good as dead if Joab ever got hold of him.

"Asahel's armor bearer saw it," Abishai said. He raked a hand through ash-coated hair, sending flecks of dirt onto the bearskin rug beneath their feet. "Asahel chased Abner from the battle, almost caught him too. Abner warned him to stop, to go after one of Abner's men instead, but you know how stubborn Asahel can be . . . could be." Abishai looked down and twisted the fringe of his cloak between his large, rough hands, as though the very words were being wrenched from someplace outside himself.

Joab stood despite his obvious weariness and moved behind the couches to pace the open area between the window and the furnishings.

"Asahel would not stop," Abishai continued after a silence so brittle that the air crackled with it. "Abner shoved the butt of his spear into Asahel's belly, and it came out his back. He died on the spot." Abishai looked up, his gaze only half as murderous as Joab's. Exhaustion was evident in dark circles beneath his sober eyes. "We walked all night to Bethlehem to bury Asahel in our father's tomb. Then we continued to return here." He leaned back in the chair, shoulders slumped.

The heavy weight of dread made sense now, and the grief that followed knotted David's stomach. He covered his face with both hands, listening to Joab's incessant pacing and wondering how the man had a fragment of energy left to move.

"There is more, David." Abishai's quiet voice carried a different tone, one less angry but with equal foreboding. He lifted his head, surprised to see that Joab had come back to the seat and practically fallen onto the couch, his strength finally spent.

"Worse than Asahel?" Though he couldn't possibly imagine what, since his top two commanders were sitting here facing him.

"For you, perhaps. For your wife, yes." Abishai folded his hands in his lap, no longer twisting them in his cloak.

"The man was a fool from the start, so one can hardly wonder that he would be among the fallen. He volunteered to be part of the contest that started it all, but it ended up being *Helkath Hazzurim*." In Joab's mouth, the name sounded like a curse.

"A field of daggers." Awareness tightened David's gut. So they held the contest he'd suggested after all. "The outcome?"

"Every man died at once. A fool's play. No strategy to such a thing." Joab's mouth twisted in a grimace of disgust. "Her brother begged me to let him be part of it. Of course I denied his request. I knew you would hold it against me to put the fool in the front lines. But he had as little sense as Asahel and Abner."

"Who had such little sense?" Though David already knew the answer, he needed to hear it firsthand from them.

"Abigail's brother, Daniel." Abishai lowered his voice and glanced at the door where Abigail had retreated. "He was among the nineteen besides Asahel we found among the dead."

David gripped the edges of the couch until his knuckles grew taut, anger and remorse coursing through him. Daniel ben Judah had tried to win his approval from the first time they'd met, always anxious to prove himself, and David had respected his strength and his ability to hold himself in check. But he'd held back from naming him to the thirty, though he knew Daniel wanted the position. Was that what happened? No doubt he meant to do something grand to gain David's notice. And it had gotten him killed.

Foolish man. And yet he wondered who was the greater fool — Daniel for having pushed to achieve what he wanted, or David for not giving him the acclaim he craved early on, to keep him from doing something rash.

He stood, dismissed his nephews with a nod, and walked to the window, where the sun fully shone now over the horizon. This battle had hardly been a victory. And what of the 360 men of Benjamin who had died because Abner would not submit to his rule?

Irritation tightened his muscles again, and a headache began at the base of his neck. Somehow he had to break the news to Abigail and her family. He whirled about and walked to the door to his side chambers where Abigail surely waited for him. No sense putting off a difficult task. He closed his eyes, breathed a prayer for strength, and opened the door.

Abigail stood at the window overlooking the family courtyard where David would meet with his wives most evenings or the women would gather to work or gossip. Abigail had often met with her parents there, and sometimes Daniel would bring Talya and Micah to visit for a day. But the visits had only managed to heighten her sense of loneliness and the longing for a normal family of her own.

She chided herself for being so ungrateful, for thinking anyone could compare to David or give her what he could not. She had lived with wealth and been the lone wife to a powerful man, at least on the surface, and nothing in that situation had satisfied her either. For David to even want her had seemed impossible when Nabal first died, for she feared no man would ever want her again. So why did she find sharing him so distasteful? Did she honestly think she was worthy of his love alone? He was the king! Kings took many wives. She'd known it from the beginning and accepted her lot with joy — at first. She had no right to be jealous of Talya's singular relationship with her brother now.

Truth be told, when she examined her heart she found it squirming with similar selfish thoughts. David had already taken to wife Maacah — a princess from Geshur, a foreign people — and Haggith would soon join their ranks. But it was Michal whose heart he still yearned for. She knew it whenever she glimpsed that faraway look in his eyes and on the few occasions he had spoken her name. Though he had reassured Abigail that he wanted Michal's return simply because she belonged to him and he needed to strengthen his kingdom, Abigail knew better. Michal still held a piece of his heart — a piece she wished belonged only to her.

She turned at the sound of the opening

door and footsteps crossing the mosaic tile. Her heart leaped at the sight of David standing there dressed in full royal garb, his handsome face wreathed in concern and his dark eyes glinting in sorrow. She could not deny her attraction to this man or suppress her longings for him when he wasn't at her side. Even in his presence she felt a giant need to cling to him, to feel his strength, to impress on her heart and mind every detail, every word spoken, every quick smile or loving look, every comforting touch.

She stepped away from the window and moved slowly toward him, meeting him in the middle of the room. He reached for her hands and clasped them in his own, his fathomless gaze searching hers.

"What is it?" Something troubled him, and she was glad she was here and that he had sought her out in his time of need. "You know you can tell me."

He leaned forward to kiss her cheek, then stroked her face with his fingers. "Come sit with me, Abigail." He led her to a cushioned couch and settled close to her, again taking her hands in his. His stance and the look in his eyes sent waves of caution through her. Something was wrong. Terribly so.

"What?" She choked out the question this time, an unnamed fear snaking through her.

His gaze never wavered, and he squeezed her hands as though to keep her from pulling away. "Joab and Abishai returned from the battle."

"Yes, I know."

He nodded. "They brought news . . . My nephew Asahel is dead."

Compassion filled her, along with a bit of relief. But why did he act as though she should be so disturbed by such news? She liked Asahel well enough, and at one time he had been interested in her maid, but it wasn't like she knew him beyond a cursory relationship. Was David looking to her for sympathy for himself?

"I'm sorry to hear that, my lord. I know you were fond of him." She gave his hands a little squeeze to convey her sympathy. She was unnerved by the steady look he gave her that told her he was looking for more than comforting words, but she was at a loss as to what. "Is there something else I can do for you, David? How can I help?"

"There's more, Abigail." At this he released her hands and rested one hand on her knees. He averted his gaze briefly, his throat working as though he were searching for the right words.

"Please, just tell me." She worried the belt of her robe, trying to ignore the tight knot in her stomach.

"The battle was fierce. Abner lost three hundred sixty men to our twenty, including Asahel."

"That's good then, right? Though I'm sorry for Abner's losses, it is good for you that we lost so few."

He regarded her with interest, as though a woman shouldn't understand such things or be interested in aspects of war. "Yes, of course, but sometimes losing a few is worse than losing many, if you love the few who are lost."

His look sent a stab of fear to her heart.

"I'm sorry that you lost Asahel, my lord. It must be a terrible blow. I can only imagine how that would feel if Micah were old enough to go to war and —"

He raised a finger to her lips. "Daniel was killed in the battle, beloved." Abigail's mind reeled, and she was suddenly grateful for the couch holding her to keep her from sinking to the floor, as her legs would certainly not have held her up. A shaking began, causing her to tremble all over. She felt David's arms come around her, holding her close. She reached for him, clung to him, feeling his strength.

"I don't know how it happened. Joab didn't discover the bodies until after sundown. They walked all night to Bethlehem to bury Asahel, then brought Daniel and the other dead bodies here. I'm so sorry, Abigail. I purposely kept Daniel out of harm's way as best I could, but he was determined to prove himself and —"

She pulled back, a horrible thought coursing through her. Did he blame Daniel for his own death? "What are you saying?"

He met her gaze with a searching one of his own that carried a hint of irritation, even anger if she read him right. Was he angry with her or with Daniel for wanting to fight for David's cause, to defend his right to rule?

"Nothing," David said, suddenly leaning away from her as though he realized he'd said too much. "I'm not saying anything or trying to infer anything, Abigail. Daniel was a good solider who fought hard for the kingdom. It is only unfortunate that he didn't live to be rewarded as he should have been." A look of sadness crossed his face, regret in his eyes. He reached for her again, pulled her close, and kissed her cheek, then slowly, gently, with a look of pure tenderness, his lips met hers. When he lifted his head, he caught her tears with his thumbs. "We'll need to tell your parents and Daniel's wife and proceed with the burial. I've sent runners to bring them here. Does your father have a tomb where we can take Daniel's body for burial?"

She nodded, unable to speak past the lump in her throat. She swallowed several times. "We have a burial cave in Maon. The other babes are buried there."

A look of surprise and compassion crossed his face. "I'm so sorry, beloved. I didn't know."

"You would have no need to know. Mama lost three babes between Daniel and me." She suppressed a sob, but when he pulled her to him again and stroked her hair, she could hold back no longer, and she wept in his arms.

31

The wind blew between the hills and ruffled the king's banner carried on a pole by one of David's armor bearers. The funeral bier where Daniel's body rested stood at the front of the crowd, men and women filling in behind to pay her brother the last respects he deserved.

Abigail's eyes filled, emotion clogging her throat. She made no attempt to swipe the tears away or dry them with her tunic's sleeve. If tears alone could bring Daniel back, he would be standing before her now, proud and strong, one arm around Talya's waist, the other holding Micah. He would give her that overconfident smile she knew so well, assuring her that he knew her mind better than she did. And he would keep Talya safe so David didn't have to.

"We have lost a great man today." David's voice cut into her thoughts. She shifted her gaze from the bier to him, longing to feel the warmth of his touch, the assurance of his embrace. "Daniel ben Judah fought valiantly for the kingdom, for Judah. May Adonai's grace rest on his widow, his son, and his family." He looked over the crowd, his gaze resting on her father. "My father, you are to be commended for raising such a fine son. May you know that your family shall never want for anything and will always be honored guests at my table."

Her father nodded, swiping first one hand and then the other across his face, mopping his tears with his brown tunic. The stone over the cave's entrance squealed and groaned as four of David's mighty men shoved it aside, as though the earth protested having to swallow her brother's body, a body far too young to rest in Sheol.

Abigail's strength waned, and she slipped from beside her mother to touch her father's arm. His chest heaved in a great sob, and his strong arms encased her. She wept against his chest, clinging to him. "Abba." Her throat closed off more words.

"Abigail." He cleared his throat, pulled her closer, and patted her back. "You're all I have left."

The words made her tears come again, silent streams she seemed powerless to control.

The telltale groan and scraping of heavy stone upon stone pulled Abigail from her father's arms, and she saw David's men, Daniel's body no longer between them, roll the stone back over the cave's entrance.

"Daniel!" Talya's voice pierced the air, setting off the wails of the professional mourners.

"Abba!" Micah broke free of his mother's hand and ran to the cave, beating small fists on the stone, his wails rising, high-pitched and pitiful. Abigail's heart felt cracked, splintered in two. She looked to her father, to Talya. Someone should go to Micah, but she stood watching, helpless. Mama moved forward, but David beat her to him. He scooped the small child into his arms, held him against his chest, and patted his back. He walked back to Talya and opened one arm to her. She stepped into David's embrace, weeping against David's chest. Exactly what Daniel would have done, should have done, if he were still here to comfort his wife and son.

David bent low, speaking something in Talya's ear, too far away for Abigail to hear. The action shouldn't have sparked her jealousy, and it shamed her to think she was so callous, so selfish not to be able share her husband's kindness with her grieving

nephew and sister-in-law. But did his kindness mean something more? He had offered
to protect her through marriage when Nabal
died. Would he offer the same to Talya now?

Stricken by her own wild thoughts, Abigail fought the urge to rush over and inter-
rupt them, but a moment later she lost the
battle and moved from her father's embrace
to take a step closer to her husband. Her
father's hand restrained her. "Give her time,
Abigail. Let her weep."

Talya could weep all she wanted, just not
in David's arms. But one look at her father
stayed her feet. Micah's screams had quieted, and he now sobbed softly against David's chest, exactly as he would have done
in his father's arms.

She squirmed at the sting of such jealousy.
David said something else in Talya's ear,
gave Micah another squeeze, then handed
him back to his mother. Kissing the top of
Micah's forehead, he turned to rejoin his
men.

Hurt singed her heart that he did not
come to comfort her as well. Despite her
father's arm around her shoulders, she
needed her husband. She needed to know
she was still important to him.

The guilt of her selfishness brought a
sense of frustration and self-loathing, and it

only added to her grief. *Daniel! Why did you have to die?*

What would she do if David asked Talya for her hand in marriage? Who could refuse the king?

Dusk descended as the king's entourage plodded beneath Hebron's city gates. Men dispersed to their homes inside and outside city walls, while David's guards accompanied the king, Abigail, and her family back to the king's house. David had invited Abigail's parents and Talya to stay with them until the next day.

Alone with him now in his bedchamber, Abigail's tension rose and fell as she contemplated the wisdom of asking him, or even how to ask him, about his intentions toward her sister-in-law. Talya's comments on the return journey had been short at best, and try as she might, Abigail couldn't pull from her what David had said. The suspense, the need to know, had her brittle and tense. And how to ask, how to speak without angering him, tightened her nerves even more.

He sat among the cushions of his couch, a silver goblet of wine in his hand. His hair was still damp from a visit to the mikvah, which she had recently emerged from as well. She pulled a fresh night tunic over her head, its white linen soft against her clean skin. Emotions warred within her — she was grateful for another night with David yet was overwhelmed by her own inner turmoil.

He looked up, caught her gaze, and motioned for her to sit beside him. She went willingly, warmed when his arm went around her and he pulled her head against his chest. His fingers caressed her arm, sending a shiver of delight through her. A soft sigh escaped him. She waited, expecting him to speak, but he sipped from his goblet instead, his fingers playing absently along her arm.

"It's been a tough day." His voice held a tender quality, and she leaned away from him to look into his handsome face.

"Yes, it has."

He placed a light hand against her cheek. "I know it wasn't easy for you . . . or your family."

Indecision flitted through her, and she averted her gaze, not wanting him to read the turmoil she couldn't keep from tugging at her.

He coaxed her gaze back to his with gentle fingers. "Something troubles you. What is it?"

She searched his dark eyes, weighing the

wisdom of speaking her thoughts. He wouldn't grow angry with her on such a night, would he? His promise never to treat her as Nabal had done momentarily bolstered her courage. Normally he was the epitome of kindness. But even a hint of his displeasure might ruin this night, and she was loath to do anything that might mar her time with him. But if she didn't speak now, the time wasn't likely to come again. And if he married Talya . . . She couldn't bear the thought.

"I wondered what you said to my sister-in-law when you comforted her at the grave site. She seemed relieved about something but refused to speak much at all on the return journey." She watched him for some type of reaction, something that would give an inkling to his thoughts.

"I told her she need not fear the future, that she and her son would always be provided for and would be welcome guests at my table." He returned her scrutinizing gaze with one of his own. "Why?"

Abigail's stomach did an unwelcome flip. She pulled slightly away from him, no longer able to hold his gaze. She was a fool to have asked. Next, he would certainly tell her that he had also asked Talya to marry him.

His hand brushed her bare arm. "Abigail, did you think I asked your sister-in-law to become my wife?"

She swallowed hard, unable to look at him.

"You did, didn't you?" His tone gentled as he pulled her again into his arms. "Beloved, I would not do that to you." He tilted her chin to look her in the eye. "You know that, don't you?"

She blinked, feeling the sting of tears. "You asked me to marry you soon after Nabal died, so I thought . . . I didn't know . . ." She stopped, suddenly embarrassed that she could have entertained such a notion.

"I wasn't already married to your sister," he said, as though she should have already realized that fact. "If my studies of the law have taught me anything, it is that Jacob had far more trouble than he needed trying to appease sisters." He chuckled, but the humor was lost on her.

"More than one wife carries its own problems." She spoke low but knew by the way he stiffened against her that he had heard every word.

"You knew I had other wives when you agreed to become one of them." Never mind that Michal belonged to another, so in essence there were only two of them. Until he became king.

"I did not realize how hard it would be to share you . . . with so many more." She clasped her hands and picked at her nails, knowing for certain she had ruined whatever joy they might have derived from this night. She could not suppress a deep shudder and a sigh.

He moved his arm to rest on the back of the couch. His silence forced her to glance up and find he was looking at her with an intensity that took her breath. "Sometimes kings have to make choices to keep peace among tribes and nations. You know how often I am called away to war, how many times I left you alone in Ziklag to fight a battle. If I can make a treaty with those who might normally oppose us, or please a tribe who might prefer Saul's son by taking to wife one of their daughters, am I not wise to do so?" His voice held a challenge, and she knew he would expect her — the wife he considered wise, the one who had played the peacemaker among the women of his band the whole time they were in the wilderness — to agree with his wisdom.

Her hands moved to squeeze the folds of her tunic, and she drew in a breath, trying to formulate her words. "I suppose so, my lord." She looked up again at the touch of his hand on her arm once more. "I just don't like to share you."

He smiled at that, and she knew she had appeased him. He scooted her toward him and pulled her onto his lap. "You have me now, beloved. And know this" — he brushed her lips with his — "I often wish I had married only you. Let's not speak of this again, agreed?"

His kiss silenced her answer, and his words, whether he meant them or not, gave her hope.

32

Three months later, Abigail sat in the shade of the family courtyard, waiting for David's evening visit. She cradled a protective hand over her slightly bulging middle, longing to feel the babe move beneath her hand. The two weeks David had kept her in his chambers had produced the child she'd longed for, though the pregnancy had already taken its toll. She prayed the babe wouldn't suffer as she had with sickness and a certain weakness that left her limp in the summer heat.

Servants hovered nearby, wielding palm fronds to cool the air, and her maid Rosah rinsed a cloth in water to place across the back of her neck, to keep her from overheating. She had missed the last several of David's visits, but tonight she longed to see him again, to hope perhaps he might call for her to spend time with him.

The courtyard buzzed with the voices of David's other wives. Besides Ahinoam and

Maacah — who was rumored to be with child now as well — in the past three months he had added Haggith, Abital, and Eglah to their ranks. Each wife had barely finished her wedding week when another wedding took place, adding another wife to contend with, to vie for David's affections. The situation left Abigail listless and depressed on those days when the child already sapped her strength.

She sighed, shooing a fly away from her face as she forced her jealousies into submission. She looked toward the door where David's guard Benaiah now appeared, preceding David's approach. She straightened the jeweled headpiece, a gift David had given her to wear at his coronation, making sure the sapphire stone lay evenly in the center of her forehead.

"Do I look all right?" she whispered to Rosah, who hovered ever close. The young girl was approaching marriageable age, a lovely girl with hair the color of almond husks and eyes so dark and large they would surely captivate many a man. Hopefully not Abigail's husband. She stifled the rueful thought. Was she becoming cynical?

"You look beautiful as always, my lady." Rosah bent to turn the fold of the blue robe Abigail wore, smoothing the lines. "The king is here," she whispered, and turned to face the entrance. Abigail did not miss the look of excitement in the girl's eyes, making her wonder if her previous thoughts were not far off.

David strode into the courtyard, several servants trailing behind. He approached Ahinoam first, taking young Amnon from her arms. He held the boy against his shoulder, bouncing him gently but looking uneasy and anxious at the child's piercing cries. Moments later he handed the boy to his nurse who stood near Ahinoam, spoke a few words to his wife, and moved to Abigail.

His smile was nearly her undoing, and she couldn't stop the immediate, sudden longing for him. Amnon's cries continued, and David narrowed his eyes, clearly irritated by the sound. Was he such a stranger to his own son that the child would wail on sight of him?

David summoned the women's servant Hannah and spoke something in her ear. The woman nodded and crossed the court to the place near Ahinoam's room.

"I will not leave. I have as much a right to be with my husband as anyone else, and more so as I am the only one who has borne him a son." Ahinoam's shrill voice made

Amnon's wailing rise in pitch. Abigail winced at the sound, watching a scowl cross David's face.

"The king merely asks that your nurse calm the child or take him someplace else. The boy is making it impossible for the king to speak with his other wives." Hannah spoke loudly enough that the words carried to David and Abigail, who sat several cubits away near a spreading olive tree.

"Maybe the king needs to stop taking other wives and spend some decent time with the one who has given him an heir. His son doesn't even know him. He wouldn't wail so if he did."

Abigail's eyes went wide at the venomous words, words she'd never expected to hear from Ahinoam's lips. But words similar to those she had thought just the same. David did not seem impressed, and if his deepening scowl were any indication, he was close to losing his temper or leaving altogether.

Impulsively she placed a hand on his arm. "Please don't go, my lord."

He swung his gaze from Ahinoam to her, the lines around his eyes softening and his smile returning. "I'm not leaving, beloved. But the babe needs tending, and Ahinoam should learn to curb her tongue." He clapped his hands together. Benaiah hurried to his side.

David exchanged a look with Benaiah, and the guard nodded once, then moved toward Ahinoam. Moments later, Ahinoam's nurse took the still-wailing Amnon toward Ahinoam's apartment, and Benaiah held Ahinoam by the arm to escort her from the courtyard.

"No! He can't do this to me. He never calls for me, never gives me more than a few moments. He can't —"

"He can and he will, mistress. Now either you can leave quietly or I will forcibly remove you." Benaiah's deep voice carried across the court, sending a prickle of fear through Abigail. Was this how David had determined to handle his multiple wives — cow them into submission? Was there no recourse, no ability to confront his excesses, no chance to share the concerns of their hearts? Would he relegate them all to their rooms and forbid them to speak?

She looked at her husband, an unnamed fear working through her. Nabal had been controlling, cruel, mean-spirited, and abusive physically and emotionally. David had promised he would never hurt her, but wasn't he equally controlling and cruel in a different sort of way? What could possibly have made him think that a wife could subsist on only a few moments of his time and go quietly to her rooms so he could see the next wife?

A hollow feeling settled in her heart, and she wondered what fate awaited her and her child in this place. Would David grow impatient with his child's cries? Would he confine them to a place far from him?

"How are you feeling, beloved?" David's question snapped her thoughts to the present, bringing them into clearer focus. His smile was trained wholly on her. The irritation around his mouth and eyes was gone, and his attention was hers.

She drew in a breath, trying to block out what she had just witnessed. She forced herself to mask the apprehension and concern drawing her up short. "I am well, my lord. Thank you for asking. The child has drained less energy today."

He touched her arm, then his fingers traveled to the secret place where the child lay. "Does it move yet?" His look of wonder reminded her of a little boy, and she couldn't stop the amusement it sparked inside of her.

"Not yet. Though I have coaxed him often enough." She smiled, her longing for her husband rising again. Try as she might, she couldn't stop loving this man, even through the pain of sharing him.

"Perhaps if I try." He winked at her and moved his hand slowly in a circular motion over her middle, sending pinpricks of delight through her and raising her emotions to new heights. Something stirred inside her, the slightest flutter, the first sign of movement.

She placed her hand over his as she bent close to his ear. "I felt something." Was it simply joy and desire at his touch? Or did the babe recognize the tender love of his father? "There it is again!"

His hand stilled, as though waiting to feel it too, but the kick was too gentle, meant for her alone.

"In time I will share your joy," he said, moving his hand to her shoulder. He took her in his arms and kissed her. "I'm glad you're feeling better, my love." He touched a finger to her nose and backed away. "Rest well tonight. I will see you again tomorrow." With that, he stood, nodded his farewell, and moved across the court to where Maacah sat outside her rooms.

He would make the rounds, going from first wife to sixth, giving them all a few moments of his precious time — the only glimpse they would have of him. The rest of his day would be taken up with military strategy meetings with his mighty men, political discussions with his advisors, and interviews with men coming to seek judgment over one issue or another. His life was planned for him from the break of dawn to the setting sun. Even then, after his visit to the family courtyard when he had chosen a wife to join him in his chambers, the time was not his own but was devoted to pleasing whichever wife he had called. Some nights no one was summoned, though each one of them would spend hours grooming themselves in hopes of being picked.

She glanced across the court where Maacah sat in her seductive pose. She was unable to stop the knifelike pain that struck her as David laughed at something Maacah had said. Abigail looked away, wishing she could wipe the beguiling smile from the woman's haughty face. But as the moments ticked past, her curiosity would not allow her to ignore her husband, even if it meant seeing him interact with another wife. But when she saw David's hand moving in circles over Maacah's middle — the same intimate gesture he had shared with her, as if to awaken Maacah's child — she felt stung. The child of the spoiled princess of Geshur was not nearly far enough along for movement, which David should know from Ahinoam, if he was paying attention.

She stood, bile rising in the back of her throat as the moment of joy quickly shifted to pain. "Help me to bed, Rosah." She stumbled forward, a hand over her mouth, begging her roiling stomach to lie still until she could make it to the seclusion of her rooms.

"Are you all right, my lady?" Rosah gripped her arm and steadied her as the two hurried to cross the stones of the court into the safety of Abigail's chambers.

33

David smiled at Maacah, trying to remember why he had ever thought another wife would only complicate his life. This woman did add to his confusion at times, but she had a way about her and knew how to coax feelings from him that he didn't know existed. Sometimes she carried a dark side, a sense of humor that bordered on that of a man, but he found the distinction intriguing, and the rest of her was by no means masculine.

Sometimes her boldness made him pause, as it did now as she grasped his hand and placed it over her belly, where she claimed his child grew. If she spoke the truth, the child would be too small to feel. Hadn't it been only a few weeks since she had purified herself from her uncleanness, as he had made sure she knew to do when she joined his house? Foreign princess or not, his wife would keep the laws of Adonai. If Maacah carried his child, she could not have known for long.

He laughed as she moved his fingers beneath her palm in the same circular motion he had done with Abigail — of his own accord. Had she seen that exchange? He glanced to his left toward Abigail's rooms in time to see Abigail place a hand over her mouth and hurry from the courtyard. He gauged the distance between the two women. Each one could definitely see what the other did. The court was not big enough for privacy. The house was not big enough for six wives.

He looked back at Maacah, trying to focus on her words, but he couldn't get his mind off Abigail. Why had she rushed off like that? Was she ill again? The pregnancy had already caused her much distress. Would she lose the babe as she'd said her mother had often done? Would he lose Abigail in the process? He'd rarely lost a ewe in the throes of birth, but Abigail was not a sheep, and as much as he'd cared for his flock, he couldn't bear to lose a wife. Especially not that one.

"If you like, my lord, I have some sweet cakes filled with pistachios and honey that I made just for you, a recipe from my people. Come to my chambers and I will feed them to you." Maacah traced her finger along the

side of his face, coaxing him to look at her
again. "You are much distracted tonight,
David. Let me warm your bed and you will
have no more distractions." Her coy smile
made his blood rush quicker through his
body. Desire filled him as she moved both
hands to his face and slowly rubbed her
fingers along his temples, soothing him.

But he had three more wives to see, and
he should really check on Abigail to know
what had caused her sudden change in
mood. Though one look at Maacah, and he
could guess. Abigail did not approve of his
new wives and hated being one of six
instead of one of two. The knowledge always
carried with it a hint of guilt that she was
right, but she should know by now that a
king's life was not always his own. She
wanted peace as much as he did, and this
way was far more pleasant than going to
war. Then again . . .

He closed his eyes, momentarily accepting
Maacah's soothing ministrations, but concern over Abigail would not let him rest. He
looked into Maacah's dark, oriental eyes
and then put his hands over hers to still
their movement. He placed her hands in
her lap and bent to kiss her, then stood
quickly before she could protest. "I will see
you tomorrow," he said, suddenly hating

that he'd caused the hurt in her eyes. He moved on to Haggith before she could snag him again, fighting a growing sense of disillusionment.

The sun had faded to the west and the family courtyard was bathed in shadows when David finally bid Eglah goodnight and walked back toward Abigail's rooms. A sigh, deep and troubling, worked its way through him as he paused at Abigail's threshold. He needed her, truth be told. She didn't believe him when he said it, so he had stopped voicing the fact that he often wished he had married only her. Somehow that declaration only managed to distance them more, something he didn't understand. Why did she think that she was the only one troubled by his many wives? Ahinoam nearly always frustrated him, and Maacah did not bring out his best qualities. He never felt the oneness of spirit with either of them — with any of his wives — that he did with Abigail. Abigail shared his love for Yahweh, his devotion to what was true and right.

He nodded to Benaiah, who moved to position himself inside Abigail's small courtyard, near enough to guard and to be summoned. David knocked on the door. Though he told himself he had the right to enter unannounced, he didn't use it. He waited a moment, then knocked again. Hurried footsteps sounded on the other side of the door, and Abigail's young maid thrust it open out of breath.

She bowed low to the ground. "My lord the king! I . . . we . . . didn't expect you."

"Take me to your mistress." He was suddenly tired of the formalities that surrounded his kingship.

"Yes, my lord." She scrambled to her feet, her face flushed crimson, her large, dark eyes lit with excitement. "This way." He knew the way, of course, but he allowed the girl to lead him. When they reached the door to Abigail's chambers, he stopped.

"Leave us now."

The girl gave a slight bow and backed away from him. He pushed open the door and found Abigail sitting near the window, fabric stretched across her lap, her hands stitching a rhythmic pattern. Her face looked pale in the dim light, and her mouth was drawn into a tight line. She looked up as he entered, surprise filling her eyes.

"David . . . I . . . you're here." Her hands stilled, a look of bewilderment passing over her face. "I didn't expect you." She started to rise. "I should call Rosah, we should get you some wine or sweet cakes —"

He waved her suggestions away with his

hand as he closed the door and stepped into the room. "Don't trouble yourself, Abigail. I can summon the servants as well as you can. I saw you leave the courtyard. You looked ill." He knelt at her side. "Are you ill?" He placed a hand on her knee. "You had me worried."

Her face flushed as though he had embarrassed her, and she looked briefly away, then faced him again. She watched him for a moment as though trying to read his expression, then drew in a deep breath and slowly let it out. "All of a sudden, I didn't feel well. I was afraid I would be sick again, so I hurried here for privacy. I didn't want to disturb you, my lord."

She was speaking the truth, but not all of it. Her eyes told him there was more, but suddenly he didn't want to know the cause of her illness. She appeared to be fine now, which was what mattered. "The babe is all right then?"

"He seems to be fine." She smiled. "He knows his father's touch."

He returned her smile and stood. "Perhaps he should also get to know his father's voice." He walked to the door and summoned Rosah to tell Benaiah to fetch his writing utensils and his lyre. He returned to Abigail and sank onto a chair opposite her.

"A song has been forming in my mind." He stretched his legs out before him and crossed his ankles. "If you don't mind if I stay, I would like to share it with you."

Her eyes brightened, giving him an immense feeling of satisfaction. "I would like to hear it. Can you sing it to me?"

"Now?"

She nodded. "You can sing it again when they bring your lyre."

"The words are sketchy. I don't have them written yet."

"That doesn't matter. I want to hear it." She laid her stitching aside and folded her hands across her lap in a protective gesture, reminding him again of the babe.

He looked at her and smiled, then lifted his eyes to the window, toward the heavens.

"O Adonai, You have searched me and You know me. You know when I sit and when I rise. You perceive my thoughts from afar. You discern my going out and my lying down. You are familiar with all my ways. Before a word is on my tongue, You know it completely, O Adonai. You hem me in — behind and before; You have laid Your hand upon me. Such knowledge is too wonderful for me. Where can I go from Your Spirit? Where can I flee from Your presence? For You created my inmost being, You knit me together in my mother's womb. I praise You because I am fearfully and wonderfully made. Your works are wonderful, I know that full well."

David looked at her again. "It needs more," he said. "I couldn't stop thinking about the babe, and it made me think of how Adonai forms us in the secret place. Is it not wonderful, Abigail? I can only imagine what is going on inside of you right now."

Tears glistened in her eyes, stirring him. He came to her then, knowing that she needed him, probably more than he needed her.

"It's beautiful, David. Many generations will be encouraged by such words."

He pulled her to her feet, slowly enfolding her in his arms. "Come, let me love you, Abigail." He kissed her then, relieved when she responded in kind. His fears for her subsided. The babe would be fine. She would be well, and he would enjoy this night in peace.

34

"How is she?" David met Naamah, Abigail's mother, at the door to Abigail's rooms and had all he could do not to push his way past her to rush to his beloved's side. Abigail's screams and moans had lasted through the night — the second night of her travail — far longer than Ahinoam's had. He'd walked away more than once, tried to drown his concern in the camaraderie of his men, but all the masculine humor in the world couldn't remove the guilt he felt for being a man and making her go through this in the first place. "Tell me the travail has ended."

"And what good would it do to tell you a lie? Ach! You men are all alike. You want sons? Then you must put up with the burden of listening to the travail. Be grateful you aren't the one having to push your son into the world to see the light of day." Naamah raised her hands to her head, then flung them upward in exasperation. "Now go. You will only make her worry over you." She moved her hand toward his chest as if to push him away, then apparently thought better of it and moved to close the door on him instead.

He placed a hand on the door to stop her. "If you promise me she is all right, Mother, I will go." He couldn't bear to lose her or the babe.

Naamah's features softened and she patted his arm, but quickly tensed as another cry came from Abigail in the back room. Concern etched her features, spiking David's fear. "Tell me the truth, woman!" Every broken cry coming from his wife ripped another piece from his heart.

She shook her head. "You want the truth? The truth is her waters have broken, her labor is fierce, yet the babe will not come. I must go to her." She turned to go and he determined to follow, but she swiveled back to face him, this time apparently not caring that she touched him as she placed a hand on his chest. "Stay here. You will do her no good."

Abigail's maid Rosah met Naamah in the hall. "Come quickly." She glanced back at David, then spoke to Naamah. "How could you speak to him that way? He is the king!"

"He is the king — nonsense! He is a man,

and he wants to ease his guilt. He will just get in the way." The door to Abigail's room closed on Naamah's words.

David stood outside the room, listening to Abigail, his heart twisting with every cry. He knew better than to be here, had heard the advice to the contrary from his men and knew he ought to hop on his mule and ride into the hills until the ordeal was over. Even Judah, Abigail's father, had suggested the two of them do just that, but he couldn't bring himself to give in to the idea. Perhaps it was because this was Abigail, and other than Michal, he had never loved a woman quite like he loved her. But he suspected the real reason for his worries had to do with Abigail's illness and weakness during the pregnancy, something that had troubled him then and worried him now.

His hand reached for the latch but stopped cold at a scream that pierced like a dagger straight to his gut. Heart pounding, he whirled about and paced to the front of the house. With one last look back at the room where his wife strained to bring his child into the world, he walked to the seclusion of his rooms, got down on his knees, and prayed.

Sweat filled Abigail's face, and pain, so

fierce it took every effort she had to breathe, ripped through her body like a hundred knife blades.

"He's coming, Abigail, just a few more pushes and it will all be over." Her mother's voice had become her one constant these past two days when the pains first began, and she let them guide her, blindly believing everything would be all right.

When at last she felt a small window of ease, she drew in a deep breath and let it slowly out. Once more the urge to push overtook her.

"Bear down!"

Talya thrust a cloth between her teeth so she wouldn't chomp on her tongue. She pushed on Abigail's shoulders and rubbed her back to make the burden of giving birth somehow easier to bear.

"Harder, Abigail. I can see his head." Her mother's excited voice lifted her spirits, and joy mingled with fear as she summoned energy she didn't think she had to push through one more time.

A tearing, gushing sound filled her ears on the final push. "He's here! You have a son, Abigail!"

Relief flooded her, and she went limp against Talya, who was holding her upright on the birthing stool. The baby's soft whimpers filled the room as Abigail worked to expel the afterbirth. Her mother took the baby, and in one corner of the room Abigail could see her clean the child and rub him with salt, while the midwife and Talya cleaned her up and dressed her in a fresh gown. When she was at last settled in her bed, her mother brought the baby to her to nurse.

Abigail inspected the child from head to toe, awed by his perfect little body. His eyes were like hers, but his mouth and nose were David's.

"He's beautiful," her mother said, planting a kiss on the baby's soft head. "His father is anxious to see him, I am sure."

"He's perfect." Abigail stroked the baby's cheek and guided his mewing mouth to her breast. "His father has perfected him." She smiled, remembering the way David's touch had made the child move, and how his words had stirred her heart. "David will be pleased." She made a poor attempt to stifle a yawn.

"David needs to be told. The man has been here at least three times since your travail began, and the last time I had to practically shove him away. By now his guilt is great."

"His guilt, Mama?" She jerked as the babe

latched on to nurse, surprised at the strength of his pull.

"All men feel guilt at what we have to go through to give them sons. It's God's way of humbling them — though it never lasts." Her mother's rueful chuckle made her smile, even as exhaustion overtook her. She couldn't imagine David feeling guilty over the pleasure that led to pregnancy. If he did, he wouldn't want to put so many women through such a thing . . . unless he thought to spare them by allowing them go through it only once.

The thought troubled her, though she would readily admit she did not want to go through such an episode of giving birth again, not as it had been with this child. She studied him, drinking in the sight of his small body — was he smaller than most babies? For as much trouble as he had been to come, she expected him to be bigger.

"What will you name him?" Talya asked, interrupting her musing. "Daniel would be proud of you, Abigail."

Abigail pulled her gaze from her infant son to look at her sister-in-law. "Two names — Chileab, whom the father has perfected, and Daniel." She smiled at Talya's look of tender pride, then turned back to Chileab.

"Rest now, Abigail." Her mother's voice

grew distant as she fought to stay awake, but she was losing the battle. "While you sleep, I will take the child to his father." Her mother's hand reached for the baby, but Abigail roused at her words and clutched the child closer.

"Bring his father to him." She wanted to see David's reaction to the gift of her son. In the meantime, she closed her eyes and drifted off to sleep.

David stood at the window in his chamber looking out over Hebron's bustling city, wondering not for the first time if Abigail's child ever meant to be born.

Adonai, please be with her and the child. Have mercy on them.

This whole pregnancy had been hard on her, reminding him of some difficult births with his lambs, a rare few ending in the deaths of both mother and offspring. If Abigail did live through this, he wasn't sure he could put her through it again. He had other wives who could bear him children. And as much as he would prefer they share Abigail's blood, he would rather have her at his side than lose her through childbirth.

He glanced toward the distant hills, then let his gaze travel to the cloud-studded blue sky. Adonai had blessed him repeatedly since Saul's death, despite the long war that had ensued between the tribes of Israel and Judah. But that didn't mean he was now immune to grief — Asahel and Abigail's brother Daniel being two examples. There was no reason for God to preserve each of his wives or the children they might bear him, except for His own great mercy.

A merchant caravan made its way through Hebron's winding streets to the marketplace. The heat of summer was fast approaching, and what little breeze did manage to fan the otherwise still air came most easily through this window. It lifted the hairs on his arms now and cooled his damp brow.

A knock on the door behind him made him tune his ear to listen as a servant went to answer.

"I must speak a word with the king, if I may." David recognized the voice of Abigail's mother and whirled around, not waiting for the servant to respond. His long strides carried him quickly to the door.

"How is she?" He should have donned his royal robe again, but at this moment he didn't care what the woman thought of him. "The child?"

"You have a son, my lord." Naamah bowed her head in an act of respect, then straightened, placing a hand on her back as though the act of standing upright caused her pain. Exhaustion lined her features. "He is small, but well."

"Where is he?" Every child was brought to its father at birth so the man could bless the child on his knees. "Why have you not brought him to me?" He almost flinched at the flash of irritation in Naamah's eyes, until he remembered that he had a right to some demands of his own. This woman seemed to enjoy forgetting that he was the king. "Bring him to me at once." He dismissed her with a wave and whirled about to change into his royal attire.

"If it please you, my lord . . ."

David paused and turned back at Naamah's persistence.

"Abigail asked that you come to her. After such a long ordeal, she is beyond exhaustion and surely not thinking clearly, my lord, but she would not allow me to take the child from her." Naamah's flushed face told him that she did indeed realize that he had a right to expect proper tradition to be upheld, but her whole body sagged as she stood before him. She'd been working for two days straight and looked like she might fall into a heap at any moment.

"Why didn't you send a servant to tell me this? You are worn out, Naamah. Go home to your husband." He summoned Benaiah, ever present in the halls outside his rooms, to have someone escort Naamah home.

"Forgive my Abigail, my lord. She —"

David touched Naamah's shoulder. "I forgive her, Mother. I will still bless my son on my knees. Now go. Rest." He nodded to Benaiah, then turned back to finish dressing.

Summoning his advisors and mighty men, he led them to Abigail's courtyard to wait while he returned with the child. After he secured him from Abigail's arms.

David stopped short of touching Abigail as he gazed down at her sleeping form. The lines he had seen far too often along her brow in recent days had softened. Her mouth tilted upward in a slight smile, and a look of peace covered her beautiful face. Her dark, auburn-tinged hair lay in curled tendrils over her shoulders to the middle of her back, a few strands lying gently over the babe's small body. The scene made his heart twist with longing and pride, and he wanted nothing more than to pull them both into his arms and cradle them there.

His Abigail was like one of the lambs he used to carry across his shoulders after an injury — a woman who had endured so much, who deserved to feel secure and at peace. He could give her that. He could keep her close to him, raise her to the status of queen, declare her son heir to his throne. She would never need to bear another child after this, never need to endure the suffering he had put her through to bring forth the tiny cherub she held close to her now.

"David?" Her eyes fluttered open, and he smiled at her.

"I'm here, beloved. May I see our son?" He didn't move to touch her due to her uncleanness, but nodded to a servant to retrieve the child for him. When the girl moved to Abigail's side, David held up a hand for her to wait. He wanted Abigail to release the boy to him, not take him forcibly from her.

Abigail scooted to sit up on the bed, lifting the child into her arms. She looked down at the boy and caressed his cheek, then met David's gaze and offered the boy toward him. David glanced at the servant who stood waiting for his word, but he changed his mind and waved her away, stepping closer to take the boy from Abigail's own hands.

Their fingers touched as she released him, her look open and vulnerable as though she were entrusting him with her most precious possession. A hint of longing surfaced in him that she should feel the same way about him, but he squelched the thought as the epitome of selfishness.

"Be careful with him, my lord," she said, her voice low and tremulous.

Did she think him incompetent? But of course, she was just feeling protective. He pulled the baby close to his heart as he'd done so often with a young lamb. The child stirred and stretched, his eyes closed in sleep, his mouth tipped at the corners as though he alone were privy to a sweet secret. David couldn't stop a smile of his own as he bent to kiss the child's soft head.

He lifted his face to look once again at his wife, so weak and pale among the cushions. "How are you feeling?"

"As though all energy has bled from my limbs." She met his gaze, but only for the briefest moment before her eyes moved to the child in his arms. "He was worth it, though."

The child felt so light compared to a lamb, a mere wisp compared to Ahinoam's son. "What will you call him?"

She shifted her gaze to meet his again. "Two names, my lord. Chileab — he is perfect because of you — and Daniel after my brother." She paused, seeming to think about it. "If you approve, of course."

He nodded. "I approve." She could have picked one and waited to name a second son after her brother. Or was she suggesting that she would not care to go through this again, as he had anticipated? He could give her that freedom, but he would surely miss the closeness they shared and the intimacy of the marriage bed. Still, there were his other wives to consider, and it didn't mean he couldn't share himself with her in other ways.

If he were to groom Chileab to succeed him . . . The thought gave him pause, and he looked down into the small face. The boy had lifted a hand to his mouth and quietly sucked on his fist. Chileab was not a king's name, though Daniel was. He rallied to the idea as he glanced again at Abigail. "He will want to eat soon. My men are waiting in the courtyard. Let me take him to them to bless him on my knee."

She nodded, joy lighting her eyes. "Thank you, my lord. And he will be blessed to have you as his father."

Her words bolstered his sense of pride, and he took the child and walked to the door. "I'll be back soon," he said over his shoulder, then turned and made his way to the courtyard to bless his son.

■ ■ ■ ■

PART V

■ ■ ■ ■

Sons were born to David in Hebron: His firstborn was Amnon by Ahinoam the Jezreelitess; his second, Chileab, by Abigail the widow of Nabal the Carmelite; the third, Absalom the son of Maacah, the daughter of Talmai, king of Geshur; the fourth, Adonijah the son of Haggith; the fifth, Shephatiah the son of Abital; and the sixth, Ithream, by David's wife Eglah. These were born to David in Hebron.

2 Samuel 3:2–5 NKJV

These were the sons of David born to him in Hebron: The firstborn was Amnon the

son of Ahinoam of Jezreel; the second,
Daniel the son of Abigail of Carmel.

1 Chronicles 3:1

35

Hebron's streets overflowed with traffic — merchant carts pulled by donkeys and camels heavy laden with dangling wares, leading caravans from far-off places. Abigail and her mother with five-year-old Chileab between them followed David's guards, female servants, and other wives into the marketplace, awed by the sights and sounds. The women were rarely given such an opportunity, and the excitement coming from David's other wives and children had managed to heighten Abigail's as well.

During five of the seven years of David's reign in Hebron, civil war had been nearly constant and at times fierce. Despite Hebron's relative safety, David had continually refused to allow his wives freedom to roam about the city for fear of kidnapping or harm done by enemy forces. Even when Abigail had asked him about his policy — after being coaxed to do so by the other women — she sensed his closed attitude. The kidnapping in Ziklag held too strong a hold in his memory, and nothing she said had managed to reassure him, despite Hebron's guards and walls.

But rumor had it that Abner had finally come to his senses and had sent word of reconciliation to David. Michal was somehow part of the bargaining price, and the women's quarters had been abuzz for weeks about her return.

Abigail took in the smells and sounds of colorful wares in the marketplace around her, wondering if the weightier, wealthier items hadn't been brought in because of Michal. It was no secret that David still yearned for his first wife, Saul's daughter. The rooms he had built for her, the private gardens . . . He had spared no expense creating a place that outshone the apartments of his other wives.

The thought brought the familiar twinge of jealousy to Abigail's heart. She squeezed Chileab's hand tighter, pulling him close as they wove in and around the merchant tables. David had hinted at making Abigail his queen, at declaring Chileab to be his rightful heir once he took the throne of all Israel. Michal and Ahinoam would surely balk at such a thing, but Michal had no heir, and Ahinoam's son Amnon was not David's first choice.

Abigail captured Chileab's small but sturdy frame with one look, her heart swelling with pride. He was beautiful, the image of his father in so many ways, though his hair curled more than David's soft waves, and its color was a lighter brown. His early love of music and nature gave him a common bond with his father, and the two had already become close.

When David came to visit, he spent more time with Chileab than he did with her, often finding excuses to leave before the night was over. If he did share her bed, he did so without the intimacy she longed for.

Did he find her so repulsive? Why had he shut her out in this way?

"Abigail, look! These fabrics are as fine as beaten papyrus, only soft as fine linen — softer, in fact. They would make an excellent princely robe for Chileab — even the king might appreciate something of this quality. The colors, particularly the purple, are regal." Her mother chattered on, moving to some colored beads and bronze headpieces, oohing and aahing like one of the young maids.

Abigail stepped out of the wide road and ducked into the booth with the unusual fabric. She fingered a large swatch, imagining what a fine robe she could fashion for her son. "May I?" She looked at the merchant, a man with graying hair, heavy jowls, and a middle that showed he loved food more than manual labor.

"Of course, of course. Here, let me help you with that. What you have here is of the finest quality. Fabric fit for a king." He looked down at Chileab. "Or a prince, of course." The man smiled, revealing a gap between his stained front teeth. "Shall I wrap it up for you?"

Abigail released Chileab's hand and allowed the man to drape the fabric over her outstretched arms. The shimmering purple shone in the early morning light, and the softness felt like a gentle caress. David would appreciate such finery.

Her mother came up beside her, while Chileab stood close by where Abigail could keep him in sight. She had no doubt he would obey her instructions not to wander among the stalls. He was as curious as any other five-year-old, but shy enough to prefer her company to that of strangers. Soon enough she would have to give him into Jehiel's care, the man David had commissioned to teach and guide his sons, as he had already begun to do with Amnon. But

Chileab was nearly two years younger than Amnon, and Abigail meant to keep him close as long as possible.

She turned her attention back to the fabric and the merchant. After haggling over the price, she purchased enough cloth to outfit both David and Chileab in royal finery. She glanced at her mother, who had moved farther down the row. Chileab had edged closer to the road, watching a bird flit in and around a donkey and cart. He bent low to look under the cart.

"Be careful, Chileab. Don't get too close."

He looked up at her and smiled, a smile so similar to his father's it made her heart ache for David. He squatted again to peer beneath the cart, and Abigail turned to accept the package from the man. She would keep this one herself rather than entrust it to Rosah. Where was that girl, anyway? She was usually close by, but this was her first visit to this market, so Abigail had allowed her to do a little of her own shopping.

She stepped toward the road to collect Chileab and search the other stalls for Rosah but stopped short. Where was Chileab? She looked at the wooden cart parked to the side of the stall where he had just been. He wouldn't wander off, so where was he?

"Chileab?" She called his name. No answer. "Chileab!" Louder this time.

She heard his young voice as though from a distance. "Over here, Mama."

Her mother's head appeared on the other side of the cart, closer to the middle of the road. She bent low, disappearing from Abigail's view. Noises grew louder around her, and Abigail turned at the sound of horses and chariot wheels turning over the cobbled stones of the road, coming toward them. David's standard flew from the chariot's back pole, and David rode behind the driver, decked out in kingly fare. Was he come to seek out a particular merchant? Guards on horseback flocked him before and behind like a small military parade.

A squeaking noise like that of a turning wheel pierced the air, closer than David's chariot. A child's high-pitched, pitiful wail cut straight to Abigail's heart. The next moment blurred before her eyes, and the world seemed to tilt and move slower than normal. She felt her legs propelling her forward toward the child's cries, heard the crunch, saw the cart move. Her mother's frantic screams jerked her out of the sudden fog that had enveloped her. The cart moved again. Another horrifying scream. A sickening thud.

Abigail's knees buckled as she reached the

cart and saw her son and her mother wedged beneath it. She scrambled forward, dropped the package, and flung herself toward her son, screaming for help. The merchant had stopped the donkey's movements, and shouts other than her own filled the air around her.

"Chileab, can you hear me?" The child's pitiful cries grew fainter, and Abigail realized to her horror that she couldn't pull him from beneath the wheels. Horses came to a halt nearby, and suddenly David's guards surrounded the area.

She drew in a shallow breath and pulled back from peering under the cart. Her son and her mother lay so still she was certain they were both dead. Her limbs grew cold and she pulled her knees to her chest, rocking back and forth, weeping Chileab's name. Her teeth rattled from the shaking that overtook her, a trembling so fierce she could not stop it.

Strong arms came around her — whose, she couldn't tell, until she felt herself being lifted into a chariot and covered with a blanket. David's voice floated to her from somewhere high above.

"Stay with me, Abigail." He stroked her face, smearing her tears. She was crying? "Don't leave me, beloved."

His soothing voice awakened a small piece of her spirit. She looked at him and swallowed hard. A servant handed her a chalice of wine from somewhere, probably from another one of the merchants, and she sipped it obediently. "Chileab."

"The men are bringing him to you now."

"He's alive?" She wasn't sure how she managed the words past the grit on her tongue.

David gripped her hand and nodded. "He's alive. We'll have you home in a heartbeat."

Dare she believe him? But a moment later Benaiah walked toward her cradling Chileab and laid him in Abigail's waiting arms. His eyes were closed, but she could tell by the slow rise and fall of his chest that he was breathing. Yet his left arm was sorely misshapen, having been crushed beneath the wheel of the cart. A little cry escaped before she could stop it. She looked at David, who had obviously seen the damaged limb. She tried to interpret his reaction, but his face was unreadable.

He hopped onto the cart and ordered his driver to take them home.

"Mama! What of Mama, David?" Sudden fear snaked through her as she remembered her mother's still form.

"The men will bring her. There is no more room here." He rose to stand behind his driver, leaving her settled on the floor of the chariot, cradling their son.

Abigail sat at Chileab's side, unwilling to leave despite the physician's protests. She stroked her son's forehead while the man gave him something strong to drink to help with the pain, then worked as best he could to straighten the broken bones. But after hours of careful work, there was little that could be done. Chileab's arm would never be whole again, its shape unnaturally grotesque.

The news distressed her, not because she cared whether Chileab followed his father as king but because she feared — no, she knew — deep in her heart that this would change David's view of their son. Would he spend less time with them now, unwilling to see the child without looking on her with blame? If she had kept him with her, never let go of his hand, none of this would have happened. And Mama wouldn't be fighting for her life in the next room.

Her mother's injuries shouldn't have been life-threatening, but when she'd tried to free Chileab's arm from the cart's wheel, her own hand had been crushed. The pain and cut of the wound had become inflamed, and now her whole body had been claimed by a fever that left her delirious.

Chileab stirred in the bed beside her. Abigail rose and knelt over him, feeling his cheeks for any sign of the fever that was claiming her mother. Rosah appeared in the doorway, looking weary and troubled.

"Get me water and a cool cloth," Abigail said. "He seems to be fine, but let me bathe his face just the same."

The girl nodded and hurried away. Abigail turned back to her son, tears filling her eyes. "I'm so sorry, Chileab. Your mama should have watched over you better. Whatever made you go under that cart?" She whispered the words, not wanting to wake him, but the herbs had put him to sleep hours before, so he was unlikely to hear her or rise to consciousness.

Rosah appeared moments later with the supplies. "I can do that for you, my lady."

"No, I want to." She took the cloth and dunked it in the cool water, then squeezed out the excess and carefully placed it over Chileab's cheeks, gently stroking his soft skin. After she was satisfied that he did not possess a fever, she wrung the cloth out into the bowl and spread it to dry over a peg hanging on the wall. She tiptoed out of the room and retreated to her sitting room, startled to find David waiting for her on her couch, dressed in full regal garb.

"How is he?" His dark eyes assessed her but revealed nothing. She desperately needed his concern, his loving embrace, his forgiveness.

"He sleeps from the herbs and wine mixture the physician gave him. But he is not feverish like Mama." She watched him closely, debating whether to sit opposite him or next to him. She wanted him to welcome her again but feared he never would. Did he blame her for all of this?

Well, why not? She was guilty enough.

He held out a package to her. "My men found this near the accident. The merchant said you had purchased it."

The fabric for the robes she had planned to make for David and Chileab. Kingly robes for the king and his heir. She took the canvas wrappings from his hands and set it in a basket on the floor. They would have little use of it now.

"Thank you." She straightened and smoothed her robe, avoiding his gaze.

He leaned against the couch, legs stretched out before him, studying her. Was he judging her as her king or assessing her needs as a husband might do? *If* a husband took the time and cared.

"Come here, Abigail." His command held little warmth, and she almost felt like a child about to be reprimanded. The tone reminded her briefly of Nabal, and the thought made her pause, her feet suddenly unwilling or unable to move her forward.

"Why?" Her voice sounded weak and afraid even to her own ears, and she saw in him the warrior she had once appeased. She fell to her face before him, unable to stop the chill working through her. Would he cast her out? Would he find her unfit to be wife to the king because she did not keep better watch over his special son?

She heard him shift his position on the couch. Silence fell between them until she felt his touch on her head. "Come here," he said again, his voice less gruff this time, "because I asked you to."

She rose to her knees and forced her wobbly legs to stand. She stood before him, clasped her hands in front of her, and bowed her head, unable to look him in the eye. He must think her the worst of fools. He had already spent years denying her the right to share his bed — for reasons she could only surmise — and now, after what she had done . . .

"Sit beside me, Abigail." He reached for

438

her hand and pulled her next to him.

She sat stiff, fearful of him. "I'm sorry, my lord. I should have watched over him better. I'm a terrible mother. I don't know how he got away from me —"

He held a hand to her lips. "Shhh . . . you are not a terrible mother, beloved. It was an accident. There was nothing you could have done." He took her face in his hands, and for the first time since the accident, she read compassion in his gaze. "I forgive you, Abigail. And we can be grateful that Adonai spared him. He will never be the same, no, and he will never be king, but he will live and grow up and love and give us grandchildren." He brushed his thumb along her cheek, then bent to kiss her. "He will be all right."

"You're not angry with me?"

He regarded her for a moment. "I'm angry and I'm grieved, but not at you, Abigail. Not at you."

"At Chileab then? He's just a boy, David, and he was probably chasing some fool bird. You know how he is with watching things — he gets so caught up." She choked on a sob. "Please don't hold it against your son, my lord."

He silenced her again with a finger to her lips. "I'm not angry at Chileab. He is too young to know better. Nor am I angry at your mother or your servant. The donkey has been hamstrung and the merchant's cart destroyed. I no longer allow merchants to keep carts beside their stalls." He ran a hand over the back of his neck. "I do not pretend to understand why Adonai allowed such a thing. Surely He could have stopped it from happening."

So he was angry at the merchant, but in a deeper sense was he also angry at God? But that would be foolish. Adonai might have been able to stop it, but He didn't.

"Perhaps I have sinned," she said, begging God in silence to forgive her yet again. "Perhaps if we offered Him a sacrifice . . . We mustn't hold it against Adonai, my lord. We deserve nothing from Him. We can only beg for His mercy." She looked at him, praying she had not offended him with her gentle reprimand. Someday he would grow weary of her wisdom if she wasn't careful.

His hands rested on her shoulders, his look thoughtful. "We will ask Abiathar to offer a sacrifice on your behalf."

She nodded and lowered her gaze. So he believed the sin was hers alone. But what of the way he had kept himself from her? Did Adonai approve of a husband keeping himself from a wife? It had been so long since he had kissed her or loved her the way she longed for him to do. She lifted her face to his, knowing she could not keep her longing for him hidden from her eyes.

He caressed her cheek with one hand, his look filling her with hope. She wrapped her hands around his neck and looked into those fathomless eyes, begging him to fulfill her desire. Dare she speak of it?

"I need you, David. Please love me as you used to."

A soft wince crossed his handsome face at her words, as though the very thought would be his undoing. Before he could deny her, she reached up to kiss him, a slow, lingering kiss. How she needed his companionship right now. What was it about grief that made a person long for intimacy? She didn't know, but she thrilled the moment she felt him deepen the kiss and respond to her in kind.

An internal battle waged in David's mind, common sense warring with desire. He'd avoided Abigail's bed to protect her, to keep from putting her through the agony of childbirth again. Yet here she was, still young and beautiful and arousing his own need of her. If Yahweh saw fit to give her another son, the boy would never usurp his older brother's rights to inherit his throne. And suppose Abigail was right? If her sin had caused Chileab's accident, what might happen to the next child born to them? What sin had she committed to cause Yahweh to allow such a thing?

He knew that sometimes Adonai visited the sins of the fathers to the third and fourth generation. But that curse was for the unrighteous. Surely Abigail was righteous. Hadn't they both done their best to keep Adonai's laws?

Guilt pricked his conscience even as his flesh yearned for her. He too had broken Adonai's laws, if he were truly honest with himself. What man could stand righteous before the Most High? He had accepted more horses and wives and gold than a king ought to, and he was certain his thoughts were not nearly perfect, as God was perfect. Even allowing Abigail to shoulder the blame and accept his judgment of her proved his own self-righteousness. They both were guilty before the Almighty.

The thought sobered him.

He drew back from kissing her to look into her soulful eyes. Her longing for him was more evident than he'd ever seen in her. It would be a risk to love her as she asked, a risk for her health and, if anything should happen to her, a risk for his heart.

She leaned closer, her sweet breath mingling with his until she tasted his lips again and he could not pull away. A soft groan escaped him — the war was surely lost. Scooping her into his arms, he carried her to her room and shut the door.

36

Abigail woke with a start long before dawn, her breath coming fast and sweat slithering down the middle of her back. It hadn't been a dream, had it? No, the fear had been something tangible, something so real it had stolen her breath. She rolled over on her bed and swung her legs to the cool tiles, padding softly to Chileab's room. The child had recovered from the injury remarkably well, though his left arm would never be whole. It was useless where it hung from his elbow to his hand.

She tiptoed to stand over him, looking down on his cherub face draped in moon-light. His look of peace made her heart yearn for such innocence, such ability to block the trauma and tragedy of life from her mind. On the days when she did not dwell on the things that tormented her, she found them pushing their way to the surface at night, when she was defenseless to stop them.

Oh, Adonai, why?

It was a question she felt unworthy to ask and yet at the same time longed to know. Why had her father felt so weak that his only solution to his own problems was to give her to Nabal in marriage? Why had Nabal treated her with such cruelty? Why had David lost faith in Yahweh and taken them to seek refuge among their enemies, leaving them vulnerable to the kidnapping that surely could have been avoided if he'd stayed in Israel? Why had David taken so many new wives after becoming king, and why had he brought back Michal to make their lives even more miserable?

Why did Daniel and Mama have to die?

The last thought brought the bitter surge of bile to her throat. She shoved a fist to her mouth to stifle a sob that would surely awaken Chileab and hurried from the room. Her mother's death after the accident had been the worst. The fever had never abated after her hand had been crushed beneath the wagon. She'd died a week later, leaving Abba distraught and inconsolable.

Why, Adonai?

She wanted desperately to understand. And no matter how hard she tried to tell herself otherwise, she could not stop blaming herself. If she had never taken Chileab that day or had never let go of his hand, Mama would still be alive. Abba, David, Talya — they all blamed her, though they never said so to her face. She knew it deep inside, where her guilt lived.

The night was still except for her heavy breathing, and she held a hand to her chest as she clung to the walls to keep from falling. She eased her way back to her room, but the bed mocked her with its promise of peaceful sleep. The only peace she'd felt since the accident was the night David had stayed with her and had given in to her charms. He'd been conspicuously absent since, and Abigail couldn't help but wonder if he would ever return. He had his precious Michal back now, and if Adonai chose to smile on them, Michal would soon bear him a child who would be the obvious, rightful heir to David's throne — a mix of kingdoms, Saul's and David's. Even the favorite Absalom would lose out over any child Michal might bear.

Abigail shivered, suddenly aware of the chill that still marked these spring nights. She fell to her knees before the edge of the raised bed and buried her face in her hands. Where had so much bitterness come from?

Why was she so angry?

David's handsome face floated before her closed eyes, and she couldn't stop the ache that filled her. Every thought of him touched a chord of such longing it took her breath. He'd been everything she dreamed of those long ago days of her girlhood when she imagined herself mistress of her own household. Handsome, noble, strong yet gentle, proud yet humble, a leader men would die for, a shepherd who would die for them, a warrior, a poet, a lover, a king. Perhaps "everything" was more than she'd bargained for.

Her throat constricted with unshed tears, and she knew she would not sleep any more this night. It was wrong for her to stay bitter. She would hurt not only herself but Chileab as well. She couldn't let her son see the ugly sorrow within her heart. She didn't want to turn him against his father, considering the few moments his father managed to spend with him these days.

But God forgive her, she could not rid herself of the pain David had inflicted and kept inflicting on her every time he took another woman to wife, every time he brushed her lips with a chaste kiss and moved on to visit a rival, every time he favored one of the other women or their children above her. Sometimes, if the truth were known, she wished she had died in Mama's place.

A groan escaped her suddenly parched lips as she crawled into her bed and rolled onto her back to stare at the ceiling above her head. Something must be done. She could not continue to live as she was. She was still young and capable and could do much good if she put her mind to it. She must. For Chileab's sake.

She would consider how to handle David's attention in the future — whether to look for a way to accept her lot or find a way to change her status in his eyes, she didn't know. Or perhaps the better choice might be to seek distance from it all, to beg permission to live away from the women's quarters, from the intrigue that moved in every corner, from the bickering and gossip and the constant sharing of him. If she could have her own home away from here with Chileab, perhaps her father and Talya could join her . . . Excitement began to build in her as she contemplated the thought of escape from this place, from the turmoil that robbed her of joy and peace.

She placed her hands behind her head and glanced toward the shuttered window. Darkness still blanketed the earth, but the slightest hint of dawn's pale light seeped in along the edges. She drew in a breath and slowly released it, her heart calming as she did so. Later today she would formulate a plan to seek an audience with David and lay her ideas before him. If everything went as she hoped, she might actually work out a situation that would satisfy them both.

Abigail followed David's flag bearers and trumpeters to the threshold of his audience chamber. Michal and Ahinoam moved ahead of her while Maacah, Haggith, Abital, and Eglah trailed close behind. The trumpet sounded, announcing their presence, and Abigail's heart skipped a beat as she took her place to the right of David's gilded throne.

Ahinoam leaned toward Abigail's ear, a hand over her mouth. "I suppose our lord will name Michal his queen today. Though I don't see how she can be queen when they have no heir."

Abigail glanced at David's first wife, noting the woman's straight back and the proud tilt of her chin. Her mouth held a grim line, and her dark eyes held the telltale signs of grief.

"You would think she'd be happy on this of all days," Ahinoam added, her tone low but laced with the hint of bitterness Abigail had grown accustomed to. Somehow Ahinoam didn't seem to notice her own unhappiness.

"You can hardly blame her for grieving after losing her brother," Abigail whispered back, darting another glance at Michal, knowing all too well the pain of a brother's loss. "Rumor has it David isn't planning to pick a queen today anyway."

The trumpet sounded again, cutting off further words. Abigail turned her attention to the wide oak doors where the young princes were ushered into the audience chamber, each one guided by his personal attendant. Her heart swelled with motherly pride at the sight of Chileab dressed in blue and green stripes, the color of princes. The sleeves of the garment concealed his withered arm, the evidence that he would never be heir to the throne his father was about to ascend. But none of that mattered today. David's coronation as king over all Israel overshadowed everything, though the desire to speak of her plan with him had not waned.

The buzz of excited voices drifted through the open windows from the outer courtyard, adding to the mix of bodies pressed in close within the audience chamber, sweat and the sweet scent of incense faint in the stifling summer heat. Servants stood behind the women and children, wielding palm branches, while musicians picked up a stately tune. Trumpets sounded again, longer this time, and all heads turned to the grand oak doors.

David, dressed head to toe in regal attire, strode into the room behind his flag bearers and bodyguards into the open area of the court, his presence commanding. The crowd cheered as David strode to where the priests Zadok and Abiathar stood. An alabaster flask of cinnamon-scented oil was in Zadok's hand. Several paces away near the front of the court, roped off to keep people from defiling the place, a new altar stood. Seven bleating rams waited nearby, and Abigail's heart squeezed at their pitiful cries.

The trumpets ceased, and as Zadok raised his hands, an awed hush fell over the crowd. He looked up to face the people, a mass of men and women that extended from David's court to the front gate of the king's house, into the streets, onto the rooftops, and as far as Abigail could see.

"Hear the word of the Lord," Zadok cried, arms still lifted toward the heavens. His white garments glistened in the morning sun, and a smile poked from beneath his dark brown beard. He was a solemn man, short yet strong, and a recent addition to David's household. His dark eyes were alight with joy. But then, when had there ever been such a joyous day in Israel?

"When you come to the land Adonai your God is giving you, and possess it and dwell in it, and say, 'I will set a king over me like all the nations that are around me . . .' "

Abigail looked at David, wondering what he was thinking. She was only able to see him from the side, but his solemn look struck her as undeniably humble in the face of such grandeur, and his sense of awe made her wish once again that he belonged only to her. How easy it was to love him!

When the speech ended, David knelt before the priest, head bowed. Zadok lifted the oil and poured it over David's head until it dripped into his beard and onto the collar of his robe. A smile crossed his handsome face until the trumpet sounded again and the people shouted, "Long live King David!"

Abigail cut a glance from David to Chileab, her heart yearning for husband and son. What she wouldn't give to wrap them both in her arms right now, even as her own voice lifted with the crowd, praising the king.

David stood and raised his hands to silence the crowd. "Your throne, O God, will last forever and ever. A scepter of justice will be the scepter of Your kingdom." His gaze slid heavenward, then with a look of utter joy and compassion, he turned in a circle to encompass all those in attendance. "Establish Your servant, O Lord, over Your people, to rule in righteousness and justice."

He looked then to Zadok and Abiathar and nodded. The priests led the way to the altar where the seven rams waited. David placed his hand on one young bull to offer as a sin offering, symbolizing his need of forgiveness. David bowed his head again as Zadok prayed then slit the bull's throat. Abiathar caught the blood and sprinkled it on the altar, then the bull's flesh was placed there to burn as an offering to Yahweh.

Tears pricked Abigail's eyes as the rest of the sin and fellowship offerings were presented to the Lord. It had been so long — years, in fact — since all of the people had been led to obey the laws of Adonai. Too long since she had made atonement for her own sins.

The bitterness she tried so often to suppress toward David rushed to the surface of her thoughts. Seeing him now, humble and bowed before his God, she felt her heart constrict. David would make a good king, a great king. He was not a perfect man, but he knew how to repent with a contrite heart.

Did she? How long had she already harbored such resentment?

She glanced at her sister wives, feeling a check in her spirit. Ahinoam had been David's only wife when Abigail came to him after Nabal's death. If she had refused to marry David, would he have found it so easy to take a fourth and a fifth and a sixth and a seventh wife? She was the one who had made him into a husband with two wives, for who could count Michal at that point? Even David had never expected to get her back. Had he?

Tension knotted her shoulders, her thoughts accusing her. *You knew better.* The other women had come to David at their fathers' behest, whereas she had come of her own accord, knowing he already had a wife, knowing she would be the one to open the door to more women in the future. Sweat drew a line along her brow, and her cheeks flushed with warmth coming not from the sun's oppressive heat but from the shame deep within.

A trumpet blared, announcing the end of the sacrifices. More speeches followed as David ascended the throne prepared for him and the men of Israel bowed at his feet to pledge their allegiance.

Abigail's head spun as she tried to focus on the things her heart told her were true. All of her jealousies, all of her bitter resentment toward David's other wives — they were her own doing. If she had restrained her own desire, her own desperate need for love, had not given in to his lure and charm . . . She could have refused to marry him. Instead, she had made it all the easier for him to take more women to wife. And she had done so without thought of the consequence.

O Adonai, please forgive me.

Remorse clung to her, an unwashed stain upon her heart. She longed to undo the past, to fix what she could no longer touch, to return to better days.

Voices of men praising the king drowned out the voices of reason in her head. Chileab's quiet cry snapped her thoughts back to her surroundings.

"Stop pushing me." Chileab's gaze rested on his younger brother Absalom, who had managed to wedge his way between Chileab and Amnon.

"It's my turn. I want to see Abba." Absalom's confident insistence, as though the place between his older brothers was rightfully his, mimicked his arrogant mother's overconfidence too well.

Abigail took a step forward, wishing for an excuse to distract her tumultuous thoughts. She intended to pull Chileab away from his brothers and escape the hot room and noisy crowd, but the children's maids got to them first and hurried them from the audience chamber. Defeat settled over her. She closed her eyes, willing it away, and searched for the good of the moment, the joy that was evident all around her.

It would be rude to leave, and she didn't dare anger David on such a day. Still, she was more determined than ever to leave the oppression and intrigue of the king's household, to live away from the gossiping, grasping women who vied for his attention. She would give him one less wife to trouble himself with. If he would allow it, she would simply take Chileab and go to live with her father and Talya and Micah. He might even enjoy having a place to come to, away from the trappings of royalty — a place of peace.

She drew in a breath and let it slowly release. The royal entourage finally moved from the audience chamber, and Abigail followed the guards to the banquet hall. If she could catch David's eye, perhaps he would visit her again soon, and when he did, she would do what she could to make things right.

37

Three days into the feasting, David stood on his roof overlooking the women's courtyard. Many of the warriors of Israel had returned to their homes, but the town of Hebron and some men from various tribes remained. The celebration would last seven days, and he had determined to give each night to one wife with a little extra time to spend with the children. He thought they would be pleased, glad to be with him, and happy that the kingdom had finally come together in peace.

He glimpsed Michal's apartment, disappointment nipping at him. She had come when he called, but the meeting he'd envisioned was not what he'd gotten.

"You wanted to see me, my lord?" She'd stood before him dressed in ornate, gilded robes, as though letting him know once again where she stood in relation to his other wives. The thought grated, but he squelched his irritation in the desire to be with her again. So much had come between them.

He moved across the room to where she waited stiff and wary. He gently gripped her shoulders and pulled her close. "I thought to share the joy of celebration with you." He kissed her nose and pulled back, searching her dark eyes. "Adonai has finally brought the kingdom together again, beloved. We have much to praise Him for."

She turned her cheek to his kiss, raising his ire. He released his hold on her and took a step back. "Disdain is unbecoming to you, Michal."

Her gaze snapped to his at that, and her eyes flashed with what he deduced was anger. But the fleeting look soon softened, as though she thought better of her actions. He allowed himself to relax and motioned her to sit with him among the cushions of his couch.

He sat near her and brushed his fingers along her arm. "What can I give you, Michal? How can I bring pleasure to your heart this glorious day?" Though in truth, he wasn't sure why her smile did not already reach her eyes. The dream they had both longed for in the early days of their marriage had finally been realized. What more could she want? Though he already knew the answer and prayed she wouldn't ask it again.

"You could give me a son and make me your queen. There is nothing more I want from you, David."

He should have known better than to ask.

"You know my answer to that already, Michal. Am I in the place of God to give you a son? And without an heir, how could I make you queen?" He shook his head and put distance between them.

The rest of the evening had been a test in patience as she lamented Abner and Ish-bosheth, and if he had allowed it, she probably would have bemoaned her no-good usurping husband Paltiel. He could not undo what had happened to her, but he didn't have to listen to her complaints or comparisons either. He'd finally sent her back to her rooms without the benefit of sharing his bed. Her demeanor had made her desires abundantly clear, and he balked at her insistent demands.

He had uselessly hoped Ahinoam would be different, but the next evening had proved even worse.

"You really should declare an heir now that Adonai has established the kingdom in your hands, my lord," she'd said, after the night had waned and dawn found her nestled in his arms. "Since Amnon is your firstborn, he would seem the logical choice, don't you agree?"

He'd been forced to grit his teeth against a bitter retort about the way she was raising his firstborn. Though the boy was only seven, he was often sulky and selfish, reminding him too much of David's older brother Eliab. If David had to relinquish the throne to one of his sons this moment, his choice would not be Amnon.

His jaw clenched now at the memories, and his fists clamped together until his nails dug into his palms. He drew in a breath and closed his eyes, willing his anger to abate. The sun still warmed the edge of the western foothills. Soon it would be time to visit Abigail and Chileab. The thought filled him with longing and hope that this wife would not set a list of demands before him but would simply welcome him with joy. No doubt Chileab would be happy to see him, and though the sight of the boy's withered arm always brought a stab of pain to his heart, he was genuinely glad to see that this son would not be spoiled like Amnon or too charming for his own good like Absalom. Would the people accept a maimed king?

He shook his head, dismissing the

thought, then glanced at the sky and followed the voices to the women's court once again. They would gather to greet him soon, but he was not in the mood to be hammered with questions tonight. He would go to Abigail, and for tonight he would pretend he was a lowly shepherd with one wife and son and worry about pleasing the rest of them tomorrow.

Abigail heard the knock before Rosah did, but Chileab beat them both to the door. David entered her rooms dressed in a simple robe more reminiscent of their life in the desert foothills than of his recently appointed role as king. He looked hopeful and at peace when he smiled at her, yet there were dark shadows beneath his eyes and a wary glint in their depths.

"Abba, come see what I made today." Chileab grasped David's fingers with his good hand and tugged him toward a table where mosaic tiles were spread out and an image was taking shape in a wooden frame. "I added the tree and two birds, see?"

David bent over the table to examine his son's work, a simple reconstruction of the things he'd seen in nature, then straightened and smiled. "You did a fine job." He ruffled Chileab's dark hair. "You are a gifted artist, my son."

Chileab beamed at the high praise, and Abigail's heart swelled with pride. She settled on the couch to listen to the exchange between her husband and son, feet tucked beneath her robe. Already she imagined how it might be if David could get away to be with them like this more often — away from the bickering of the other women. She smiled to herself, barely able to contain her excitement at presenting her idea, and prayed he would agree.

"How was your day?" Abigail asked when Chileab had finally tired and Rosah had put him to bed.

David leaned against the couch and stretched his hands behind his head, looking at her. "Long," he said at last, his muscular chest lifting in a sigh. "It is a wonderful feast, though, and the people seem glad to have it extend for a week. We will soon reinstate the feasts Adonai initiated long ago, celebrations we have neglected in our disregard of Him."

She smiled, pleased with the direction of his thoughts. "It is good to see you finally realize the dreams Yahweh placed on your heart, David. As you lead the people back to true worship, you will unite them and give them a kingdom of peace."

He moved his arms to rest along the back of the couch. "Yes, peace. Once we subdue our enemies and take back the territory that Adonai deeded to us, then the kingdom will know peace. I'm not sure I will see that peace in my lifetime, but surely the one who reigns after me will." His tender look warmed her. "I only wish Chileab would have been that man."

The reminder pricked her soul, but when she searched his face, she saw no reprimand there, only resigned sadness. "I'm sorry too, my lord. But apparently it wasn't meant to be."

"Apparently not."

Silence settled between them then, silence born of understanding and acceptance. She took courage in his subdued mood and rose from her chair to sit beside him, taking his hand in hers. He lifted one eyebrow but seemed pleased with her boldness, an amused tilt to his mouth as though he wanted to smile but wouldn't.

"David . . ."

He nodded, acknowledging that she should continue, but held his tongue.

"I know you would like nothing better than to live in peace, and I fully agree. And I know that we, your wives, are often a greater trial to you than some of the enemies you fight in battle."

He allowed the smile to show through at that. "An interesting observation."

She met his smile with one of her own. "Yes, well, I know that at times I have been no better than the others, and I will admit, it is not easy to share a man you love with all your heart."

His eyes softened, his look tender. He seemed as though he would speak, but then he nodded for her to continue.

"I've been thinking about the situation, my lord, and I don't have a ready solution to keep the women from complaining short of cutting out our tongues — which I would not recommend, for then you would never hear the good things we have to say either." She didn't want to give him any bad ideas!

"That thought is tempting." He chuckled, and she slowly relaxed, releasing a breath. Sometimes the idea seemed like it wasn't such a bad one where Maacah and Ahinoam were concerned.

"What I have thought of was a solution that might please us both . . . and be good for Chileab since he cannot do as much as the other boys and is sometimes bullied by Amnon and Absalom."

His brow quirked again, and she inwardly kicked herself for mentioning something that could distress him. But if it brought his attention to see things her way, perhaps it was worth the risk.

"Just say it, Abigail. What is it you want me to do?"

Her heart sank. She had tried to present this to him in a positive way, and already he was weary of the exchange. She stifled the urge to sigh and instead clasped both of her hands around his and kissed his signet ring.

"I would like you to allow Chileab and me to live away from this house, to move back with my father and Talya. Abba could be a good help to Chileab, to teach him things you do not have time to do, and he would be a companion to Micah. Talya and I could care for Abba in his old age, and we would make the place a sanctuary for you to come whenever you needed to get away. We would be free of the bickering and squabbling here, which always troubles Chileab's gentle spirit, and you would have a home where there was peace. It would mean one less wife to worry about." She inwardly flinched at how that sounded. "Not that you do not provide a fine home for us, my lord, just that —"

He held up his free hand to silence her. "You've made your point." He looked at her for the longest moment, but she could not read his expression. He was becoming a master at disguising his emotions, only letting her glimpse his inner self when he wanted her to see his thoughts. That saddened her because she wanted to share every part of his life, but she understood his need to protect himself from those who would seek his ruin. Kings had many enemies. Even beloved kings.

"I've offended you." She spoke the words as a statement, though she meant it as a question and longed to hear him say it wasn't true.

"You have asked me to allow my dearest wife to move away from my protection, out of my home, to go back to her father. You want to take my beloved son from me so that your father can raise him because I am too busy or perhaps unfit to teach him. You cannot live with the turmoil of my house because you blame me for taking more women to my bed and you hate having to share my love. Yet you love me with all your heart." He pulled his hand from her grasp and adjusted the signet ring. For a moment he studied it, then her. "If loving me with all your heart means leaving me, you do not understand the meaning of the word." He stood then, clearly agitated, and walked to the door.

How had he taken what she said and twisted it so? This was not what she intended at all!

He opened the door, then turned to face her again. "You want to leave? Then go! Have your things packed by morning." He whirled about, stepped across the threshold, and slammed the door behind him.

Abigail stared at the closed door, too numb and confused to move. He was sending her away? So quickly? And not with the joy she expected or with the hope of letting her create for him a sanctuary of peace, but with anger and despair.

What had she done?

She picked up an embroidered pillow and hugged it to herself to still the sudden trembling. Her intentions had been to please him — and herself, if the truth were known. She had thought he would appreciate a place of refuge from the demands of his kingly life. She could give that to him in a home of her own. So what if she cared for her father in the process? Why couldn't he see that she spoke wisdom?

She did, didn't she?

Memories and uncertainty swept over her in little waves — times of trying so hard to appease angry men, of working to keep her heart from being broken again and again, of believing promises no man could keep. And what had it brought her?

A knock at the door drew her gaze from the pillow to the place David had just stood. Rosah pattered over the tile floors to answer the knock.

"We are here to assist the lady Abigail." Two female servants stepped into the room, arms loaded with straw baskets. "The king has sent us to help pack your things."

"Pack your things?" Rosah looked at her askance. Had she not heard the conversation?

"The king is sending us away." Abigail heard her own flat tone acknowledge the unbelievable truth. She stared at the two servants in silence.

"Away? Where? Why?" Rosah moved closer and knelt beside the couch at her feet. "You must call him back. You must fix whatever is wrong. Please, my lady."

Abigail looked into Rosah's impassioned face. "Why do you care so? You will still be cared for. Just not here."

Rosah's cheeks flushed, and she leaned back on her heels. "I only thought . . . it isn't good for your son to be away from his father. Forgive me, my lady." She backed away, and Abigail wondered not for the first time if Rosah had feelings for her husband.

But then all the young women were enamored with the king. She would outgrow it in time when she married and had a home of her own.

Which apparently Abigail would finally have as well — a home of her own to do with as she pleased. She would make the place a safe haven for her son and her father, while her husband went off to live his life as king away from her.

The thought left her empty and desolate. But she would not weep. She had done nothing wrong.

With new resolve, she rose from her seat and went to help the servants pack. There would be no rest for her this night.

David stood near the parapet of his roof, looking down at the small entourage ready to carry his wife and son to her father's home outside of his palatial compound. An ache began along the back of his neck, and he could feel the tension knotting his shoulders. He wanted nothing more than to forget their conversation of the night before and return to the joy he'd felt when he'd first entered her apartment. How had this peace-loving woman managed to ruin his sense of well-being? Was he overreacting?

She didn't realize, couldn't possibly know,

what this request had cost him. To allow her to return to her father was to let another man control what belonged to him. He would lose her when he moved his family to Jerusalem, something he had only recently shared with his advisors.

The thought of the future eased some of his tension. They had so much to look forward to. Why did she want to retreat? She needed to embrace these new challenges, to help him plan a new palace and give him some insight into how to bring the women into worship.

But all she could see was her fellow wives. Instead of embracing them as sisters, she wanted to see them as rivals for his affection, and though in her mind that may have been true, couldn't she see that she already owned an important part of his heart? Who else among his wives loved Adonai and sought Him with heart and soul as she did? He never worried about Chileab learning to follow Yahweh as long as Abigail was close by. He counted on her wisdom to keep peace with the other women. Why did she want to give it all up?

The servants helped Abigail mount a donkey, then lifted Chileab into her arms. Her young maid rode behind her, and Benaiah and several of his bodyguards surrounded the small group.

David's heart squeezed at the sight. How could she do this to him? Why did she test his goodwill? He gripped the edge of the parapet and blew out a breath. He could see them clearly from where he stood, but Abigail did not look up, apparently not caring whether she saw him again or not.

"Are you going to see them off, my lord?" His friend Hushai came up beside him and rested a hand on his arm. "Are you sure you won't reconsider?"

Hushai had listened to his complaints without comment when David had returned the night before. David glanced at the man now and sighed. "She has made her decision. Let her go."

Hushai hoisted his sagging middle and tucked his bulk beneath his belt. "It seems to me, my lord, that you made the decision for her. If what you told me is correct, she asked you to consider letting her live apart from your other wives, to care for her father, but you told her to get out today. I hardly think the lady Abigail meant for you to send her off during the feast with such animosity between you." He looked at David then, his pointed, honest expression reminding David in the smallest way of Jonathan.

David turned his head, heat creeping up

his neck, feeling more like a reprimanded child than a newly crowned king. "Nevertheless, she should not have asked. She implied that I am unfit to raise her son, unfit to be husband to her since she is forced to share me." His own words mocked him, and he couldn't bear to see their truth mirrored in Hushai's kind face. He glanced down at the group again instead, watching as the donkeys moved forward toward the palace gate, feeling the dagger of Hushai's words and his own petulant admission twist in his heart.

"We both know the law, my lord," Hushai said, his gentle tone belying the sharp implication. " 'Kings must not multiply wives to themselves,' yet you have seven wives and have considered more. Adonai gave that law for a reason."

"So that the women would not turn the king's heart away from Him. My wives have not done that. I am fully devoted to the Lord my God. So where is the problem?" Irritation pricked the back of David's neck, followed quickly by a heavy weight of guilt. Was that the only reason God had given such a law? Might David have used his own desire to justify his choices?

"I think you know that answer as well as I do, my lord." Hushai backed away from him

473

and nodded. "I will leave you to think on these things in peace."

Hushai left the roof, and David turned back to watch the road. The caravan carrying his wife and son grew smaller in the distance. He rubbed the back of his neck again and glanced toward the heavens.

My heart is devoted to You, O Adonai. Surely You know this.

His wives had not turned him away. On the contrary, he had insisted the foreigner Maacah learn the ways of Yahweh. But it was Abigail who had shared his love for the Most High, his yearning for his Creator.

And he was sending her away.

But he was only giving her what she'd requested.

Turmoil churned his gut as he left the roof.

38

Abigail clutched Chileab to her chest as the donkey slowly plodded to the king's gate, leaving David's property and his protection. That he'd sent his trusted bodyguards to escort her gave her a small measure of comfort, but as they passed beneath the thick stone arches, she couldn't stop the sudden doubt assailing her. Even now, should she beg Benaiah to return her to David to fall at his feet and beg his forgiveness? Surely he would restore her to her former place, allow her to stay with him as before.

Was it her pride that kept her from doing just that? The breeze cooled her hot cheeks, and she squeezed Chileab closer, drinking in his scent and wishing she could keep the truth of all that had happened from him forever. But he would one day want to know why he rarely saw his father, why he lived away from the palace, what had become of his brothers . . .

Was she doing the right thing?

But what choice did she have? David was sending her away. She would risk everything if she tried to get back in his good graces, and she wasn't sure she could do such a thing.

"Mama?" Chileab's young voice cut into her musings, and she leaned forward to hear him better.

"What is it, sweetheart?"

"Where is Abba?" He twisted in her arms to look into her face. "Why are we leaving our house?"

"I told you, beloved. We're going to live with your grandfather. You'll get to see your cousin Micah. You'll like that, won't you?"

He nodded, but his gaze was uncertain. "But will we be gone long? I didn't get to tell Abba good-bye."

I didn't either, baby. But she couldn't voice the words or give vent to the feelings they evoked. She swallowed hard. "We'll see Abba again sometime."

"When?"

"I don't know."

He fell silent and twisted around to look ahead again, apparently satisfied with her answers. She gripped the reins, tempted to turn and look behind her at the home she had occupied for the past seven years. But if he would not come to her, she would not look for him. She fought the temptation and stared straight ahead, unable to stop the sinking feeling in her heart.

David forced himself to act as though nothing unusual had happened as he returned to his dining hall that evening for the fourth day of the feast. He tried desperately to pay attention to the men sitting closest to him, but his stomach knotted with every bite of food, and the wine tasted like gall in his mouth. Abigail had trotted out of the city's gates without a backward glance as though he meant nothing to her at all, taking their son with her. And he had let her go. How had it come to this?

He lifted a silver chalice to his lips, staring into the dark liquid and seeing Abigail's reflection in his mind's eye. He was unable to wipe away the image of the shocked look that had crossed her lovely face at his sudden demand she leave. He took a long drink, wishing he could drown his memories, but the hurt in her eyes stabbed him in the heart. He had once promised her he would never hurt her. So what had he done? He was no brute like Nabal, but hurt came in many forms.

He rose, suddenly disgusted with himself, and shoved away from the table. His servants and guards scrambled to keep up with his long strides.

"My lord, how can I help you?" a servant asked, puffing at his side.

"Get me my copy of the law, and do it quickly." He would do his guilt no good to remind himself of Adonai's commands, but experience told him that if he wanted answers, Adonai's law was the best place to start.

His manservant brought a lounging robe for him, and he settled onto a plush couch in his bedchamber just as a scribe entered, carrying the scroll. He unrolled it carefully, spread it on a low table, knelt on a soft bearskin rug, and pored over the words. Words that now came into clearer focus, accusing him, convicting him.

"Neither shall he multiply wives for himself, lest his heart turn away . . ."

O Lord, surely You desire truth in the inmost place. And in truth, I have not kept this whole law. Surely I was sinful at birth. And the consequences have cost me much heartache and have hurt the ones I love.

He did love her. Now he realized just how much. Had he told her so? Did she know it? If sharing him meant never knowing for sure, she could not possibly know it or believe it.

Cleanse me from my sin. Wash me, make me whiter than snow.

He should have told her every moment she was with him, should have made her believe it, should have never allowed such hurt to darken those luminous brown eyes. His breath came slow and deep, and he bent his head over the parchment, his heart broken and bare.

Create a clean heart in me, O God. Teach me Your ways.

How could he possibly set things right again? He could not undo the marriages he had already made, but he could refuse to accept such future alliances. He recalled the pressure his advisors had placed on him to accept Maacah years ago and how easily the rest had been added after that. Maacah, the spoiled foreign princess who would expect him tonight.

He released a troubled sigh. To please and to appease them had cost him what he held most dear — a wife and son he dearly loved.

If he kept himself from adding more wives, would Abigail see it as enough? Would loving her be enough for him? He couldn't ignore his other wives. There would always be reason to share his time. Always the struggle to give her the peace she craved.

So did he act on this law or continue as he had done all along?

Oh, Adonai, show me what to do.

The longing to set things right between them warred with his pride. Pride told him to let her be, to wait for her to come to him. Wisdom told him to set pride aside and go to her, to not let another sundown give root to bitterness. Voices of reason and want clashed within him, and he wasn't sure which side would win.

He wasn't sure which side he *wanted* to win.

Abigail tucked her feet beneath her on her father's wood bench, listening as rain drummed a rapid rhythm on her father's roof. Chileab and Micah sat on the floor playing war games with sticks and stones. Talya sat opposite her, stitching one of Micah's worn tunics, while her father whittled a piece of olive wood into another soldier for his grandsons.

"Of course you are welcome here, Abigail. You know that. But we don't have the room you are used to or the wealth. Can you live with that?"

"I have lived with little and with much, Abba. I can be content with either."

480

"Then why were you not content to stay with the king?" Talya's soft voice held neither reprimand nor accusation but rather took on a curious tone. "Was life in David's household so terrible?" She looked up, breaking off a thread with her teeth. "I imagine it must have been hard to watch him with all of those other women."

Chileab's head tilted, and Abigail wondered how much he heard and understood. He looked at her with an innocent, questioning look, intensifying her sense of guilt. Should she have tried to reason with David, to appease his anger as she had so often done over the years? She was weary of playing peacemaker.

"You don't have to explain, Abigail." Talya met her gaze with a look of understanding and concern. "We are glad to have you here."

"Thank you." Abigail shifted in her seat, then stood, suddenly agitated. She walked to the window overlooking the outer courtyard and gazed into the dusk. Damp air greeted her as she pulled the shutter open farther, letting the breeze fan her face. Normal night sounds were masked by the patter of rain, and Abigail wished the water could wash the pain and hurt from her heart.

She moved from the window to the doorway and slipped into the courtyard. She stood beneath the awning, feeling the dampness seep into her skin. She pulled the scarf around her neck, covered her face, and looked up into the darkness, a darkness that matched her mood. If only she had kept her mouth shut, had not spoken of her concerns. Not during the feast. Not when David had come to her to rejoice and share the good fortune of finally seeing the kingdom united. When would she learn to curb her tongue?

A clap of thunder accompanied flashes of memory:

Nabal standing above her again, his arm raised to strike, casting insults and demanding that she do that very thing — curb her tongue.

You want to leave? Then go! David's words hurled at her in brittle tones.

She closed her eyes and leaned against the wet limestone of her father's house, clinging to its support. Weariness enveloped her, and she knew her lack of sleep from the night before coupled with her battered heart were taking its toll. Why did she love a man she couldn't satisfy? Why did she long for him even as he disappointed her again and again? Why did she punish herself with the desire to please rather than act as her sister wives and live to please herself?

Search me, O God, and know my heart. Test me, and know my anxious thoughts. David's words came back to her, words he'd shared with her long ago when Chileab still slept in her womb. *See if there is any offensive way in me, and lead me in the way everlasting.*

She looked up again at the heavens as the rain petered to a stop. A handful of stars poked through the dissipating clouds, and she felt the tug on her heart, the yearning for Yahweh. Life would be so much better if David had not taken so many wives. But she could not change him, even as she could not have changed Nabal from his abusive ways. She had accepted her lot with Nabal yet chafed at her lot with David. Why?

She examined her heart as she moved away from the wall and walked through the court to the small lane connecting her father's house to his neighbors. She had accepted Nabal because she didn't love him. She had managed him as best she could.

"But I loved you, David," she spoke softly to the empty night.

"Loved, or still love?"

She stilled, knowing the voice but not believing her own ears. Her heart thudded wildly as she slowly turned, and there he stood, hands extended, dressed as a shepherd rather than a king.

She looked into his handsome face. His dark eyes assessed her, and his outstretched hands beckoned her. She placed her hands in his, and her stomach did a little flip as his fingers covered hers. But he didn't close the distance between them.

"How did you get here? I didn't hear you come."

"Benaiah helped me escape the feast. It took a little doing, but no one expected the king to dress as a lowly shepherd. I slipped away rather easily." He squeezed her fingers. "I had to come, Abigail." His Adam's apple moved, and he cleared his throat, his gaze skipping beyond her. The moon bathed his face in ethereal light. "I . . ." He looked at her then, his expression open and vulnerable, no longer the unreadable mask she had grown accustomed to. "I spent some time tonight reading the book of the law that I copied when I took the throne of Judah seven years ago." He paused at her curious expression. "Despite what you may think, I do know the law and have hidden it in my heart." His smile was guarded. "I know my many wives trouble you —"

"David, I —"

He held a finger to her lips to stop her

words. "If you don't let me finish, I may not have the courage to say this to you again."

She nodded, her pulse kicking up a notch. Her eyes searched his and read only truth there.

"When I read the words that warned kings not to take many wives, I assumed it meant not to do so only to prevent the king's heart from straying from Yahweh. Since I decided I would never allow such a thing, I saw no reason not to unite tribes and nations with marriage treaties." He glanced briefly away from her. "Though that's not the whole truth." He pulled one hand away to rub the back of his neck. "Truth is, Abigail, I gave in to desire as well." He looked beyond her at the heavens, then finally let his gaze settle on her face. A sigh lifted his shoulders, as though the words were too painful to say. "I was wrong, Abigail. Taking so many wives . . . I broke Yahweh's law. The hard part is, there is nothing to be done about it now. There are seven of you, and that is the truth of it."

He searched her face, and her heart yearned for him to pull her close, but she would not squelch the effort this was costing him or ruin this moment to read into his soul. She was certain he was right — this chance would never come again.

"I cannot even promise you that I won't fail to keep this command in the future. I know the pressure placed on kings for treaties of peace among nations and tribes . . . and I know my own weakness." He dropped his head then, as though to admit such a thing was the epitome of grief to him. "But if you will return, I will do my best to keep the law from now on, to add no more wives, to treat you all with the care you deserve." He lifted his gaze then, his expression hopeful. "I love you, Abigail." His voice grew husky. "Will you come?"

Her heart soared with his words. Had he spoken them in that way to her before? Surely she knew that he loved her, but she couldn't remember him ever having said the words. Her throat closed as she squeezed his hand and pulled the scarf from her face, exposing her emotions in the look she gave him and allowing him to read the fragile trust in her soul. "You honor me, my lord, more than I deserve. Surely I have tested your patience and grieved you in my desire to steal so much of your time. I know my own weakness. I am not better than you."

Her heart throbbed as emotion pulsed between them. He lifted a hand to her face and traced a finger along her jaw, his gaze unutterably tender. And in that moment she believed him. Not in the sense of a man who might say words to get his way and later break his promise, but in the sense of a man who means what he says with all of his heart. He had come to her when he could have let her go, and here he stood, longing to take her back. And she knew without doubt she wanted nothing better. Despite the circumstances, she wanted him and wanted to be near him all the days of her life.

She stepped forward and held her palms open in a gesture of acceptance and peace.

"I love you still, David."

He reached for her and pulled her into the warmth of his embrace, and she caught the steady cadence of his heart beating beneath his rough tunic.

"I will come," she whispered, kissing his bearded cheek. "And I will serve Adonai at your side, David, all the days of my life."

EPILOGUE

One Year Later

Abigail held her infant daughter Anna tightly against her breast and stood at the altar at the tabernacle in Gibeon. David stood at her side, one arm around her waist, stripped of royal garb, head bowed. Zadok the priest took the lamb and the turtledove they had brought for her purification — the lamb for a burnt offering, the dove for a sin offering — and placed them before Abigail. She laid a hand first on the dove, then on the lamb, then watched the priest slit the animals' throats, spilling their blood to cover her sins.

Tears filled Abigail's eyes as she considered the high price of her redemption. Sin she had inherited at birth, dating all the way back to the first mother, Eve. Sin she had carried all on her own as Yahweh tenderly broke her stubbornness and her discontent to teach her obedience, much like her father once broke the leg of a ewe lamb to teach it not to wander from the shepherd. She glanced down at her sleeping daughter, knowing all too well how soon this child would display her own penchant to disobey the laws of Adonai.

The pungent aroma of burning flesh filled the air as the smoke from the sacrifice wafted upward. Abigail followed the path of the smoke, lifting her eyes to the heavens.

Oh, Adonai, please help me to teach this child to love You. Help her to have a heart like her father David.

She glanced at her husband and met his gaze. He smiled at her and squeezed her closer to him.

"Thank you for my daughter, David." Her delivery had been easier this time, much to her and David's relief. The reinstitution of purification offerings after childbirth had helped to alleviate the guilt they both felt at neglecting the law with Chileab's birth, to remind them where to put their trust. They would not always obey, that was certain. Their own human weaknesses had proven how easily they lost that obedience and trust.

David leaned closer to push the blanket away from Anna's face, his smile prouder than it should have been for a daughter.

"She has her mother's beauty already. Every young man in Israel will be vying for her hand." He winked at her, then looked back at the sacrifice.

Musicians took up a song David had written, and his quiet tenor blended with them. It was the song he had begun when she still carried Chileab in her womb, a song now completed with Anna's birth.

"How precious are Your thoughts to me, O God! How vast is the sum of them! Were I to count them, they would outnumber the grains of sand. When I awake, I am still with You."

She glanced at David, noting the sheen of tears dampening his lashes. She was grateful beyond words for her husband, a man willing to admit his faults and repent of his sins, a man after God's own heart. How grateful she was for the change in him. No new wives had joined them since David's promise that night in her father's courtyard. She could only hope he would stay strong and true to the laws of Adonai.

"Search me, O God, and know my heart. Test me, and know my anxious thoughts. See if there is any offensive way in me, and lead me in the way everlasting."

When the song ended, David took the child from her as the two of them knelt before the Lord. Abigail's heart was humbled to know how far Adonai had brought her — from a broken spirit and wounded heart to a woman who had learned to trust Him even when she didn't always understand, a woman at peace with her husband and her God.

While her time with David was never long enough, she had learned to be grateful for what he could give her and accept it as a gift from Yahweh's hand. He would never be perfect, but what man was? He was her husband — shepherd, warrior, poet, lover, and king — and she would accept what she could not change. But she would not cower in fear of his reprisals, knowing now how much he depended on her. She would work to change what she could and would serve him as she served Adonai.

Smiling now, with a heart turning in surrender to the Lord, Abigail lifted her eyes and hands to the heavens and worshiped.

ACKNOWLEDGMENTS

Abigail's story has been a long time coming. I originally imagined her life — the how and why behind what happened in Scripture — during the first five years I homeschooled my sons. I learned point of view and much more about the craft of writing during the first draft of *Abigail*. After the Wives of King David series sold to Revell, I reexamined and rewrote the story. The journey into exploring her life, first with Nabal and then with David, has been eye-opening, especially as I studied polygamy in both ancient and modern times. Despite three thousand years spanning between us, human nature has not changed. Men and women will always find ways to justify their actions and even try to use the Bible to excuse them.

During the months of rewriting *Abigail,* I relied on the encouragement and prayers of many people, particularly my prayer team, the members of Transforming Grace —

what an army of prayer warriors you are; my friends, who love me just because; and my precious family. Thanks to all of you — you and your prayers are priceless. I love you!

A special thanks to Kristin Hill Gorin, who believed in me years before *Michal* saw print.

To my editors at Revell, Lonnie Hull Du-Pont and Jessica Miles, for your help with pacing and other issues. Your gentle comments always opened my eyes to ways I could show the story better. You have my highest respect and thanks!

To Wendy Lawton, my faithful agent whose advice has helped guide my career far better than I could do myself. You encourage me in ways I will always treasure. Thank you for supporting me and rejoicing with me.

To the marketing team at Revell — what would I do without you? Cheryl Van Andel, your cover designs should earn you awards! The cover for *Abigail* is every bit as wonderful as that of *Michal*. Thank you! Twila Bennett, Claudia Marsh, Michele Misiak, Deonne Beron, Carmen Sechrist — thank you for so expertly promoting my work. You are the best!

To my critique partner, Jill Stengl, who

made me believe Abigail's story had merit and loved it even amid my self-doubts and second-guessing. I love you, dear friend.

To Mom and Dad — words cannot express how proud I am to be your daughter. Dad, you remain a godly example to me in every circumstance life sends your way. Mom, you instilled in me the love of books, and you always remind me that God knows best.

To Randy, Jeff, Chris, and Ryan — without you, there would be no story.

And lastly but most precious of all, to *Adonai Elohai,* the Lord my God, whose grace never ceases to amaze me, who truly can do "exceedingly more than I could ever ask or imagine."

Ta'amu ur' u ki tov Adonai — "Taste and see that the *Lord* is good" (Psalm 34:8).

In whose grace I stand,
Jill Eileen Smith

ABOUT THE AUTHOR

Jill Eileen Smith is the bestselling author of *Michal,* book 1 in the Wives of King David series. When she isn't writing, she enjoys spending time with her family — in person, over the webcam, or by hopping a plane to fly across the country. She can often be found reading Christian fiction, testing new recipes, grabbing lunch with friends, or snuggling one or both of her adorable cats. She lives with her family in southeast Michigan.

The employees of Thorndike Press hope you have enjoyed this Large Print book. All our Thorndike, Wheeler, and Kennebec Large Print titles are designed for easy reading, and all our books are made to last. Other Thorndike Press Large Print books are available at your library, through selected bookstores, or directly from us.

For information about titles, please call:
(800) 223-1244

or visit our Web site at:
http://gale.cengage.com/thorndike

To share your comments, please write:
Publisher
Thorndike Press
295 Kennedy Memorial Drive
Waterville, ME 04901